I am a dog mum who loves to read. During the wonderful time of COVID-19, I found my passion for writing and never stopped. I have never believed in being saved, so I wrote books where the heroine saves themselves. And when I am not writing, I am probably out with my bestie, causing all sorts of mischief and mayhem.

Thankyou for the support.
enjoy Gx

G.P.Bundy

This book is dedicated and inspired by the most important and wonderful people in my life. My nan and grandad are my rocks and my biggest supporters, and without them, I don't think I would have had the confidence to publish my work. They taught me to be strong and to strive for what I want, and to never let a 'no' stop me. My whole life, I have tried to be the best version of myself, to be the person they knew I could be. My nan is the strongest person I have had the wonderful pleasure of knowing; the way she has always held herself and worked harder than most is beyond inspirational. And my grandad, well, he was my best friend. The person I knew I could rely on, and someone who always told me how proud he was. And with this book, I can always keep a small part of them alive; a piece of them that will never leave. I worked hard to embody my nan's determination and drive into E and recreate my grandad's heart and kindness into K. I love all the characters I have created, but I have a huge soft spot for K, and I hope you all do as well.

I have spent nearly five years writing and editing this, wanting it to be perfect, something I and my entire family can be proud of. I hope that each and every reader loves and enjoys my book. I want people to know that no matter the trial and tribulations in life, there is always a way out. There is always light at the end of the tunnel, and the only person who can truly save you is yourself. Everyone is a strong and powerful person; you just have to believe in yourself.

Now sit back and enjoy E's story; you're in for a bumpy ride.

All my love,
G.P. Bundy

G.P. Bundy

THE ALLIANCE

Love and Revenge

AUSTIN MACAULEY PUBLISHERS

LONDON * CAMBRIDGE * NEW YORK * SHARJAH

A CIP catalogue record for this title is available from the British Library.

ISBN 9781035865932 (Paperback)
ISBN 9781035865949 (e pub e-book)

www.austinmacauley.com

First Published 2025
Austin Macauley Publishers Ltd®
1 Canada Square
Canary Wharf
London
E14 5AA

Prologue

Monday mornings were always horrible. My aunt was usually in a foul mood, but Mondays, she was like a demon. The way she always took her rage out on me, it used to hurt me. But the longer I have been here with her, the more used to it I got. I know she hates me; I don't know how a nine-year-old can cause so much anger in a woman. The look of distain in her eyes whenever I would cross her path, it was more than I could bare. So, in the end, I learned to just avoid her, pretend I don't exist—makes life a little more bearable. She always resented me, she calls me the burden of her life, which she isn't wrong.

I was only meant to be with her for a short while, but my parents died two days before they were meant to collect me, that was two months ago. I don't quite know the ins and outs of how they died, but it took its toll on Maggie. She's been a drinker since I can remember, but the past two months, she has been worse.

"Here's your shit, leave!" she shouted, commanding me out the door. Being nine, I'm not really meant to go to school on my own, but I have a friend's mum who comes to pick me up each morning. I only have one friend at school. We spend all our time together. It's lovely being with her. She helps me to forget for just a short while what is waiting at home for me. I don't know if I will stay with Maggie, but she is the only family I have left. I won't find out for a few weeks what is happening. Rick, Maggie's husband, likes to keep me up to date with everything. He says I am old enough to understand what is happening; he sees me as an 'adult in training'—his words not mine.

I don't even acknowledge her as I leave. She looks particularly dishevelled today. Her brunette hair is in a messy bun that she clearly slept in, most of her hair is hanging out of it. Dark circles under her light green eyes show me what I already know, she's probably been drinking till silly o'clock this morning. Doesn't surprise me in the slightest—she spends most of her time that way these days. It's hard seeing her like this. I used to watch my mum try and help her. But it never worked, clearly. Maybe if I stay with her and Rick, I can help her get clean. I know it would make my mum proud if she stopped, but Maggie doesn't want to.

Maggie is a hard woman, but I am becoming acclimatised to it. Keep your head down and everything will be okay. After being here two months, I am beginning to spot the moments before her anger flares, the moments when I know she will lose her shit with me. So I tend to find something else to do, be out of her way, mainly so I don't have to have the wrath of her or her tongue.

Getting to my friend's mum's, car I open the door and buckle in. I had to move the dress that she always puts me in to get secure. I hate this dress. Its pink with yellow pockets. I have about three of them, all the same. I go to a private school, and uniforms aren't used here. Most kids are rich and snobbish. I hate that about this place. They seem to all be born with a silver spoon up their asses— well everyone apart from Lulu. She is the only real person there, the only girl I get on with. Her family is well off, but nothing like the posh snobs that also attend.

Lulu's mother is lovely, always smiling and happy and it makes me wish that I had someone like her to live with. Looking at Lulu's mum makes me miss mine all the more. I'm now an orphan, but I didn't want the other children to know. I don't want to be treated differently or to be pitied. I need to be strong and hold my head up. Rick says it's bad now, but it will get better. I'm just holding out for that day, but I doubt that day will happen.

"Morning, Emie sweetie, you okay?" she calls back, looking at me through the rear view. Kate always asks me every morning. Its sweet, you can see in her grey eyes that she can tell something is wrong. However, she's not the sort of woman to push anything. She knows I'm from a rough background and I'm pushed from pillar to post with my parents. They have phoned her many times to have me at night so they can go out, she doesn't mind but she does worry. It's nice to know that even when my aunt doesn't care about me, at least one adult does.

"I'm okay, thanks," I reply, never telling her how I truly feel. She wouldn't understand. I know no one would. The woman I live with is horrible, my parents are dead, my life is in ruins and my anger is getting harder to control; it's becoming all-consuming.

The drive to school is short but Lulu and I chat about all the fun things we're going to do today. Come to think about it, school is my only escape from my terrible life back home. It's a way to be me, a way to not feel the relentless torment of my life. It's freeing to be able to just go and let loose, to not have to think about the loss of my parents. I don't have to think about the hell that awaits me just a short car ride away; it's my only moment of sanity in an otherwise atrocious existence.

After spending my day at school, I arrive back home. Something isn't right. Something just feels off, like the air around me has an ominous feeling that I cannot put my finger on. A couple of cars are parked outside the house. We don't have visitors. Maggie doesn't like them; she says they interrupt her day. What she means is they 'interrupt' her drink fest. All that woman ever thinks about is drinking, so it's not a surprise that she hates guests. It's lucky I have Rick, really; he is the only one out of the two who bothers with me. He's the only one who cares, always teaching me new skills. He puts me first and tries to help me cope with my anger, cope with the tidal wave of feelings that plague my mind relentlessly.

Walking into the house, I see Maggie's face. Fear consumes me as I realise she is sober. Something must be seriously wrong if that woman put down the bottle. The sombre look that contorts her face puts me on edge, and a sick foreboding feeling engulfs me. I have never seen Maggie look at me with anything other than distain, so for her to look at me with nothing but sadness, it fills me with dread.

Rick is in the corner behind me just staring at me, his eyes are full of tears; looks like he has been crying for some time. Looking around the rest of the room, I see two tall gentlemen and a woman sitting on the sofa, drinking tea from the fine China that we never get out.

"You must be Emie. I'm Detective Jonson. These are my fellow detectives, Neil and Lawrence. We are here because we have some news about your parents' deaths." The gentleman says, sitting on the right side of the sofa. He had black hair slicked back and the most piercing blue eyes. He motioned towards the other man first, then to the woman giving me an indication as to who the others were called; they all looked so sullen.

My parents died about two months ago, and I never knew what happened. All I was told was that they were shot. According to the report made at the time of their deaths, it took my mother two bullets to die. My father died instantly. I never understood why my parents were murdered. They were sweet, and kind people. My heart breaks every time I think about them. Maybe it was the wrong place at the wrong time. It's the only thing that makes sense. Who would want to hurt two kind-hearted people just wanting to come home to their daughter.

"We shouldn't tell her. She's too young," Maggie chimes in before anyone else can say anything. Clearly, she is trying to protect me for the first time in forever. If you could die of shock, I would have in that moment. She has never tried to protect me; if she had, she would have given up the drink.

Rick moves from the corner of the room to stand on my right and puts his hand on my shoulder. It's comforting but I'm yet to find out what I am being comforted for. "She deserves to know. She's an adult in training. It's her parents, Maggie, she has a right to all the facts. Or else one day, when she's older, she will resent us for not telling her," Rick says back to her. He always has my best interests at heart. And yes, I would be very upset to learn these facts when I'm older. I may be nine, but I am not stupid, I can handle anything they throw at me. My parents are dead, how much worse could it be?

The detectives look between each other, clearly undecided whether to proceed or not. I look at him with my cold expression. I'm starting to get impatient here. What's the hold up? "We are saddened to say that your father got caught up in some bad business and apparently ended up paying for it. Your mother took the brunt of the attack. I am so sorry. I won't go into too much detail; the act was heinous. Your father was shot in the head, so we believe that it was him they were after."

Taking a moment to run his fingers under the collar of his suit, clearly uncomfortable with telling a young child about the brutal way her parents died. I understand this might be hard for them to say. I can't imagine it's pleasant no matter who you are telling it to. But Detective Jonson really needs to man up, not like it was his parents that were brutally murdered. It was my life that was turned to shit, not his, so he just needs to spit it out already.

"I'm so sorry to tell you all this and that you had to go through this at such a young age, but our colleagues promised never to keep anything from you. And I will personally honour that, Emilia. Is there anything you wish to ask us?" says Detective Lawrence who finally spoke. He must have picked up that Jonson was obviously uncomfortable with this. He was clearly a tall man, judging by the way his legs protruded over the edge of the chair, with light brown hair and eyes to match. His suit is more tailored to his body than Jonson's; he clearly holds himself in better regards. I also notice that he irons his, whereas Jonson doesn't;

the wrinkles in his shirt obvious. It shows a lack of care, and maybe that reflects in his work. Mum always said you can tell a person by the way they dress.

"Yes," I say, looking at them. My face was controlled, not showing one ounce of emotion. This was a skill Rick taught me when dealing with Maggie's bad days. Finding it useful now more than ever. I don't think I have ever looked at someone with such a straight face while screaming in my head. Fury and venom flowing through me, like a torrent of water battering against a wall just waiting to be released.

"Who was it?" I asked, gritting my teeth. For a nine-year-old, I've always been so grown up. I had to be; Mum and Dad were always away, never sticking around for longer than a month. I was never allowed with them, so I guess that made me mature mentally faster. Learning to take care of myself, but I also learnt that I am truly alone in this world. A world that is full of hurt and now death. A world that has started to attract demons to me; they plague my thoughts. But something else is settling into me, a different need. Something that I need to do in order to survive, in order to not allow the darkness to take me.

"Harry Steadwell," Detective Jonson replied. I will remember that name. I will destroy him. I will watch his world burn to the ground the same as mine has. I will make sure he knows what he took from me. And most of all, I will make him pay for this, and the only payment acceptable, his life!

Chapter 1

When I awoke this morning, my mind was running a million miles an hour. Each passing day becomes easier, and I can keep going. However, I still have my hard days, and today was definitely going to be one of those. I was about to meet with the devil's son. I never usually go to meetings, but I decided to make an exception. I have seen pictures and researched him, but nothing ever prepares you fully. All the research in the world can't stop something from going tits up, it can't prepare you for the unknown. Especially when you deal with someone so powerful, someone with a shit tonne of influence and very high-profile. Like the person I am meeting today.

Luther Steadwell, he is one of New York's most eligible bachelors. I am a woman. I have eyes, so I can see how good looking he is. But men are the least of my concerns. They will only stop me from getting my revenge, or at least that's what has been drilled into me since I was fifteen. And I don't think I can ever be with a man, not after my first love, the man who stole my heart and kept it for years. He will never feel anywhere near what I do, but I don't think I could ever be with anyone else either.

But right now, I can't think about him. I need to focus on the matter at hand. And that is getting Luther to work with me; his help would make my job of killing his father so much easier. When he took my parents from me, I declared vengeance. I've waited many years and built my company from the ground up. Now I'm at the top of my game and considered the only female mafia boss in New York. Everyone in my world knows not to fuck with me. I get what I want, and I don't care who stands in my way. I have worked too fucking hard to have some pretty boy stop me.

I am snapped out of my thoughts by the flight attendant. "Ma'am, we will be landing shortly. The time will be 7 am in New York." I turn to the steward and nod; I was meant to be flying first class, but I couldn't be bothered after the time I've had in London with Maggie, Marcus and Aid.

Marcus and Aid took me under their wings many years ago, so they became like extended family. Plus, we had some business to speak about, so when that ran over, they offered to get me home so I would be on time for my meeting.

I told Luther to meet me at 7:15 am today at a café I own. I prefer having meetings there because I am the only one who sees the camera footage. I can also make sure that no one else can interrupt or hear what is spoken about. I pay the staff that work there handsomely to keep quiet; it's not surprising how money can buy silence. And if I'm honest, many of the people who work at the café have been there for years, so they understand that they don't speak about the matters discussed.

Getting off the plane, K greets me with my Harley Davidson, my favourite bike. "Hey, boss, hope you had an enjoyable time with Maggie. H is with Willow now but said if you need anything, to call. Do you need anything else?" K's chocolate eyes look into my green ones, his hair is in a messy bun, and a few wispy strands have slipped out. How this man has held my heart for 15 years is beyond me. Although he does look like a Greek god. His muscles are straining through his black top, all the men wear black tops and trousers; it's the uniform. But K looks damn fine in them. Looking at him, I want to run my hands through his thick hair and kiss those soft, luscious lips of his. But I've grown to know that it would never happen. He only sees me as his boss. And sometimes it breaks my heart. Sadly, over the years, I've found it easier to swallow my feelings for him. My heart may be heavy with feelings, but I am also too cowardly to speak about them either. Catch-22 or what.

"No, let him be. Can you get James and his team ready at the house? Once the meeting is over, I need to get to the office. Thanks." With that, I grab the helmet and drive off to the café. I don't like sticking around with K alone. I don't always trust myself around him. He makes me think about my feelings, and I hate thinking about those. They are the bane of my existence sometimes.

Passing through the city, I notice how the sun is just rising above the skyline. It sends a soft glow around the buildings. The city can be so beautiful but it's also insanely busy. Even London isn't like being here. The city never sleeps, the traffic never dies, and no one stands still. It's fascinating watching everyone just run around. I don't usually have the time to sit, and people-watch. And if I'm completely honest, since I was 13, I've never had the time to.

Since my parents died, I became a mess. I rebelled in school and got into fights, and then met Marcus and Aid. They taught me how to build my company and how to control and direct my anger. They also sent me into the armed forces. That didn't help with my stability. It may have made me always think the worst of people and made me far too accustomed to death. Not a bad trait in my current line of work, but still. Bottom line is, I kill more than I should because I know how to do it efficiently and effectively. They made me into the powerhouse that I am today, and I owe them a lot. I wouldn't be here today without them.

Pulling up to the café, I noticed that he's not here yet, and I'm not surprised. Mr Steadwell Jr isn't exactly known for being up so early in the morning. He is usually passed out from the night before in his room, and a woman draped over him. I can't be angry though. I am early. Having my bike makes it easier for me to weave through traffic.

Walking in, Hannah greets me, her smiling face always seems so happy. *Isn't it tiring to keep that up?* I couldn't think of anything worse. "Hey, E, you want your usual?" her chipper voice calls as I take my seat and open the top of my leather jumpsuit. I show just enough cleavage to hopefully throw Steadwell Jr off, but not too much that he actually thinks he has a chance with me. I have seen what he brings home, and I am scared I would catch something.

"Please, Hannah." She shuffles off to get my usual pancakes, bacon, and maple syrup, with a cup of tea. I may have lived in America for a long time now, but I still love a good cup of tea. Maggie always said to me, you can take the girl out of London, but you can't take London out of the girl. And I know she's right; coffee is nice, but it's not the same.

After a couple of minutes, she drops my breakfast in front of me. It smells divine. As I'm pouring my syrup onto my pancakes, I hear the door open. It must be him. No one else would come in as the sign said closed and Hannah would have told them to leave.

"Mr Steadwell, please take a seat." I point to the seat across from me. Not taking my eyes off my pancakes as I pour my syrup on. I am extremely precise, maybe to the point of OCD about it. Bad trait, but sometimes I can't help it. I have to be in control of everything.

Looking up, I take in how good he looks; he is more handsome in person than I thought he would be. His brown hair is styled precisely, not a strand out of place. He is clean shaven, showing off his chiselled jaw line with a small mole on his cheek. His suit is crisp and clearly designer. It screams money. I've never understood why people who have money decide to spend so much on clothes, fancy cars and jewellery. I have more money than most people. I'm actually the second richest person in New York. But because my identity is hidden, no one knows, and because I don't want people knowing who I am, I don't spend my money frivolously.

"Early, I see. I do appreciate that. Would you like some breakfast? I have dragged you out of bed rather early this morning," I say, glancing into his hazel eyes. He just looks at me. His eyes move down my body, taking in my appearance. I am used to men looking at me like I'm a piece of meat. Luther, however, looks at me like he's appreciating what he sees; it's refreshing.

"No thank you. I can pick something up after this," his voice is deep but with a hint of softness to it. If my heart didn't belong to someone else, I could see myself swooning over this man. I can see the appeal: good looks, money, and charisma. The trifecta of a man, but I can't afford to think this way. I have a job to do.

Shrugging, I glance at him while cutting my pancakes into bite size pieces, my OCD in overdrive. "Your loss. They are amazing." I place a piece into my mouth, savouring the taste. Pinning him with my eyes for a second, I try to gauge him. *Can I trust him? Can I believe what he says?*

"Actually, I will, seeing as you gave them such good reviews." He chuckles. It's low and kind of sexy. *Stop it,* I chastise myself. Shaking off the thoughts in my head, I raise my hand and click my fingers; Hannah comes running over. My eyes never leave Steadwell Jr, but his eyes never leave mine either. It seems he's trying to gauge me as well.

"Same again for Mr Steadwell, please." I hear Hannah scurry away while I eat another piece of my breakfast again. He studies me carefully, watching me with an intensity that is slightly uncomfortable. I don't let men make me feel like that though. I learned many years ago how to handle them and their eyes.

"So, what can I do you for, Miss Clawson? There must be a reason you asked to see me." His question doesn't take me by surprise. I knew we would get down to business soon, but I didn't think he would have the balls to ask me. Most men who do have the luxury of meeting me are always intimidated, and I do enjoy that. It makes my life so much easier when they are frightened of me.

Taking a slurp of my tea, I raise my eyebrow. "Well, Mr Steadwell," I say, taking another sip, as I debate how I'm going to word this. "I believe we could be of mutual benefit to each other. I know you want Daddy's empire, and I am willing to help you get it from him. And why shouldn't you have it? You have worked hard for the company for years. Graduated Harvard with honours, was an unpaid intern for four years before Daddy finally gave you anything for your time and efforts. You grafted hard, brought in 158 new clients. You even paid two clients out of your own pocket for their claims. I know everything, Mr Steadwell, all the things you have done and all the dodgy shit your father has done. And believe me, his list is endless at this point."

His face gives everything away. His eyes are round and wide, and if his mouth hangs open for much longer, he will start catching flies. "I'm happy the way things are, Miss Clawson." His response is cute. Does he really think I am that naïve? His lie is commendable because he doesn't know me, but sadly for him, I expect him to collaborate with me. And if it takes more than one meeting, so be it. I am a patient woman when it comes to my revenge.

"Mr Steadwell, this will only work if we don't lie to each other. I'm a very powerful woman. I can make your dreams a reality, but it requires honesty on your part. My part will be behind closed doors, makes things easier for all parties involved. Once this is all over, you will never hear or see me again." I enjoy being invisible. Some high-profile people know who I am, but they don't say anything because money definitely does help keep shit silent.

Luther doesn't need to work with me. I could just go and kill his dad, but then it would cause too much drama. He is very well-known, so his death would be high-profile and that means media and tabloids would swarm, and that would expose too much. So, with Luther involved, it means I can slip in and do what I need and leave – no mess, no drama, and no evidence of what I did.

"Okay, but how do I know you will not screw me over and leave me to take the fall if it goes tits up?"

I chuckle at him. *Why would I 'screw him over' as he so eloquently put it?* "Mr Steadwell, you're quite right not to trust me. We have only met today and I'm offering you everything you want. However, I am not going to 'screw' you over; that would defeat the objective of what I want in return. Plus, it's counterproductive." I glance at him and finish the last of my pancakes. Picking up my tea, I take a sip.

"Look, trust me or don't, either way is fine by me. Just your participation helps me out better than doing this alone. Makes things less complicated, really. How's this? I will give you today to think about my offer. I'm a very busy woman, Luther, and either way, I will get what I want. With or without your help. Your father owes me something and I plan to take it back by any means. Pick your side of the fence wisely."

Suddenly being aware of the time, I notice its 7:30 am, and I need to get moving. I have my 'normal person' job to get to. "Oh, would you look at the time! I must get going. Speak soon, Luther, and remember, your next choice will change your life either way." And with that, I stand up and leave. He will work with me; I gave him all he ever wanted. It's a hard offer to refuse. All he has ever wanted was being handed to him on a silver platter. He would be dim-witted to turn me down. I guess I will see what he decides soon enough.

Chapter 2

My meeting with Luther went comparatively well. If I'm honest, I have never had a meeting quite like that. He was far more handsome in person and taller than I thought; towering a whole six-foot, compared to my five-foot-four. The grey suit looked amazing on him, fitting so well to his muscular physique. He must love working out as much as I do. With each movement he made, I could watch each pop and flex of his muscles. And his punctuality is impeccable. I love a person who is on time. I believe it shows a level of respect; it shows you mean business. I have turned down clients over being late; it's a pet peeve of mine.

Mounting my motorcycle, which I parked just out of sight, my mind constantly on the man I just met. I'm not blind. I appreciate his good looks and the general sex appeal of Luther. Part of me is slightly bewitched by his good looks. *But will I go there?* I don't know. It's my job to stay the hell away, to never get involved other than to do the nitty-gritty work. But his father is what I want, so I decided it was best to deal with this in person. I'm going to make his father realise he pissed off the wrong woman, and going through his son is going to be the best way of doing it.

It's taken me over twenty years to get where I am today. Meeting the correct people, doing the right jobs, investing my money wisely. Now I'm at the top of my field, and yet I still didn't feel like I was ready for that, for Luther. I've had years of practice with my emotionless mask that Rick taught me, often finding myself never really taking it off. Even in my cover job, I use it. I'm a receptionist at Scott and Wildes, a big law firm in the city. I only do this because it's so easy to get information, tap a few phones, and speak to some people and boom! All the info I need right in my hand. *Simple.* Thinking about it, I'm supposed to be there in an hour, and I haven't even gotten ready. Lucky for me, K organised my makeup team to meet me in my house. I cover all my tattoos and put a wig on to cover-up the right side of my head that I shaved off. I know not everyone likes it, but I love that it shows off my tattoo, and also, it's different. Makes me look bad ass. It's about a 25-minute process with four people working on me at once.

Pulling into my driveway, I turn my Harley Davison off and stroll to my front door. Even being who I am, knowing that people do want me dead, I never have any guards. I'm called one-shot for a reason. Equally, people don't expect the most notorious hitman in the states to be a woman, which gives me the upper hand. I may be a mafia boss these days, but as I said earlier, everyone does things for the right money. And I am no exception.

Strolling into my house, I see my team is already there with my adopted brother, M, in the living room. These people have been with me since I became wealthy a few years ago. I don't trust M, not in the slightest. I suppose too much water had passed under the bridge to allow me to. But that's definitely a story for another time. Let's just say, he pissed me off one too many times and lessons had to be taught. Put a foul taste in my mouth ever since.

Maggie took him in a year after my parents died. She thought he would help me get out of my shell I had created, but he didn't. Then he just became a burden. A burden I have never been able to get rid of, probably because he has been around since I was ten, and how do you get rid of someone who's meant to be family? Well, we'll use the word family very loosely; don't want to give him too much standing. His ego is big enough.

"E, what a pleasure to see you this fine morning," he says, spotting me entering the room. *He's awfully chipper this morning, heaven knows why.* His black hair is cut short and he has dark circles under his eyes. I know he was out till late this morning; seems to have been doing that for a while now. *Something dubious is going on, let's hope it doesn't turn problematic.*

All my men apart from M live here, and hang out together. K told me a while ago that M hasn't been present as much, and he also hasn't been going back to his flat as often. That's how I know he's up to something. K always keeps me in the loop, my eyes and ears among the elite, as it were. It's nice to have them around, but I sadly don't get five seconds to myself. I do love the fact I have a full house. I cook for all of them. I enjoy it if I'm honest. It helps me to think, and sometimes I need that time to sort out my head and what my next moves will be. Plus, none of the lads bother me while I am cooking, scared I will throw a knife at them. You do it once and you can't live it down.

"What is it, M, I'm busy?" I say as I sit in my makeup chair that has been set up in the middle of the living room. I let my makeup artists work their magic to make me look like a regular innocent woman, not the stone-cold killer I am. Luther's father did this to me, he made me pursue being a killer. I own a couple of billion-dollar companies, one is on a need-to-know basis and the other is 'Secret', most high-powered people are members. Secret is a club that lets any person get exactly what their heart desires in the bedroom. Your wife won't peg you, we have you covered. Your husband won't tie you up and ravish your body, sweetheart, we have you sorted. If you can dream it, we can make it happen. The only stipulation is, keep shut about us. And all our members are happy to; I think a lot of them don't want their significant other to find out their weird kinks and fetishes.

Secret is run by Martin who keeps me up to date on everything going on with the men and women who work there. He's been my main man there since I opened it seven years ago with what little money I had. Now Secret has about forty men and women working there. And before you ask, all the staff are here by their own free will. If I am completely honest, they all love it. Massive wads of money, and all the kinky sex they want. What's not to love?

"Well, the good news is we have located the girl; she works three blocks from here in a library. Apparently, she was taken in by a nice family at a few months old, and has been with them ever since. However, we haven't found a reason as to why Kathy and John didn't keep her when you both were born," M says with a puzzled look on his face, his dark brown eyes looked like they were hiding something from me, which I never liked him doing. I don't like things being kept from me – it's fine for me to keep them. I am the boss after all. Looking at him through the mirror on my table, I raise my eyebrow.

"What are you hiding? M, we never keep secrets." His eyes flick over the people in the room. I never really notice my makeup artists. They aren't usually here for too long and judging by my reflection, it seemed they were done. Sighing, I turned to my main stylist.

"James, just put my clothes for the day on the sofa with my black bag and leave us. Thank you." He does a curt nod and ushers his fellow colleagues out the door. "Tell me." I watch as his chest rises and falls with nervousness. I know I'm a hard person to read, but I didn't think that he would be scared to talk to me.

"She looks similar to you. But, instead of your green eyes, hers are deep blue and she's got golden hair. She wouldn't pose well as a body double. Also, she has an American accent, so she doesn't sound like you in any way." I move away from my makeshift dressing table and start to get dressed for my morning at the office. James picked out a navy skirt and matching blazer, paired with a soft ivory silk blouse. All finished off with a pair of nude stilettos; simple yet elegant as he always dresses me.

Was he really that worried about saying this? *Good God, he is pathetic.* I still do not know why I keep his useless, idiotic ass around.

"That's all you are fucking worried about? She can dye her hair, and have you ever heard of contacts? And I will have someone teach her to speak as I do." I return, strolling off to the bathroom across the hall to put on the finishing touches, a small amount of perfume and some deodorant. All done and ready for the office. I do look particularly good today; I love the slightly smoky eye makeup that James went with. And my hair in loose ringlets makes me look incredibly beautiful; sometimes I think they know magic or something. How they manage to stop me looking like a killer is beyond me.

As I stroll back, he looks a little more relaxed but still has one more question. "How would contacts change her eyes? She is also an inch shorter than you, so that might be a problem."

"Colour contacts." I roll my eyes. *God, is he really so dense?* He really isn't the full shilling, as Rick use to say. "Even if she's slightly smaller than me, no one will notice when she's sat behind a desk. And when she's not, heels. For God's sake, M, is this all that concerns you these days? We have done far riskier things than this," I state, Well, I say we, more like me and, I just carry his arse. Marcus and Aid have always said he was dead weight, but I couldn't bring myself to abandon him.

I straighten his tie, pat him on the shoulder and smile. With that we leave the house, locking the door and setting the security alarm and cameras. Walking towards the car, I think about what M said, my blood starts to boil at the way he was with the situation. His inadequacy really starting to antagonize me, and I can see myself imploding with rage soon.

I have a hybrid Nissan with all the bells and whistles included. I don't drive a Jaguar like Luther, yes, I looked at his car. But I also knew because I own his driver, best to have at least one connection to him. It was easy to get someone into his camp. He was advertising for a driver a couple of years ago. Graham, a good friend of mine needed a job, so it worked out for the best. I get to know where he is at all times, and he gets to live like the playboy millionaire he likes to be.

The office is a suitable place to work part time. It's a law firm in New York City. The CEO owed me a favour, so it was easy for me to get in. Not that I needed the money, just the connection to the big wigs of New York. It's always best to have some dirt on people, never know when you might need to blackmail someone.

I usually have others that I pay to work here and feed me information. I have too much to do, but for twelve hours a week, I come here. It gets me out of the house, and away from most of the men. The only one that is here with me is B. He works security for me. Doesn't like me being in the normal world unprotected, scared I might get hurt or kidnapped. It has happened before, so I guess I understand. I've tapped all the phones, so I know everything that goes on and hear it all, but being young and sweet also has its advantages. The bosses love to give me all the details and tell me dark secrets to try and impress me. Fluttering my eyelashes and whispering sweet nothings into people's ears works wonders here.

My main reason for wanting to be here is because Harry Steadwell is a client. I want and need to know all about his dirty business, so I can work out the best way to ruin his life, before I take it. But no one here knows that. I'm just a lovely young lady who shows people to the right rooms and picks up the phone when needed.

The women here don't even notice me much, too clicky and I don't vibe with that. So they stay clear of me. I appreciate it. . Women talk, and I can do without that shit. "Alexia, can you take these to Mr Thorn's office. Then you are done for the day. Sam will take over," Patrick, my manager, says with a smile.

Christ, had I been here for five hours already? His grey hair is impeccably styled, slicked back with a light amount of what I can assume is hair spray. His navy suit is well tailored to his fine body. For a man in his near fifties, he looks damn fine. And I don't know what aftershave he uses, but it smells delightful, and his beard is trimmed and tamed effortlessly making him look all the more distinguished.

I remember the one year he dressed in a red suit for Christmas and looked like a sexy Santa. Even I appreciated the way he looked, all steamy and suggestive. No wonder he has women of all ages after him, and those deep blue eyes can render any woman immobile. If K looked this good at that age, I would be happy to stare at him for the rest of my life. I know nothing will ever happen, but it doesn't mean I can't look at him, imagine what it's like to kiss him, sleep with him. Some nights, I lie in bed and picture him, his hard cock, what he would do to me. I can always imagine; it helps sometimes to cope with the knowledge that I will never have the man I love.

Coughing, I pull myself from my traitorous imagination. "Yes of course," I replied with a sweet smile. I hate this part, pretending to be nice to everyone when I know a lot of the people here deserve a bullet for the shit they pull. Alexia Jones is my name in 'normal' life. It allows me to be in places I shouldn't be and stops people from knowing me or asking questions. If I'm honest though, Clawson isn't even my real name. It just helps to distinguish between my real meetings and working here. I have many aliases that allow me to move through the shadows; many names that can't be traced back to me. I am like fog – around but never caught. Names are traceable and you can be found by a quick search; everyone is on social media or job sites. Everyone here has their face on a website. I can find anyone I please with a quick look on the computer. And my face is on the Scott and Wildes website; me smiling and my name underneath. But with my hair, and makeup, I don't look exactly like myself.

Making my way to Mr Thorn's office, I keep smiling and it's hurting my face. When I get to the room, I notice he's in a meeting with someone. I knock on the door. I never usually check on Mr Thorn. He doesn't do dealings with Mr H Steadwell or anyone of significant importance, but the more I eavesdrop, the more I recognise the voice in the room. "Enter. This must be Alexia with my files for you," he states to the other person in the room.

As I enter the room, I suddenly see who it is. Luther is sitting at the desk. Turning his head to look at me. I smile as I enter, watching as Luther's eyes examine me, scepticism written across his face. Clearly, he sees something that he recognises, but not enough to ask me directly if I am who he met this morning. "Have we met? You look familiar," he states with puzzlement in his voice. Nobody ever recognises me because they never see me, but this is one of the only clients I've met in person, and he better not blow my cover.

"No, sir, I believe I would remember meeting a face as handsome as yours," I say in a girly voice that makes me want to vomit in my mouth. *How do people do this all the time?* Honestly it baffles me more than M right now. I can't stand being nice. Smiling at that comment, I think I've thrown him off the scent. He shrugs and turns back around as I hand Thorn the folder, that then being my queue to leave.

Picking up my burner phone, I call K. "Listen in on Thorn's phone, he's in there with Luther Steadwell. I want to know why," I all but demand, just gracing over pleasantries.

"Yes, E," he replies before I hang up.

Moving back to the main floor, I see Sam already sat at my desk. I smile again. *This shit is getting annoying.* My bag is already on the table ready for me to leave. Sam is another one of my workers, not an agent. He just works here when I don't, feeding me information. I have people dotted all over the place, so I constantly have news coming in. This operation has been years in the planning and nothing is going to fuck this up.

"Have a pleasant afternoon, Alexia. Don't do anything I wouldn't do." Sam smiles from the desk. He is a fine one to talk, him, his boyfriend and girlfriend are game for pretty much anything. I would know, they come to the club now and again. I allow them in because Sam's boyfriend is a member and a close friend. Dwayne Stanley, a tech mogul in New York. He builds firewalls for huge companies, and anti-virus software. If you have a phone, you have Dwayne's tech in it. And let me tell you, the sky is the limit on what those three will do at my club.

"You would do pretty much anything, Sam. Thanks for coming in," I reply with a chuckle, and another smile I sure as hell can't wait to get rid of the minute I leave this building. I lean over Sam and log out of the computer before grabbing my bag, ready to leave.

"You're right there, Alexia, but where's the fun in not doing everything and anything. See you next week, honey." Sam chuckles as I get to the front door. I raise my hand and wave goodbye.

Thank goodness I'm out of here. Now I can get out of this monkey suit and put on my proper clothes that are more comfortable. Feeling someone behind me, the same scent fills my lungs. The smell of mint and spice, it's an unusual combination, but for some strange reason it smells tantalizing. I remember it from my meeting this morning with Mr Steadwell.

Turning, I see him standing way too close to me. Retreating a step or two, I face him. I am intrigued with what he wants. Why is he staring at me so intently? Seems I won't get out of this easily. I best bite the bullet and speak to him.

Chapter 3

His eyes are looking into mine like he knows who I am. And even if pretty boy did put two and two together, Julius, the CEO, wouldn't do anything. Julius is a good friend; we have known each other for a few years now. Julius is low-key scared of me. Don't know why, I've done nothing to him, yet anyway.

Luther tries to take a step closer to me. Noticing him moving, I retreat another step. "Miss Alexia, isn't it?" His voice holding such cynicism. His eyes boring into mine, begging me to answer him. I, however, don't have any intention of giving myself away. I would be stupid to do that. It would ruin everything I have worked for.

"Yes, sir, Alexia Jones. Is there something I can help you with? I am currently off shift." I'm really trying to hold back from knocking him out, but if I did that, it would be on camera and then I would have to dig my way out of that. People are bustling past us, and right now, I need to get going. I have training and a party to get to, which I don't want to go to, but I must. I also know that Steadwell senior and junior are going to be there.

"Yes, you can. I can't seem to shake this feeling that we have met before. Are you sure we haven't?" I roll my eyes at him; will he not stop being so persistent? I can't cope with him badgering me with all these questions. If I wasn't trying to stay unseen, I would have thrown him up a wall and told him to shut his fucking mouth.

"Mr Steadwell, I said before that we haven't. I remember the faces of all the people that pass through this law firm. It's my job to know everyone. I make sure I remember for my boss's. And you haven't ever visited us before, so I know we haven't." My voice remains flat; my irritation thinly concealed at this point. His face still holds so many questions, like he doesn't believe me. I wouldn't trust me either, but I know who I am, he doesn't.

"Also, judging by the designer clothes, I know we don't even hang out in the same social circles. So no way we could have met outside the office either." My smile doesn't waver, being here has allowed me to learn how to hold my smile without letting it fall, even when people like Luther piss me off and make my patience wear thin.

"Fair enough, Alexia, you would be right. Maybe you have a sister I met instead." Good God! Is he never going to let up? My patience is only going to last so long before I punch him.

"No, sir, I'm an only child. No sisters or brothers. Just me. Now if you don't mind, sir, I would love to stay and chat, but I have a hair appointment to attend. See you around, Mr Steadwell." Without giving him a second to respond, I turn on my heels and leave.

Once I'm in the car, I drive back home. It's 2 pm. Gosh! Today has been long. Been at the office since 9 am and missed lunch with the guys. K probably cooked. He is a great cook and makes my favourite foods. If I'm lucky, he will have saved me some for when I get in. The house is only a 15-minute drive from the office, so I pull up not long after leaving Luther. I used the drive to calm my racing mind; so much is going on right now. I just don't know what to do, between M and Luther, I am starting to get stressed.

Entering the house, I spot H and K laughing in the kitchen and M is nowhere to be seen. That's odd, as he's usually always at home when I get back. Lately, he's been out more and home later. I am going to investigate that, but right now I'm starving.

"E, food is in the oven. Want me to heat it up for you while you get changed?" K asks when he notices me. His dark eyes glancing at me, an unreadable expression etched onto his face.

Sometimes I mistake his looks for love, but then I remember he probably only sees me as his boss and nothing more. I nod and move into my bedroom; the room is cleaned every day by me. Well, I make the bed and make sure that things are put away, that's about it. I do have a cleaner who comes and sorts out my house once a week. I would do it myself, but sometimes I just don't have the time, so Gloria comes once a week and cleans and stocks up the food. I have five men who live here, so I go through food fast.

Stripping out of my body suit, I move to the bathroom. Washing my makeup off, I glance at myself. I can see why men look. I have a small nose, large bright green eyes and beautiful, long shiny near black hair. But I think my tattoos put people off – they run over my left arm. I also have one that runs from my left ear down my head, neck, chest and left ribs. It's not finished, but it will never be;

it's my reminder of the good things I do. It's a vine and each leaf is a life I've saved, but the tally on my arm is the lives I've taken. I always remember; it helps to keep me sane. I have more leaves than tally marks. I live with the belief that I should always save more than I take. I may do some despicable things, but I want to do more good than bad. I am not completely evil.

Once I've washed and made sure I smell good, I move into the bedroom. Opening my small walk-in closet, I grab a black top and jeans. Putting them on, I move back into the house and sit at the kitchen island. K places my dinner in front of me. It's some chicken and Chinese style noodles. This will definitely keep me going for a while. I demolish it quickly; I loved it. But to be honest, I think I would love anything K cooks me, probably because it is him. I swear I embarrassed myself by making happy food noises, and if you don't know what those are, it's basically orgasm noises when you're eating. What can I say, I was ravenous, and it tasted great.

"Do you like it?" I raise my eyebrow at K, watching him shift from one foot to the other. Nervousness evident on his face as he asks me. His cooking always tastes amazing, so why he was nervous was beyond me. For some reason, he always asks for my approval on his food.

"K, of course I liked it. You are a great cook. Is this a new recipe?" That would probably be why he asked, because it was something he hadn't cooked before for me. He blushed at my comment. I love it when he does. His cheeks go a lovely shade of red and he can never look me in the eye. He coughs and turns around; H chuckles and sits next to me. He nudges my arm and glances at me. I give him a questioning look. H shakes his head and smiles at me. H and K are my best friends and my right hands. M likes to think he is, but if I'm honest, he's far from it. We may have grown up together, but he's always been a hindrance, never making things easier, just harder. He always tries to copy K and H, but he just isn't as useful as they are. And come to think of it, I have always had to clean up his messes – all the times he has not completed a task or done as he is told. It's hard to carry his dead weight all the time. I know it pisses the lads off no end.

"H, go to Luther Steadwell's and drop him a note and a pocket square on his outfit for tonight. I need him to know how easy it is for me to get to him." H nods and follows me into my office.

Grabbing a piece of paper from my supplies, I write my note:

Mr Steadwell,

I have taken the liberty of placing a red pocket square with your suit. If you wish for us to continue with what was discussed, then wear it. My offer stands until midnight. Discard this letter immediately when you have decided. Choose wisely, Luther, you will not get this offer again.

I fold it up and seal it with a wax stamp. I know that it's very old-fashioned, but it allows many people to know who wrote it. It's like an old movie calling card. Come on! They are cool, plus they are fun. H did show me a couple of TikTok videos that show people doing them, and I just fell in love with them. Definitely seemed like a me thing. For my birthday, K got me a lot of different waxes so I could mix them and create new patterns and colours. Now I send all my letters with them; it became a given.

I pass the note and pocket square to H, who then leaves the office. Hopefully this will make him realise how easy it is for me to get close to him without him even knowing.

Glancing at the time, I see I have a couple of hours before I need to get ready for the charity gala. I run a children's charity which homes many orphaned children. It's called Open Arms, and the hoity-toity snobs of New York have chosen to hold an event to raise money for it. I can't for the life of me fathom why. We have more than enough money. But unfortunately, I can't deny them, so I must attend as Katie Oswald, the CEO of the charity. It's a complete ball ache. I am an extremely busy woman. And being the CEO means I have to go, plus it's black tie, which is even worse. I have to wrangle K and H into suits, that's no mean feat.

I will have my tattoos out and look like I usually do. No one who is attending knows me. No mob bosses are going to be there, so no one will question me or expose me.

Walking into the open plan kitchen and living room, I see K cleaning up from dinner. I go over and start drying the dishes he washed. We do have a dish washer, but K always refuses to use it; apparently it doesn't clean better than he does. Drying the plates in silence is slightly awkward, but nothing unusual. Whenever we are alone at home, we have these moments where we don't know what to say to each other. It is cute, the way he gets all quiet and nervous to talk to me, but another part of me gets frustrated. Sometimes when I look at him in these moments, I want to kiss him. I want to tell him all the feelings inside and allow him to know exactly what I think. Not that I am particularly good at feelings, or just being vulnerable in general. I get snappy when I am sick, so speaking about what's on my mind is even worse.

"Thanks for lunch, K," I say with a small smile at him. As he turns, our eyes lock. Another look passes through, but is gone in a split second. I don't dwell on it.

"It's my pleasure. You always cook for us." He looks away and focuses on what he's washing up, keeping his hands busy so he doesn't have to look at me.

His side profile is as handsome as the rest of him. His beard is trimmed today, keeping it shorter than normal. His chiselled jaw line is still very defined, but his arm muscles flexing with each of his movements mesmerizes me. Watching him move and lift each item he cleans enthrals my attention. After realising I've been subtly staring at him from the corner of my eye for a while, I put the plate I'm drying, away. I won't lie, I have been drying this dish for longer than I care to admit. We finish the dishes before I move back into my room, needing to get my mind off the Greek god that occupies too much of my mind lately. After a few minutes, Klaire and James walk into my room to get me ready for the event.

"Hey, E, I brought the silver dress with matching heels for tonight. I also found these beauties in the storage locker; thought they would just finish the look off." Klaire is my personal assistant, so she does all my wardrobe and organises my events and meetings. She's worked for me for nine years and is always shit hot at her job. Sometimes I don't know what I did before her. She keeps all my diaries organised. She also deals with all the people wanting to get a hold of me. She has saved my ass regarding business affairs more times than I would care to remember.

She shows me a red box. I can't remember what is inside. Klaire opens it and my eyes catch what it is. Shock fills me as I thought I'd lost it. It's a diamond choker and matching tennis bracelet, the ones Rick got me for my twentieth birthday. A tear rolls down my cheek as I look at them. They are as magnificent as the day I opened them. I think they are all the more stunning, because Rick isn't around anymore.

"Brilliant! Just leave my hair in loose curls clipped on the side and flowing down my back, and some light makeup. I'm not covering my tattoos or my shaved head. No one attending other than Luther knows who I am. Also, did you bring K and H their suits?"

Klaire nods and holds up the two other bags. I know that they hate wearing suits, but they will need to get used to it. Sometimes we have to do what we don't want to. If I must go then, so do they. Klaire walks out to give K his suit and to put H's on his bed. I am so glad that Klaire is dealing with K and the whole suit thing. I won't deal with his toddler temper tantrum. He always throws his toys out the pram when it comes to dressing up. You hear everything: 'It's too tight on my neck', 'I don't get why I need to wear this', 'Can't someone else go', and so many more. He makes me want to backhand him into next week sometimes. So the less I have to deal with that, the better, plus Klaire isn't in love with him, so she isn't scared to put his childish ass in its place.

James does my hair and makeup; I have a dark smoky look, making my green eyes pop. My dark hair falls down my back in loose curls, elongating my neck and shows off my necklace, which sparkles beautifully. Klaire helps me into my dress when James is finished. It fits my body exactly. The back is cut out low near enough to my bum and the front is a little low, showing off some cleavage, and barely held up by the spaghetti straps. Klaire did put some tape on my breasts to make sure the dress doesn't move; I would hate to flash someone. The dress is a full-length A-line style with a large slit up the right leg. Klaire has to basically tape the dress to my bum and hip, so that part doesn't move either – the slit is that risky. Looking in my full-length mirror, I notice how good I look. I'm not a vain person, but right now, I know I look fire. The dress makes me look sexy, but not too slutty. It hugs me in all the right places and gives me an amazing figure. And finished off with the nine-inch stilettos and jewellery, I feel like a million-dollars, and I also look just as good.

"Right, boss, you are all done. And may I just say how stunning you look," James says, giving me one last look over, to make sure I am all sorted. His eyes scan me from head to toe. With one final nod, he moves and opens the door.

Moving into the living room, I see H fixing K's bowtie while K huffs and puffs about wearing it. They both look great, but K looks striking. The way he left his hair down, with light shining off it, makes it look just like silk. His beard looks full and luscious. K also trimmed it shorter than usual. I don't like it. I've always loved his long beard. Not long like Gandalf, but long enough to potentially tie it with a hair bobble. But what captures my attention is the way his glorious body is in that suit. His muscles showing off through the blazer jacket. God, it's panty melting. He has left the black blazer open, his waist coat buttoned up, and finished with a white shirt and black bowtie. I bite my lip as I think about ripping it off his sexy body, devouring every inch of him.

H notices me walking in and nudges K while smiling at me. H is dating a girl I have working at Secret, so he isn't here all the time these days, but is always on hand when I need him. I do hear him bring her back sometimes though, and they have kept me up a few times, but I can't be bothered to say anything.

K turns and looks at me. His face stills for a second before his eyes travel down me, taking in what I'm wearing. I watch as he gulps while taking me in, an intense look crosses his handsome face. My panties getting wetter with his zealous gaze, my mind still consumed with thoughts of him looking at me like that while his thick cock buried deep inside me.

"You look great, mate, doesn't she, K?" H bumps his elbow into K, knocking him slightly. This brings him back, and he averts his gaze to the floor and coughs.

"Yeah, you look great, boss." His eyes move up and lock with mine; heat rushes to my cheeks. His eyes make me feel warm wherever they are. I look away slightly, not wanting to show him how much he affects me. Trying to hide how much I want him; how much I dream about him.

"Thanks, we best get going. Charles is waiting for us outside." I turn and walk towards the front door; my heels click off the tiled floor. I can hear them following me. It's not always this awkward with K, but sometimes we have these days. And it's especially when we aren't doing much, or when I have to dress up. When he's in his suit, I struggle to keep my desire hidden, so I act super awkward, or I just turn and leave. I've never been very good with boys, and I'm even worse with K. This will be a long night.

Chapter 4

Pulling up at the venue that is holding the event, I pass the invitations to the guard on the door. He nods and signals us to enter. The party is in full swing and naturally the hoity-toity snobs have gone all out – a massive ballroom filled with people. The lights are low, an orchestra is playing soft music in the background, and servers are passing around canapés. There is a huge chandelier hanging from the centre of the ceiling, and small lights dotted around the room, giving off a small glow. Flowers are in huge vases in the corners. They are beautifully arranged and add to the aesthetic. To be frank, they did an amazing job making this fundraiser. It's beautiful. It's a shame that everyone here is an asshole with too much money. Now that brings down the appeal of the place.

I walk to the bar and order a glass of champagne. K and H order a scotch and start to move around the room checking our surroundings. I'm not worried about being here. This is all for show, anyway. No one gives a shit about the charity. It's just a way for people to show off; to make each family jealous of the other. It's entirely a joke and I wish I wasn't even part of it, but here I am, and there is no backing out now.

I walk round for about an hour or so mingling with the elite of New York. They all ask me about the charity or me as a person. Luckily, the charity is real, so I don't have to bullshit about that, but when they ask about me, my whole back story is rehearsed, so many would think that it actually happened, and if I'm honest, I can be quite a good actress. I tell them about my life, and what inspired me to start the charity work. It's such a beautiful story about a girl who knew someone who had no home, and who struggled throughout life. So, she decided to make a difference. She decided to create something to help children who needed it. For children who had no one to turn to and give them not just a home, but a chance in life. Told you, a proper good story – shame it's all fake. I really made the charity for children like me; I know how hard life can be when you are alone. The world is huge and when you have nothing, it feels a hell of a lot bigger. I started to build homes for children who needed somewhere safe, somewhere stable they could turn to. A place they could always rely on, even when they have grown up and left. We never turn our backs; we have the mantra 'the door is always open'. And we stand by that. No child should be left to struggle.

I smile and talk to many people. K and H always in my sight but far enough away to not cause any suspicions on who they are. Not that anyone would ask. They are two handsome men. The women here love them. K has two women hanging off his arms. And yes, before you say it, I am jealous. Why wouldn't I be? And H, well he has a cute red head practically drooling over him. I think she is the daughter of Cole Anders. He works in the private security sector and has made a mint doing it. Now, many big wigs use his company to secure their buildings. He seems to only be humouring her, maybe the relationship with Willow is serious.

Just as I finish talking to Ella Nickolas, the heiress to the Nickolas fortune, a tap on my shoulder snatches my attention. Turning around, I come face to face with the devil himself. Harry Steadwell stands a few inches taller than me, dressed in his Armani suit. His hair is gelled back and he is freshly shaven. His dark nearly black eyes look into mine. A sickening feeling fills my gut, and the hatred I feel for him starts to sink in.

"Mr Steadwell, what a pleasure to make your acquaintance." I smile at him, extending my hand for him to shake. My mask is well and truly locked in. I keep my demeanour light, not giving away my disgust for this man.

"Miss Oswald, the pleasure is all mine. I've heard what amazing work you do for those children. Must be such a rewarding job." His eyes still hard. I'm not going to let him intimidate me.

I smile brighter, trying to keep this charade up. "Why yes, my job is so rewarding. Helping those little ones brings me such joy. But I bet your work is just as fulfilling, helping people out who have lost their possessions due to fire, floods and other problems." I hide my sarcasm in my response because this piece of shit never pays out. People insure their home with him and then if something happens, he does nothing. He fights them tooth and nail on the pay-out. Just shy of 30% of all claims are paid, and of that 30% only 22% of those are paid in full. He's a scumbag on every level.

"Yes, it's nice to be able to bring people some relief when they think there is none. Anyway, you must meet my son, Luther." He looks around before spotting him. He was leaning against a pillar not far from us. He has the red pocket square in and a red tie to match; it goes well against his all-black suit. He has black Christian Louboutin's to complete the outfit. Does he think I needed the extra reassurance with all that red? I can admit he looks quite dashing in that suit, and with his five o'clock shadow, he looks very distinguished. His hair is styled nicely, a lot better than his father's anyway. He has a small amount of gel in compared to Harry Steadwell; he looks like he used a whole tub. If the sun hits his hair just right, the fucking thing will go up in smoke. I try to supress a chuckle as the thought crosses my mind.

Once Luther has joined us, Steadwell senior introduces us. "Luther, this is Katie Oswald. Miss Oswald, this is my son, Luther. Katie was just talking to me about how rewarding it is to work for the charity we are raising money for tonight."

Luther looks at me, his eyes full of questions, but he doesn't give anything away. He smiles and shakes my hand. "What a pleasure to meet the son of such a generous man. You must be really proud." I give him my sweetest smile and softest voice, praying to God he buys this shit. Luther smiles and takes a swig from his drink, his eyes roaming up and down me before returning to mine. A lustful look fills his eyes as he takes me in, and right now, I am not opposed to it.

"Why yes, I am. He's doing quite a few good things lately, a couple more charity events coming up."

I smile and take a small sip of my drink, giving Luther the best flirting eyes I can; the thought of coming to another one of these gives me the chills. But I need to keep up appearances. I know what he said about being proud is bullshit, but damn did it sound convincing.

"Well hopefully I may get another invitation if I behave myself." I giggle slightly and look at Harry with a super sweet smile, I know he loves a younger woman. The last woman he fucked was about 28 and he's 59, so yeah, if he thinks I'm just a sweet innocent charity worker, then that's all the better. But each time I try to be sweet, I want to vomit on the floor. He makes my fucking skin crawl.

"I'm sure you will. We could do with a few more pretty young things like you at these events, my darling," Harry states, raising my hand and kissing my knuckles. An urge to throw up passes through me. He is the worst man I know, and here I am chatting with him while he kisses my hand. I wish I could just slice his lips off so he can't kiss anyone else and cut out his tongue so he can't speak to anyone. Sadly, I can't, so I just smile at him. But I think Luther may have seem my face contort for a split second; it was fast, but it wasn't unnoticeable. I just hope he doesn't mention it.

"I love the matching tie and pocket square, Luther. Colour suits you nicely," I state, making sure Luther knows I spotted it. If I need the extra reassurance then so does he. I won't lie, it looks great on him and sets the suit off nicely.

"Thanks, thought a pop of colour would be good for a change."

"Why yes, it is. Anyway, if you will excuse me, gentlemen, I would like to speak to some other people about the charity and try to get as much money as I can. Hope to see you at the auction, Luther." He was clearly getting uncomfortable with this situation, so I decided that I should take this as my cue to leave. I smiled and turned, strutting away, glad to be away from his poisonous snake of a father. Thank God Luther played innocent; seems he might not be as dumb as I thought.

Chapter 5

As I walk away, I take out my burner phone. I text Luther; I got his number from K after he overheard him tell Thorn what it was.

Thursday 8 am–8:45 am, Café Richie. Do not reply.

With that, I put my phone away. The moment it's away, I'm asked to go on stage and talk to the masses about the charity before the auction. I really didn't want to do this, any of it, but my charity was chosen to host the auction. Apparently, the big wigs of New York choose a charity each quarter to have a fundraiser for, and mine has happened to be chosen. What an honour – not.

Standing on stage looking at all the people around me, I imagine I'm giving a prep meeting for my staff like I usually do once a month. It usually consists of me telling them what our next move is. "Thank you, ladies and gentlemen, for attending today in honour of our charity. We take in children whose parents have abandoned them or passed away; some are with us because their parents are just unequipped to look after them. We give them not only a safe place to live, but also the tools to get through in life, and people who they can turn to. Not just when they are with us, but also throughout their lives," I state, looking at the room. Pictures of the children are showing behind me and all the wonderful things we do within our seven boarding homes of 56 rooms.

People are looking and awing at what I'm showing them. Yes, I care about the charity I founded and got it off the ground. I made it what it is today, but I don't care about these rich scumbags standing in front of me. I only came for Harry Steadwell. I wanted him to look me in the eyes. So when I do kill him, the shock at it being me might just kill him off quicker.

The last picture that comes up is of me and a small child. We are both smiling. I remember that day fondly. Faith was adopted, and I was saying goodbye to her. She was such a bright wonderful child, and the family are good friends of mine. I still stay connected with her. She is doing well and loving her new home. Apparently, she is getting straight A's at school and her parents think she will get into an Ivy League school. I couldn't be prouder. She is proof of all the work we do here.

"I founded the charity because all children deserve a stable and safe home to live in. They deserve to have a great start in life, and the ability to become the person they want to be. I hope you find it in your hearts to donate as much as you can today, so we can help make more children as happy as all the children in these photos. Thank you."

Once I had finished my presentation to the mass gathering in the room, I step backstage as Mr Steadwell senior and Luther stepped onto the stage. I felt Luther's eyes on me like fire blistering my skin. I had a close call this morning with him nearly recognising me, meaning I needed to get the girl fast and bring her into the fold but that would take a few days, maybe even weeks. She may be hard to turn around or she may be willing to work for me but then I have to get her changed to look exactly like me. It's doable, but it could take a while to get the results I want, meaning I have to be smart about it. I've ordered my man to take her to mine tonight while I'm here. Hopefully she comes willingly with the offer I am putting on the table, but I can't be one hundred percent certain.

"Thank you, Miss Oswald, for that illuminating presentation and speech. Yes, my friends, this money is going to an excellent charity that will greatly benefit from your generosity. Right, on with the auction. We have thirty-nine wonderful women waiting to go out with some lucky man or woman. Shall we start with 108?" Thank God it wasn't me. I thought that prick would put me up first. I'm 405 so hopefully he forgets I'm even part of this.

Watching as each woman is picked by random powerful men and one even gets a woman, I realise I'm the last one. Oh for Christ sakes! Now I must go up there. Plastering a smile on my face, I hear my number called, "405 is our last lady. Miss Katie Oswald, doesn't she look divine today, ladies and gentlemen? Who's going to start us off?" Harry Steadwell says as I'm stood in the middle of the stage.

"$400,000," Luther interjects, raising his paddle from the side of the stage, causing a whoop to erupt from the crowd.

"Best bid of the night, ladies and gents. Who wants to bid higher?" Harry asks. God, these people have more money than sense. But hopefully, no one bids again. That was insanely high.

"$450,000," returns another random man a few feet from the stage slightly right from the centre. God, he looks like a sleaze; probably hoping I'll give him a good time. The thought makes me a little sick. He even looks like a guy who expects a girl to put out because he paid. His whole look sends a shiver of dread right down my spine.

"$500,000," calls Luther again a second after that man bid. I'm kind of hoping that he would win because I would rather hang out with him than any other man in this joint. No one bids for a few seconds, so Harry Steadwell decides that I'm basically sold.

"Okay, for $500,000, Miss Oswald is going once, going twice, and SOLD to Mr Luther Steadwell. You may take your date off the stage." This in no way made me feel like a prized cow going away for slaughter. This must be the most degrading thing I have ever done.

Luther struts towards me with a smile for the crowd and takes my arm, and waves as we walk off. My smile instantly gone; distain replaces it. "Pleasure to see you here, Miss Clawson, so you really own a charity? But looking you up, not one Miss Clawson matching your description in the whole of New York. With that in mind, who are you really? Miss Clawson, Miss Oswald, it's all very confusing." Luther whispers right into my ear, his voice is like hot chocolate slipping straight into my core, making me slightly wet. I dismiss that thought rather quickly. *You never mix business and pleasure,* my mind reminds me. God, I have too much pent up sexual tension.

"Depends. I told you I don't want people to know me. I have no name and by the fact you tried to look me up and came out with shit, I am pretty fucking good at not being found, aren't I?" I reply, my tone harsh. But being up there in front of them men who only look at my body kind of pisses me off. Turning to face him, I grab his jacket and shove him into a dark corner. He hits the wall a little hard. My patience finally breaking, tonight has been a lot.

"If you are wise, Mr Steadwell, you won't poke your nose into my business or question how I do it. You call me whatever name I tell you, smile and wave like a good boy. If our deal is to work, that's what you will have to do. I won't fuck you over. The only person who'll do that is you by being where you shouldn't. Now let's get the last of this shit show done so I can get the hell out of here and back to where I need to be. My associates will finish up," I say sternly, which causes a corner of his mouth to turn up into a smile.

"I do enjoy our little chats, Miss Clawson. Let's finish saying our goodbyes and then maybe we can chat after?" he asks with a mischievous tone to his slick voice, and straightening his tie with a glint in his eye. This man really knows exactly what buttons to push, and I could swing for him sometimes.

"And what would you like to chat about, Luther, the weather perhaps?" I say sarcastically, resulting in a bigger smile from him.

"Well, I would like to know where you would like to go on a date, or maybe you would like a surprise. Also, when are you free for it?" God, he's infuriating. An exasperated sigh escapes my lips looking him in the eye.

"I will be in touch with details. Also, never text me back. I hate replies. If I want an answer, I will call, understood?" He looks slightly puzzled but replies with a nod. Linking his arm, I face the crowd. "Let's get this over with then," I say to myself more than him.

God, that was fucking horrible, but I'm glad to be going home. It went quite smoothly though. Many congratulated Luther on getting a girl like me. One even said he must love playing with fire to which Luther laughed slightly and said, "Well it makes it more fun." That annoyed me but men can be arrogant pigs, especially when they have money.

We did bump into a couple of Luther's friends; one was Jack the other was Tyler. Jack was the same size and build as Luther. Apparently, they went to college together. He was very talkative; we had a good chat, and I could see why they were such good friends.

"Hey Luth, Katie here doesn't seem like your normal type. Which is good, blond bimbos won't make you happy for long," he says with a chuckle. Luther however didn't laugh. He looked sort of embarrassed. I laughed. And I know exactly who he is referring to. That would be Sonya about ten feet behind me giving me the evil eye. Five-foot-eight blonde bimbo. From my intel, she cheated on Luther so many times I lost count. She would be the perfect photo wife for him, but she's obsessed with sex. You know the wife that goes to events with her husband, and you never see any other time, that's all that tramp is any good for.

"Well, I do have my blonde moments. For one, I decided to come here," I say with a chuckle, causing Luther, Jack and Tyler all to laugh.

"Fair point," Tyler says with a chuckle. He's not as tall as Jack and Luther, also he's lighter haired compared to their dark hair. Very kind blue eyes though.

"You happy Luther paid for you?" Tyler asks, his eyes flicking between me and Luther.

"Damn right, I am. Luther seemed to be my best possibility. Also, the other guy bidding looked like he was hoping for a 'good time', but I don't think his idea and mine of a 'good time' are aligned. Also, I would be worried his hip wouldn't hold out if we did," I reply, air quoting for emphasis on good time. This causes me to get another laugh from everyone.

"I like this one, Luther, try not to fuck it up. She might be good for you," Jack says with a smile. I will be good for him, his career that is, not his sex life, or in any romantic sense. I don't do love, feelings or any of that romantic shit; never have and never will.

We all chatted for a while; it was a nice time with them actually. I even had a couple of drinks, and usually I try to nurse the same drink all night. You just put it to your lips and pretend to take a sip. If you don't stay with someone too long, no one notices.

After I was done chatting to Luther and his mates, K and H signalled it was time to go. I made my excuses and took my leave, and I won't lie, it did turn out to be a pretty good night. Something I wasn't expecting.

Chapter 6

Entering my home, I see a woman sitting on a chair in my large living room, looking rather at home on my crushed velvet sofa. K and H look at her before making their way upstairs, giving us the privacy we need. As she hears me enter the room, she turns, and true to M's word, she looks just like me, with two major differences. One being her blonde hair, while mine is near enough black, and the other her bright blue eyes, nothing like my green ones. "H-hello," she says as she stands looking at me with amazement in her eyes.

"Hello, Jasmine, I'm E. You are probably wondering why I brought you to my home. I would like to ask you something," I say, stepping into the living room. Instead of sitting on a chair, I walk towards a mini fridge that sits in the opposite corner to the door. Opening it up, I get myself a Pepsi Max out. "Care for a drink?" I ask, purely out of politeness.

"Please, do you have cherry Pepsi?" Of course, that's a silly question. I toss her one and take a seat across from her on the other sofa and open my can. Her blue eyes keep wondering around the room, every few seconds they flick back to me.

"You said you wanted to ask me something, ma'am, but can I just say how weird it is we look remarkably similar. And, how amazing you look in that dress," she says with puzzlement in her voice. Apparently, she can't put two and two together. At least she is pretty; Mum and Dad didn't bless her with brains.

"Darling, you're my twin sister. You were put into care at three months old. Sadly, we still don't understand why, but according to records, our parents left you over here while keeping me. I'm looking into why, but that may take me some time. Going back over thirty years in records is not an easy job. And thank you, I have just been to a charity gala. I hate these things with a passion. Anyway, I need you to join me and my business. It would be of great benefit to me and also to you," I replied, taking a sip from my can and setting it down on the coffee table. Her eyes are wide with surprise, and she also has a slight tremble in her hands. Now I know I am a hard woman to deal with, but I didn't realise I was that intimidating. She will need to toughen up when being in my company. I can't have any weak links, well any more than I already have.

"Why do you want me? I'm nobody." There is moisture evident in her eyes, apparently something I said upset her. Fuck me! She needs to get a backbone and stop the waterworks; I don't do tears. Crying is the one thing I lack empathy with. Okay fine! I lack empathy, period!

"Actually, you would be of great use to me, Jasmine. I would like you to do my job at a law firm. You would be a receptionist. A very simple job, but it requires one thing from you," I say, looking her in the eyes. She seems intrigued by my statement. I just hope she takes it. I'm glad she's not actually started to cry yet, but I don't think she looks particularly shocked by what I'm asking. Maybe someone else spoke to her. I did ask M to track her down and keep an eye on her. Then today, I asked him to bring her in. Has he betrayed my trust and spoken to her before me? I hope for his sake he hasn't, I can't be dealing with having to teach him a lesson again.

"Okay. What would I have to do?" She took a sip of her drink. She is still shaking slightly, but she doesn't seem as nervous now.

"Well, you would have to answer the phones at this job, but also listen in to calls I request. I will provide you with an earpiece that will allow you to listen without anyone noticing. Also, you will have to dye your hair and wear contacts. Plus, you will have to have elocution lessons to sound British. Apparently, that's what yanks love about me. I would obviously make it worth your while, but my offer comes at a high price, and this is the bit you will need to think about."

I take another sip of my drink. She looks like she will accept my offer. I can see the cogs in her brain turning, thinking about all that I said. She bites her lip while she thinks of her response. I can see why men would find her attractive. She is the complete opposite to me. She looks sweet and kind, and her eyes glimmer when she talks. Her heart is clearly on her sleeve, while I am harder, stronger willed, and have an edge to my look. Only our faces are the same. She's slim, but not quite as slim as I am. She has slightly more ample breasts, not that mine are small. But maybe she uses a push up bra, not that she needs it. And is maybe an inch shorter than me. But that's hard to tell since she's sat down. I only know because M told me earlier. "What's that high price?" I think I may win here.

"You will have to cut all ties with your family. It's for their safety as well as yours. You will have to have a phone I provide, identification I provide, and do the jobs I assign you. I know it's hard to wrap your head around, so I will give you a couple of days to think about it. In the meantime, you are free to stay here and get to know the people you could potentially work with, or I could send you home, the choice is yours." It's as if I can see her brain working, deciding if she should or shouldn't do this.

I get up to leave, but she looks at me and asks a question I knew she would. "What do I do about money? I have college fees to pay and rent, other amenities to. I need a proper job."

Chuckling, I return to her. "Darling, you think I would ask you to do this for free? If you take my offer, your college fees are paid off, your rent will be paid. As for everything else, you will get a wage through from the company. What they pay me for the job I do there, I will just move it to your new bank account. Obviously with a small fee taken. Think of it as a protection price. You won't ever have to worry about money. Just think about it and let me know Friday morning. If you take my offer, we will start you that day and money will be paid to you from Monday. If not, you will go back home and never hear from me again." Pausing, I take a long look at her. "There is one more thing, you must never tell anyone about me, my name or what I do, nothing. I'm a ghost in this world. I walk in the shadows, and no one must ever know about me. I want complete loyalty, do you understand?" She looks at me and smiles before nodding. She may come in useful after all.

"M will sort you out whatever you decide. Hope I can trust you, Jasmine, or should I say, Alexia Jones. You will have to get used to hearing that name, darling." And with a smile, I leave the room.

On the walk to my bedroom, I think about Luther, the way he handled all the men looking at me and making remarks. He was a true gentleman, and I appreciated it.

Lying in bed, I think back at Luther and how he looked at me tonight, his eyes full of lust and appreciation for my looks. He did look good in that suit, but Luther's face was suddenly replaced by K and him in his tuxedo. I try to focus back on Luther because I can't have another night of thinking about a man I can't have. I want to use Luther as a distraction, forcing my brain to think about Luther. I start to picture all the things I would do to him and have him do to me.

Just as I'm about to pleasure myself, another noise rips through the house; this time it's not me making moans of pleasure. It sounds like Jasmine upstairs. It's also accompanied by sounds of a bed thudding off the floor. I own a sex den; I damn well know what is happening above me. But who the hell has she brought in with her, but more importantly, could they be any louder? It's as if they don't care that I am right underneath them or that this is my house – a little bit of notice would have been nice. And also a little less noise so I can sleep; fucking frustrating the hell out of me, the longer I listen.

Grabbing my blankets and glasses, I move into my office down the hall. Hopefully the noise doesn't get that far so I can get some sleep. It's already late and I have a meeting early tomorrow morning and can really do without her keeping me up all night, then I am hopping back to London. If this is constant, I may have to soundproof the whole house or just build a shag shack outside in the yard. I lock my door to the office and lie on the couch. This could be a long night.

Chapter 7

It's been a couple of days since I took Jasmine and went to the fundraiser. I've been out of New York City doing business with some of my associates in England and seeing Maggie. I like to keep an eye on Maggie. She wasn't too bad to me once we learned about my parents that night when I was little. I try to keep her safe as much as possible. I packed my bags and left when I was thirteen to be with my old boss and pay my way. She misses me more now than when I initially left. I am not a thirty-minute drive away anymore, but I do go back to England for coffee and to catch up once a month and call her when I can. She's been sober now for over ten years, and I couldn't be prouder. Things with her took a turn after that fateful day and for the better. It was hard for us all, but she decided to cut back on the booze before finally quitting.

We lost Rick six years ago and it was hard for Maggie, but I came back for a few weeks to be with her. I was proud that she didn't go back to the drink. She's been my rock for so many years, and I wouldn't be where I am, without her. She became the mum I needed, and our relationship grew tenfold.

Being in London was great. I usually only go for a day or so. I stopped with Maggie, and we chatted and had a laugh. "So, Emie, tell me about this Luther then. He sounds dishy," Maggie says with a grin, causing me to chuckle.

"Mum, he's not that amazing, he's Harry's son. He seems like a lovely guy, but you know how I feel about relationships and all that." I sigh. Maggie knew exactly how I felt. Her support over the years has been phenomenal. She has never judged my life choices, only ever encouraged them.

"Sweetie, listen, not every man is like his father. Rick wasn't. His father was an asshole who used to beat his wife and had a mistress. Whereas Rick was the sweetest man ever, loved me no matter what and he also loved you. I am so sorry for the way I was when we had you. Drinking was the worst thing I could have done." Her eyes filled with tears. I don't blame her for anything. She's been an amazing mother figure to me. I started calling her mum a few years after we found out about my parents. She was getting sober and actually looking after me and our love for each other grew. Couldn't imagine calling her anything else. I take her hand in mine, and she sets her tea down on the side.

"Mum, listen, you have been amazing to me and to Matt. We wouldn't be the people we are today without you. You gave us so much love. I can't thank you enough for all you have done for us." Maggie took Mathew in after my mother and father died. I never wanted anyone else around. I hated sharing Rick and Maggie's attention, but she felt it might help. It didn't, clearly seeing as I am still as cold and withdrawn as I was back then. He just drove me crazy, and still does. He goes by M these days, but to Maggie, he's Mathew and I am Emie, or Emilia, if I'm in trouble. I may be in my thirties, but it doesn't stop Maggie from telling me off now and again. I still get the same pit in my stomach when she calls me Emilia, the same as when I was a child. And with Maggie, I am more scared than I ever was with my mum, but she wasn't around like Maggie always was.

"You both are the sweetest children ever. It's a shame he couldn't make it this time. What's he doing again?" Maggie asked with a puzzled look on her face; her green eyes look at her cup when she asks. She has the same green eyes as my mother. Since she's been sober, she reminds me more of my mother each and every day. And it makes my heart swell with more love. She is my last link to them, and I treasure that constantly.

"He's taking care of Jasmine. Remember, I told you the other day I found my sister?" I say with a smile. Her memory isn't that great these days, but she does try. Suppose the drink boggled her mind over the years.

"Oh yes, didn't realise that Kathy had another daughter. Wonder why she gave her up." Maggie scratches her head, but something in her eyes makes me question her reaction. Does she know something that I don't? I don't think she would lie to me but there must be something. There must be a reason why Mum never took Jasmine, and Maggie would probably know.

"I'm looking into it. She's my twin, so surely, they would have taken both of us. It is odd but I want to know," I reply, taking a sip of my tea.

"Of course you do, sweetie, my bright beautiful girl always has to know everything. But maybe things are more complicated than they appear, just remember that, my darling," Maggie says, taking a sip of her tea, clearly ending the conversation. I drop it and we chat about anything and everything else, she knows something but won't tell me. I guess it will come out in the wash.

The next morning, Maggie is waving me off from the tarmac. She always has a cry, but she knows I will be back in a few weeks to see her. She is my mum, after all.

Getting back to my home, I notice that M is already there clearly, his piece of shit car is so badly parked, I damn near rear-ended him. He must have business to discuss, and I wasn't meeting with Luther for another 40 minutes, so I had some time.

Strolling into my house, I see him and Jasmine deep in conversation. She decided to stay for a while, and I appreciate it. Yes, I think about business a lot but, she's still my sister when it comes down to it also its company. Clearing my throat, I make them both jump like I've caught them at a bad time. I raise my eyebrow to them and Jasmine blushes.

"What's going on here then?" I ask, stepping into the kitchen. My house is average sized, sort of like something a normal person with a family would own. I love the fact I live on the outskirts of the city, still inside my territory. I couldn't be dealing with the hustle and bustle. I also don't mind the commute to New York; helps me get my mind straight before meetings and other important things. Yes, I do have too much on my mind but soon enough, it will all be over with.

"Sorry, E, we didn't hear you come in," M says with a slight blush in his cheeks. He also takes a step away from Jasmine. They were standing close but nothing I was particularly concerned about; maybe now I should be concerned. Was he who she was fucking the other night? Bile rises in my mouth at the mere thought of M and Jasmine. It's a little too close to home in my books, but whatever makes you happy.

"Clearly not. Why are you here before eight?" I retorted, getting a cup of coffee from the pot they brewed. It seems very fresh as it's still steaming.

"Well, erm. Couldn't sleep." M clears his throat before continuing, my eyes boring into him. I swear I saw Jasmine blush. He is shifting on his feet and looking super nefarious. "We were just talking about what it's like working for you, all good stuff, of course."

"Yes, M was just telling me how nice you are to the staff, really sweet actually," Jasmine interjects.

You buying this crap? Me, nice, is this a fucking joke? The voice in my head says. "Really? But that still doesn't answer my question. Why are you here before 8 am?" I ask again, looking over the top of my mug at both of them. Jasmine is still in her nightwear. Hair messy, no makeup and a mug of coffee in hand. M is fully dressed in his work clothes, but he looks a bit weird like he got dressed in a hurry. If people are in relationships, they should declare them to me. We are mafia, which means that we have certain rules to follow. And although I don't always like and agree with the rules or even being called mafia, I still expect people to follow them, and M knows this. When we first moved to New York, M and I shared a flat, but once the business started to grow, I bought my house and M stayed in the flat. H, K, and the others live with me here, but M didn't want to live with his sister, and I was always okay with that. Gave me space from his useless arse.

"There has been a development with Harry Steadwell. He's been doing more dodgy dealings and one is with the charity you are patron of. Erm…how do I put this nicely, he's erm…" His eyes flit to Jasmine, who also looks equally as nervous about this. We did speak a few days ago, and I filled her in on everything I could. She may be related to me, but trust is something you have to earn with me. And if he's been spilling his information with her, I'm going to be pissed off. Jasmine is new, so she shouldn't know everything. But clearly, she does know a lot so there is no reason to hide this from her now.

"Oh, for Christ sakes, spit it out, man," I say, setting the mug down on the kitchen table harshly. He knows it pisses me off when he doesn't just say it right away.

"He's sleeping with the manager, and they are taking money off the top." The room goes black for a minute as anger boils in my blood. Who the fuck is this prick? Thinking he is taking money from a fucking charity. Picking my mug back up, I smash it off the wall. How sick do you have to be to skim money off a charity, especially one for children, no less? Taking a couple of deep breaths in and out, I turn to Jasmine.

"Have you made your decision yet?" I need to move this on fast, I've got places to be today. "Walk with me." They both follow as I move to my bedroom. Jasmine and M stop in the doorway while I strip and change into something new.

"Yes, I have. I would like to take you up on your offer. But how will my family know it's me who's dead?" Looking at her as I'm putting my black T-shirt on, I see she's worried, but I have men who deal with this all the time. M has his back to me so he doesn't have to see me change, not like he will see anything anyway. I roll my eyes at him.

"Why don't you focus on what you need to do, and I will deal with those details. M, make the calls to get this one ready. I want her hair dyed and contacts made by the end of the day. We can work on the voice tomorrow. She will also need a new wardrobe. Get Klaire to sort it," I say to him as I exit the room. I only have 15 minutes till my meeting with that asshole's son.

"Yes, E, right away." And with that, he leaves us.

"Will I be able to see my family before all this happens?" Jasmine looks so sad, but she has made the right choice.

"Yes, but it will be with one of my men. You can spin the reason they are with you any way you like, but you will not be going alone. Do you understand?" I know I sound harsh, but I will explain it all over dinner. Grabbing her by the arms, I look into her eyes. "Look, I know I sound brutal and drastic, but it's business. And your safety, and my team's safety is a big deal to me. I will explain everything that will happen from here on out over dinner, okay?" With a small smile, she nods, seeming still slightly sad. A cough grabs my attention. M is standing by the door, his dark eyes flitting between Jasmine and I.

"E, we are ready to take you to your meeting and Jasmine to her appointments." With a curt nod, I move out of the room.

Pulling up at the café, I nod at both my sister and M, asking them to be here at eight thirty and no later. M agrees and drives off. Luther's Jaguar isn't here yet, so I stroll in and take my seat.

Again, like last time, he arrives five minutes early and I already have a coffee settled down on the table waiting for him. He's wearing a shirt buttoned up to the second to last one, black trousers that are tight but not too tight that they remove all the imagination, and a leather jacket similar to the one I own. God, he's like walking sex. *Stop it and calm down for fuck sakes. He's just a man!* My mind shouts. Clearly I'm going into overdrive thinking about this man.

"Mr Steadwell, early again I see. I took the liberty of getting you a coffee. Please take a seat." I gesture to him; he nods and shrugs out of his jacket setting it on the chair before sitting. Clearly this man is getting too comfortable in my presents, and it aggravates me somewhat. I hate people getting too friendly with me; its bad business.

"Good morning, Miss Clawson. Looking radiant as ever," he replies with a smile. What does he want? No one is nice to me when I have meetings with them, not even my staff. He's up to something. Narrowing my eyes as I looked him up and down. His eyes never leave me. I can sense there is some tension, whether it is sexual or otherwise. The tension is so high I can barely breathe.

After a few minutes, I break the silence surrounding us. "Thank you for being so punctual. We need to discuss what your role will be in this operation seeing as you agreed to this with the red cloth. I also want to make you aware of what I expect out of this deal. I don't do anything for free, no matter how good looking the client is."

"Yes, I look forward to talking to you about it, but on one condition. You go out for dinner with me Saturday night, say nine o'clock." Who the hell does he think he is making conditions of his own? I am the one with all the cards, he's just my way in. I have the men, the arm power, and the ability to bring his father to his fucking knees. But this man thinks he's in the position to make his own. *You know you want to.* That pesky voice in my head calls. Sure he is built like a god, with a face that was carved by angels. But this makes for bad business, doesn't it? Plus, wouldn't it help me get over K? Would it stop me fantasising about him every time I see him?

Chapter 8

His eyes are boring into my soul as he sits and waits for my response. Yes, maybe going out with Luther would be a welcomed distraction from my constant thinking of K. But I don't wish to put my revenge in jeopardy, no matter how sexy the man is. However, thinking about it, maybe if I had some fun, I could finally get back at the lads for fucking loudly above me. Moreover, it's been worse now that Jasmine is here. I don't care what she does in her personal life or more specifically who she is doing, but keep it the fuck down. I have been putting my needs off all my life. It's just dinner with Luther; nothing bad ever came from just dinner.

"Fine, Mr Steadwell, you have a deal. I'll text you later. Now down to the matter at hand. I found out some information about your father. I was hoping you would shed some light on it." I give him a pointed look; I'm fuming about what his father has been doing. And I even broke my favourite mug over the situation. It's fine because K has gone out to replace it, but that's not the point. That money was for little children, kids that don't have any family, no real homes. And I even use that money to put the kids through college. Well, some of them, I've found most of the kids in the orphanage work exceptionally hard and get scholarships. They have this urge to prove themselves and make a better life. It's beautiful to watch, and to have that son of a bitch steal money from them makes my blood boil. "Your father has been taking money from certain charities, skimming it off the top, more precisely. One I happen to be a patron of. You know anything about this?"

His jaw goes slack for a second before he regains his composure. Judging by his reaction, he knew nothing about what his father did. "I don't know anything about stealing from the charities, although he is shady as fuck sometimes, so I wouldn't put it past him. However, I do know he's seeing a lady called Sandra. I believe she works for your charity you spoke about the other night at the fundraiser. I just hope my mother doesn't find out; it would hurt her." His eyes are sad for a second. Did he not know that Sarah was fucking Oscar, her personal trainer? And before him, she was doing George. He was the UPS driver that definitely wasn't delivering after a while. Neither of them are saints in their marriage, but Sarah is happy with how things are between her and Harry. She gets money each week, and he doesn't ask about her boy toys on the side and has the trophy wife. Seems like a win-win for both of them.

I am not going to burst the bubble of his saintly mother, bearing in mind his mother is anything but. She has had more men than hot dinners. "Yes, I knew about that. I would like to think that you weren't part of this, Mr Steadwell, would hate to have to show you what happens to someone who crosses me." I keep my face emotionless; I would hate to think that he crossed me this early on. He doesn't understand how far I am willing to go to get his father, the lengths I will travel to succeed in what I have planned.

"No, I don't have anything to do with what my father does, and it disgusts me that he would do that. However, I can't do much about it either."

"But on the contrary, Luther, there is always something you can do. Try and gain your fathers trust, get personal information when you can. Sadly, for me you're my only inside man in his house. I know how that is possible." Yes, I have men in his companies and close to him, but Luther is going to be the closest person I have. Also, I don't wish to show Luther my entire hand. As Rick said, make everyone think you are playing chequers, when in fact you are playing chess.

I need him to butter his old man up, make sure he is gaining his trust. I know his father is a bastard most of the time, but he will have to weasel his way in. I need contact information, and associates he has. Really, I need everything he can get his hands on. "I have been waiting twenty-three years for this to happen. I can wait a little longer. This needs to go off without a hitch. We will work this slowly and carefully, more precisely than anything else I have ever done. Then when the moment is right, we will strike, or more so I will, and you will seize control of his company and his assets."

"Okay, Miss Clawson. I will follow your lead, but how do I get close to my father without raising suspicion? He's not an easy man to get around. He will sense something is wrong."

"In this industry, Luther, it's like chess. Just make sure your dad thinks you're playing checkers. That is something you may have to do alone; think of something you can do with him. Try to be perceptive. How I do it is, to think how they think, then do it better than them. Try thinking of this like trying to get a woman into bed, surely the great Luther Steadwell has game. Be creative, but most of all, don't fuck it up." I can see he's worried, it's written all over his face. But everything I said was true. Always act like you are trying to fuck someone, say things they want to hear, be close-by all the time. Be the person they feel like they can rely on, the only person, in fact. Massage someone's ego a little, then they will always let you in, even the great Harry Steadwell loves an ego massage, even from men, if you know what I mean. My goal is all I see, and nothing and no one will stand in my way. I stand up and walk past the table. I stop and put my hand on his jacket. Looking him in the eye, I nod before ending our meeting.

"Right, with that, I will be off, pleasure as always. See you Saturday at nine sharp. I like dancing, for your information. I'll be in touch." I don't even spare him a glance as I leave; he will do this, or he is useless to me.

Chapter 9

Standing in this dimly lit room is thrilling; I love the outing each week with the boys. Some of the women tag along but not all of them. This is the time we practice our shooting skills and it's exhilarating. I love working alone while the boys try to shoot me. Picture laser tag but more painful. I've had bullets that are made to imitate being shot; it injects you with a small amount of liquid that replicates the pain. With the added benefit of only lasting a few seconds, it's fucking agony. I've got five out of the ten men that came. We have one rule in this game: no head shots. Shit gets nasty when you get one of these in the head. B went temporarily blind the first time we used them; Q shot him. After that, we stopped and gave the no-sensitive-area rule, especially after we saw how he reacted to it. It wasn't pretty.

I heard, what I believe, a couple of men approaching round the corner. They are not even trying to be quiet. Stepping out, I see two men, one about six feet away, and one about ten, easy targets and with two bullets, they are out. I got one in the leg and the other in the chest. They both hit the deck like a tonne of bricks.

"We are already out, boss. H got us. Christ, this shit hurts," A yells, B gasping for breath next to him. I'm straight faced. I don't give a shit if they are out, you cross me while I'm still playing. You will get shot either way. This means there are three left. Great! They must be in the stairwell up ahead. They should know you never try to take me out on stairs, they are my best friend. I've always been good at getting people here; stairs offer an amazing amount of cover and the ability to echo people moving on them.

Moving swiftly, I make it to the door, no one is left on this level. The door is heavy, but I move it without a single noise. I've been doing this for years; you would think my men knew better. Coming to the stairs, I hear the rustling of clothes. It's a distraction. No way clothes rustle that loud or quickly, even when running. Rule 1 when fighting: Always listen to your surroundings. These rules will keep you alive. I've tried to instil these into my men for years. Such a shame they never listen. That's maybe why they will never beat me. I move up one flight, keeping my back to the wall and my gun raised. The hairs on my neck stand up; someone is close. Turning fast, I spot the movement of one of my men. He's just a few stairs up from me. His breathing is loud and fast, he's on edge and too right he should be. I aim my gun at him and with a pull of the trigger, I know I made my target.

Catching him in the back of his leg, he yells and falls down, clutching the area I shot. I smile, knowing it was K I just shot. I would recognise that voice anywhere. It's as if they never learn. Maybe I should trade them all in for monkeys. At least they would learn what I show them. In real life, I would have gone over and finished the job, but it's training and one of these bad boys is enough to make a grown man cry, and clearly it does, seeing as K is clutching his leg like I shot it off and he's about to bleed to death. "Really? That's the best you got after all these years?" I whisper into his ear, a light snigger leaving me as I stand.

Moving further up, I hear what I assume is whispering. Silly boys, it's hand signals or nothing at all. God, it's like I teach them nothing. I only whisper to my men when I know no one is near me, plus they would never catch me. I move into the room in front of me; this abandoned office building in the middle of butt fuck nowhere is amazing for this.

I see someone out of the corner of my eye, slightly too far away to use my pistol, but I have my baby with me today, a sniper. There is a rather large hole in the middle of the open plan corridor, it would be a nasty fall from so far up. If this was real, I would have used this to my advantage; lure someone over towards it then trick them into falling. Clean, efficient and leaves no evidence, they are the best types of death. Means all I have to do is wipe my tracks of being there, i.e. CCTV cameras around the property. Then grab all my men and equipment then leave the police to come up with nothing. Quite poetic really, the dead tells no secrets, and I'm one big walking secret.

I move further back and get cover behind a pillar. He moves into range and with one bullet, he's also out. The screams my men give me are thrilling. Even from what could be 50 feet away, his screams echo around as he falls to the floor. I love the noise; I know I shouldn't, but it's like music to my ears. I know I am a sadistic fucker. Just H left to go. This will be interesting.

Moving away from the hole in the middle of the corridor into the room behind me, I smell him. I smell the fear in my men. This is only fun, but no one has ever beaten me in the whole time we have been doing this. But I'm known as one-shot for a fucking reason, *THERE!* My head screams as I catch a glimpse of him. He's about ten feet away on the other side of the room. Maybe I'll play with him. My phone vibrates, giving me away. *FUCK!* Ducking, I grab cover behind a discarded table. This place is full of random stuff left behind. I glance at my watch which shows who just texted. Mr Steadwell, you have some fucking timing.

I hear the bang of his gun before I feel the whoosh of air as the bullet leaves the barrel and whips past me. Close, yet not close enough. "E, you can't win now. I know you're here!" H shouts. He's my best shooter, well after me that is. He's also very good with tech. He's very versatile and that's why I like him. He's a challenge. H works out with me and K; his skills are particularly good. And I know if anything happens to me, the company is safe with him and K.

"Oh, I will. You will make one wrong move and you're going down, motherfucker!" I shout back. If I'm honest, we always get to this. The boys must duck out so they can watch our face-offs on the CCTV cameras I've had put in; they get very heated.

"E, we have been here many times before. I've learned all your moves by now. I know exactly how you work; I know exactly how you operate," H states as I creep around the room looking for the best place to stand. I'm so close to him I could almost touch him. Stupid boy, he never notices me move. I think I'm going to play with him for a bit. I tap his shoulder and slide under a nearby table.

"You are so close to me, E; you are making this too easy," he states as he fires and misses me by a good foot. I know it's dark but come on! It's child's play. I go for his leg with the butt of my gun, knocking his knee out from under him.

"Come on, H, you can't possibly think you're better than me," I say while I stand up quickly. He's on his knees with his back to me, so naturally I'm going to take this further than I should. I cap him straight in the ass cheek. He should know that he would never win against me.

"YOU'RE OUT, MOTHERFUCKER!" I yell, walking over to the lights.

"Right in the arse, E, why?" he retorts, pulling the bullet off him.

"It's funny every time I do it. You don't listen to where my voice is coming from. You don't listen for my movements or my breath and until you learn that skill, buddy, I'm going to keep doing it. This is why you just aren't quite good enough to beat me. And we will keep practicing this until you are as good if not better than me. You know how hard I was trained. What I put you guys through is child's play. Maybe I should get Marcus here and let him train you for a week or so," I say, slapping his shoulder.

"I would rather eat my own shit, E, but thanks for the offer." H chuckles while walking out to the van with me.

"Well, if you all are going to be this stupid every time, I may have to consider it. I need every single one of you better than this. If anything ever happens and one of you dies, I'm sure as shit gonna resurrect you and kill you myself." I chuckle, but it's true. I may not say it aloud, but their safety is my utmost concern. And I do actually care about them, but don't tell the lads – their egos are big enough.

I've only ever been shot three times in my life doing my job: once in my arm and twice in my abdomen, and I learned from my mistakes. I also learned that that shit hurts like a bitch. This exercise allows my men to learn how to survive without actually getting hurt. We tried paintballs, but it wasn't quite the effect I wanted. They just saw it as fun and not a lesson. They enjoyed being shot. I wanted them to feel the pain of their fuck ups. I lost something horrid the third time I ever got shot. Part of me was left behind with that bullet and I will never forget. I don't want my men or women to ever go through that pain. I will do anything so they can stand strong and not be hurt. My men are my family, and you protect what's yours.

We chat like mates again on the way to the van. It's awesome having days like this where I get to bond with my team and have a laugh. Reaching the van, I realise I have to text Luther back. I hate texting, but I will let him off just this once. Texting back and forth with Luther, I could see my men smiling at me through the minibus's rear-view mirror. I may not be driving, but I always like to see behind me, so sitting near the front, I have a perfect view of all angles.

"What the fuck you all laughing and smiling about?" I ask, kind of frustrated with this situation I was in. What is so funny? Am I smiling? If I'm honest, I don't know if my muscles even know how to smile.

"E, why are you giving this posh jumped-up-little-prick your time of day? He's wanting to get in your pants and you're kind of blushing," states H. Me blushing? No, never – am I?

"You know he paid for me like I'm some prized fucking cow. I know it's just a dinner, but I don't want him to think I do feelings and shit. Because let's be honest, I don't and the thought of him getting attached makes my skin crawl.

Dinner can just be a business transaction, right?" I ask the lads. For once, I do need a second opinion. I feel more comfortable asking them than the women. But it doesn't mean that I am comfortable talking to him about it.

"Depends, mate. Do you want him to get attached? If not, then make it clear at dinner that that is all it is. If you want more, then instigate more. The thing is, E, you are in control. Either go and see what happens or tell him where he and you stand. You never have had a problem with putting people in their place before," K says. It is hard to talk about another man with him. It's a tad awkward, but what else can I do? I need advice and we are kind of trapped in the van together, so he will hear everything anyway.

"I'll be honest, K, I don't know what I want from him. Yes, I could take his father out, but it's better Luther is involved, so I can give him the business and it looks less suspicious. I mean, he's good looking, but he's so fucking annoying. He texts me, asks me questions. Also, he demanded he buy my dress and said he would only take my offer if I accepted this. If I didn't want him to take over Harry's company, and I hadn't made a promise to someone, I would have put a bullet through his skull for opening his mouth without asking. Do I look like the kind of girl who is into romance, anyway?" I say, although I could also use his mouth for other things, I guess. *Hell yes, you could…*the voice in my head cries.

"Look, we can't tell you what to do, but maybe when all this is over, you could go and do what makes you happy. Also, take a holiday. You haven't, since the day you started. And seeing Maggie doesn't count. You're thirty-two, you should be enjoying yourself. And no, you don't look like the romantic type, but that could change." Maybe I'm going to do just that; the holiday, not the whole romantic crap with a husband, family, and a dog. I couldn't think of anything worse really. I would also never give up my company. It's all I have really. I will just find something else to do, someone else to kill.

"You're right about the enjoying myself, but I doubt the whole romance thing will ever change. I need a man who would rather go to the gym than dinner, prefers sweatpants to fancy outfits. And definitely someone who is more like me, who grew up in this world and understands the risks and implications of it. Someone who understands I have a company to run, people to protect." The last one is most important because I would never give up what I do for anyone. I've worked too hard to have it taken away from me. Let's be honest, I need a man who shuts his mouth and just does as he is told, and Luther has too many opinions. I call Klaire to get her to Luther's house. I could do with a holiday, but when that motherfucker is dead and his head is on my mantelpiece. Until then, I can't let anything get in my way.

Chapter 10

When I arrive at the house with the lads, I notice that Jasmine and M are home. M did not come today as I had him running errands and helping Jasmine sort some things out before she works for me full time. "Lads, I think something is happening between Jasmine and M. They always look so guilty when I catch them together," I state, turning to them. My suspicions have been growing tenfold lately.

"E, we know there is something going on. M told us. He also said he didn't know how to tell you in case you lost your shit at him," K says, taking me back a bit. Do they all think I'm some hard-faced bitch that doesn't want people to be happy? I just think it's weird you want to shag a girl who is the spitting image of the girl you grew up with. That's the part I still can't seem to wrap my head around.

Oh, so that's who she has been fucking all night, and keeping me awake. "I don't give a fuck that they are banging, but when they keep me up all night and I must sleep in my office, it pisses me off. What I'm more annoyed about is that I think he's spilling shit to her, and I can't trust her. Do I come across as someone who he can't talk to? Am I really that hard?"

"No, no, boss. It's not like that. He just doesn't want you to feel weird about it. Also, it's only early days. And I can't see him leaking her information. He hasn't got the balls to cross you, and we all know it," H added to K's original statement.

"Fine okay, let's go in. I need a drink after that." And with that, I lead them into the house. Opening the door, I see Jasmine swiftly jump off M's lap, clearly startled by my sudden arrival. I don't even acknowledge it, what's the point? They already think I'm some bitch that will shut their love affair down before it's even started, so I'm not adding gas to that fire.

"E, you're back early," M says as I walk into the room, finishing his conversation with an awkward cough. I don't even look at him. I just grab the bottle of scotch, pour myself a glass and move into my office. I was planning on sitting with the lads but I do have files to print off.

My office is white with a solid oak desk in the middle and a couple of bookcases on either side of the door. And a full-length window that looks onto my garden. It's nothing special, just grass and a fence of trees that enclose my house. It's quaint but I love it. When I was little, I always wanted a home like this, with a husband and children, especially by the age I am now. I'm 32 with no children, no husband and no want for love. Hell, I've never even been with a man, and if I'm honest, I don't think I want to be. Not that I don't find men attractive, just I don't want a man that's going to be clingy and always around. Couldn't think of anything worse. I go away at random times and don't come home for days on end and if I had someone, I would have to tell them where I am going. I don't tell anyone now and that's how I will stop. I need a man like K, he never questions me, and lets me do what I need to. But I soon stamp that feeling away; it's never going to happen.

I walk over to the printer and turn it on. I have some information going astray and I need to find out who the leaky tap is before something bad happens. I have come too far to have it ruined now. Looking at myself in the window, I see I look okay; maybe my hair is a little messy. Also, I have some dirt on my face. I should probably get that off before I leave. I do have time to get ready for my meeting. My office has two doors: one is to the living room which I just entered through, and one leads to a small room that has a wash basin and a mirror. Also, there is some white cupboards that hold various items: clothes if I need to change in a hurry and some sanitary products if I need to clean myself up after a messy day. Grabbing a baby wipe out of the cupboard on the right, I wipe my face. Looking in the mirror, my small scar under my eye is slightly dirty. Wiping it, I still remember how I got it.

"You, young lady, will get yourself killed if you don't start watching your opponent. You are talented, Emilia, but don't let that be your downfall. Again," Marcus says with a swipe of his knife. I love close combat fighting; he's trying to train me for when I'm allowed on jobs of my own. Being 15 means I still have a lot of training to go, but I am already better than most of his men. I'm even better than Matt, and he's two years older than me.

"Eyes up, hands here," Marcus says while moving my hands into place. "And begin." With that, I swipe my knife at him, trying to catch him with it. He's

fast, but I'm faster. I catch his arm and I slice his chest, cutting through his top in the process. I catch him a few more times. Something catches my attention from my right side, causing me to lose concentration for a second. It's Kieran. He's a few years older than me, with bright blond hair falling to his shoulders and blue eyes like waterfalls that I could get lost in. He is 18 and is filling out, his muscles are starting to show. His lips are plump and extremely kissable. He turns and his eyes lock with mine. He smiles at me, causing me to drop my guard. I know he did this on purpose to distract me. We get on well enough, but not entirely. That's probably why I want him, because I can't have him. My lapse in concentration caused Marcus to slice my face under my eye.

"Ah, SHIT," I yelled at the top of my lungs. That fucking hurt. I know that using knives that are razor sharp is dangerous, but this was taking the piss. I can't believe that I allowed a man to get in my way. How could I be so stupid?

"EMILIA, you need to pay attention. Christ, now that's going to need stitches, stupid girl. You want to make something of yourself, don't you?" Marcus glared at me.

"Well, of course I do. I don't want to be a nobody and also, I need to get him back. However long it takes," turning my attention back to him.

"Well, then, get your head out of your ass and do the training. Men will only bring you down and stop you from achieving what you work hard for. Stay away or kiss your sweet revenge goodbye." I knew he was trying to help, but at this moment in time, it wasn't helping at all. I felt like a child being punished for having a crush. But Marcus was right. I did need to forget about men and what they look like and focus on my payback. No matter how long it takes.

"Again," I retorted to Marcus. With a laugh, we continued training and from that day, I kept my distance from men. My mission was far more important.

Finishing up in the washroom, I walked back into my office. The printing was nearly done. Taking my drink into my hand, I took a sip. Scotch wasn't my usual drink, but today felt like an unusual kind of day. Still remembering Marcus' words, I picked up the printing. The list is about seven pages of all the people I need looking into. Putting it into my briefcase, I finish off my glass, then walk into the living room.

"E, you okay?" M asks with a smile. Apparently the awkwardness has gone from his voice. Maybe the men had told him I knew. Or at least that I knew something was going on. Either way, I felt slightly better about the situation.

"Yeah, yeah, just a weird kind of day. That's all. How's you?" If I'm honest, I don't usually do pleasantries, but I thought I would give it a try. And I fucking hate it. God, why do people feel the urge to have small talk.

"Yeah, I'm good. Why you ask? Something wrong?" M clearly is confused about why I am suddenly being nice. His eyes are full of confusion. Okay yes, I don't ask how people are, but sometimes I do. I'm hoping more to throw him off, so he will tell me about Jasmine.

"Nope, nothing is wrong. Thought I would try this thing called kindness. Clearly by your face it's not working, so I won't bother trying again," I respond with a smile, which gets a chuckle out of all my men. Taking the last sip of my scotch, I place the glass on the coffee table.

We chat for a few minutes when I hear something in my earpiece. I have been slightly listening into what Klaire and Luther have been talking about since Klaire told him about X. I'm not too bothered that she did, maybe it will deter him from crossing me. But this bit piques my interest. I have been hearing them squabbling like siblings for the last few minutes. And to be frank, Klaire is beginning to get rude. Putting my finger up to the lads to indicate they should be quiet, I grab my phone and call Luther. It rings for all of two seconds before he answers. "Luther, put Klaire on please." I hear him pass the phone over.

"Yes, Boss." I'm not very good with patience, and I'm definitely quick to anger so I take a deep breath in to control myself.

"Listen, Klaire, I know you think you know best, but right now you are being rude. I've been listening to you since you mentioned to Luther about X and what happened, which is true, I did shoot him in the head. You need to calm your ass down and leave him to it. Lucy worked for me a few years ago. She knows everything about my wardrobe. Hell, she dressed me at Secret for long enough before I stopped working there. Go find me some outfits to wear from the shop and leave them alone." I sigh, maybe I shouldn't have sent her. Maybe I should have sent James, but what's done is done.

"Put Luther back on the phone now." And with that, she passes it back. "Sorry about her, Luther, I'm sure any outfit you pick will be sufficient. She gets a bit carried away with herself, but she means well." And I know she does. I log into Lucy's CCTV and laugh in my head about how confused he looks. The view from the camera behind the counter has a perfect view of his face.

"Don't look so confused, I can hear everything. I don't always need to be in a room to know what is happening. You have much to learn about me, my dear, let's start slowly. Move slightly to your left and look up thirty degrees." He follows my directions, and you can physically watch the realisation cross his face. "Finally, you see, Luther, you have money, as do I. But money can only get you so far in this game. Sometimes you need something more and I have that in buckets. Pick what you like, but just so you know, I do like the colour blue. Reminds me of the ocean, calm, tranquil, but can cause havoc when needed. Have a good day, Mr Steadwell." Hanging up the phone, I grab my glass. Each of my men are looking at me with puzzlement now.

"What was that, E? Blue is your favourite colour? It's calm and tranquil, bla bla bla, come on! What is happening to you? Suddenly all nice and sentimental, you…" I don't even let M finish before I dive across the coffee table and punch him square in the face. His nose starts bleeding. Be confused by all means, hell even I'm confused as to why I said it, but don't question me on it.

"Fuck off, M, and get me another drink," I demand, setting his nose back with a loud crunch. He grabs my scotch glass and re-fills it before bringing it to me like the good dog that he is. No one questions me, not even my own brother.

After an hour, I pick up my stuff to leave. Even with the friendly chatter, there is an air of reservation and mistrustfulness. "I'm off to a meeting, someone do the washing up while I'm gone. M, I will meet you at the club in an hour. Jasmine, just chill here, K will show you where the movies are and books, depending on what you would like before they leave. What am I saying, you fuckers never leave. I was meant to live alone but evidently not. Don't wait up," I say and walk out of the door. Something feels off and I will find out what.

Chapter 11

"E, what a pleasure, what can I do for you this fine Thursday evening?" Freddy Edwards gleams from his chair at the bar. We always meet in Kugars. It's a nice bar but also sleazy enough that no one cares what we are doing. I mean people here are probably doing much worse. It's in the back ends of New York and even off duty police are here doing bad business. I meet a couple of them here to give them bribes to cover things up.

Mr Edwards is an older gentleman with grey hair slicked back, always wearing a suit. Today's suit is black with a white shirt and a black tie, his top button is undone, and his tie is pulled down. I place the briefcase on the bar and settle into the seat next to him. Looking at the waitress, I put my hand up slightly to call them over. This petite woman with blonde hair strolls over. She's slim with a large chest; her top is ridiculously low. Clearly, she thinks this will get her lots of tips.

"What can I get for you, Ma'am?" she asks in an innocent voice.

"Rum and coke, please." With a nod, she walks away. I turn my attention to Mr Edwards. "Shall we sit in that booth? I'm sure she will bring my drink over." I get up and move with Mr Edwards in tow.

Taking our seats, he glances at my briefcase; I only ever use this when I have business I need him to take care of. Briefcases are bulky and annoying to constantly have with you. "So, I'm assuming you have something in there for me, E," he says in a deep voice as the bartender drops my drink on the table and walks away. I don't even look at her.

"Yes, I have a mole, Freddy. I need you to go through all my associates and find out who it is. I know they are working for Steadwell. I just need a name and then I can fix the issue," I state with a stern edge in my voice. My eyes held anger; I can't believe after all these years I actually have a rat now. No one has ever crossed me before, so why start now? The mole only started a few months ago, but I don't know who it is.

"You know I'm always happy to help especially you, however my services aren't cheap." I slide a wad of cash across the table. I know he's not cheap, but he does a thorough job. I've worked with him for nine years in my own business. He's never let anyone down, and he certainly won't do it for me now that I've paid him double.

"There is double there. I need you to do it without raising suspicion. None of my men know I'm onto this, and I wish for it to stay that way. No one knows I'm here either. I hope you won't let me down." I glare over the top of my glass, before taking a sip.

"Of course not, you're a good friend and godmother to my two grandchildren. I will be back in touch with you in a few days. If you get anything else you need doing, just let me know."

I pass him the file and finish my drink. I do love his children and grandchildren. His family has been good to me, and his eldest daughter Zoe is a good friend of mine. We exchange goodbyes. I leave a small tip, and I head towards the door.

As I am leaving, I glance towards the bar. I see the back of someone who looks very familiar. Suddenly, a pulse heads down my body to its core, only two men in my life have ever caused me to get turned on, and one is here, of all places. He turns around and I see him. Luther is sat at the bar with his father. Why is he here in this crap hole? And what are they talking about? I must know.

Chapter 12

Walking out of the club, I glance at the bar. Luther and his father are just sitting down. Just as I am about to leave, his eyes meet mine, and a surprised look enters his eyes. I don't hang around and exit. Just as I leave, I notice that Jack, Tyler and another guy I haven't met, walk into the club. They all have money, so why are they meeting in a place known for violence and illegal activity? You don't have to be in the mafia to know about this place. Everyone in New York knows this area of the city is rough. Oh, what was that English saying? Yes, it's so rough, even dogs walk round in pairs. And that would be true, judging by the women in there. I chuckle to myself as I think about it.

Moving outside without making eye contact with them, I see Leon waiting for me. He is stood next to the passenger door, opening it for me to get into the car. "Secret, thank you, Leon." He nods and shuts the door after I'm seated in the car. The car is a large SUV with quite comfy leather seats. I lean forward and close the partition glass. Grabbing my phone, I listen in on the device I placed on Luther in our meeting. I put it on the back of his chair so when he sat down, it would clip onto him. I connect it to my earpiece and listen in.

"Luther, we have much to discuss." His father's voice bellows through my earpiece, his voice sends shivers down my spine and not in a good way. He makes my skin crawl; the thought of having to have another conversation with him makes me want to cut out my own tongue. "You need to give me your schedule every day, and you need to attend some meetings that I can't, for a while. I will be busy for a while and you will need to pick up the slack, and as my son, it is expected. Luther, are you even listening to me?" Annoyance heavily embedded in his voice.

"Sorry, I erm…Never mind," Luther stutters as he finally starts listening to his father. If I'm honest though, I wouldn't listen to him if he was my father either. His voice is annoying as hell, like nails down a chalk board.

"As I was saying, I want you to take up more meetings with certain clients. More specifically the meetings that I don't have time to attend, but I want you to keep me in the loop of who you are meeting. I mean all your meetings, Luther." Oh shit, he must know something is going on, seeing as he wants his schedule. This isn't good, although Miss L Clawson doesn't exist, I can do without him looking into that name. A lot of people who have power know me as L Clawson, and I can't 100% be sure that someone wouldn't tell him I exist.

"Thank you for giving me more responsibility, I appreciate it. I don't understand though, why you want to know everything I do. What's brought this chat on and why do we have to have it here?" To say I'm pleased he didn't say something to him is an understatement. He knows when to keep his mouth shut and I appreciate it. *Good choice, Luther*, I thought to myself, wise choice to keep quiet. But maybe he didn't think that his father was on about me, and sometimes ignorance is bliss. I am also surprised he is being given more responsibility now, only hours after I told him to weasel his way in. What is his father up to?

I'm bored of listening to them, so I shut off the earpiece and log into Luther's diary. I remove myself from it. I will have to tell him that I am going to be sending him one to forward to his father, then it will take the heat off me. I can't have that prick looking into me or I will lose my patience. I've worked too hard to have Luther or anyone ruin my plans now. While I'm sorting out a few things on my phone and text Luther about his dad, a tap comes through the tinted window.

"Ma'am, we have arrived," Leon states as he opens the door for me.

"Thank you, Leon, can you go back to Kugars and pick up Luther Steadwell? Say nothing to him and get him here." Leon just nods and gets back behind the wheel. Walking up to the guards on the door, they nod their heads in respect and open the door.

"Hank, Luther Steadwell is coming. Leon is dropping him off. Search him and then point him in the direction of my office."

Hank is a six-foot-two bald bloke of very few words, and that's what I like the most about him. He has worked for me since this place opened and thank goodness he has. He isn't frightened to get into fights with people, even if they are naked. And that helps tremendously with this line of work. "Yes, boss." With them aware of what's happening, I move into the club. It's busy tonight. Well, it's always busy, but today is gents' night. So, most of the women are wearing next to nothing and the men who work here are wearing just boxers. If I'm honest, most of the men who come here like to – how do I put it – try new things. So, a lot of the male workers are busy today. All the tablets are being used, people booking rooms to experiment. Many couples are scattered around having fun.

As I move through, looking around at the stages and booths, I see the women are working hard, collecting many tips from paying customers. Willow is always the most popular. She is the classically pretty woman. Blonde hair, big blue doe eyes, tiny waist and naturally larger breasts and bottom. She is always soft spoken and is down for anything. I will never understand her and H's relationship. They are very happy together, but Willow still works here. I couldn't do it, but hey, it makes them happy, so who am I to judge? Willow is currently dancing with the mayor's son. He's here every night without fail. She looks up and spots me. Smiling at her, I walk down the back stairs to my office.

Stepping inside, I see M lounging lazily on the couch. His eyes look tired like he's been up all night. And I full well know he was; he's been keeping me up for days as well. "Maybe tonight you could try sleeping, M." Sarcasm dripping from my voice as I raise my eyebrow. His face pales for a second, but he quickly composes himself. His dark eyes hold so much embarrassment, it is painful to look at. But I equally don't care; my sleep is important, and he hasn't allowed me to get any. But at least I know who Jasmine is bringing home with her. It makes me worry less, seeing as she's bringing him into my house and not some random dude.

"Erm…E, what do you mean?" I just roll my eyes at him; does he think I'm stupid? I won't lie, M has always underestimated me.

I ignore him and call Luther. Leon should be here now or not far. After a couple of rings, he picks up. "Hello, sorry I can't hear you. Two seconds," Luther yells down the phone/ I know the signal is a bit shit. But it's not that bad, so clearly, he doesn't want to be heard.

"Hello?" he asks again, clearly, he hasn't saved my number.

"Luther, in twenty minutes, please leave the club you are in with your friends. Someone will be waiting for you. I believe we need a chat." My voice doesn't hold much patience in it. I don't have time for him to argue with me.

"It's meant to be lads' night; I haven't seen them in ages." His voice pleads with me, but I don't give a fuck what he wants.

"Hey, what did I say to you the other night? Do as you are goddamn told, yes?" I really will punch him if he keeps going. I'm getting bored of him already and we have known each other less than a week.

"Fine, you know I love it when you are forceful with me. Also, what do I call you, seeing as Miss Clawson is a bit of a mouthful every time we speak?" I roll my eyes. If I rolled them any harder, they will roll right out of my head. If this man wants to get on my last goddamn nerve, he's getting there. M is looking at me with a smile. I narrow my eyes at him. What is he smiling at?

"E, just call me E." With that said, I cut the call; this man is literally driving me insane. I know he wants me. I can feel the sexual tension. I see it in his eyes. Let's be honest, I have never allowed myself to let men into my life other than work, but maybe one time won't hurt. But don't people who start doing drugs or drink say that – oh, my brain is in such a pickle!

"Just call me E? Really sis. You were even nicer on the phone to him. You want him, and here I thought K was the only man for you." I snap my head to him. M is wanting death, right? Is he asking for me to shoot his arse?

"Shut the fuck up. For one, it's nothing to do with you. And for two, we both know very well that I put those feelings for K to bed a very long time ago."

"Yeah, sure you have. Don't lie to me, Emie. I see the way you look at him. He has always had your cold dead heart, but I guess Luther could be a good distraction for you. You have pined over him for 15 years, why not have some fun with someone else because we both know you don't have the balls to talk to K about your feelings." His whole face holds his enjoyment of pushing my buttons; the whole time he never moved from his lazy position on the couch.

"Do you want to die today, Matthew? Brother or not, I will knock the shit out of you for speaking like that to me. You will treat me with some fucking respect. I won't let any of the other men say those things, and don't think I will let it slide with you." My face screams my anger. Yes, I know he's right. I never have dropped those feelings, but I also don't need him to point it out. Without letting him reply, I walk into my adjoining bedroom; my whole body shakes with vehemence. Who the fuck does he think he is? I will beat his ass, not like I haven't done it before.

Once I'm in the bedroom, I log into the CCTV in the SUV. Watching Luther brings a smile to my face. His nervous demeanour makes me chuckle. I text him not to worry, he's almost here. He doesn't seem to calm much but his head looks around the car trying to figure out what is happening, and how I am seeing him. He is so cute when he's clueless. *Did I say cute?* Cute, really? But I guess he is, with that frantic look in his eyes. He's not far away and the guards have their orders for when he gets here.

Soon after he pulls up to the club, I don't bother to watch any longer. What's the point? He will be here not long after, and I know everyone is going to say I'm in a foul mood upstairs because I haven't done my usual rounds checking on the girls. I just couldn't be bothered really. I move to the bed and take a seat, going back to do the work I started earlier. My plan is moving along nicely, but there are still many things that I need to get aligned before I can start moving further.

Hearing chattering outside, I move to the door. I hear Luther. "Yes, it is different. But that doesn't explain why I am here in the middle of nowhere." Opening the door, I stroll in, his eyes lock with mine. Confusion laced in them. A smile tugs at my lips as I watch him for a second. Apparently, the club makes him feel slightly uncomfortable, but I don't see why it would. I've investigated his past and I don't see why he would be, he's had so many conquests in the past. His latest was a large threat to him. She was crazy and after the charity event, she followed Luther. The big busty blonde with only one working brain cell, who was giving me the stink eye. Yeah, her. But I soon made that stop. She won't be bothering him again, hell she probably won't be bothering anyone ever. If you know what I mean.

"Well, that would be my doing, Luther. I would have waited until our next meeting. But sadly, this can't wait." His face flashes with concern. I know I'm scary, but he doesn't ask me anything. "As I said before, Mr Steadwell, our relationship can only last if we don't keep secrets from each other. So, I must ask, what does your father know about me? Have you said anything?"

I know he hasn't as I have been listening and monitoring his phone, but he doesn't need to know this.

Yes, I did enter the room like a bad arse. I threw the doors open and strolled in; his face is pale looking at me. "No, I haven't said anything. And he doesn't know anything, he just knows a powerful woman is coming for him."

I throw my head back and laugh. "Oh, your father has no idea." A tear slips down my face as I laugh hard. "I planted a listening device on you this morning, so I know your whole conversation in Kugars. And don't be shocked, I would hate for you to underestimate me, Luther. I asked to see if you would lie to me. You didn't, so we can proceed as planned." He physically seems to relax, but not too much. "I have taken the liberty of redoing your staff rota, so the ones that work for me are on when I need you. I won't pretend like I give a shit whether

71

you care or not. You will do as you are told. You will do as I ask and follow my command. It could very well save your life."

His features hold a lot of confusion, question and shock at the statement I just made, but I don't care. My men do as they are told, and he will follow suit. "You seem to forget what type of world I live in. It's a dog-eat-dog world. And we don't always play by normal world rules. We lie, cheat and kill each other. Yes, we have treaties and try to live as harmoniously as possible, but the mafia don't always stay peaceful. So, if you want my help, Mr Steadwell, you will act as directed. Is that understood?"

His head bobs up and down while he sits on the couch next to M. I've never seen someone so scared in a long time. "Good, I am so pleased we are on the same page. It definitely makes my life so much easier; would hate to have to teach you what world you have walked into." I take a seat on the adjacent couch and sip my drink. He will learn what world I live in soon, but will he survive?

Chapter 13

I don't think Luther will ever understand my world or where I come from. He is still naive about what I do, which is nice, easier to keep him safe. "Luther, have you ever wondered what happens to people like me when we get caught, either by the authorities or other mob bosses?" I glance at him with intensity. He ponders this for a few seconds. I can physically see his brain mull this over, his leg twitches as he probably thinks of the worst thing possible. And let's be honest, he probably isn't far from the truth.

"No, I don't know what happens. But equally, I don't think I want to know; I would like to know what this place is though. And why you asked me here?" he asks with a raised eyebrow.

"Very wise to not ask what would happen. Well, I brought you here because I needed to know about your father and what he knows about me. Other than that, it's probably because your company is alright. You are free to leave whenever you feel like it. However, in a couple of minutes, M and I are going upstairs if you wish to join us. I am surprised you don't know about this place; your father is a member," I state. It is strange that he doesn't know about this club.

He is wealthy enough to afford to come, and seeing as his dad also frequents here, it is slightly surprising. However, not too much of a surprise seeing as it's called Secret and members here are not meant to mention that this place exists. I make all my clients here sign an NDA. It does state that if someone mentions this place, I will sort them out. It doesn't state however, how I would do so.

His face is filled with astonishment. This is the most explicit club in the whole of New York. Only the best and most powerful men and women attend. Mostly, it's just men looking for a good time, and my women gather whatever information they can from them. But we do have women who come as well, some to piss off their husbands, some come to have needs met, and others, well, let's just say they are here for something other than a hard dick.

When men think they are getting a good time, they tend to spill their guts. And women are gossip fountains. If there is something to know, most women here are happy to tell. A knock on the door interrupts us. "Yes?" I shout to the person on the other side of the door.

Martin's head pops round the door. He looks super nervous. Am I really that scary? I mean I like being feared but not from my closest workers, and Martin has worked for me since this place opened and I've only lost my shit once. Okay twice…although there was that one time…fine, I've lost it a few times but not ever at him, maybe just in his direction. Fine, I'm a stress head and I get emotional, passionate – alright…angry. I get angry at everyone.

"E, your new woman is here to see you." Oh shit, yes, I had a new girl working for me.

"Send her in."

"Miss Clawson, what an honour it is…" I cut her off by raising my hand.

"Sit, I don't have long. One question, are you willing to report to me in any and all situations?" I ask with a stone-cold look in my eye.

"Yes ma'am. What would I need to do?" Is she for real. She hasn't ever heard of us, but I don't even bother to answer her question. I just move on.

"Right, who sent you?"

"Willow, she said you were a good boss and the pay is great. You don't force people to do anything but ask that we are loyal. So, I would like to know what it is I am required to do and what is optional." That doesn't make any sense. Willow is my best worker. She always gets the best information and asks me if I need to know anything from certain people, she then makes a beeline for them. Cannot fault her at all, but she's territorial. I will have to speak to her when I go upstairs. Also, no one says I'm a good boss. They just say I'm E. No one can find words to describe me and if they did, 'good' sure as hell wouldn't be one of them.

"Okay, so you won't get the same pay as Willow. She has earned her money with me. However, you will get a good rate of pay and also tips from customers. You are here to please whoever wants you, but you have the right to say no. However, if you do say no, the tips are shit. Any client tells you anything of importance, you report back to me. Finally, you will be living with the other girls and will be required to work five nights a week minimum, more if you wish. Speak to Willow, and she will explain all."

She looks super confused, and I can imagine why. This club offers everything a person could want sexually; it's a devil's hut. If you can think of it, it's probably under this roof. The girl in front of me is skinny, maybe a little too skinny, but living here she will put on a small amount of weight. Bleach blonde hair and big blue eyes, she will get plenty of attention. "Go with Martin and he will show you around. If there is anything you wish to perform for the people out there, sex wise, speak to him and he will be happy to sort it out." She looks even more confused; her light blue eyes fill with nervousness. This doesn't feel right. Surely if any of my girls sent her, they would have told her about what I do here. But something isn't adding up. I will have to speak to Willow about it.

"Are you a virgin?"

Luther goes bright red, maybe I should have sent him and M out the room. If I'm honest, I forgot they were there.

"Yes," she says timidly.

"Ah, makes sense. I can tell. You seem nervous but I can be quite intimidating. Do you feel comfortable having sex or even selling your virginity? It's all your choice, but if you want to, I can arrange some of my top men to put in an offer and you can pick one. Obviously, all the men that will bid for you are wealthy and are vetted to make sure they will look after you. But as I say, everything is your choice. Everything you do will be done here and nowhere else, anything goes amiss then you will report it to me, or Martin and we will sort it. Also, you will have to have a full STD check every seven days, non-negotiable. Also, if you have sex outside of your job, you must do another STD check. But if you work hard, you won't want to." She nods and stands up.

"One more thing," I say as she's walking towards the door. She stops and turns around. "Call me, E, Georgia, this place is nice, and the girls will treat you well. Come see me tomorrow at two and we will talk privately. I have something in mind that will suit you very well." She smiles, nods and leaves the room. Martin opens the door and collects her.

I turn my attention back to Luther and M. "Right, are we going upstairs?" Luther looks a little shell shocked at what I said to Georgia.

"What's up, Luther?" I ask as I glance at him. His eyes flick to me then flick away.

"Why did you have to ask her all that? And why would she sell her virginity?" I suppose he doesn't know what I truly do here. I sit in front of him on the coffee table and pat his hand.

"Look, the girls who work for me here don't do anything they don't wish to. However, if they have anything they want to do, such as sell their virginity, it works well in my favour also. I get information and the girls get a shit load of cash. Here they get everything they always wanted, and I get all the information I need. You flaunt your body and men spill their guts. Look, it's probably best I just show you what we do."

I can tell he's a little unsure on how to take this. I am by no means a saint but everything that happens under this roof is consensual, and I damn well make sure of it. "Okay, Luther, come with me." I stand and gesture him towards the door with M in tow. We make our way up the stairs into the main room. Men and women are everywhere. I've been here so long that I don't tend to notice all the attention I get or the men running around naked. I glance back to see both M and Luther looking awkward. You would have thought that M would be okay with all this seeing as he has slept with most the women here. But maybe because he is seeing Jasmine, he is a little strange around the women now. He must still think I don't see what is going on, but neither of them are exactly hiding the fact that they are together.

Maybe it's the fact I have caught Jasmine creeping in at 5 am this morning, or the fact that the night before, I heard them going at it so loud, they may as well have been doing it on my bedroom floor when they thought I was sleeping. I know they have only known each other a couple of days, but my Christ! Since she has been staying with me, I constantly hear them going at it. I mean who the hell sleeps through a noise like that? But I didn't bring it up after my cheap dig earlier. I guess I like the thought of them being happy. Still having the spare room soundproofed, I may only sleep a few hours a night, but I would still like to get those in.

I spot who I am looking for and make a beeline straight for her. Willow is stood with the chief of police and he is slipping her some cash. Captain Roger Kenning is New York's highest police captain and oversees most of the departments. He's also a good friend of mine.

"Roger, can I please steal Willow for just a few moments?" I ask with a smile; he looks nervous to see me. I will investigate that later.

"Sure, E, no problem. But just a friendly heads-up, someone is looking for you, so keep a low profile," Roger replies with a smile.

"Who is after me, Roger?" I'm curious on who is looking for me because no one ever has the balls to try and step up to me.

"Harry Steadwell. He has cops working for him. He's trying to find leads back to you. He's found a small amount of CCTV that has you and his son leaving a café, moments apart, but that doesn't mean anything. He apparently doesn't have your face in the footage but is still trying." I knew this son of a bitch was looking for me, but didn't realise how close he had come though. Might have to get him off my tail, can't have him poking his nose where it doesn't belong.

"Thanks, I appreciate it. Keep me updated. And let me know the names of the cops he has in his pocket if you don't mind. Anyway, it's Willow I wish to speak with for five minutes tonight."

"Oh yes, of course, E. And I will give you the names if you promise not to harm them."

"No, of course not. They are still police." I turn around with Luther, M, and Willow in tow.

"Willow, Georgia came to see me tonight. What do you know about her? Also, what did you tell her about me and the company?" By her reaction I can tell that she doesn't have a clue who I am talking about. I knew something was off with her.

"I'm sorry, E, I have no idea what you are talking about. I don't know any Georgia; I don't usually bring people to see you anyway. One, because I don't want another girl stepping on my territory and two, because I don't trust people not to say something to someone they shouldn't. A lot of what happens here isn't above board and I love what I do." Oh shit. I knew there was something fishy going on, but Willow is right. I'm not meant to get women to fuck men for money, but half the men that know about this place are clients. So, they wouldn't do anything to ruin the fun they have.

"Right, thank you. I have something to attend to. Come by and see me when you are finished with the captain. We have business to discuss. Also, is H bringing you to Sunday lunch?" She smiles and walks away. I'm just glad they make each other happy.

I turn my attention back to M. "Get Martin on the line and find me that girl. We need a chat, woman to woman. Get her in one of the rooms. I will deal with her in a bit." With that, M leaves me and Luther alone.

"So, Luther, would you like a drink?" I ask, purely because I will be getting one. Clearly all this may have been too much for him, but he needs to get used to the world I am in.

"Definitely," Luther replies, maybe he needs one as much as I do.

Chapter 14

We walk to the bar that sits in the middle of the massive main room. This whole place is in the middle of a shipping yard. So naturally this building is an old container, no partitioning walls. Just one massive open space with tables and chairs scattered around. On the edges of the room is some curtained booths, but hardly anyone uses them. Most here love the thrill of fucking while others watch. I guess that's another appeal to this place. The red and black theme just adds to the sin feeling, and the dim lights give a sexy ambiance. I have rooms built under the container for more ambitious and erotic sex. They are usually always booked up. And the bondage room is always booked weeks in advance. I am planning on having more built in the near future. I also allow smoking inside so there is a low amount of smoke in the air. When I thought of this place, I wanted 'sex meets a speakeasy'. Somewhere to fuck and have fun, and judging by how much I make here, everyone loves it. The low music mixed with the sounds of sex seems to just turn people into horny animals, and right this second as I am leaning on the bar, there are two orgies happening. Luther is pale watching, but I also watch him adjust himself.

I signal Darley to come over. She's a tall, busty red head with bright red lipstick on which makes her deep blue and green eyes pop. She has heterochromia, which means that her eyes are different colours, and most men love it. She always has them throwing themselves at her. She does well behind the bar, but her trustworthiness leaves much to be desired.

"Yes, boss, what can I get you?" her thick Southern accent asks. Her eyes racking over Luther before peeling back to mine reluctantly. Luther is still watching what is happening all around us. He probably either hates this place or loves it. And right now, I really can't tell which one it is, but this is how I make money, so he has to accept it.

"Whiskey, just bring the bottle and a couple of glasses to my office," I say before turning and leaving the bar. Luther follows me quickly, his eyes still roaming around. I notice he's looking at a particular girl called Steph. She does look very similar to me. Dark hair, green eyes (but hers aren't as powerful as mine.) Her tiny waist and round, full breasts are very desirable. She's not as popular as Willow but close enough. She's also a good friend of mine and Willow's. Well as friends as anyone, I don't usually do friends, but they have both been here since I opened.

"Who's that?" His eyes never moving from her as she dances around her pole effortlessly. Her tiny silver bikini leaves very little to the imagination.

Chuckling, I look at her, "That's Steph, 29. She's worked with me for seven years now. She is very popular. Why you ask?" I raise my eyebrow at him. His face goes red, embarrassment creeping in. "If you fancy some fun, I can book you in. I'll check the iPad to see her next slot." Luther's eyes snap to me, and the colour drains from his face.

"No. No, nothing like that. I was more admiring how much she looks similar to you. Plus, I was hoping for fun with someone else." I smile and raise my eyebrow at him again. Well, if that's the case I will sort it for him. A treat on me for helping me get my goal.

"Sure, who you looking for? Point to a girl you want, and I'll make it happen." A sly smile spreads across his face. He raises his hand and points at me. My heart stops for a moment, I erm...I've never had visitors. But I guess there is a first for everything. I turn and walk away. After a few steps I realise he isn't following me.

"You coming?" A smile tugs at the corner of my mouth. His eyes light up as he follows me across the dance floor and to the spiral staircase. This set of stairs are only privy to me. Even the guys don't come down here. Getting to the bottom of the stairs, I put my thumb on the door handle and the red light turns green, granting me access. I don't want anyone to accidently walk into my room, so I have it as thumb print access.

Opening the door, I walk into the bedroom; my white bed sits in the middle with white walls and light wooden floors. There is also a couple of bed side tables and three doors: one leads to the office I was in with Luther earlier, a bathroom and small walk-in wardrobe. I let Luther walk into the room. His face is shocked as he takes the room in. It's probably not what he was expecting, but this is where I stayed for a while when I first opened this place. The girls are in the rooms built under the shipping container next to this one.

Shutting the door, I grab Luther's jacket and pulled him backwards, throwing him against the door. I may have been a bit hard as I hear the air leave his lungs. "I don't do feelings, or commitment, Mr Steadwell. So, anything that happens right now won't happen again, and we won't discuss it either." My eyes bore into his, showing the level of sincerity I mean.

"Things can always change, E."

"Don't hold your breath, Steadwell, this is just some fun. Don't look too far into it." And with that, I smash my lips into his, silencing him. He responds immediately. His lips moulding with mine; the kiss is heavy and all-consuming. He spins us, slamming my back against the wall. His hands run down my body, sending shivers down my spine. I moan into his mouth as his hands reach my ass. He lifts me, and I instinctively wrap my legs around his waist. I can already tell how sculpted he is. My hands run over his shoulders and down his chest. I can feel each well-defined muscle, and with each breath he takes, I can feel his abs more on my lower body. My hand starts to undo the buttons of his shirt before I run my hands over his shoulders, forcing his shirt off.

Pulling away from his lips, I take in his chest. Those mouth-watering abs and pecks stare at me causing me to blush slightly. Luther grabs my T-shirt, pulling it up and over my head. My maroon lacy bra now on full display. Luther's eyes trail down my chest, admiring me.

"Fuck, you are sexy." I just chuckle at him as he pulls me off the wall and walks us over to the bed; his lips capturing mine again. My back comes into contact with my soft duvet. We don't break contact for a second as Luther's lips descend onto my neck. He sucks on my throat slightly causing me to moan, his hands start to massage my breasts through my bra as he rests between my legs. My moans get louder, my core getting wetter with each passing moment. I slide my hands down his body till I reach his trousers. In one swift flick, I open his trouser button and slide his zip down. Slowly, I slide my hand into his boxers and grab hold of his cock, running my hand up and down his shaft, Luther's breathing hitches.

"E, God," Luther grunts against my neck before his lips collide back into mine. The kiss is filled with so much unbridled passion, something I never thought I would feel from another person. Luther bites down on my lower lip, drawing forth a moan of pleasure from me, awakening a fire inside. Grasping his moment, Luther slides his tongue into my mouth. His tongue waging war with mine for dominance, a war I might just let him win tonight. I let my desire and sexual needs win, might as well allow him too as well.

Luther moves back to undo my trousers. After a second, he pulls them down, leaving me in just my maroon lacy bra and panties. My breathing stopped for a second as I felt something lightly stroke across my folds. Glancing down, I see Luther has his right hand in my panties. His fingers slide between my folds before stroking my clit. I let out a breathy moan as he builds my pleasure. "Fuck, E, you're so wet for me. But I want to taste your sweet pussy before I fuck it."

"Mhmm," was all I could muster as he pleasured me. I push my panties down so he can get to me better. Luther takes them the rest of the way off before spreading my legs further and resting himself between them. Trailing kisses down my body, he nips and sucks on my skin until he reaches my thighs. Feeling each press of his lips as he kisses, jolts a pulse right to my core, my need building and pulsating through my entire body. Each of my nerves in overdrive as he prolongs my wait for sweet relief. I didn't know it could feel this good. I didn't know it could be this intense. With each and every movement of his lips along my skin, my anticipation builds, my wanton desire going into complete overdrive. I throw my head back into the pillows, unable to watch his torturous onslaught of his mouth. I need him to give me my delicious release.

His lips suddenly clamp on my nerves before he sucks hard, making me moan louder than I ever had before. His act of war against my pussy begins as he runs his slick tongue against me. He stops every so often to suck and nip my clit. Throwing my head back even deeper into my pillows, I moan and grip the duvet cover; my pleasure building higher and higher with every stroke and suck of his tongue and mouth.

Sensing my pleasure, Luther slides a finger into my tight channel, the invasion makes me moan again. My breath stops for a second or two as he starts to move his finger in and out of me, his mouth never leaves me for even a second. I start to climb to my impending release; my breathing becomes harsh and ragged as my pleasure increases, my back arches with every moan. After what seems like an eternity, I release one more moan, my orgasm hitting me like a train. The power of my climax is like nothing I have ever felt before, the sheer force makes my toes curl. I am surprised I didn't break Luther's fingers with how hard my pussy clenched him, but I think even if I did, he wouldn't care. His tongue laps me up, he drinks every last drop of my release like a starved man. My pussy all the more sensitive after what he has just done to me, like every nerve ending is on high alert.

"God, you taste good," Luther says with a husky voice, so full of lust and desire. He moves back up to me and kisses my lips. His kiss is hard and heavy leaving me breathless. I can taste my sweet nectar on him; the taste is actually delightful, and I taste more with each stroke of his tongue against mine.

When he pulls away and lines his cock up to my entrance. He slowly starts to push into me; the resistance is evident. A tear slips down my cheek as the pain soars through me. "What? Are you a…" His words trail off as he looks down at me, his tip still inside me.

I look into his eyes. "Yes, I am a virgin. Is that a problem?" My eyebrow raises as I look into his eyes.

"No, just surprised, that's all." His eyes go a shade darker as he looks at me. He locks his lips with me as he slowly starts to move, his length sliding into me as he uses his mouth to help ease my pain. "Just breathe, baby, it won't hurt for long." As he moves into me painstakingly, slowly inch by inch, I feel something pop, like a barrier that was once there is now gone. I gasp as the pain rockets through me, but the moment I feel it, it dissipates, leaving nothing but pleasure.

Once he reaches the hilt of his cock, he stops moving, allowing me to adjust to his length. He stretched me more than I thought was possible. His lips leave mine as he moans at me. Slowly, he starts moving, rocking his hips back and forth. I moan as he does this, my pleasure building up again. I've never felt so full, his cock moving within me brings me closer to the impending edge. The feeling of his cock moving back and forth brings me more pleasure than I have ever felt. I've had many dreams about what it would be like to finally have sex. I never thought it would be this fucking good. I rock my hips, allowing Luther to enter me more, my climax hurtling towards me.

"FUCK FASTER," I basically yell as he grunts and starts to plough into me at a punishing speed. I know I will feel this tomorrow, but right now I'm loving this with every fibre of my being. I am loving the way his cock fills me to the brink of too much. I love the sensation of him gliding within me. Feeling him against my walls as he takes what he wants from me, showing little sign of slowing down or stopping. I can't seem to get enough of this euphoric feeling, of being so high. I feel like I am on some drug, and I don't wish to stop taking it. The way I am climbing higher and higher with each of his powerful thrusts, his grunts and moans making it hard to stay in control of my subsequent climax.

Each noise he makes, each thrust of his hips, just propelling me closer to my destination. A sweet oblivion I have never been before, a place I am yet to experience.

I grip the back of Luther's head tightly, his groan resonates around the room. With each passing second, my grip on his glorious hair tightens. His speed picked up as he threw my legs onto his shoulders, his cock going even further into me, hitting me at new angles. His resplendent cock sending me hurtling towards my mind-blowing orgasm, stars forthcoming blinding my vision momentarily as I feel the rippling waves of my happy-ending washing through me. "I'm cumming. Shit, Luther," I moan as Luther prolongs my second climax, making sure that the glorious feeling of my orgasm is felt to its fullest. He gives a final few rough thrusts, before I feel him release his own orgasm.

Once he finishes, Luther releases me and lies next to me on the bed. Our breathing is ragged as we try to catch our breath. My mind spins at a hundred miles an hour. Not only did I break a promise I made to myself, but I did it with the son of the man who destroyed my life. Maybe I'm in well over my head, but I am definitely thinking sex isn't a bad thing. Some fun is always good. Right?

Chapter 15

Getting up, I look at Luther. A small amount of panic crosses his face, "What's up?" I ask while grabbing my clothes off the floor. I thought it was great. Maybe he didn't.

"Nothing. I just wasn't wearing protection. So erm, yeah." He looks super awkward. His eyes flicker with an emotion I am not quite familiar with.

"Don't worry about that. It's fine. Anyway, we best get back. Our drinks are outside. M will probably be in the office by now." I don't know what to think, yes, it is just sex, but hell I want that again. It was amazing. Don't know why he would worry about not having protection. *Maybe because he doesn't want kids, dickhead*...my brain responds. I chuckle to myself for a second causing Luther to look at me for the first time since we finished.

"What's so funny?" Luther asks, raising an eyebrow. Is he trying to copy me with that? It's not as intimidating as when I do it; he has more of a cute edge to him when he tries.

"You are worrying about not having protection. Trust me, I can't." I put on my trousers and T-shirt and head through the middle door into my office.

M is stood in the office with a smile on his face. "Yes, I know. Shut the fuck up and never speak of this to anyone," I say with a glare. M must have brought our drinks in with him as they are now sat on the coffee table. I hear the door behind me. Luther emerges next to me before picking up his glass. I usually order rum, but today I didn't, I felt like I needed something stronger. I take a seat; this feels super awkward in here. "Right, it's awkward and I don't like it. M, I know you're fucking my sister, and I fucked Luther. Now that's in the open, anyone want to add something to this or are we just going to move on?"

The colour drains from M's face. "What?" he asks with a cough. Clearly, I caught him by surprise. Maybe my hint earlier wasn't strong enough for his tiny brain.

"Oh, do you think I can't hear you fucking above my head? Who can sleep through you two, really. I have never heard anyone say 'oh God' so much in my life. But hey, as long as you are having fun and are happy, I don't care. I'll just sleep in the office, harder to hear you from all that distance."

M and Luther both cough, clearly embarrassed by my comment. "E, I'm sorry. I wanted to tell you, but I didn't know how to. And hold on, you two are fucking? E, you have never so much as looked at a man. What the hell changed? Also, what about you-know-who?"

"Wouldn't say fucking, more friends with benefits," Luther interjects with a sly smile. I actually don't mind it being portrayed as that if I'm honest. Sounds less sordid that way.

"Christ. Am I such a cold-hearted bitch? I have needs, you know, M, things I need a man to help me with. And for your information, I've never been against having sex, just never found most men attractive in that respect and now I have, so fuck you. Thanks for the support, BROTHER. Also, that's none of your concern, is it?" I emphasise the word brother. Luther is clearly lost in the conversation now, but it's fine, he will catch up eventually.

"No, I didn't say that. I just know your views on relationships, that's all, but apparently that has changed." I believe it has, but it won't throw me off my game.

"Right, if that's all sorted, I have business to attend to. You two can stay here, or I can call a cab and drop you both off at your respective homes. Choice is yours," I say, looking at them both. Neither of them move or say anything. "Staying it is then. I won't be long. I have a lying bitch to take care of." And with that, I leave.

I pick up my phone once I am out of the office. There is a message on it and it's from Martin. **Room 3**. I like Martin's texts, always straight and to the point. I look at the door. She has some explaining to do. I grab the handle and open the door. What I see makes my blood boil. Georgia is lying on the floor, blood pooling around her and spreading; dread starts to fill me. Walking over to her, I see where it's coming from. Her throat has been slit.

"Fuck sakes," I say as I step even closer. Suddenly I see something. Her chest is still moving. She's alive but barely. Pulling my phone out, I call Martin. "Get to room 3 and bring a doctor. Someone has been in here and it's not great." I then put my phone away and pull my top off, pushing it to her throat hard enough to stop her bleeding so fast but not too hard to stop her breathing, I need this girl alive.

86

Two minutes later, Martin and a doctor walk in. "E, what the hell happened?" Martin asks. I scowl at him.

"I don't fucking know, Martin, I walk in and she's like this. If I was going to do it, I would have done it properly. Just make sure she fucking lives, okay?" And with that, I hand her over to the doctor and leave. Luckily, my office is only a couple of doors away; I can do without walking around this place with no top on and blood all over my hands. I reach the office door and open it. Both M and Luther are laughing away with a drink in their hands. Their faces drop when they see me.

"What happened, E?" M clearly spotting my blood covered hands. A strange look that I cannot decipher, passes over his face momentarily.

"Someone went into the room I was holding Georgia in and slit her throat. She's still breathing, thank God. I just need to find out who went in so I can repay the favour." God, I'm vexed now. Who the fuck managed to do this? I need Freddy to come back to me soon about the fucking mole. I can't have people coming into my establishment and slitting people's throats. All the years of being a mafia boss and not once has someone ever been attacked here; never once has this been so close to home. The thought of someone so close doing something like this scares me slightly; a hesitant and fearful feeling washes over me. I can't allow someone to have such a hold on my emotions. Soon enough, I will know who is working against me. But alas, right now it's just a waiting game. Moves and countermoves, that's all this is.

I disappear into the bedroom I was in with Luther earlier; still smells like it did, not too long ago. And the sheets are a mess. I still don't know if it was as good for him as it was for me. I mean he's had sex before, I hadn't. Maybe the fact I was a virgin has put him off. I take the door to the right of the office one and walk into the bathroom. Sometimes I get a tad messy, let's say, and that's why I had a bathroom put in when I built this place. I also point blank refused to share with the other girls, not that I felt I was better than them. More of a 'I don't share' kind of thing.

Turning on the sink tap, I rinse Georgia's blood off my hands. My Christ, she better make it. Would hate for the person who did this to get a head start on me. Also, she seemed like a nice enough girl, so I would hate for her to die a senseless death. I mean hers would be without meaning and death should always mean something; whether it's a warning or a deployment of power or for the greater good of everyone.

I feel better now that her blood is off my hands. Turning the tap off, I grab the white hand towel. I dry my hands and grab a clean top off the side of the dresser on my way through the bedroom. This was rather inconvenient, I must say. I make my way back to my office where Luther and M are chatting away.

"Yeah, it's weird being around E. She's very blunt a lot of the time, and I can never read what she's thinking. It's hard to gauge whether she's happy or sad, vexed or joyful. How do you cope, man?" Luther really got that with only four days of knowing me. Christ I must have gotten cold over the years. But being cold keeps you alive in this game. I stay behind the door so I can continue to listen.

"Yeah, she is a hard person to understand, trust me, I've known her since she was ten. But she's a great person and has a big heart, even if she doesn't show it all the time. She's always there and completely loyal. That's why she asks for the same in return and for you to be completely honest with her. Being a leading woman in her world is super hard. Many men have tried to break her and take her down. But she's shown all of them she's just as badass as they are – maybe even more so. Just give her time, mate, and she will warm up to you." M chuckles to himself. "I mean fucking hell, you actually got her into bed with you. That's no mean feat, I tell you. X tried once, and let's say he's lost the requirement for oxygen. He did do something major though. But that however is a story for another day."

X was a complete wanker. He deserved to die for what he did. Pushing that memory away, I put my hand on the door and was about to walk in when Luther stopped me in my tracks. "Yeah, and trust me, it was great, but I don't know, I guess it's weird talking to you about this. You know, being her brother, but I just don't know if she thinks how I do. I mean like, I didn't wear anything, and she just brushed it off like it was nothing. She does know what happens, right? And I don't want her to think I'm being a dick or anything, but if I'm to have kids, I want to be serious with their mum, you know?" Oh, shit I didn't explain why I was so flippant with his comment about protection. Also, I didn't know men had such deep conversations. I always thought they just spoke about football and shit, nothing like this. Or is that just an E thing, to push your feelings down to your feet and never deal or think about them.

M chuckles again. "I'm her adoptive brother not blood, so don't worry. It's only slightly weird, but that's only because no one has ever turned E's head, well not since she was in the force, although one did before him, but that's not my story to tell either. Things like feelings were knocked out of her. Men are a hindrance in her eyes. And honestly, don't worry about the kid's thing with E, she can't—" I barge in before M could finish his conversation.

"Right, I'm off home for the night. It's getting late. Who wants a lift?" M glances at Luther with an apologetic smile.

"Yeah, I'll have a lift back, please," says Luther, looking at me with a questioning gaze.

"M, you coming to my place or going back to yours?" He's been stopping over quite a lot and to say it's nice is hard, seeing as every time he's over, I don't get a wink of sleep.

"Erm, Jas wants me to stop again, but I won't if you don't want me to." M looks down. I can't with this man right now.

"For fuck sakes, if you want to stop, stop. But keep the noise down, that's all I ask. Got fuck all sleep last night. I only sleep for a few hours a night anyway, but I would like to get those in if you wouldn't mind." I then start to laugh, hard. I can't understand why, I guess it is awkward talking about this with M.

"Okay, but you are more than welcome to crash at mine, only if you want."

"Fuck off, M. If you two want to fuck so loud, why don't you go to yours? Oh wait, I remember, your neighbour is a dick." M's neighbour is a complete asshat. He complains about everything. I turned up at 11 pm one night, needing him to sort something out and he banged on the door saying that it was wrong that I turned up at the apartment at such a late hour. It wasn't even like I was noisy; we spoke quietly and didn't even have the TV on. I am so glad M moved in after I left, else if I had stayed any longer, I probably would have shot him.

"M, just go to mine. I probably won't sleep in my room tonight anyway. I have a few things to sort in my office." Luther hadn't said anything, so when I glance at him, he just stares at me. "I will drop you home, Luther, and we can convene our conversation in the next couple of days." And with that, I grab the office handle and walk into the corridor.

Walking past room 3, I notice Georgia was no longer lying on the floor, but her blood was still there. I'm assuming she is on her way to hospital; I grab the handle for that door and slam it shut. "Martin, lock this door please, and clean that fucking carpet," I shout, knowing he isn't far away; he wouldn't leave this door open if he left. The noises coming from the rooms around us are suddenly a lot louder than they were before. If I'm honest, I never noticed them earlier, maybe because I wasn't too interested in it before Luther. Now it suddenly makes me feel super uncomfortable, and also super turned on.

Emerging from the stairs, I notice the bar is fairly empty, which isn't unusual this late at night. It's around 11 pm and most of the men are in rooms with my girls, or just off fucking around the room. It's always that way around this time. Everyone has their drinks and are now just having their fun. Imagine playboy on steroids, that's what's happening now.

But something else caught my eye. Darley, the bartender who got my drinks earlier is now in the till. Hold the phone, did I just see that? "E, did she just slip that into her pocket?" Luther asks from my right.

"Why yes, I think she did. Let's go have a chat with her."

M grabs my shoulder. "Let me chat with her. She may explain more to me than you. No offence." What the fuck? I can talk to her myself. He looks at me like he is my boss, a hard edge to his usual demeanour. Is this man for real right now? Does he think he can sit at my table? I am her boss, so I can fucking well speak to her. But I need to pick my battles with him wisely right now. He is up to something. I can feel it. So, I might just let this play out.

"Fine, whatever," I say without looking and walk away. God, what the fuck is going on at the moment? What's gone down in the past few days to cause people to stop speaking to me? Before this I was feared and now, I'm not able to even speak to anyone. M has never stopped me speaking to anyone before, so why now? Something isn't adding up. Is M trying to take my seat at the big boys' table?

What if M is trying to remove me from power? I mean, why wouldn't he? He's been in my shadow for years. Maybe he wants to prove something. What? I don't know. Every mafia boss knows he is useless. So no one would stand with him if he tried to take me down. He's not skilled where it counts in this game. He's never taken a life, never tortured someone. He's never so much as lead a training session; he's fucking useless. The only skills he is good in is sweet talking the ladies. Other than that, I wouldn't trust him to run a bath, let alone a mafia empire like mine. He could try to have a seat with me and the other bosses, but I give it a week before he falls. And that's me being generous.

Making my way out, Leon is waiting out the front for me, M, and Luther. "Drop M and Luther off for me. I'm going to take the bike. M is going to my place."

With that, I turn and walk round the side of the building. One of my bikes is parked round there. It's a good job I always keep my helmet in the seat. I need some space away from all the people I know right now. Something is going on, and I need to find out what, away from here and away from all distractions. I need to sort this out and eliminate the problem, and I can't do that if I'm lusting after Luther and thinking that M is coming for my throne. Not that he would ever have a chance of taking it, we all know that by now.

I would usually put my earpiece in so I can answer the phone while driving, but I don't want to speak to anyone right now. Putting the helmet on, I hear my name being shouted. "E, WHERE ARE YOU GOING? COME ON!" M shouts. I can't deal with them either right now. I need to blow off some steam. Getting on the bike and starting the motor, I see Luther and M staring at me like I'm never coming back at all. I just need a minute. I don't know what I want to do but I believe I need to have a break for a couple of days. I know that maybe I should tell someone I'm going away. Yet all I can think about is getting the fuck out of here, away from everything. Run away for a short time, clear my head and come up with a plan – a way to navigate this shit storm. I need to know who's trying to ruin me and possibly trying to eliminate me.

Chapter 16

Getting to the tarmac, I call Rod. He answers and I ask if I can borrow his plane. He obviously says yes after I saved his life last year. He also suggests I stop at a hotel of a friend he knows. It's Washington, DC, and I decide to do it. I could use some time out of state. I ask him to book me a room and that I'll be there in a few hours. He obliges and we hang up. My next phone call is to K.

"Hey, boss, what's up?" His voice is filled with sleep. I know he's tired because he was up late last night for me, I had a job for him. I can only imagine how handsome he looks right now. His dark eyes, bed hair plus that deep gravel voice. My core clenches at the thought of him lying there in his bed. I would love to think he sleeps naked. I shake that thought away before continuing our conversation.

"I am leaving for Washington. Don't tell anyone, especially M. Keep him at a distance. H will be in charge. I have another job for you. Monitor M. I want to know his every move. Who he speaks to, where he goes when he isn't at my house, and make sure you aren't seen. I don't want him to know I am onto him. If you need me for an emergency, call me. Other than that, I will be MIA to everyone else." As I say this, Rod's plane pulls up, ready for me. "Can you grab my bike from the tarmac for me, please?"

"Yes, boss, if you need anything, just call. I will inform H. Let us know when you decide to come back." He sounds like he wanted to say something, but refrains from saying whatever is on his mind. Whenever I leave, he usually sounds like this. He always comes across like he thinks I won't be back; I may have abandoned him once when we first met. But since then, I have always come back. I have always been around, even when he thinks I am not.

"Thanks, mate, I should be back Monday." And with that, I hang up. H and K are so used to me just getting up and leaving. I've done it far too often over the years; now it's normal.

Getting on the plane, I am greeted by the stewards. They smile and welcome me aboard. I nod and take my seat. Opening my phone, I text Marcus that I will be calling him and Aid in a couple of hours.

Glancing around, I notice how nice this plane is; the cream carpets and white walls. The seats are also cream leather, with small white tables around. It's clean and crisp. Rod is clearly a fan of minimalism. A male steward walks towards me. He has glittery eyeshadow on and black eyeliner. He's slim and about 5 ft 9 inches tall, dark skin and short black hair. His uniform is immaculate, and he clearly takes pride in his looks. His smile is sweet.

"Ma'am, is there anything I can get you? We will be taking off in about five minutes." His voice is smooth like butter, and his big brown eyes sparkle as he talks. Even this late at night, he still looks well rested and is far too chipper for my liking. No one should be this happy at nearly 3 am in the morning, it's maddening. Crazy how the time flies when you are alone with your thoughts. I left the club at just after eleven. And now it's the middle of the night, and I am still wide awake and plagued with thoughts and a need for answers.

"No thank you, I am fine." I smile back. He nods and leaves me alone. Not long after, we start taxing down the runway, and off we fly. I turn the lights off in the cabin and close my eyes. Soon, sleep consumes me. Finally, some sleep after the past two days.

I am woken by the soft voice of the steward. "Ma'am, wake up. We are about to land." I stretch and smile at him. He smiles back, his eyes glimmer in the dim light of the cabin.

"Thank you."

"Not a problem, Ma'am. The time in Washington is 01:28 am." He turns and leaves me to get myself ready. I remember I didn't actually bring anything with me. So, I should go tomorrow and get some stuff. I don't even have a toothbrush.

Once we land, I exit the plane and see a car waiting for me with an elderly gentleman standing nearby. I assume it's for me, seeing as I landed on a private strip and no one else is there. "Miss E, my name is Karl. I will be your driver. Mr Powell sent me." He opens the door for me, and I slide into the back of the black coupé; the black leather seats are heated so it's warm when I sit down. I could get used to this. I chuckle to myself.

We drive for about ten minutes before we pull up to a large hotel. The name Castelo is in big bold gold letters above the entrance. I walk in and notice how modern it looks. White marble floors with white walls and a large abstract painting on my left. The front desk is a light wood, and the name of the hotel is in big gold letters behind the reception. I don't think I've ever stopped in somewhere so lovely. It's usually sleepy motels and dodgy hotels that no one in their right mind would stop in.

I glance at my phone and I have a text message from Rod. *'I checked you in under T Parker. It's the name you used at the casino the first time we met. I thought it would be harder to track you if you went by a name you never really use any more.'* Rod knows me well; he was a friend of Marcus back in the day. And when we found out someone was after him, Marcus asked me to protect him, so that's what I did.

Walking up to the front desk, I look at the receptionist. Her deep red hair shines bright in the artificial light. Her green eyes smile at me as she notices me there. "Hello Ma'am, welcome to Castelo. How may I help you?" Her voice is soft and light, and she has a bright smile.

"Yes, I'm booked in under T Parker." She looks at me, then the computer. Her face pales for a second before she regains her composure.

"Okay Ma'am, you are booked into the Diana suite. Do you have any bags to check in?" I just shake my head. She slides me a key and smiles again. "Very well, breakfast is served between 6 and 9 am. Your room is all paid for, and you're booked in until Monday, so please enjoy your stay, Ma'am. And anything you need, please don't hesitate to ask."

"Erm, do you have a toothbrush and toothpaste. I'm sort of here on a whim." I smile and she nods. Reaching under the desk, she pulls out a bag of products. It's got a toothbrush, toothpaste, shampoo, conditioner, small brush and small mouthwash. All the necessities for a small stay. I thank her and head to the lift. Getting in, I hit the floor with my suite on. The lift plays soft music as it ascends. It's small but with it being light and a mirror wall, it seems bigger.

Opening at my floor, I notice just two doors: one to the Diana suite and the other to the Presidential suite. I put my key card to the door but it doesn't open. I try it three more times. I then try the other door, just in case the lady at reception made a mistake, but alas that doesn't open either. I'm too tired to go back down and I'm kind of getting pissed off with it, with all the shit going on, so I decide to take it out on the lock. Grabbing my gun, I check the cameras. The only one here is coincidentally facing the floor. I raise my gun and smack it down on the lock. It clicks, and the door opens. Once I open the door, I look at the card reader and realise it's actually broken. Oops, I didn't mean to do that, just hoped if I hit it, it would work. It's a good thing there is a chain on the inside, so I don't have to worry, and the lock doesn't look broken, which is a win. The only way I could tell it doesn't work is the light isn't on – oops, my bad!

Walking in, I go straight to the bedroom. I don't even look around. I'm too tired. The bathroom is huge. It's white like the rest of the hotel with small blue and white tiles. It's gorgeous here. There's a massive walk-in shower and large Jacuzzi bath. I remove my contacts and run myself a bath. As it fills, I decide to call Marcus. He picks up after two rings.

"Hello, Little Bird, how are you?" his deep voice speaks through the speaker. I keep my eye on the bath. I can do without flooding the place when I have already damaged the door.

"Not great, pops. I think M is plotting against me. I saw Darley stealing from the till in Secret, and he said he would deal with it. I think he's coming for my throne. There are more oddities that have happened, but I won't bore you with those tonight. And yes, before you ask, I did do something rash. I got on a plane and left before I shot him. Can you come here so we can work on a game plan? But I need to check on the lads, so go there first."

Marcus just sighs down the phone. I know his feelings on M. I think his last words on him was something along the lines of 'He's a leech, little bird; he will suck you dry of everything. You are carrying him. Just dump his arse off somewhere and don't look back. He's useless.'

"I will pop to the lads first and make sure they are all busy and whip them into shape, then I will come with Aid over to Washington to see you. Did you put K or H in charge?"

"H, I have something else for K to do." I walk over and turn the tap to the bath off and drop some bubble bath in that I found on the side next to the sink.

"Good. H will do well. I'll call him to let him know I'm coming, then when they are sorted, I'll be over with Aid. If Matthew is crossing you, I will kill him personally." He growls through the phone, and I don't doubt he would hurt M. His hate for M runs deep. I was surprised that he even let M work for him when we did.

"I'm sure you will enjoy telling him that you are coming. You know how much they enjoy you training them. But on a serious note, I am looking into M right now. I am very wary of him, so I've told K to keep him at arm's length, and also follow him. Something isn't adding up here, and my suspicions are running high. We need to get ahead of this before it becomes a monumental problem." I chuckle at the thought of their faces when Marcus says he's on his way to them; he drills them harder than me. He likes to watch them in pain; it's a sick sadistic side of him. He may be married to a man, but he also loves torturing them.

"Oh, you know how much I enjoy tormenting your guys. Okay, little bird, I'll be with you Saturday lunch time. We can discuss this then. Bye."

"Bye, pops." And with that, I hang up and place my phone on the countertop. I strip and slide into the bath. The warm water eases my tension and loosens my mind for a brief moment.

I never thought I would be in this situation with M. Yes, he is pretty useless. He's never been to battle, he's never killed anyone and the only person he did get assigned to kill, he let him go. I, of course, had to go and pick up the pieces. I killed him, and beat M up for punishment. I think that punishment was more for me than M. It solidified this coldness I feel towards him. I was fuming the day he did that; he was meant to take him out for 1.2 million and he fucked it. Marcus came storming up to me while I was with Big Trey and Brad, yelling his head off. I remember it like it was yesterday.

"Emilia, your stupid, useless brother has fucked up more than ever," Marcus has a murderous look in his eye. His fists are clenched with his knuckles turning white. Brad and Trey have confused looks on their faces. They are my best friends along with Nath. I raise my eyebrow at Marcus. "He fucked up, and because he's your brother, you will clean up his mess. Then you will dish out his punishment." His glare is intimidating to most people, but to me it's not. He's like another dad to me. He picked me up when I was at the lowest point in my life.

"Fine, what's he fucked up? And what's his punishment?" I know Matt is not the sharpest tool in the box, but I've never known him to mess up this bad. I've also never had Marcus yell at me like this.

"Sort it." He throws me a file before continuing. "And you will take him to a cell and beat him every day for a week. And I will make sure you don't go easy on him; he needs to learn his lesson. If he fucks up again, you will kill him. Am I understood?" I just nod and open the file; this is an easy kill. Dave Morestone has a routine and never strays from it.

"Can I use Trey and Brad to do this?" I ask. Usually, Marcus lets me have whoever I want with me.

"Just get it done." He turns and storms away; his shoulders never lose their tension as he walks.

I call Nath and get him to put Matt into a cell. Trey, Brad and I go and sort out Dave Morestone. It was super easy and the clean-up was quick. When we get back to the compound, I made my way down with the guys to see Matt. Marcus and Aid were already there waiting for me. I look through the one-way mirror and Matt is tied to a chair and is sobbing lightly; he looks so weak right now. Marcus grabs my arm, his eyes boring into me. "He is your brother; you knew the agreement we made when I took him in as well as you. His fuck ups fall on your shoulders, so you will be the executioner." I nod and open the door; all the guys follow me in.

I don't even look at him as I upper cut his face. His head snaps back and his nose bleeds. "Emie, why are you doing this?" Matt asks with a pleading look in his eyes. His face is puffy from his crying. Right here, I see how weak he truly is and it repulses me.

"You fucked up. You know the rules here. You do the job and that's it. Now because you haven't done what was asked, I have to dish out your punishment. And to say I'm let down is an understatement. I put my neck out for you and you can't do something so simple," I state, punching him again. His head flops to the left as his eye swells from the impact. I'm seething at him; Marcus didn't like M from the moment he met him. I bargained that if he took both of us, I would take full responsibility for M, and this is the first time that M has been caught not pulling his weight. Usually, he takes me with him, and I do all his dirty work, but now because he didn't, Marcus learned he can't kill. When he tried, he shakes and runs away. "You will never be strong enough, Matthew, and hopefully this will teach you to be stronger."

I spent a week beating Matt to the point he lost consciousness; the worst part is I didn't feel bad about it. He deserved it, and each of the men was brought down to witness what would happen if they don't pull their weight. To say it was effective falls short of the impact it had. Each man was even more terrified of me more than they were before. I was meant to be leaving for boot camp this week, so this just made me more determined than ever to be better.

Matt is in the infirmary right now; his punishment ended this morning and straight after, he was taken to be seen by the doctor. Packing my bags to leave for the forces, someone knocks on my door. Marcus pokes his head round.

"Little bird, can we talk?" His eyes hold a plea, but I don't know why. I'm not angry at him. I'm angry that Matt put me in that position. He shouldn't have fucked up in the first place.

"Sure, what's wrong?" I turn and look at him, a small smile on my face. He's really turning into a father figure for me. He trains me one on one; he taught me to cook and honed my skills. I know I will be the best of the best in whatever I do, but I also know that no matter what, I will get my revenge thanks to him.

"Just wanted to make sure you're okay. Aid made me realise that I was very harsh on you, making you punish Matthew. I shouldn't have done that." I chuckle at him and roll my eyes.

"Pops, listen, I am the reason that Matt is here. He isn't capable, and he isn't able to do the jobs required. So, it was my fault he failed. Don't worry about me. I don't care. In fact, I went easy on him, and we both know it," Marcus nods and leaves. I finish packing.

Matt learned his lesson and when he let Marcus down a second time, I didn't go easy on him. That time, I put him in a coma for nearly two months. I think that was the last straw on my resentment for him. I couldn't hold back my feelings, and I think he has always known I hold ill feelings towards him. Even K and H know this, and they understand why. They have watched me tear him a new asshole over some very small things, but there were also things that could have been avoided. If he is crosses me, I will kill him without batting an eyelid. He's had this coming for years, and if he didn't know before, he will definitely know now.

Getting out of the bath, I get dried and go straight to bed. I set an alarm for 5 am and plan to go to a Walmart or something to grab some clothes before heading to the gym. I spot a sign that says there was one when I was in the lobby, apparently. They also have a swimming pool which I plan to utilise as well.

Chapter 17

I love being in the gym and at this time in the morning, there is no one present. I went to Walmart this morning and bought some black tops and trousers, gym and swimming clothes. And a few other things I needed. It was weird shopping, but when times are tough, I do what I need to. Walking through the shops, I realise that I don't do all the things that normal people do, mainly because I pay Klaire to do it. She enjoys doing this for me – heaven knows why. But I know I should do more, but I'm usually too busy.

Punching bag at the gym is really helping to get rid of some of my anger. M maybe trying to steal my life, but I will certainly give him a run for it. Right now, I need to come up with an action plan. The gym is near enough empty, apart from a few gym junkies that walked in about ten minutes ago. They are clearly taking something to be as muscular as they are. One of them to my right keeps looking at me and it's starting to annoy me. I can see him in the floor-length mirror lifting weights, but his eyes haven't left my ass for at least ten minutes. What the hell is this guy's problem? Not being able to stand his eyes on me anymore, I turn to go on the rowing machine.

It's not my best option. I do hate it, but I need to keep my leg strength up and it's far enough away to stop seeing him, and I will be obstructed by enough pieces of kit to keep his eyes away. Putting my wireless earphones in, I turn up my music. Panic at the Disco is playing at the moment. I know it's weird, but I have a guilty pleasure for them and Fall Out Boy. Bet you never thought someone like me would enjoy music like that, but hey, we all have our surprises.

The lack of that weirdo's attention doesn't last long, as he moves to the piece of kit right next to me. Does he wish to talk, because I don't? Yes, he's good looking, I won't deny that. But I'm not interested. Most men can't take no for an answer, thinking they are God's gift to women. Never taking my eyes off the screen, I feel a tap on my left shoulder. I turn to see him staring at me with a big white grin on his face. Blond hair is slightly sweaty, but not enough to say he's worked out enough yet. His tank top doesn't even have sweat marks, whereas my black sports top is drenched and so are my leggings. I don't even take my earpiece out to talk to him. I just turn my head back to my machine and carry on. God, can't men just go live on another planet, please! I can do without this today.

Suddenly, I feel my earphones come out from my ear, then his voice catches me off guard. It's so close to my ear it makes me jump out of my skin. "Hey, how are you? See you're working hard. You in the forces or something?" What the hell does he think he's doing? His breath stinks, for one. If I had a mint, I would shove it down his throat before talking.

"Hi, I'm good and in a manner of speaking. Anyway, I must get back. I have a busy day ahead." I try to grab my earphone, but he moves it out of my reach.

"Ah, come on, can't you stop and chat for a few minutes? I promise I won't bite. Also, you're too sexy to be in the forces. How can a beauty like that do something so ugly?" Clearly, he's trying to pull and right now I couldn't think of anything worse than being around him.

"Look, mate, give me my earphone back and fuck off. I've not got time to deal with a man who thinks he's God's gift to womankind, and if that's your best pick up line, you clearly haven't had any in a while."

Apparently, this offended him because a dark look came to his eyes. "Listen here, you little bitch. I'm trying to be nice and you can't even take a compliment..." I don't even let him finish before I jab him in the throat. I was aware of where the cameras are and made sure my back was to them so if I did have to fight my way out, I wouldn't be seen doing anything. I wish I had shut his airways down, but then I would be found out or at least charged with something. I just hit him hard enough for him to drop my earphone and gasp for breath for a few seconds.

"You fucking bitch," he croaks out, still unable to catch his breath. I step off my machine. I grab my earphone that he dropped when he gasped for breath for a moment.

"It is a shame that you can't take steroids to fix that personality of yours. It would have helped you far more with the ladies." I whisper in his ear as he tries to catch his breath. I get up to leave, but before I can, his hand grabs my right wrist. I've had children grab me with more strength than that. My lip twitches in amusement, knowing his next move. Honestly, this steroid king is really getting on my last goddamn nerve.

"Oh, you think you get to do that and walk away? I don't think so, sweetheart." All the other people in the gym are now looking our way. Yes, I could fight them all off. After all, I'm a master at close combat, but I don't wish to be found. I simply look at him, my eyes boring straight into his.

"You don't want to start something I will have to finish, pal. You don't know me. Just let go of my arm and we can all be on our way. Okay?" A laugh erupts from his chest. Why are men so cocky when they gym. He looks at everyone else and they all start laughing. There are about three other men in the room, clearly all friends.

"Well, can't say I didn't warn you." And with that, I twist his arm he's holding me with and bring my left elbow down on his elbow. A snap echoes round the room, followed by his scream of pain. He lets go of my right wrist and I bring my foot down on his left knee. This time, I hear a pop. I only dislocate it. That's a plus; if the police do come, they can't get me done for anything major, plus the camera has him grabbing me. I can claim self-defence. He is now lying on the floor, crying, clutching his arm that is very clearly broken; also his knee is swelling and bent at a very weird angle.

"Anyone else fancy a shot? No? Didn't think so," I ask, looking at all of them. Just then, a hotel attendant runs in, panic stretched across his face. "He grabbed me, sir, it was self-defence. I am so sorry. I just felt so helpless." I cry, running towards him. I have mastered the art of crying on command as well. Comes in handy when a man picks a fight with little old me.

"Hey, hey, it's fine. I will get my manager to see the footage and I'm sure nothing will happen. Why don't I escort you back to your room, Miss Parker, and get you a complimentary evening meal for later," the attendant says with a soft smile. Through my crocodile tears I glance up at him.

"Thank you. That would be very kind, but there is no need. Honestly, I'm just going to go for a swim, then I will be back in my room. You are too kind." I squint at his name tag, 'Jacob' and with that, I leave the room. I wipe my tears and go to the pool.

My phone rings again. I turned my main one off that most of my men use to contact me. I don't wish to be spoken to by them until I have a few things cleared up. "Go," I say, clicking the earpiece into my ear.

"Right, E, Aid and I will be in Washington around noon on Saturday. I will call H and keep them busy," Marcus says. He would do anything for me. I just feel bad I brought him out of semi-retirement for this.

"Thanks, Marcus. I knew I could rely on you. I just need to know what M's plans are. Something is going, on and I don't like it." I hear his pause on the other end of the phone.

"Yes, I get the feeling he's up to something. Don't worry. We will get to the bottom of this. I will join Aid at the landing strip in Washington and meet you at the hotel."

Chapter 18

With that, the phone call was over. I am very happy that Marcus and Aid are coming. They are the only men in my life I know wouldn't fuck me over. I've called Marcus and Aid, pops for many years. After they took me in, they have always been there for me and helped me more times than I would care to imagine. Don't know if I could do what I do without them.

Getting to the pool, I notice just a few people are here, even though it's only about 9:30 am. I thought there would be more people around. An old couple are just doing laps, and a stunningly handsome man is also here. I mean, he's sort of on par with Luther; maybe not as handsome, but definitely close. I strip out of my gym gear and enter the pool from the shallow end. The chill of the pool feels great on my burning muscles. Maybe I went a little overboard with my workout this morning, I was there since 6 am and went hard with my workout trying to burn my anger away. The handsome guy glances at me as I enter the pool, giving me a warm smile. Usually, I wouldn't smile back, but he seems like a genuinely nice guy who's just being polite. I give a small smile back and start swimming.

I'm not in anything spectacular, just a black bikini and my hair in a messy bun. I just need to take my mind off things for the day. Starting to swim slowly, I notice that the group from the gym have entered the pool area. Apparently, I wasn't clear with my actions earlier. For fuck sakes, can't I catch a break anywhere I go? "Oi, you bitch. We want a word," one of them shouts, causing the gentleman and the elderly couple to look my way.

"Hey, watch who you are talking to. Hope you don't speak to every woman you meet with that tone," says the handsome gentleman. It was nice, but I don't need a man to fight my battles for me. I swim over to the side of the pool they are standing on. Jumping out, I walk up to them. Everyone is watching me including the lifeguard that is on duty. If I'm being honest, there isn't enough of us here to warrant a guard, but hey, pool policy, I guess.

"Look, mate, I'm on holiday. I wish to relax and not do anything that requires too much energy. So, if you don't mind, I would like to get back to my swim." I am trying so damn hard to keep calm. I can see the anger in his eyes. I'm getting the feeling they won't be leaving me alone anytime soon.

"You broke my friend's arm and leg, and now we want payback."

I start to laugh. "Yes, I broke his arm, but he shouldn't have grabbed mine. However, I didn't break his leg. I dislocated his knee cap. Maybe he should have thought about that before manhandling me," I say with a smile, causing them to get angrier with me.

"You are a psycho. We will teach you a fucking lesson," the one on the right says with a grin while cracking his knuckles.

"Oi, watch how you speak to this woman. Do you kiss your mother with that mouth? Also, if she did that to your friend, I would love to see what she could do to you three," the gentleman says as he approaches, looking directly at me. I didn't even notice he got out of the pool.

"Well, let's see." I cross my arms and tap my foot as I think about what I would do. "This one here on the right, I'm going to wind him, break his nose and probably throw him into the pool. The one in the middle, I am going to break his knee and dislocate his shoulder as I throw him through those doors on my left. And the one on my left that you just walked past, gets all the fun. I'm going to hit him with that chair over there," I say, pointing to the chair that is a little way behind me on the left. "Then, I'm going to boot him in the kidney, causing it to fail and him needing a lengthy stay in hospital."

I turn to the gentlemen trying to fight me. "Does that sound okay with you?" I ask with a smile, looking at them directly. They all look dumbfounded; the guy next to me smiles a big smile.

"Well, sounds very impressive, sweetheart, maybe you should show them exactly how that would go down," he says with a chuckle. Clearly, he would like to see me in action but I'm not into doing that today.

"Oh, I would love to, but I'm far too polite to throw the first punch. I like the losing team to get one in first, it's only good manners," I say with a smile. The lads who came to pick the fight, never said a single word since I told them what I would do to them. This always makes men feel weary of me when I describe it in detail. Some take me up on my offer, some walk away and some run. I like it when they run – the coward's way out.

"So, fellas, you going to take this beauty up on her offer, or are you going to walk away?" he asks with a smile and a twinkle in his eye. I hadn't even noticed that two security guards and an attendant had walked in. Apparently, the lifeguard had alerted them to the altercation. I turned around and the guy on the right grabbed my wrist. Right, I best put my threat into action. I turn and hit him in the stomach hard, winding him, then I grab his black hair while he's doubled over and raise my knee to his face, breaking his nose. Once he's bleeding from his nose, I grab his top and launch him into the pool. Good job men who work out and take supplements are top heavy. They always skip leg day. I find it amusing that they are fighting me one at a time. It feels so easy. I could do this in my sleep.

The one in the middle comes at me next. He takes a swing at me and as I duck, I bring my foot up and put it through his knee, hearing that all too familiar snap, and it breaks. Swiftly, I grab his hair with my left and his shoulder with my right, and throw him through the door on my left. Good thing that it was open, because if it wasn't, I could have caused him a lot more damage. I did however hear the pop of his shoulder as I pulled it out of socket when he went through the door. The hot gentleman is just watching, standing back away from me. I've never had an interested audience before.

The last one manages to clock me in the side of the mouth with his right hand. Pushing me back slightly with the force – exactly what I wanted. I grab the chair to my left, raising it up and smack him over the head with it like something from TV wrestling. He hits the floor, and I kick him in the back right over his kidney. He jolts with the power I put into it; I know I definitely caused some damage with that one. *Oh well,* I think to myself, *the holiday was fun while it lasted.* I start to walk away when the gentleman, who sort of defended me, catches my attention. He's clapping.

"That was mighty impressive; never seen a girl fight like that before. You do have a split lip, however. She's fine. You may go now," he directs to the security guards and the attendant. "My name is Xander. This is my hotel. Don't worry about this, I won't let them kick you out for it. Anyway, you did tell them exactly what you were going to do to them." He chuckles again, clearly much doesn't fuss this man.

"Thanks, I appreciate that. I don't usually go around knocking men out. Just don't like being grabbed without my consent, you know," I replied with a smile.

That is a lie. I love beating people up. I guess Marcus rubbed off on me more than I thought. I do have a sadistic side.

"I completely understand. Look, if you're not doing much, maybe once you have finished your swim, we could go for a drink? I know a great little bar in the city that we could go to. My treat." Hope evident in his hazel eyes.

"This has sort of put me off swimming today. I have some time before 2 today if you want to grab breakfast." I know I shouldn't, but he seems nice and I'm on holiday, of sorts.

"Sure, breakfast sounds good. I'll walk you to your room if you like. What floor are you on?"

"48th, Diana Suite," I reply. This causes another chuckle from Xander.

"So, you won't be impressed by my money then." I of course, found this funny.

"No, I have enough myself. Also, money doesn't bother me either. I guess you're going to have to rely on your personality to get you through a meal with me." I laugh harder this time; he is super-hot and kind of funny. He puts his arm out for me, and I link mine through his. The elderly couple just go back to swimming now that the show is over. If I'm honest, that was a great way to blow off steam. I grab my clothes and we walk towards the lobby. Should have done that sooner, I chuckle to myself.

"What's funny?" Xander's confused face glances down at me as we walk through the lobby in just our swimming suits, holding our clothes we picked up on the way to the door.

"Nothing really, but I feel weird walking through this pretty fancy hotel in just my swimsuit." Xander then chuckles.

"Yes, I guess you're right, but we are at the lifts now, so we might as well finish the journey in our suits. Anyway, I must ask, how did you learn to do that? Not many women can fight off three fully grown men that easily. And only walk away with a split lip. It was pretty awesome."

I guess it was. I've never thought about it before. I suppose because I'm not a normal girl, I've never seen it from someone else's perspective. "I learned when I was little, and never really thought about it before. I've always been able to look after myself and make my money doing it for others as well. And they didn't exactly put up much of a fight – all talk no action. Most men are like that." That was the best way I could have put it without being, 'oh yeah, I'm an ex-hit-woman for hire. Then I went into just doing bad shit for worse people. Also, I run a fancy brothel where lots of important influential people go to do bad shit.'

Obviously, that is not the way I want this guy to look at me. Also, if he ever found out, he would stop breathing – no one should know what I do.

The ding of the lift brings me out of my train of thought. The lift doors open, and we step in, clicking our floors. Xander clicks the 48th and 49th floors. "This place is beautiful; the designer is super talented. I must get their number so they can do some work on a new house I've bought," I say, glancing up at Xander.

"Actually, I designed this place. I may be a man but I know what looks good. By the way, did I tell you how amazing you look in this swimsuit – stunning." I'm not very good at compliments, but the twinkle in his eye makes me think he wants more than breakfast. He's quite tall compared to me. Got to be at least six-foot-four, maybe taller, and he's quite muscular. The tan of his skin shows each of his abs nicely, and his trunks are quite low, so it shows the top of his happy trail. He is definitely built like every book boyfriend ever. "By the way, is that an English accent I hear?" Xander asks. If I'm honest, most men in America ask me about it. I smile and look back at his eyes, just so I can stop looking at his abs and other bits of him.

"Yes, it is, Xander. If I'm honest, everyone in America comments on it, but if I go home, everyone comments on my American accent. I guess I have a mix of both, still can't get over the way you guys say things though. And I've lived here for nearly twenty years now."

"Twenty years, really? Wouldn't have said you was much over that if I'm honest." I laugh hard at that. Christ, he's really trying here.

"Why thank you. Knocked ten years off my age there." His eyes go wide for a second before a dazzling smile crosses his lips.

"So how old are you?" I ask. He's got to be late twenties, early thirties, maybe.

"34, why you ask?" Xander does look remarkably good for 34, I must say.

"Just curious, you do look very good for your age."

"I could say the same. They do say age is just a number. Anyway, we are nearly at your floor. I will pick you up in about an hour. Say 10 am, should give you enough time to get ready," Xander says as the lift comes to a stop, there is still a glint in his eye. Does he wish for me to invite him in? Because that is not happening.

"Yes, that sounds good, thank you. I'll be in the lobby at 10 am." And with that, the lift dings and I step out. I pull my key card out of my bikini top and go to open the door.

"See you then, beautiful." Watching as the lift doors shut and Xander is gone. This might be an interesting break away after all.

Chapter 19

Once Xander is gone, I push the door open and walk into my suite. It's beautiful. Two large white chairs sit in the middle of the room with a very fluffy rug between them and a small glass coffee table on top. The window is floor to ceiling, looking over Washington. It's a glorious view, seeing everything going on in the town below. It's nowhere near as busy as New York, but it's still busy. I guess big cities like this never sleep. The floor is a light wood, and the walls are white. I must say Xander does have a very good eye for detail.

Walking into the bedroom, which is to the right of the giant windows, it's exactly the same glorious white bed, massive window and wooden floor. I am very glad Roy went with the suite; being cooped up in one room would have been annoying. I'm booked in until Monday so I can get my head straight. But hey, why not have a little fun while I'm here? Everyone is right. I am all business and Xander seems like a perfect distraction.

I know, I know; I said that about Luther, and that it would be a onetime thing, but now that I'm here, I may as well enjoy myself while others work on the mole problem. I walk into the en-suite bathroom, which is equally as elegant as the rest of the hotel, with a marble floor and white walls, and even a beautiful walk-in shower, I may be a cold-hearted bitch, but I know elegance when I see it. I turn on the shower and strip out of my wet bikini. The bathroom starts to steam up, indicating the shower is hot.

Getting under the water, I feel all my stresses from the past couple of days start to slip away. I'd been stressed since I had first spoken to Luther on Monday. My plan was coming together nicely, but I think it will be a while before it comes to fruition, which is nice because it means that for the next day or so, I can just let everyone do what I have assigned and do what I need to. I know K and H won't talk to anyone if I contact them; at least I have a few trusted in my camp. Getting out of the shower, I glance in the vanity mirror. I do look tired, but I didn't really sleep last night. I was on the phone to Marcus till late, explaining what's going on and that we need to look more deeply into M and Jasmine.

I dry my hair quickly, leaving in my natural curls and put some moisturiser on my face. If I'm going to look presentable, I should do a little more. I put on a small amount of mascara and eyeliner; I glance at my lip gloss then go without it, because I have a split lip. There is also a slight bruise starting there. Christ, people are either going to think that I am abused or that I am clumsy. I do hope it's the latter one. Walking into the bedroom with my towel around me, I open the bags from earlier and start to get dressed. Grabbing my black skinny jeans, black T-shirt, and black underwear, I start to get dressed.

My phone rings again. "Go." I know I'm blunt, but I can't stand wasting time.

"Little bird, it's Aid. I know you didn't check who was calling. I have been checking your house CCTV and obviously the wires we have in everyone's phones. M is clearly wanting to know where you are. He is calling anyone who knows of you, but I will keep my eyes open. Luther has gone to work so we can slip that letter in while he's out. He did however receive a phone call from M this morning, but he obviously knows nothing, so I'm not worried there. Marcus is going to pay him a visit later to see what he does. Clearly, he's also worried and Jasmine has just sat in her room. She told M she doesn't know what to do, and she doesn't want to offend you by leaving or going somewhere she shouldn't. What do you want me to do?" Okay, so this is not how I expected things to go. I thought she would incriminate herself. Or perhaps that was me hoping she would, hoping she would tell me either her or M were crossing me. But I need to keep everyone busy so they don't know I am investigating them; distracting them will make it easier. If Jasmine crosses me, I need her away from her family anyway. I don't need them trying to look into where she is. Especially if I kill her, too many questions would arise and well, I don't have the time or energy to handle that as well as Steadwell Sr.

"Right, get H to lead some team exercises and Jasmine to say goodbye to her family. Luther, get him to go to some bullshit meetings with some random associates just to keep his mind off where I am. I'm going to be coming home Monday anyway, so we can arrange for him to meet me, Monday evening. Let's just pretend I'm away on important business."

"Right, I am on it. Stay safe, and see you tomorrow." And with that, the call ends.

Aid is amazing like Marcus. He's straight to the point and doesn't ask questions. I know I can rely on both of them. So that work sorted. I have ten minutes to get downstairs for my breakfast date. That's fine; I'm ready, I may as well go down now and wait. I can catch up on some reading, and maybe send a few emails I have been putting off sending. Making my way to the lift, I pick up my phone and my key card. I do almost everything from my phone anyway, but I do have some cash. I grab a twenty from my bag by the door and leave the room. Getting down the lift seemed to be so much quicker this way, maybe because Xander wasn't in the lift with me. The doors open at the lobby, and I walk over to the seating area. A conversation grabs my attention; lifting my phone I pretend to be on a call while I eavesdrop.

"You should have seen her, man. She kicked arse by the pool, and I even watched what happened in the gym. She is a complete fox. I'm not even lying; she's got this edge about her that makes you want to stay the hell away, but also get to know her. I'm taking her out to breakfast and see where that takes me." I recognise that voice and only one man was there when I kicked those guy's asses and knew about the gym, was Xander.

"She sounds like a handful, mate, but if you are into that, why the hell not!" says another bloke. I know that voice; a shiver runs down my spine.

Looking up slightly, I see them leaning against one of the marble pillars in the middle of the lobby. The man he's talking to is shorter than him with jet-black hair slicked back and in a black suit. Clearly, he's a businessman. "Yeah, I am. She doesn't give a shit about money; she has her own. I can tell she's got a lot. She's in the Diana suite and dresses minimally. Like she never wants to be noticed; that clearly indicates a woman who has money but doesn't want to flaunt it. Also, she has these piercing green eyes that could cut through a man's soul. I don't know but she seems like the kind of woman that's all business. She's also got a lot of tattoos, but they look super sexy. She's not like the normal bimbos you get round here. She's fierce and intelligent, which is a rare combo."

For crying out loud! I met this man an hour ago, and even he got that vibe. Maybe I don't know how to deal with people, but I was taught by a man who always said men are the spawn of Satan and will only use me and cast me aside when they are done.

Glancing at the time on my phone, I notice it's exactly 10:00 am. Ten minutes go fast when you are eavesdropping on a conversation about yourself. I stand up and walk over to him; his eyes meet mine as I walk across the lobby.

His light hazel eyes are swirling with emotions and darting all over my face like he's trying to read what I am thinking. "Hey, Xander. Nice to see you again." I follow with the sweetest smile I can muster.

"Yeah, hey. Ready to go? Oh, by the way, I never caught your name." Oh shit, I only ever made a surname for my trip here, quick, quick think of one.

"Yeah, it's Taylor, Taylor Parker. Sorry, did I forget to tell you earlier." I laugh. Phew, that was close. Why the hell Taylor, isn't that a boy's name, although I guess it could be unisex. Hey, I'm just going to roll with it. I look at the guy he's talking to and finally get a good look at his face. *FUCK…I know him. We did business a couple of years ago. Maybe he won't say anything…but he never saw my face, just heard my voice…*I think to myself. Mr Wilson, complete sleaze bag. While I look at him, he clears his throat, looking extremely uncomfortable.

"Hi, I'm David. I was just…erm…Leaving. Catch you later, Xander." And with that, he slithers away like the snake he is. He must have recognised my voice. I watch him scurry off, my eyes watching his retreating figure. I don't have any issues with the bloke, but how he conducts his business.

"Well, that was weird. Sorry about him. We do business sometimes, and we are friends. He's never usually like that, Taylor." I laugh slightly, if only he knew.

"Honestly, it's fine. I wouldn't worry about it. He's not the first man to run away from me, and he probably won't be the last." This seems to put him slightly at ease.

"Shall we?" he asks with his arm out. I laugh and take it. Is this what being normal feels like? Probably not, but it's different to my version of normal.

We get out onto the street. It's warm here, but not too warm; it is only May. Summer hasn't even begun, but I wish I had something other than jeans to wear, but then I would feel self-conscious. Yes, even the infamous E has insecurities.

"So, what do you do for work other than protect people?" Xander asks, guiding me through the bustling streets of Washington.

"I help out at a charity. It's for orphan children. I read to them and try to keep them calm when they first arrive. I kind of get how they feel so it's easy to sympathise with them." I do know how they feel. I was orphaned at nine; that's why I founded the charity. I wanted to help children like Maggie helped me and M. Marcus also helped. He helped me channel my anger and also do some good with the skills I had, apart from shooting cans off walls and trees in Maggie's back garden with Rick's guns. I won't lie, I was really good, dead centre all the time. That's how Marcus found me; he saw me shooting in a back alley in London centre. I was a bit of a criminal even before Marcus. I had a criminal record before I was fifteen. Often being brought home in the back of a cop car, I am surprised it didn't make Maggie drink. She had to deal with my wayward ways. Damn! I would have drank having to deal with me! The rest, as they say, is history.

"That's amazing. The kids must really appreciate that. Someone knowing how they feel and all that. I won't ask how, you know though." Xander looks at me with an apologetic smile.

"It's fine. My parents died when I was young, and my aunt and uncle raised me for a while. It was nice actually then. When I was a bit older, I went off to go make my money and now I'm here." It feels good to actually talk like this, not worrying about anything too much. If I'm honest, after Monday, I probably won't see Xander again, so what's it matter as long as I skirt round the truth.

"I'm really sorry to hear that, Taylor. Must have been hard. Changing the subject, where would you like to eat? They have some great places around here, depends what you fancy." I smile, like an actual smile. It feels nice just being a normal woman chatting to a normal man; not a man who I do business with or with one of my men.

"I'm not from around here, so you pick." I smile up at him as he smiles down at me with that glint in his eye from earlier.

"Okay, your wish is my command."

After about ten more minutes of walking, we enter a quaint little artisan coffee shop. It's got art all over the walls and there's an amazing smell of coffee. A cute blonde girl is behind the counter. "Hey guys, welcome to Bistro. Would you like to eat in or take out today?" She smiles at Xander first then looks at me with a slightly smaller smile. Maybe she thinks this man I'm with is as sexy as I do, but me being here, she clearly doesn't want to flirt with him in front of me.

"We will be eating in; I'll take a flat white please. Taylor?" he asks, looking down at me expectantly.

"I'll take a cup of English tea please." I smile at the girl.

"We only do pots if that's okay? And it's Yorkshire Tea."

"Perfect." I could do with a lot of tea this morning. Even living in the states I still can't get enough. Coffee just isn't the same.

"Right, if you go sit down, I will bring that over." I'm actually enjoying not being E today. I'm going to be Taylor the charity worker who protects people on the side. I would laugh if I wasn't trying to keep up the charade of being her.

"So still into tea even after twenty years?" Xander asks once we have sat on a little round table next to the window. It's nice here just looking out the window watching the people go by not worrying who's pointing a gun at me.

"Yeah, coffee just doesn't do it for me. It's nice and if I've had a long night then I will grab one, but usually I always have tea. In New York, I've found this shop that sells English food and I always shop there for a lot of my tea and other items I miss from home, or my mum will send it over for me." I smile, just thinking about all the times Maggie has sent food packages over makes me smile. She always knows what to send. My guilty pleasure is jammy dodgers. I know they are childish, but I can't get enough, and I can never find them anywhere. For my birthday last year, she sent ten boxes of them; must have lasted about two weeks before I ran out.

"Really, your mum sends you food like if you were at college. That's super cute." Xander laughs. I guess it is, but Maggie always does it even without asking. She knows my issues with jammies and waggon wheels.

"Yeah, she gets me. Even in my thirties she treats me like a kid. But I can't complain. It stops me missing home too much." I sigh. Sometimes I do miss home. I miss Maggie dancing around the kitchen. I miss hearing her laugh every day. I miss the lack of responsibility that came with being in England, but I won't change anything either. I still see Maggie when I can and speak to her loads. I do really miss Rick sometimes. He always believed in me and was so proud when I made it big over here. He was always fully aware of what I do and never questioned it; he always saw the good in me even when I couldn't.

"So, you call your aunt mum then?"

"Well yeah, I guess. She did raise me from the age of nine until I moved over here. Then she was still always around, visiting whenever she could and sending food from home. It's nice really." I really do always appreciate everything Maggie does for me.

Suddenly, the waitress is next to our table. Jesus, I really haven't been paying attention to my surroundings. Normally, no one ever gets the jump on me, but this petite blonde woman definitely caught me by surprise. Xander smiles bigger than he already was. "She made you jump?" He chuckles.

"Yes." I turn my attention to her.

"Thank you, just put them on the table."

"Anything else I can get you this morning?" she asks with the biggest smile I've ever seen on someone. Her eyes staying on Xander. Clearly, she is hoping he will take a shine to her, but he is too focused on the menu to even notice her; he is so funny. He takes a hot second to figure out what he wants; his fingers gripping his chin as he ponders his choice. And a level of concentration I haven't seen on someone's face for a long time, taking this decision extremely seriously.

"I'll have a breakfast, eggs over easy. And two rounds of white toast," he states with a smile of accomplishment. I chuckle as he folds the menu up and hands it back to the waitress, whose name I have already forgotten. Xander can eat. I would never order breakfast. They are too big here in the States. He turns to me.

"You want the same?"

I shake my head.

"No thanks. I'll have some pancakes with bananas, strawberries and blueberries on the top. And some maple syrup on the side, please." I smile and grab my pot of tea. It's in a small English style teapot. It has some seventies style pattern on, kind of what you would see in the movies. I know we Brits like our tea but it's kind of a cliché.

My phone rings while I'm pouring my tea. I click my earpiece, getting a small, confused look off Xander. I hold up my finger to indicate that I will only be a minute. "Yep."

"E, why the hell is Marcus here telling us all to do training exercises for the next three days? I know you're pissed, but you should be here doing them as well. Also, why is H in charge? I'm your right hand. I should be leading this if anyone." God, M is such a whiny bitch this morning. Sighing, I pour some milk into my tea. Looking at Xander, he's still as shocked that I didn't even pick up the phone. I need to know how M got this number; the only people who have it are Marcus and Aid. I furrow my brows as I think about it, but with my response, I give nothing away. He doesn't need to know I am on to him. Well, not yet anyway.

"Just do as your fucking told, okay? I'm busy at the moment and that's all you need to know. I made my choice, and you will either accept it or we can discuss this when I get home. Now fuck off and get on with whatever H tells you to do. Bye." And with that, I hang up.

"Sorry about that. Business is a tad annoying right now. I'm meant to be on holiday. Clearly, people don't understand the whole 'I'm away from the office' thing," I say with a shrug and a chuckle.

"Don't worry. I completely get it. It's the same when I go away. But I don't usually speak so roughly to my staff," he says with another chuckle at the end. I laugh along.

"It's my brother. He's a whiny bitch when he doesn't get what he wants. They say don't work with family and my God, they are right."

Breakfast with Xander was nice. We talked like normal people. No business, no shop talk, just like friends. It was definitely what I needed. My phone did ring a few more times but I just ignored it. Apparently, they must have got the message. Looking into Xander's eyes was like looking into a forest in summer, so full of life. So many emotions that I forgot what the time was, and before I knew, it was nearly dinner time. We had been sat in the cafe for hours. I'd had many pots of tea and he had a few coffees.

"Oh shoot, is that the time? I've really got to go. This was lovely and probably the better part of my holiday. Thank you, Xander, maybe we can meet again before I go home?" I am slightly wanting to see him again. It's like I can be a completely different person with him. I don't have to be E. I can be anyone else. Even a normal woman. Maybe I would treat myself to some nicer clothes for our next date. *No, this wasn't a date; it was just a friendly breakfast…we don't do romance…we didn't even do sex until last night…slow down, girl…*my head says, putting me back into my place. Yes, romance is definitely off the cards but maybe a quick fling would be nice.

"Yes, I would love that. Maybe we could go for a proper meal and a drink before you leave." Xander reciprocates the look I have in my eyes. Or at least I hope I have. If I'm honest, I don't know what look I have; I'm not great at emotions.

"Well, I don't have to leave till Monday so maybe we can go out Sunday night around 9 pm, or earlier if you would prefer. Sunday is the only day I'm not too busy." I can't seem to stop smiling. What the hell is wrong with me? I'm like a little girl all over again and I don't like it. I feel like I did when I was fifteen and Kieran walked into the room.

"Sounds great to me. Want me to pick you up from the hotel? Also, wear something less black. Maybe we could go somewhere a bit more upmarket than a café." With a smile, I look down at my watch. I really do have to leave.

"That will be fine. Right, I will see you there, Xander, 9 pm Sunday night. I'll be in touch." And with that, I pop my twenty on the table and leave. This is going to require me going shopping, something I haven't done in a very long time. Usually, I get other people to do it but today I will sort it myself.

Chapter 20

Yesterday wasn't too bad. After breakfast with Xander, I met up with some old friends, as close to friends as I get. I also spoke to Marcus about what's happening in New York. He came over to see me at lunch today. Apparently, Marcus had told H that today Luther was to go training with them and he was to learn how to shoot a gun and to do close combat. I didn't think that was a bad idea. In all honesty, he did need to know just in case we aren't always there to protect him. His father is a threat to him, so he needs to be safe at all times.

All three of us are now sat in a bar somewhere in downtown Washington, which, if I'm honest, is quite a sketchy place. Even at around 2 pm on a Saturday, it seems to have some very questionable people in, and that's saying something for me. "E, the lads are on the phone. They want to know if they can go to Secret for some time. I believe Luther is going with them from the sounds of it," Marcus says with his phone held to his shoulder.

"Is M planning on going?" I ask only because I don't want him anywhere near that place at the moment. I found the footage of what happened to Georgia. K has traced back to M or at least him phoning someone to sort her out. Worse part is that the fucker who did it knew where the cameras are, so I didn't see his face, and only a select few know, M being one of them. Right now, I'm deciding whether I want to kill him or beat the shit out of him. Marcus put the phone back to his ear.

"Not if you don't want him to."

"Great, I'll text him to do something meaningless. Yes, it's fine if the others go."

I don't mind if they go to Secret, they usually enjoy hanging out there anyway and chatting up the young women there.

"You okay, E?" Aid asks with a small smile; he's like my other father figure. Marcus and Aid have been together for years. Marcus said that's how come he knew men were no good. Not only because he is one, but he's also married to one. Aid and Marcus are definitely a strange pairing, but despite it all, they have made it work and raised me, not into a typical woman but into the person I'm meant to be.

"Yes, I'm okay, just a bit concerned about M and what I'm going to do. I know he's crossed me, but I want to know why before I make my first move. But I will be locking him in a cell and teaching him a lesson, either way," I reply looking between the two men sat in front of me. I pick up my phone and text M.

You will be sitting outside of Harry Steadwell's house tonight. I want to know all his movements. You will also be listening in on his conversations and what he's doing in his house. Take Jasmine with you. Don't mess this up. — E.

I can really do without him going out with the lads. He's not getting away with this, at all. And if he takes her with him, then she is out of my house and away from anything important. I don't trust her either. "Why don't you interrogate him? We know how it breaks him. He would spill his guts if you had him tied up. You're a bit ruthless when it comes to getting information out of people." Aid has a point. If I'm being honest, I don't tend to stop beating someone up until I have what I want out of them.

"I may do that actually; he deserves to be beaten up regardless." I will get to the bottom of this, one way or another.

"So, what are your plans for the rest of the day then?" Marcus asks. I don't know what I want to do. I may just go back to the hotel and use the facilities. But I do need to get something to wear for tomorrow night. I said I was busy until then, which I technically am because I'm looking into things in my hotel room but not too busy. I'm just trying to take a small break from everything and get back to normal.

"Probably go shopping at the mall, then go to the gym and swim later. Nothing exciting until Monday when I'm home." I chuckle. That's when I will kidnap M and ask him a few questions, sibling to sibling.

"You are going shopping, really? You only ever send Klaire to do that. You call it a meaningless task that is performed by meaningless people. What's really going on?" Aid asks with a shocked look on his face.

"Fine, maybe I want to act like a normal person for five minutes and not a raging murderer. Apparently, I'm not approachable and maybe this way I can have a go at being a woman." I roll my eyes; they may be the closest guys I have but sometimes I don't think I should have to explain myself to anyone.

"E, you haven't been normal since you were thirteen, I made sure of that. Are you sure there is no other reason?" Marcus is right there. I'm not normal and never will be, but maybe I want to have a go at it and see what I'm missing out on. See what all the fuss is about.

"Yes, I've been like this for years, also I'm going out tomorrow and I can't exactly wear this." I point to my current attire, which is the same as every day. Black top, black trousers. After a bit of a chat, I say my goodbyes. I tell them that I will see them at the hotel tomorrow to discuss what they have found and leave.

The mall is a small cab ride away. It's huge and I don't exactly know what I am doing. I usually send Klaire out shopping for me. She knows what suits me but she's not here, so I will be doing it alone. Walking into Prada, I notice a beautiful black dress. I know I'm meant to be staying away from black but it's too pretty not to buy.

"Hello Ma'am, what are you looking for today? Anything I can help you with?" a tiny woman with bright red hair asks. She's dressed in black. She has a name tag on which says Rabecka.

"Yes, please, I love this dress so I will take that in a four, and I need something for a dinner date tomorrow. Classy yet sexy, you know." She smiles.

"Yes, we can do that. I will get the black one put behind the till for when you pay and we will find you something for your date." I am super nervous; I don't do this and this woman knows nothing about me at all.

She walks me over to the other side of the shop. There are rows of very elegant dresses that are stunning. I check the price tag on a dark blue floor length dress which I also like. *How fucking much*…my head yells. I've never seen so much money spent on a dress before, but I guess I don't buy my own so I would never know what they cost. "What colour are you looking for? We have some lovely blues or maybe a green to match your eyes? The choice is completely yours," she says with another smile.

"I'll be honest, Rabecka; I've never bought my own clothes so I've no idea what I'm looking for. Maybe a nice green, or maybe red? Probably best if you choose." I shrug.

"Well, I think we should try a couple on and see how you feel. Now is this date formal or casual?" I actually hadn't thought of that.

"Hmm I actually don't know. I don't usually date either – too much work not enough play." I chuckle, glancing at something that catches my eye.

I walk over and pick it up. It's a soft pink mid length dress with sleeves. It dips at the chest low, maybe a little too low, but I actually really like it. The dress is skin-tight. I know it will show-off my figure.

"This dress would be stunning on you. It's formal yet casual, and slightly revealing. Your date will love it."

"Should I try it on then?" I really don't know what to do when I'm shopping. The most shopping I do is food or for weapons. This is unfamiliar territory for me.

"Yes definitely, changing rooms are right over there. I'll be outside. Just come out when you're ready," she says, leading me to a room with a lockable door.

Walking in, I see the bench to put my stuff on and a floor length mirror to see what I look like. Why am I so nervous to try something on? It's pretty and I have worn many pretty things before. Maybe it's because I have chosen it, not Klaire. Nothing has ever been this pretty or expensive, although a few of my dresses are designer, so they maybe this much. I wouldn't know, Klaire and James just arrive at mine with them in hand. Some of my clothes could have cost thousands and I would never know. I don't ask. Why would I, I know I can afford it and I suppose sometimes I need clothes like this. Come to think of it, the one I wore for the gala was probably twice this. I guess it's just something I never think about or think to ask about.

Slipping out of my jeans and T-shirt, I get a good look at my scar that runs across my stomach. I've had it since I was 20. But it carries some significance, a part of my past I wish I never endured. A part of me I wish I could forget about, but alas I cannot. I must live with the pain every day and remember it every time I look in the mirror.

Waking up in a medical hut with doctors all around me, Kyle stood to my side with a sad look on his face. I don't remember what happened, just a searing pain in my abdomen, then nothing. A doctor walks over to me. He's clearly in his early forties. "Emilia, welcome back. Didn't know if you were going to make it. The operation was a huge success, and we stopped the bleeding. However, we did have to do a full hysterectomy to stop the infection from spreading. The bullet hit one of your ovaries and caused a lot of damage, because you didn't come in straight away. Which yes, I know here is hard to do, but it caused an infection, which meant you needed both removed and your womb. I'm so sorry, you won't ever have children." The sad look in his eyes made the news a little harder to understand. Never have children? I was only 20. I never thought about it really but now I have no option.

"Emie, I'm so sorry. I'm here if you need to chat," Kyle says with a small smile.

"How did I get here anyway, Kyle; we were in battle, last thing I remember. At least 50–60 miles away from base camp." Another look passed Kyle's eyes. Clearly, he was upset with what happened. I am grateful he's here and also, that we are both alive. I helped him over a year ago, when I found him lying on the ground with a bullet in his side. I got him back to camp and got him stitched up. I did abandon him when he woke up, but he swore to find me. Nearly a year later, he tracked me down, surprising me, Byron and Silas. After that, we all agreed he could stay. He proved he was an asset. We have been best mates ever since. He even clicked with Byron and Silas, my other two army brothers.

"You jumped in front of a bullet for me, Emie, again. I then carried you back to the tank and Byron drove us all back here. You were bleeding so much that the team and I thought you would die. I couldn't let that happen; we got you back here about a week ago. You've been in a coma since then." A coma! Really? I tried to sit up, but the pain was excruciating. It felt like someone was ripping my insides out, and my breath hitched for a moment as the pain raged through my body.

"Please stay down, Emilia, you only just woke up. In a few days, you and Kyle will be flying home, your work here is done. I hear you're getting a medal for this. Well done!" And with that, the doctor walks away. Kyle's hair is ruffled, and he doesn't look like he has slept in days. He has dark circles round his eyes. And the blue of them is dull. I put my hand on his.

"Hey, we are both okay and that's all that matters. We can get the hell out of this shit hole country and back home." I smile. This clearly makes him feel a bit better.

That was the hardest day of my life. I shake my head to remove the images of that place. I'm not there now and that's all that matters. I slide the pink dress on; it's beautiful. The cut looks amazing; showing just enough leg and breast to be sexy and classy. It fits all my curves exactly; I feel amazing. I zip it up and walk out. As promised, the assistant is waiting outside the room for me. Her jaw goes slack for a second. "Wow, you look amazing. I think that's the dress for your date. He won't know what hit him. Would you like this one or do you want to keep shopping?" She smiles.

"No, I think you're right, this is the one. I'll take it as well." I return her smile I take another look in the mirror; it hugs me in all the right places. The way the low cut accentuated my round breasts, even allowing you to see some of my abs. The corset structure holds me in down to my waist, showing off my slim figure. But what captures my eyes the most is the way it hugs my round ass, showing off how plump it is. The tight fit makes my body look phenomenal and would make any man's mouth water, but it does have a small slit in the back under my ass, so I can walk. As I look closer, I notice there is a small pattern to the fabric in some sort of holographic material. The light shines off it in a beautiful way, adding to the aesthetic of the dress. The sleeves do worry me slightly, but as long as I don't flail my arms around, they should hold. They are only attached by a small amount of fabric under my arms, giving an off the shoulder look. I feel wonderful in this dress, and it is so different to anything I have ever bought before. I reach into the changing room and grab my phone; snapping a picture, I send it to Klaire. I need to know what shoes to pair this with, and she is the best person to ask.

I immediately get a response.

WOW. Damn, E, you look epic. Nude shoes, for sure. Excellent choice on the dress. Klaire.

I smile as I read the text then look at the photo. I even see a small smile on my face. What's happened to me? I never smile. Maybe it's because I feel drop-dead gorgeous, or maybe it's because right now I can be less on edge and enjoy the moment. And I should, because come Monday, it's all over.

I go back into the changing room; I can't wait to see Xander's face when I meet him in this. Getting back into my normal clothes, I remember I was meant to look into him when I had a second to make sure he was who he said he was. I know I'm probably overthinking things; he could just see me as a pretty girl who he would like to know more, but I can't run the risk of it being something else. I make my way out and over to the till.

"And how would you like to pay today?" Rabecka asks.

"Card, please." I pull out my black card. Apparently over here, cards come in colours. The more money you have the colour changes. I honestly don't know how much is on here but I know it's enough to get these dresses and the shop as well. It goes through straight away; with that, I pick up my stuff and leave.

I should get some shoes to go with it. Christian Louboutin's is across the way. Apparently, if you're not super rich, you can't shop here; everything is designer. I walk in and straight away, I see the most beautiful pair of nude high heels I've ever seen; they are only gloss finished but the minimal look is gorgeous. Next to them is a pair of black ones that are also as equally beautiful. I am a girl of simple taste, well most of the time. Occasionally, I do love something shiny. What girl doesn't love sparkles?

I look for a store assistant so I can ask for them in a size seven. This has always confused me because back home I'm a size five shoe, which is average over there. Sizes confuse me; they change in most countries, and I just can't wrap my head around it. Good thing I have Klaire.

I locate someone to help me. She's, again, slim, but she's tall – taller than me and has lovely brunette hair with matching eyes. The look in her eye, however, reminds me of a look I use to get when I was young. A look of disdain, like she thinks I don't belong here. Even with the Prada bag in my hand, honestly. I plaster on a fake smile, knowing exactly how this conversation is going to go.

"Excuse me, do you know if you have these in a size seven?" I ask, pointing at the heels I want.

"Yes, we do ma'am, but erm…" She glances at my bag then back at me. "Are you sure you can afford two pairs? They are $500 a pair." I stare at her in shock.

"Do you ask everyone that or just the woman in jeans and a T-shirt?" I ask. She again looks me up and down. I see the cogs in her brain turning as she tries to think of the answer for why she is being such a dick. "Look, just get your manager please. I don't appreciate being spoken to like that." She tuts and walks away. I am holding a Prada bag which I spent more on one dress than I will on both these shoes alone. I won't tell you how much, you might have a heart attack. I nearly did.

A few minutes later, she comes back over with an older lady with silver hair and a few wrinkles; wouldn't say she is old, but she's not in her twenties like this girl is. "Hello Ma'am, what would you like?" I smile slightly. I am pissed but I'm going to be polite.

"Yes, I would love a size seven in these shoes." I hold up the nude pair and the black pair. "I would also like a pair of those in black as well." I point at a different pair of heels. They have spikes on the back and on the toes. They are also boot style with a high chunky heal which is totally a me thing. I tend to wear boots all the time: rain, hail, or shine. I only wear stilettos when I need to. But these boots, they are different, and I love them. I may have another outfit that they will go with, or I'll just wear them because I can. The bright gold spikes are just a bold statement, and well, I am a bold kind of woman.

"Yes, of course we will get those put through for you right away. Also, those boots are limited edition, so there will only be so many pairs of those. Good choice, Ma'am." She smiles. The redhead rolls her eyes at me.

"Please, can she do it?" I ask, pointing towards the redhead.

"Why would you like that, Ma'am? She was rude to you and I have put her on a warning."

I chuckle as I reply. "I wish to see her face when I pay for my shoes. I don't care that she was rude. Yes, I'm not dressed like everyone else in here with their designer clothes, but it doesn't mean I can't afford what I want. And she needs to learn not to judge a person before they know them." I smile. If she worked for me, she would have worse than a warning. See, I am not evil, I am a teacher. I hold back a chuckle at my own thoughts. I always love teaching people a lesson: M, the guys at the gym and pool yesterday. And now I am tutoring this woman on her perception of people; think of it as my community service.

"Okay, Ma'am, I will make sure she puts it through for you. Would you like to follow me to the till?"

With that, we make our way over. The redhead is at the till bagging my shoes. She rolls her eyes again, gaining a glance from the manager. I just smile. "That's $13,000 for all that. How would you be paying?" The redhead sighs.

"Card, please." I pull out my black card. The redhead pails when she sees it. It's not a credit card, just a normal one. The name on the card is Miss T Parker; never thought about what the T stood for until Xander asked me the other day.

The card gets accepted automatically. "See, shouldn't judge a person before you know them. I work hard for my money; I shouldn't be spoken to like that. And I hope you never speak to anyone like that again. Goodbye." And with that, I grab my shoes and leave. Her face was a picture as she eyed up my card, and yes I enjoyed each and every minute of putting her in her place.

Chapter 21

Being back in the gym is great. I have my headphones in, listening to the best playlist I have. It's got lots of different artists on: some pop, RnB, and some other upbeat songs. I've been on the treadmill for a while. Glancing at the monitor, I notice I've been running for about 45 minutes; I have very good stamina, being ex-military. I had to, and I just kept up the strict training. I will stop in a few minutes and move onto another piece of kit; I've been here for about two hours. That's nothing for me. I can be in a gym for at least four maybe five hours. I need to be at my peak fitness for my job. I just wish they had high bars and a rock-climbing wall. Hitting the cool down button, the treadmill starts to slow down. As I hit a walking pace, I feel someone tapping me on my left shoulder.

Turning my head round, I see Xander smiling at me. Smiling back, I pull out my earphone. "Hey, Xander, how are you?" He's still as handsome as he was the other day, maybe even more so as he is dressed for business.

"Yeah, I'm good, thanks. I was walking past and saw you in here. Thought I might pop in and say hi. So, hi." I laugh at him. He's super cute.

"You knew it was me even from behind. Cause the door is directly behind me." He starts to blush; I think he's a little embarrassed.

"Fine, I saw you enter a couple of hours ago. I knew you hadn't left yet because the woman over there." He points to a woman about the same age as me, "is complaining you are hogging the 'good' treadmill, so I said I would talk to whoever was on here. Funny it would be you. Have you really been running for nearly an hour?" He stares at me, shocked. Hitting the stop button, I grab my drinks bottle and jacket. I get off the treadmill and smile at the woman who wanted it; she's death staring me. I just roll my eyes at her and walk away. Some women be acting crazy over nothing. It's just a machine and there are twelve of them.

Xander walks alongside me as I go towards the door. I fancy trying to swim again today. Let's hope it's not as eventful as last time. "So where are you off to now, Taylor?" I pause a second, stopping at the turn I look at him. He's in a suit and his hair is slicked back, making him look very professional.

"I'm going to go for a swim and maybe use the sauna. Never been in one so thought I may try it. Also, do you know where I can go either rock-climbing or where I can do gymnastics?" His eyebrows crease together slightly.

"The sauna is lovely, but I'm not sure about the rock-climbing or gymnastics. I will go look for you if you like." Oh well, worth a shot.

"Thanks, anyway, I'm going to head to the pool. I'll see you later." As I'm walking away, I feel his eyes on me. "By the way, you scrub up nicely, Mr Valance." With that, I keep walking. He never told me his surname, but I looked him up and found out he owns a few hotels. He is worth a pretty penny, and isn't connected to anyone who is after me. Age appropriate and seems to be quite kind. Donates to charities and holds normal people fundraisers. He does have a couple of parking fines and speeding tickets outstanding. But hey, who hasn't had a speeding ticket or two.

Getting to the pool, I remove my gym clothes. If there is a pool, I always wear my swimsuit underneath my outfit.

No one is here and it's great. I walk to the deep end and dive straight in. It's cold in here, but it's nice. My body was on fire after my intense workout. I like to swim to help my muscles relax. I also find it therapeutic. Especially when there is no one else here. I didn't put my earpiece in like I usually do. I'm expecting a phone call. I swim over to my stuff. Getting out the pool, I go into a zip pocket in my leggings. There are my wireless earphones and my singular earpiece; good thing it's waterproof. I've swam in these many times; H is great at inventing things for me. Can't be without it now.

Starting my swim again, my phone rings. Touching my earpiece, I answer it. "Yep," I answer, curt as always.

"E, it's Luther. I've been worried about you. Where are you?" He's been worried about me; he's slightly slurring his words. Apparently, he's had a few. I guess it was late back home. I know he went to Secret with the guys. How does everyone seem to have this number? I groan inwardly to myself. This is the last thing I need, a drunk Luther Steadwell calling me over fucking nothing.

"Luther, it's late and I'm just having a swim. I take it you're having a good time at the club." He laughs down the phone.

"A great time, the lads are super funny. I miss you. When are you coming home? Also, are you mad at me? I didn't mean to be a dick after what happened

Thursday night. I just went into panic mode. I'm too selfish to be a dad right now." I forgot we hadn't spoken about it since I left.

"I'm not mad at you, Luther, just needed to clear my head and sort a few things out. I will be home soon, and we can talk." I know he's smirking when he replies.

"Maybe we can do more than chat when you get home. But seriously, I can't stop thinking about you."

Oh, shit, I know he's drunk, but I can do without him getting feelings right now. "You know how I feel about this, Luther. Feelings aren't to be a part of this, I'm not good with those." If I was anyone else, I would be pleased he felt this way about me; he did take my virginity, but I can't afford to get attached. It will make me weak.

"I know, but I can't help how I feel. All other women pale in comparison to you now. I'm going to go. H brought more drinks. We will chat when your home. Come back soon." He hangs up before I can reply. Sighing, I carry on swimming.

I can feel someone's eyes on me. It's strange to know someone is staring at me. I'm trying to ignore the feeling. Diving under the water I can feel them getting closer to the pool.

When I break the water as I come up for air, I hear someone enter the pool. I'm slightly on edge right now. I dive under the water again and turn around. I see a man swimming towards me. I slowly push myself away slightly, but they make a beeline for me. I go back up for oxygen. As I get my head out of the water, I see the brightest hazel eyes right in front of me. I recognise them, my eyes flick to the rest of his face. It's Xander. I feel more at ease now.

"God, don't creep up on a woman. Christ!" I was planning how to take him out without my weapons. I probably would have strangled him with my bikini top. I know, original.

"Sorry, didn't mean to scare you. Thought you may want some company. I thought someone else was here when I walked in. But apparently you were talking to yourself." A deep chuckle comes from his throat.

"I was on the phone. Why? What did you hear?" Oh shit! I hope he didn't hear too much.

"Apparently you don't do feelings, and apparently you will be having words with someone when you get back home. So, I have to ask, why don't you do feelings?" Xander raises a single eyebrow. God, he looks so sexy when he does that. His dark hair is still slicked back like it was before. He looks hotter than he did on Friday morning.

"I just don't, never have. Would make things complicated. I'm also too busy for them." My life is very all over the place, so it's unwise to get attached.

"Well, maybe I don't want feelings, maybe I just want something fun. You intrigue me and I would love to get to know you, but I would like to show you a bit of fun before you leave. If that's what you want." Xander gets it. We are in quite deep water. If I was to kiss him, we would probably sink, because at this moment in time, we are treading water. I give Xander a cheeky grin and swim away to the shallow end of the pool. He chuckles again and follows me.

When I can finally stand up, I stop and look at him. He's still got a cheeky smile on. It's like he knows exactly what I'm thinking.

He walks right up to me; he tucks a stray wet piece of hair behind my right ear. His eyes are fixed on mine. His left hand moves to the small of my back. It feels nice. I watch as his head slowly moves towards me. I tilt my head back slightly. When our lips meet, it's hot and steamy. His lips move slowly with purpose, I meet his movements with my own. He slides his tongue into my mouth, his hands slide down to my ass and squeezes it gently. Why do I get the feeling he will be gentle with me like I'm a China doll. My arms slink around his neck to deepen the kiss. He pulls my body closer to his. I feel his rock-hard chest press against my breasts; I also feel his cock pressing against my stomach.

"So, erm…what do you want to do?" I stammer, flicking my eyes up to his. I see the look of desire in his eyes. I feel it too.

"Well, we could stay in here or go to your room or my apartment." I do like the idea of being in here. The thought of getting caught puts an edge on it.

"I do like the idea of potentially getting caught, but we can take this upstairs if you like." He starts walking forward, forcing me to walk backwards. My lower back hits the edge of the pool, I am basically naked but under his zealous gaze. I feel completely exposed. The edge of the pool is cold, but I'm feeling super-hot right now. His lips come straight down on mine with a lot more force than they did a few minutes ago. His left hand goes back to the small of my back, pulling me closer into him. His right hand goes to my right breast, his thumb brushes over my nipple, causing me to shiver. I moan into his mouth, letting him know I like it. He does it again, getting another noise from me.

Xander's lips move to my neck, sucking and nipping at the skin under my left ear. My hands move to his chest. It's hard as hell and his abs feel like they are carved from stone. I feel the strap of my bikini slide down my left arm and Xander's lips move over my shoulder and down to my breast. His hand is still on my right one, and his lips are on my left nipple. He sucks it slowly and gently starts nibbling the tip. A moan escapes my throat before I realise. My hands move further down his body, until it finds his happy trail. A deep rumble echoes round the room. His moan makes a euphoric feeling flow through me; my pleasure intensifying with each passing moment. . His lips leave my nipple with a pop and move back to my lips.

His hand leave my breast and move down my stomach. When his hand runs over my scars, he freezes. It feels weird when my scars are touched. "What are these?" Xander asks while running his fingers over them.

"Don't worry about them. They are nothing." His eyebrows scrunch together. Sighing, I look into his eyes.

"Look, I got them years ago. Something happened and I had a major operation. Nothing to think about." It looks like this satisfies him slightly. He kneels down and kisses them. It was a very strange feeling. I've never spoken about them before, and never wanted to even think about them. He brings his face back up to mine, his eyes looking into me like he's trying to see my soul; only if I had one.

"They make you, you. And I get if you don't want to talk about them, but you can with me if you ever want to."

"I've not spoken about it in 13 years. I don't see me doing it for a long time. But I would like to get back to where we were." I don't think he needed much more encouragement. His lips are back on mine. I run my hand along the top of his swim shorts.

"If you want to go further, go for it. I plan on putting my hands all over your glorious body, Taylor." His hands reaches the top of my bikini bottoms and slowly slides them down. His fingers slowly slide over my clit, causing my head to fly back and another gasp leaves my mouth. I lower my hand into his shorts, finding his cock. It's bigger than I thought. I grasp it in my hand. His head falls forward with a deep groan. His eyes look into mine as I move my hand back and forth along his cock, while his fingers slide over my clit. I'm getting wetter with every movement of his hands, and I can feel him getting harder.

"Mhmm, God I want you," Xander whispers into my ear.

"Then have me, Xander." With that, his finger slide into me; straight away he hits the good spot. His thumb moves over my nerves causing me to start moving up the hill before I fall into my orgasm. He moves his finger in and out of me faster.

"Oh God," I whisper, his second finger joins the first one inside of me, stretching me.

"You're so fucking tight." I don't quite hear him when he says it. I just start to move my hand on him faster, his next groan sounded like it didn't belong to him.

"Fuck me, Xander. Right now." I want him so much, the feeling is palpable. His lips move onto mine again, his kiss furious and full of passion. His fingers leave me, making me feel cold. Xander then grabs my bikini bottoms and pulls them all the way down.

He swaps places with me and takes a seat on the steps into the pool slightly to our right. Xander pulls me onto his lap. I grab the top of his shorts and try to pull them down slightly. He raises his hips to allow me to pull them over his thighs and down his legs. It was slightly difficult with us being in a poll, but I must get what I want; the need to be satisfied fills every part of my mind. I slide my bikini bottoms off my right leg, leaving them still around my left. I don't want them to end up across the other side of the pool. I climb back onto his lap, kissing him again. Raising up slightly, I grab his cock and put it to my entrance. I break away from our kiss for a second. Looking into his eyes, his passion never wavering, I lower myself onto his cock slowly. "Oh fuck, you feel amazing, Taylor. So tight," Xander remarks as I gasp as I slide him into me. He fills me up. Not like Luther, but still feels great. *Stop thinking about him. He's not here. God, just fuck this man who's handing himself to you on a platter*...my mind screams at me.

"OHHH," I gasp as he hits my back wall.

"Taylor, I don't want to finish inside you without protection. You may have to get off in a minute, I'm quite close." For Christ sake's are all men like this?

"Don't worry about that, I can't get pregnant." I move fast on him, making me gasp more and him moan harder. I'm so close to climax. His hand moves back down to my clit, massaging it lightly, building my climax higher. I move even faster, my breasts bouncing harder. "Oh Xander, I'm so close." He starts to rub me harder and harder. My climax hits me like a train, just as I'm coming down, Xander groans. I feel his hot cum filling me. I'm so full I feel it spilling out.

Climbing off him, I grab my bikini bottoms and slip them back on. That was good. Xander pulls his own shorts up. "Are you sure you won't get pregnant. I don't want to be a dick but I don't really want kids just yet." I sigh and get out the pool. "Taylor, stop. I'm sorry. I just worry. Been stung by women before." I turn to him when he says he's been stung by other women.

"Look, I don't usually talk about it, but maybe we should go for a drink. I'll explain." And with that I pick up my stuff and walk away. Xander is right behind me. We walk into the lobby and most of the people there are staring at us. "What are they all staring at?" I don't actually know what they would be looking at.

"Maybe it's because you have three hickies growing on your neck, or maybe because, yet again, we are walking through the lobby in our swim clothes." He chuckles.

Getting up to the elevator, Xander looks down at me. "Let's go to my room. I've got some wine up there if you like." Wine? Do I look like a wine kind of girl?

"I don't do wine. If you have rum or scotch, then I will go with you." I laugh.

"Anyone told you you're the woman of any man's dreams." He chuckles. Getting into the lift, I realise I'm a little cold now that I'm wet, the air conditioning is really making me chilly. Goosebumps appear on my arms.

"We will be in my place soon. I'm sure I have something you can borrow to wear." Xander must have noticed I'm cold; either that or he feels it too. This could be fun or the biggest mistake of my life, either way, I don't care right now. I'm just going to enjoy the ride.

Chapter 22

The lift stops a few moments later and we walk out. "Two seconds. I'll go find you something." And with that, he leaves the room. His apartment is lovely. It's white with white furniture and blue ornaments. Some pictures are hanging on the walls and a massive window wall stretches across the whole of the living room. It's amazing. If I enjoyed living in a city, this is what I would have. But I like my little house, it's cute.

A few moments later, Xander appears fully dressed with a top and jogging bottoms in his hands. "Here you go. Bathroom is just up the corridor and to the right." I shake my head. I strip right in front of him and throw the clothes he handed to me on. I've never really had any privacy before so why bother now. Also, he just had his hands all over me, no point pretending to be shy.

I walk into his small kitchen. I guess being a single man, he doesn't need much room. I walk right up to the cupboards on the wall and open the third one from the left and get out two glasses. Then I walk over to the end cupboard under the counter and pull out the scotch. "How the hell do you know where I keep my stuff?" I hadn't even noticed that he was watching.

"Lucky guess." I shrug. I pour two glasses and slide one over to him.

"You said you would explain, so why don't we sit, so you can." Grabbing his glass, he directs us to the living room. I take a seat opposite him on the white leather couch. Placing my glass on the black coaster sitting on the glass coffee table, I sigh before I relive the worse day of my life and tell a story I have refused to speak about to anyone. I don't know now why I am tell someone, but maybe if I get it off my chest, I will find it easier to cope with.

"Right, well, I've never told anyone this. Only two of my friends knows because they were there. When I was twenty, I was in Iraq serving my second tour and we came under fire." I glance out of the window. "I remember hearing all this gunfire. My friends and I were firing back. We were ducked behind this mound of dirt; it seemed like we were there for hours and maybe we were. When we thought it was over, as we stood up, I saw a guy move. I didn't even think. I just threw myself in front of my friends trying to protect them. All I felt was excruciating pain, then nothing."

I pick up my drink and take a swig. Xander doesn't say a word, just watches me. "When I woke up in the makeshift hospital, a doctor stood over me. He said he didn't think I would make it, and I had a full hysterectomy. I have no parts now to make a baby; being in the middle of a war zone meant they couldn't freeze any of my eggs." Sighing, I look back at him. "Apparently it took my friends three days to get me back to base camp. I got a massive infection and nearly died." I grab my drink again. "So when I'm asked when I want children, or men say they don't want to get me pregnant, they never have to worry. My chance to have kids left me very young."

Getting up, I walk to the window; I've never said any of that out loud. No one apart from K and B knows anything about this. I always thought it would stay that way with just K and B. They only know because they were there. They're the ones who got me home. But B was too heartbroken to sit with me; the guilt of what happened ate at him. And I guess even now it still does. He is always trying to keep me out of trouble. Trying to repay a debt he thought he owed me; little does he know I would have done it again in a heartbeat. Even if I knew what would happen, even if the outcome was worse. I would do it without a doubt, because that's what you do for family.

"You have been to war? I am sorry to hear what happened, but I'm still shocked you served our country." I laugh. It's refreshing hearing him focus on my war days and not my lack of a baby maker.

"I was in the forces from 18 until I was 25. But I did do training from the age of 16. At 25, I was honourably discharged. I served my terms and got very badly hurt on my final tour, so I was unable to continue in active duty. I trained so hard to get back to my peek physical fitness, overcame whatever stood in my way so I could do what I love." I turn back to him; he has a soft smile on his face.

"Wow, you are definitely not a woman to be reckoned with. What division were you? Army, Navy, Air Force?" I smile. I can't believe he is so interested in this and not the other thing.

"SAS, Special Ops. Usually, you have to work up to that, but I have a special skill set that allowed me to go straight to it. I was trained from a very young age, so I passed many of the tests with flying colours."

His mouth hangs open while he looks at me. "No way, SAS! Christ, you must be a beast to get in there." I laugh again. This was a lot easier to talk about than I thought it would be.

"I suppose you do. I never really thought about it. I just accepted that I was in and just sort of got on with my job. Nice to be out though, but being around normal people still weirds me out, even after being out for nearly ten years." I don't like to talk about the forces much, brings back a lot of bad memories. Things I would rather stayed in the past, and at times I wish I could forget. I may be a monster, but I still have some emotion. I do feel remorse for what I did then. Sometimes I still think about what I would have done differently; what I would have changed. But it's done now and there is nothing I can do. I can't bring back the lives I took, I can't save the ones I wanted to. No matter how hard I wish.

PTSD is a challenging thing to cope with. I may be a hard-faced bitch to almost everyone, but inside I suffer. I guess it's what makes me human. I carry a mask to hide the pain and suffering from the world. People fear me, envy me, or run from me. But I wish I could run from my past. I've been trying for years now. "That's quite an achievement to be part of that. You save lives and fight for all of us normal people. I get why you don't want to talk about it, but can I ask you a serious question?" I smile at his words; they touch something deep inside me. A part of me I have never allowed myself to feel.

"Sure." I smile as Xander chuckles.

"Don't laugh. Do you get dog tags in the SAS, and do you get to keep them when you leave?" I stifle my laugh. Of all the things to ask me about, this is what he chose. Not how many lives did you take? What was the craziest thing you have seen while serving? Not even if I miss it. Nope, just about some dog tags that are kind of a movie cliché, but yet quite efficient.

"Yes, we get dog tags. They have our code names on and an ID number. So, if we get blown to pieces, they can identify the dead. A bit morbid, I know, but it's efficient. And yes, when we retire, we are allowed to keep them; mine are at home with my uniform and medals of honour."

"Cool, I know I sound like a kid, but I've never spoken to a veteran that wasn't army or air forces before. Let alone had amazing sex with one. By the way it was great, and I'm definitely up for another round before you go home." A sly smile creeps back onto his face. I find it rather amusing that he thinks more about this than my sad parts.

I did lie to him about one thing though. I wasn't in the SAS. My unit never got a name. We were like cleaners, to put it plainly. We did a variety of tasks. Some were retrieval missions, some was dead collection, and some are still classified to this day, and I don't think they will ever be available to the public. Other units would call us sociopaths, doing the jobs no one else had the stomach to do. Going to places everyone else was too cowardly to enter, and handling things far more delicate than the other units could manage. We did what was asked, no questions asked, and never batted an eye no matter what was thrown at us. I guess I am sociopathic if I think about it. I have scraped enough guts off the floor by now to not be fazed by anything life has to throw at me. I've seen enough dead to not feel anything about it and committed enough murders by now to do it without even caring. Maybe the other units were right, but I don't care either.

"Well, that would be nice. I even went shopping for clothes for tomorrow. It was hell, if I'm completely honest with you. I don't normally go shopping other than food." I shrug. I didn't mind it up until I went to Christian Louboutin's then it went downhill fast.

Xander smiles. "I can't wait to see what you got for our outing tomorrow."

I appreciate him not calling it a date; that word terrifies me. I just chuckle at him and raise my eyebrow before moving into his bedroom. I glance over my shoulder at him. I gave him a cheeky smile before entering. I can hear his heavy footsteps; his deep chuckle reverberates around me.

The bedroom is gorgeous: white walls, deep blue bed and light wood floors and furniture. The minimalism works so well; this man has such great taste. I jump slightly as his arm snakes around my waist. His lips move down to my neck, sucking on it slightly. I moan with the feeling.

I turn in his arms. My eyes meeting his hazel ones. "Don't hold back on me, Xander, I am not a weak woman, and trust me, you won't hurt or break me." Something flares in his eyes, and within a second, he picks me up and throws me onto his bed. A small giggle leaves my lips as my back hits the extremely soft duvet. If he keeps this up, I don't think I will be able to leave tonight. A deep guttural moan leaves his lips as he advances towards me; a hard look of carnality is etched into his handsome features. His eyes turning a shade darker with each passing second. He stalks towards me like a predator hunting its next meal.

His large body lays over mine, his lips capturing me in a punishing kiss. His hands moving down my body painstakingly slowly. His sweet torment eliciting moans from me, anticipation building in my core. After what feels like an eternity of Xander feeling my body through my clothes, he grips my top. Raising, I allow him to pull it over my head. I take this opportunity to remove his top and slide my hands over his muscles. I feel each flex and movement of his muscles as my hands descend towards his hard member.

Sliding my hands into his jogging bottoms, I grab his cock. I run my hand along his member. "Fuck, Taylor, I am going to make you cum before you get me deep inside your tight pussy."

His words send shivers and pulses directly to my core. I moan as his lips start to descend down my chest. I close my eyes as I savour the feeling of his lips on my body. With each kiss, my core moistens, and my heart rate increases. Any more of this and I think my heart might actually beat out of my chest. His lips capture my right nipple, my hands sliding into his hair as his teeth clamp onto me hard.

"Ohhhh," I moan loudly as pain causes through my chest but is soon soothed by his tongue. My head falls back into the pillows as he continues his bombardment of pleasure. His lips nipping and sucking every square inch of my body, never giving me a moment to breathe. The way he is ravishing my body sends pleasure rocketing through the roof, sending me higher than I thought was possible.

Xander's face comes between my legs. "Mhmm, so wet and ready for me." His tongue strokes across me from asshole to clit. I arch my back as the pleasure moves through me. "So sweet." His lips clamp onto my clit as he starts to suck on me hard; my pussy clenching as I try to hold onto what little restraint I have.

I moan as he slowly glides two of his fingers into me. I can't believe I have deprived myself of this all these years. His fingers start to pump into me, slowly at first but building faster as he licks and sucks on my sensitive nerves. After a few more seconds of onslaught, he slides a third finger inside me while lightly biting my clit. My hands move next to my head and grip into the pillow. The intense feeling of my climax comes barrelling towards me. He starts to pump his fingers faster before sliding a fourth one inside me. He is opening me further than I think I have ever been. I am moaning louder than I have before, my voice becoming hoarse with the cries of ecstasy resonating from me. My back is arched to the ceiling, my hands move back into Xander's thick locks, holding his head to my pussy.

My hips start to rock against his hand, Xander moves his lips from my overly sensitive clit, his teeth bite into my thigh. As much as it hurt, the sensation only intensifies my pleasure.

"Fuck, Xander, I'm going to cum." I moan as my pleasure soars; his fingers start to move faster while he curls them, hitting my sweet spot. "Ah, fuck, yes." I yell as I feel my walls start to clench around his fingers. My head flies back as my core explodes. Xander's lips come around my hole as he laps up all my release. He keeps running his tongue over me and moving his fingers as I ride out my orgasm. In an instant, his fingers leave me to go under my ass and lift my hips; his mouth moving directly to my core and his tongue enters me. He drinks me like a man starved of water. Each time his tongue enters me, it prolongs my climax. I move my hips, rubbing my sensitive pussy over his face, not wanting this heaven-sent feeling to end.

Once Xander has had his fill, he moves back up to me, his lips locking with mine, his tongue fighting mine for dominance. The taste of myself on him turns me on even further. I wrap my legs around his waist and use his weight against him, flipping us over and straddling him. I move my lips down his jaw, following the same movements he did on me earlier. I take my time to love each of his abs, licking and sucking on every piece of him I can get my mouth on. I want to savour this man; I want to enjoy every single moment I can before it is gone.

Reaching his jogging bottoms, I start to pull them down. Lifting his hips, I pull them fully off. His hard cock springs free as I pull them down; a glistening on his tip catches the light. I lick the tip first, tasting his salty pre-cum on my tongue. It's not an unpleasant taste, but the way the girls at the club have acted about it, I thought it would taste like strawberries or something. I run my tongue from base to tip before sliding it into my mouth.

"Fuck." Xander groans, his hands tangling into my hair. He grabs my hair roughly. Using his hand in my hair, he starts to move my head, forcing his cock further into my mouth. Tears start to form in my eyes with the sensation of his cock sliding down my throat. I enjoy the feeling of him gliding in my mouth; the way he feels as he hits the back of my throat while I supress my gag reflex is exhilarating.

Each time I come up on his cock, I suck harder. This makes Xander moan louder each time. I can feel my juices start to spill down my thighs. I move my right hand down to my pussy; I start massaging my clit in circles as I pleasure Xander. I can feel my own orgasm rising within me again; the need to be filled by him getting stronger with each suck of his cock and movement of my fingers. I feel Xander twitch in my mouth before his cum shoots down my throat. Xander moves my head up and down his cock as he rides out his orgasm. I swallow each delicious drop, not as bad as I thought it would be. I flick my lust filled eyes up to his. Using my right hand, I use my finger to wipe a small drop of cum off my lips and into my mouth. I close my eyes and moan as I enjoy the flavours of both him and myself, before finally licking my lips while staring into his eyes.

Xander moves his hand from my head to my chin and pulls my face up to his. "God, Taylor, where have you been all my life?" A primal hunger is written all over him. His pupils dilated with the zealousness of what just happened and what is about to come.

I laugh. "Many places, now what do you want to do to me, Mr Valance?"

"Get on your knees." I do exactly as I am told, getting on my hands and knees next to where he lay. I watch him move. I feel his hands grip my hips as he kneels behind me. Once he's moved me into the right place, I feel him run his cock over my wet pussy. I arch my back at the sensation of his hard cock running through my wet folds. I start to pant with anticipation. "Do you want my cock, Taylor?"

"Yes, Xander, Fuck me right now." My breath catches as he forces himself straight into me. If Xander wasn't holding me in place, I know I would have been thrown across the bed. Xander pounds me at a punishing pace, his relentless thrusts build my orgasm higher. His hand comes down on my ass cheek; the sting mixes with my pleasure, sending me closer to my release. His hand goes to my shoulders as he pushes me down onto the bed, my ass in the air. His thrusts feel deeper than before, and with power, I feel him force the air out of my lungs. I bury my face into the bed as I scream out my passion. I feel another sharp sting on my ass; my head flying up as I suck in a breath. The pain mixed with the pleasure quickly sends me hurtling into the thrills of another orgasm, but Xander doesn't slow down. In fact, he pumps harder as I move through my release, the sounds of our bodies slapping together with each of his movements starts to build me to my third happy ending.

Once I am down from my climax, Xander pulls out of me. Annoyance fills me, I want to be in charge right now. No man pulls out of me without being done. I turn and push him backwards. Lying on his back, I straddle Xander, lowering myself on top of his erect member. His head goes back. I start to ride him as pleasure rises in me again. I am thoroughly enjoying the feeling of his rock-hard member sliding through my slick juices. The feeling of being in control of him and watching the pleasure on his face builds mine. My head goes back as I rock back and forth on him, his cock hitting my back wall every time he is fully inside me. Leaning back, I feel his thick cock rubbing against all my walls, slowly fulfilling a deep primal need I haven't felt before. Not even with Luther. My mind solely focusing on the wanton desire to be pushed to my limits, to be fucked into near oblivion.

"Oh fuck, Taylor." Xander grunts at me as I build his pleasure. Clearly not taking much more of this, he sits up. His arms wrap around my waist, his teeth sinking into my shoulder. The pain mixing with the building pleasure is intoxicating. His right hand slides between us. He starts to stroke my clit. As I ride his dick, my juices coat his cock. His hips move with mine, meeting every slick movement I make. Our bodies moving as one chasing the same goal, an earth-shattering orgasm. His teeth sink into me harder, his left arm gripping me tighter, his fingers stroke me faster as we both get close. I throw my head back, spots coming before my eyes as I release all over his glorious member. I squeeze him impossibly tight as I continue to rock my hips; my climax elongated with each movement both inside and outside of my pussy.

Xander speeds up before I feel him twitch inside me; his hot cum fills me and starts to spill down my ass cheeks. We sit there for a second catching our breath, neither of us pulling away from the other one as we come down from the intoxicating. Our breathing is ragged, and our bodies are covered in sweat, and yet I don't want this to stop. At least not right now; maybe I could get a couple more rounds from him before I leave.

"Maybe, we should continue this in the shower." I comment, getting off him. I moan as his cock leaves me; the sensation building my need to be satisfied and filled again. It seems I am a woman with far too many needs, and I doubt anyone would ever be able to keep up with me. But the look in Xander's eyes shows me he is up for the challenge.

Moving to the bathroom, I give him a cheeky smile, leaving the door open a jar. I go and start the shower. This is going to be a fun night.

Chapter 23

Last night, talking to Xander was lovely. We had an amazing chat not to mention amazing sex. He asked me all about my army days. It was nice to feel like a person, let alone a woman again, for a few hours. After Marcus trained me, he sent me off to the military to learn how to defend myself in proper battle. He said it would make me a stronger person and a stronger leader. He didn't send M to war apparently; he would never be ready. I knew this. He couldn't do the simplest task for Marcus, so I knew he would never be able to kill people, even if his life depended on it. But I always knew deep down that M was never like me, I had a mission, goals, and the drive to do what I wanted to do all these years. M on the other hand, didn't; yes, he was a care child, yes, he was troubled, but he didn't have the issues I had. I was dissociated to everyone and everything because all I could see was my end goal, my mission, and my reason for life. My revenge was all that kept me going.

I stopped the night at Xander's and now I'm finding myself creeping out at 7 am this morning. After the shower, we chatted, then things led to more fun; I think we stopped around 2 am. I've never done the walk of shame before, but now I understand why it's called that. I manage to make it to the door and slowly open it. I freeze in my tracks when I come face to face with a blonde-haired woman; clearly a dye job. Her face is just as shocked as mine. She's older than me and has similar eyes to Xander. "I'm sorry. I was just leaving." I apologise as I try to slip past her.

"Another of my son's whores, I take it? God, you're not even as pretty as the last one; at least she wasn't covered in tattoos and a stupid haircut." She huffs at me.

My back straightens. Who does this bitch think she is? I didn't even respond; I just walk away and get into the lift down one floor to my suite. Walking in, I am on edge slightly; someone is in here. Turning around, I nearly lose my shit. "Fucking hell, Marcus, what the hell you doing here? The men need you to make their hangovers hell," I yell, hand on my chest. I knew someone was here, but he sat in complete silence staring at me.

"Sorry, E, but we need to talk to you. Also, where have you been young lady? You're always up and about around 4 am."

I roll my eyes and move into the small kitchen and put the coffee machine on. "I'm an adult now, Pops, I stopped being a child you need to look after years ago. I was out enjoying myself for the first time in years. Now what did you want to talk about?" Marcus still looks at me and sees the young girl he trained, the girl he spent years looking after and moulding to being a perfect killing machine. He is a mafia crime boss in London. I was meant to be his next in line. I declined the offer though; I had my own agenda to take care of.

"We found out what's going on with M; well, it's more Jasmine. And also, we found out what actually happened when Jasmine and you were born." Marcus tilts his mug at me, indicating he wants a drink as well. I pour us a coffee once the machine is done; my mind not fully focusing on him, but more on that old hag who just called me a fucking whore. You have two days of sex and now you're the village bike, well that's what it seems anyway. Also, my tattoos are beautiful. I don't know what that bitch was talking about. I have been thinking of changing my hairstyle for a while. But growing it out would take a while, and I can't really be arsed with it. Been shaved for years, why change it now, I guess.

"So, what is that then?" I ask glancing at my phone; I left a small listening device in Xander's apartment last night. I also know he has cameras there, so I just take a few seconds hacking into them. Typing in a few different codes into my phone, I get to see the inside of Xander's apartment.

"E, you're distracted. We can talk about this later if you like." I glance up at Marcus.

"Sorry, Marcus, the guy I saw last night, his mum turned up at the door as I was leaving. So, I want to see what they both say, because if he says something I don't like, I won't be hanging around long enough to see him later." Also, she called me a whore; she is a fine one to talk.

Marcus moved round the table to me and watched the phone, turning the volume up as we both watched. "Who was that, Xander? Some dirty whore you usually spend your time with? God, she is clearly a mess. You know you can do better. You also know you need to find a wife. I want grandchildren and you aren't getting any younger." She tuts as she strolls over to the couch and sits down.

"For God's sake, Mum, she's an incredible woman. You always do this; you judge before you know someone. Also, she only wants fun just like me, and she goes home soon. Can't you just leave my life alone?" He throws himself into the seat opposite her. He got dressed into the same clothes I took off his delicious body last night. I know because he was naked when I left. His hair is still a mess, and I bet he still smells like me. My core gets wet at the thought of him sitting there, smelling of me, while his jumped-up mother is sat opposite him. Fucking bitch.

"You know I'm only looking after you; you deserve a beautiful woman who can give you babies and keep you happy." Xander huffs in response to her. Even though I never wanted that with him, it still felt like a punch to my gut. Hurting a small part of me, each word cut a little deeper. Like little, tiny paper cuts, irritating and painful.

"Maybe I want to find love, not just marry because that's what you want me to do. Maybe I'm not too bothered about having children. You cannot just let me be and just come visit because you miss me." She rolls her eyes. This woman is a living nightmare.

"I actually came to see you to tell you I have arranged for you to meet a good friend of mine's daughter. She is sweet, well-educated and will be good for you. Not like that piece of work that crept out of here this morning. She isn't going to make you happy." Oh I want to punch this woman right in the face.

"I can't tonight. I'm going out with Taylor, the girl from this morning, again."

"Well cancel it. It's not like it will work out, and you will do as I ask. I'm not even messing anymore, Xander Valance, I'm your mother, and I know what's best for you." With that, she gets up and leaves. Cancelling my connection to the camera, I call Xander.

Within two rings, he answers. "Hello?" Oh yeah, I forgot I never gave him my number.

"Hey, Xander, it's Taylor." I hear him sigh on the phone. "Don't worry about cancelling tonight. I've got something to do anyway. Your mother enjoys dictating, doesn't she?" He pauses for a few beats.

"How the hell do you know about my mum?" He seems to be slightly concerned. I chuckle.

"Don't ruin the magic of me. I know things I shouldn't a lot of the time, Xander. Also, I did have the pleasure of bumping into her on the way out this morning. I don't appreciate being called a whore, and who said I couldn't make you happy? You seemed very happy last night." He also laughs at my response, lightening up slightly.

"Yeah, she's controlling but she means well; doesn't stop it from annoying me. Sorry about tonight. I was really looking forward to it. And yes, you did." I sigh, so was I.

"Hey, don't worry about it. If you're ever in New York, maybe you could hit me up and you can take me out for that drink."

"That would be good actually. See you around, Taylor."

"So long for now, Xander." And with that, I hang up the phone. I was looking forward to the date but maybe he will come to New York some time and we can try that date again. Marcus pats my shoulder.

"Listen, E, you remember what I told you all those years ago?"

"Of course, I do. 'Men will only distract me and ruin all the hard work I have done. I don't need a man.' Do you really think I would forget. I have the scar to prove that lesson. But that doesn't mean I can't have some fun." I turn and grab my coffee, making my way over to the window. If I'm honest now, I have no reason to stick around and I could do with going home and sorting things out.

"Anyway, Marcus what was it you found out?" I stare out the window; it's been nice being away from everything. I haven't in so many years. I've the weight of the entire company on my shoulders. He stands beside me and sighs.

"E, you need to stay calm, okay. You can't lose your shit at what I'm about to tell you." I don't say anything, just keep staring at the city below. "Harry isn't Luther's dad. He's yours and Jasmine's. And that's not even the worse part." Marcus pauses for a moment before continuing, "He bargained you and gave Jasmine to care. Harry knew Kathy, and that she had a boy. Harry wanted Luther, so he bought him, and they had you. Apparently, he didn't have a person to give Jasmine to, so she was dumped at a home. He got in touch with her a few months ago; she's feeding him information here and there. Using M to give him what he wants. He doesn't want your company. He's doing what he can to make her happy."

My blood is boiling. I'm so angry, I drop my coffee mug. I've treated M like shit since Thursday night and it wasn't him; it was my snake of a sister. But he didn't stop her or tell me either, and in my eyes, that's still crossing me. I have never and would never do something like this. It's classed as treason in mafia law. Punishable by death, and the way I am feeling right now, he deserves it. Slow and painful. "Let's pack. We need to get home now."

Sitting on the plane on the way home, I'm seething. How could M sell me out? I'm going to kill him; I've stuck my neck out for him on so many occasions. I look out the window and watch as the clouds pass beneath the plane; the peace and tranquillity of the sky is nice. It's helping to tame my mind because it is definitely running a million miles an hour. My brain keeps on thinking of imaginative and impressive ways of killing him, and that bitch I brought into my house.

I should have never brought M with me to Marcus, to America or even allowed him into Maggie and Rick's house. And as for her, she should have stayed in her perfect little life, the fuck away from me, or I should have just killed her the minute I knew she existed. It's not unheard of for bosses to kill family they find; it is usually so they don't challenge them for their title. I could have done that; I should have done that. She is a problem, and I am great at removing those.

The plane is filled with a deafening silence. Neither Marcus nor I are breaking this silence. Too much has passed this morning, and we are both just letting the shit storm settle, or fester. Either way, something is coming and let's hope the explosion doesn't blow everyone too far. I would hate to have a massive clean-up. I only know one person that could clean up a massive explosion and he's not in the country; he might come here for the right price. But I would only call him when time is dire. Being my cousin, he will always try to help me, but I don't like making him leave his work for me. I guess we will see when I get home what will happen next.

Chapter 24

Landing in New York is weird; it still seems strange to me that time zones are different throughout the country. It was early morning in Washington when we left but in New York it's just past 11:30 am – it's so weird. In England, it's the same time no matter where you go, even in Scotland and Wales. Stepping off the plane, Aid is waiting for us next to my car. I walk over and give him a hug. Sometimes, you just need a hug, and Aid is not opposed, whereas Marcus is very against physical contact. Well, that is unless I haven't seen him in a while, or I've been hurt.

"Hey little bird, we will get this sorted. We always do." And he is right, he had been in Washington with me for an afternoon before he flew back to stalk M with K, while I was away. Now both he and Marcus have decided to stay to help me with the M problem.

"Hey, pops, I know we will. I just can't believe that he would sell me out. I've put that piece of shit first all of our life together. And he repays me like this. I will kill him. But first, we all know how hung everyone is going to be, so best get them sorted, then we can deal with M." Aid just chuckled, opening the car door for me; we all climb in and Graham drives us back to the house.

After the short drive home, I move into the kitchen and start cooking breakfast. I know the boys and Luther are fast asleep upstairs in their rooms. K and H share one room, A and Q have the other. There is a spare room, but I put Jasmine in it, so it's not spare anymore. I start to cook their breakfast, making pancakes, waffles, and a full English fry-up. I also put cereal and fruit on the table, and I brew two pots of coffee and put them in the flasks to keep warm. In about an hour, I've cooked and laid the table for them. Marcus and Aid walk in after washing and changing in my room. I don't usually allow men in there, but they are different, I try to keep some stuff aside for them in case they visit.

"Smells good, little bird. Want me to wake the lads?" Marcus asks, but a sly smile crept across my face.

"Na, I will do it." I grab a metal pan and a wooden spoon. Sometimes, I like to make my men jump. It's a small joy I allow myself.

Walking upstairs, I go into their room. K and H are on the beds, not in the covers, so clearly passed out the minute they came back. Luther is on the floor with a pillow and blanket. I check A and Q's bedroom and find them cuddling in the bed. I chuckle because we all know they are together, but they aren't ready to talk about it, so we all just let them be. I leave all their doors open and stand in the hallway; raising the pan and spoon, I start banging them together.

"WAKE THE FUCK'S UP, LADIES? BREAKFAST IS ON THE TABLE." I keep banging the spoon inside the pot, continuing to yell for them to wake up. I do enjoy waking them up when they are hung over. After all these years, you would have thought they would have learned. Alas! They clearly hadn't.

And with that, I stroll back downstairs. I can hear them all groaning as I descend. I chuckle to myself, but if they didn't get themselves into this state, I wouldn't find such joy in waking them. I get into the dining room and see Aid and Marcus chuckling; I raise an eyebrow and finish putting the last of breakfast out.

H, K, and Luther are the first to come down. They look a little worse for wear. Apparently, they went a little hard last night, but that doesn't stop them from working today. A and Q walk in shortly after, and everyone takes a seat; they all basically fight over the coffee and start to fill their plates with food.

"What time is it?" Luther croaks at me while sipping his coffee, clearly trying to wake up. God knows what time they got home, but judging by the black circles under their eyes, it was definitely late.

"12:30 pm, Luther. It's clear you all had a good time. I thought you would all benefit from breakfast, so dig in," I say as I place the milk in the centre of the table.

"You're home, E. When did you get back?" K's eyes meet mine, and I am lost in them for a second. I cough and bring myself back. Even after so long, when they are on me, I forget everything around me.

"Yes, I am home and have been for about an hour. You know me, K, I go and come back whenever I want. Now where is Jasmine and Matthew?" My tone drops as I mutter the traitors' names. Judging by their faces, they can feel the anger rushing off me. Everyone is just staring at me; I cock my eyebrow at them, indicating I want an answer.

"We don't know. He was in a mood since you left. And it got worse when we were training yesterday and made him train with bootleg Barbie. I think it was worse when Luther started training with us. But after he got in the car and left with Jasmine, and we took the jeep to the club. I swear he nearly cried; what you saw in him, I will never know," H states while munching on a pancake. That man is strange and eats them dry when he's hung over. He swears to God that it helps; his Southern ways make me laugh. He made me drink this weird concoction when I had a cold the other month. It tasted like ass, and I did vomit after. But I was better the next day, left with just a small sniffle. I will not ever take that shit again even if it did work.

"Right, okay then. And don't start. He was my family. But apparently that meant shit to him," I say through gritted teeth. I walk over to the TV and load up the tracking devices I had loaded on everyone. Small red dots pop up all over the map. I tap in Matthew's and Jasmine's name into the database. All other dots left, leaving just two. One is stationary while the other was on the move. Names appeared on top of the dots, showing that M was the stationary one at his flat. But Jasmine was on the move. She was moving east, clearly by foot, based on the speed the dot moved at. Clicking off the map, I load the CCTV, and yes, it is slightly illegal. But what they going to do? I'm untraceable even if they knew the cameras were being hacked. The screen splits into 24 smaller ones, each showing a different view of the area her dot came from.

"Is that her? Top left?" Luther pipes up. I know he would have seen her the other day.

"Good spot, Luther. She's moving down Jefferson Road to Lincoln way," H says, giving him a pat on the back, and it was a good spot. I keep following her from one camera to the next. She stops outside a café about 15-minute walk from M's flat. My heart drops as someone takes a seat opposite her. His face comes into focus on the screen and my heart stops. This is the proof I need. They are as good as dead right now; there is no going back. I screen-capture the image of them together, then continue to watch.

"GET M HERE NOW!" I yell, my anger reaching maximum capacity. My blood is boiling. My heart is pounding, my brain thinking of a thousand unusual ways to kill both of them. I watch as she slides a piece of paper to Steadwell who is sat directly in front of her, the deception is unforgivable.

I didn't know K was there until he walks up to me and places a hand on my shoulder, trying to calm me down. I can't contain my anger; I am on the verge of losing my shit. I shrug off K's hands and swiftly turn/ I grab Luther and throw him up a wall, my face inches from his.

"Did you know about this? Do you know why she would meet your fucking father?" My eyes boring into his as my anger radiates off me. His eyes wide and hands up in surrender to me, the look of fear is evident on his face.

"No, Christ no. I only met her yesterday at training, and I didn't even speak to her." His eyes hold only the truth, so I shove him and walk away before I do something stupid. He rubs his chest, which I must have hurt when he hit the wall. My fists were in the fabric of his top and did hit off him with his abrupt stop when he slammed against the wall. I walk into my office and grab two needles and go back to the living room; everyone's eyes are on me.

"K, go make sure M is on his way over." He nods and moves away to make a phone call. "Let's hope that he knows nothing about that little bitch meeting Steadwell, else death will be the least of his concerns." I muse while twirling the syringe round with my thumb and forefinger.

"E, don't you think this is a bit harsh? What if he doesn't know anything? What if he's as blind as we were?" H asks. *Oh! Wrong move, pal…*my brain says as I cock an eyebrow at him. Did he really just question me?

"Did you really think that comment was wise? Are you really querying my response to being crossed? I suggest you don't do that; you wouldn't like to join them down in the cells, would you?" I ask, staring right at him. My eyes don't blink or move from him. He looks away, apparently defeated by me. "That's what I thought." I walk over and get right into H's face; fear floods his eyes as I stare at him. "You ever so much as think of questioning me again, I won't hesitate to end you. Right hand or not, Henry." I watch as he gulps; realisation hits him that I am deadly serious. The way I spoke to him was more menacing than I have ever spoken to him before, but he has never crossed me before.

"Sorry E. I wasn't thinking," H stutters, sweat coating his brow at the situation.

"I gave you a second chance at life; don't think I can't take it away just as easily." I state before standing and walking away from him. I think he was getting a bit too big for his boots. No one fucking steps to me. I am the boss.

"E, we will sort this," Marcus states, putting a hand on my shoulder, trying to reassure me that all will be okay. And I know it will be, because I will make sure of it.

"I know we will. She will beg for death when I am done, and you know I will be only too happy to grant her wish. No one stands against me. You all best learn from this and fast," I state, giving each of them a pointed look. Q and A look physically panicked. I will deal with that later. When this is all done, I will call Freddy and see how long before I get back who the mole is.

I quickly walk into my office; I don't have the time to wrestle him into the cells. I need something to speed that up before Jasmine gets here. If the house is in disarray when she gets here, she will know something is wrong. Luckily for me, I have a great friend who is a chemist; he made the bullets for training but also a lovely little sleeping agent. I have kept them in my desk, hoping one day I would be able to use them and see their affects. And today is wonderfully that day. I can't wait to ram this into M and Jasmine's neck. Hopefully their bodies hit the ground hard; the feeling brings me a small amount of joy. My mouth twitches as I think about it.

I go into my desk and grab them; two small needles with clear liquid. I wasn't told how much to use, so let's do the whole thing. Dean said it won't kill them, but the more I use, the longer they will be out, and I am fine with that. Gives me more time to get my tools ready and figure out how I want to play this.

A knock at the door draws my attention. "Everyone, go sit, and let's eat." I move and sit at the table; K goes and let's M in as I believe the front door is still locked.

Luther sits opposite me, with H next to him and I'm in-between Marcus and Aid. Q and A are at either ends of the table. M and K walk in, my anger is pouring out of me but I hold my composure. M looks around the room as K sits next to Luther and starts filling his plate with food.

"E, you're home." M's voice is full of surprise; his eyebrows lift as he looks at me. Clearly, he wasn't expecting me to be sat here, but this is my house and if I want to be here, I will. He is shifting nervously from one leg to the other; his chest is heaving heavily. I cock my eyebrow and chuckle slightly at him.

"It would appear so. Where is Jasmine?" I put some pancake into my mouth; the needles rest on my lap while I eat. I need him to get her here before I knock him out; it will be easier to move him if he's asleep.

"Erm, I don't know. She wasn't there when I got up, so I naturally assumed she was here." I hear the genuineness in his voice, but I also can hear he is hiding something from me. And I hate people hiding things from me. I don't care who he is; he's not getting out of this alive.

"Why don't you call her, get her here for breakfast. We obviously have much to discuss, so we can do it over food. I will have Graham pick her up seeing as Luther is here." I notice Luther is staring at me, his face a picture of confusion. "Yes, Luther, Graham works for me. Actually, I own half of your staff; you seem to underestimate my reach. How do you think I got that note into your house? I do hope you remembered that it's your head cleaner, Faith's, birthday today. She has worked very hard for you and me over the years. You should get her something nice." His mouth hangs open. I chuckle at his realisation of how powerful I am.

"Sure, I will give her a call. We did have an argument last night. But I'm sure she will come over; she's always asking about you." M's voice draws my attention back to him. I am struggling to hold myself back. Right now, I want to rip his head off, but I need to hold off for a few moments more.

"Oh, is she now?" I grip my fork so hard, it physically snaps in half; my strength surprised even me. My knuckles are white as I stare down at the half of the fork that is lying on the table; the other half is still in my fist. Pulling back to the room, I notice everyone's eyes are on me. Most of them know I'm strong, but this is a strange situation. "I knew I needed new cutlery; damn things are old and fragile." I shrug like it was nothing and get up to get a new one; while I do that, M phones Jasmine.

She picked up in a couple of rings. "Hey, babe, what's up?" Her sweet voice calls through the phone. M always puts people on speaker. Don't know why, but at least I can hear, which is good for me; her voice makes me feel sick; acting all sweet and innocent, but I know she's not.

"Hey, I was wondering if you were coming to E's for breakfast." M glances at me. I give him a nod and he nods back. He's too stupid to be in this world. If I don't kill him, someone else will. If you think about it, I am doing him a favour by killing him.

"Sure, I'm not far away. I'll be there in ten minutes." And with that, M hangs up the phone. I grab mine and text Graham to pick her up. I give him her location and place my phone down on the table. I get up and walk over to him, placing my arm on his shoulder with the syringe in my back pocket.

"I'm sorry about the other day, M, I was in a bad mood, and it was just shitty timing. I took my anger out on you. Forgive me?" I give him my sweetest smile, even though I don't mean what I am saying. I'm never sorry, I do everything for a reason.

"Sure, sis, what are big brothers for?" He chuckles, looking at me. I chuckle as well, grabbing my needle, I flick the top off with my thumb.

"Na, I'm just kidding. I'm not sorry for that or this, brother," I state and stick the needle in his neck, pushing the liquid into him.

His shocked eyes look at me. "What the fuck you doing? I don't..." he staggers for a second before hitting the floor hard. My lips curl into a smile. I will make him pay for crossing me. I will make sure that they all know what happens when you go against me; they will all learn. I've been too lenient, and that is stopping today. Now all I need is that bitch and my collection of family traitors is complete.

Chapter 25

"Luther, K, drag his useless ass down to the cells. I have another visitor to deal with. Also, deadbolt the door and remove all access, leaving only me. I plan on dealing with him personally." K nods and nudges Luther to get up. They take him downstairs. Luther grabbing his legs and K holding his top half. When they are out of earshot, I hear them talking to each other. K is probably talking to Luther about what it is like to work for me, but also probably explaining why I decided to knock M out. I roll my eyes and check the screen to see where Jasmine is. She is starting to move in the direction of the house. Graham must have just gotten to her.

"Little bird, we are behind you in this." Aid pats my shoulder as I watch the screen. I nod and keep my eyes on her dot as it gets closer and closer. Five minutes of me death staring at the TV, her dot pulls up outside the house, switching the screen off. Watching Luther and K emerge from downstairs, I hear a knock on the door. "I'll get it," I state and move towards the front door. It's not that far from the dining room. I love how small my house is as it's easy to move around; the dining room and kitchen is just off the living room and front door. I open the door and see her sweet face as she smiles at me. To think, she won't be smiling at me after what I'm about to do.

"Hey, E," she smiles at me. I step to the side and allow her to come in.

"Through here is breakfast." I smile as we move into the dining room, keeping her directly in front of me. Her head moves as she glances around the room, her eyes taking in the whole room looking for me.

"Hey, guys, where is M? He said to meet him here." Her eyes land on me, question written all over her face. I smile slightly as I step closer so I can get easy access to her neck.

"Yeah, about that." I flick the top off the needle and embed it into her neck. The neck is best, as its faster acting. But the chemicals in this are fast acting anyway, so it wouldn't matter where I jab her. I mainly use the neck for dramatic effect.

"E, what the…" She drops like a sack of shit; I don't even attempt to catch her. I see her head smack off the floor; that amused me in all honesty. I hate her, and for her to hurt herself made me smile. Bending down, I grab her and throw her limp body over my shoulder. "Bitch is heavier than she looks." And by Christ, she is. I know she is slightly chunkier than I am, but I wasn't expecting her to be this weighty. I walk downstairs, not giving a shit if she gets hit by anything on the way down; it does bring me pleasure hurting people but mainly her.

Getting to cell 2, I dump her in the cot sat in the back left corner; the room literally has nothing in it, just a cot and a toilet. It's not a hotel. I only put a toilet, so I don't have to clean up bodily messes – well the ones I didn't cause anyway. Walking out, I completely lock her cell only granting myself access. This means that none of the lads can open the door. I also remove all dangerous items from her person: no belts, phones or anything she could use to hurt herself with. I would hate for her to kill herself before I get that luxury.

Closing the door, I look at her through the one-way glass; seeing her lying there gives me a small pang of pain. Only small, but I was hoping she would come around to my way of life so I could use her to get what I want. Clearly, though, she won't, so I can't have any more dead weight than I already have. She could have had a good life with me here. I would have given her everything and allowed her to know what happened when we were little. But now, she will die without knowing. I would have given her a new life and a good job, but she isn't like all the other guys I have taken in. She doesn't see the good I can do and that upsets me a little. All my men especially K and H are grateful for the life I have given them. But people like her aren't. They don't see the bigger picture. They only see the bad shit I do. Such a shame; but they decided to betray me in life so they will join each other in death.

Turning away, I glance at M; he was my brother. We have been together for nearly 25 years and for a bit of pussy he met last week, he turned on me. How can a small amount of sex change someone's alliance? I've never had this problem before, never had anyone turn on me like this. Well, I have had one person turn on me. X was someone I met when I was in Ohio. He was tall and well built, with the biggest blue eyes I've ever seen on a man. He was an ex-marine who was out of work. His cousin works for me as an intel person in

Steadwell corp. So, Les called me and said X needed a job and thought he could have been useful to me, and looking at his file, he could have been. He was top of his squad, hardworking and knew how to follow instructions.

I remember sitting in his living room waiting for him.

I heard the front door of the apartment opening; I'm sat in complete darkness waiting for Charlie to come in. I've decided that if he does work for me, I will change his name to X. I already had a C work for me so that wouldn't work. I'm sat in the back left corner in the single seat watching him enter the room. He hasn't turned the light on yet, which is odd. Most people turn their lights on the minute they walk in. I watch as he bends down and grabs a knife from his sock; how funny, that's where I keep mine.

"Charlie, I wouldn't do that if I was you. I'm only here to talk." His head whipped around and looks directly at me. This is not the first time I have broken into someone's home. Hell, it's not the first time I have broken into his house. I placed bugs in here a week ago, so I knew his routine. And as someone who is ex-marines, he is a stickler for them. Everything he does, he does it the same way at the same time. It's quite funny to watch, even goes shopping for food the same time, same day, every week. So predictable; makes breaking in a hell of a lot easier.

"Who are you? Why the fuck you in my home?" He tries to reach for his gun that he leaves in the top draw by the door. I laugh at him and flick on the lamp behind me.

"Looking for something?" I hold up his gun while looking at him; his eyes move over me. I don't think he was expecting someone like me. Taking him in, I notice how easy he is on the eye; his blue eyes narrow at me. His muscle-ripped arms fold over his chest as his chest heaves in a deep breath. He stands roughly 6 ft tall, not the tallest man I've ever met. His blond hair is in dreadlocks and tied back, and the sides of his head are shaved short, showing off his neck tattoos. "Now that I have your attention, maybe you should sit so we can talk. Les called and said you need work. Now I've read your file, and I am impressed. Top of your squad, also excellent at school. Shame your mum was a drug addict, but that must have given you your drive and determination."

His face is red as I talk. I must have hit a nerve. But I don't really care. If he doesn't come with me, then it doesn't matter because I won't see him again. "Who the fuck do you think you are? How dare you bring up my life when you

155

don't even know me? Who the fuck do you even work for?" His eyes boring into me, he must be trying to intimidate me. It won't work. No one has gotten to me in years and I doubt anyone would.

"Calm down, tinker bell, don't pop a blood vessel. I don't work for anyone; I am the boss. I have every right to investigate you, and I have every last sordid detail. Also, drop the bravado, you don't and won't intimidate me. I give ex-forces men jobs in my company; you are unemployed and have been for seven months. You were honourably discharged with injuries that stop you doing some of your jobs, but I can give you a new purpose. I could use a man with your skills, but if you would rather live in this tiny bedsit living off your small retirement fund, then be my guest. But I have a once in a lifetime offer for you. And just to warn you, I only offer this once because once, I leave you will never hear or see me again."

His eyes don't move from me as he walks over and takes a seat. I disarm his gun as a gesture of good will. I dump all the bullets onto the floor and disassemble it into pieces; his eyes follow my fast movements. He seems stunned by me doing that; his eyes hold shock. "So, what do you want?" Apparently, brain cells are missing. I literally just said what I wanted.

I roll my eyes and tut at him; I've been doing this for many years and it's always the same questions. "Why do all men always ask the same questions? Who are you? What do you want? Why are you here? How did you get in? For God's sake, Charlie, ask me a decent question. I've told you what I want. I told you I have read about you; I have told you I could use you. So, if you are going to ask me stupid questions, I will just leave now." I sigh. This is the same as every other man, well unlike K and H. K just followed me back from war and never left, and H just agreed to work the minute I offered him a job.

"Fine, why did you decide to come to me? I'm sure you could have any person who is ex-forces, so why me?" Still not an amazing question, but still worth answering.

"Like I said, your file impressed me. You have a great aim; you follow orders very well and proved to be loyal while overseas. You also saved five of your men when under fire, but I'm not in the saving game, so those skills are useless. But Les called, as I said, so I decided to give you a shot." I cross my legs and lift my cup of tea and take a sip. "Oh yes, I also know where everything is in your home, so, I wouldn't reach for your backup gun under the table in front of you. It's not there. I also took the liberty of removing any weapon from this house until I *leave, then you can have them back." I lift my eyebrow at him. Does he think I'm stupid. I know why he sat where he did, yes, I am sat in his seat. But the gun would have been in easy access from where he was.*

"You are good, I'll give you that, Ma'am, but you forgot…" He reaches under his seat and his face drops. I just sigh. Waiting for him to stop patting the bottom of the chair for his baseball bat, I think he thinks I'm stupid.

"Are you done patting the chair and floor? I told you I have all your weapons. I'm not stupid. Please stop trying to one up me; it won't happen. I have been doing this for far too long. You are actually boring me, Charlie. Look, I will give you two days to think about it. I will offer you good money and a decent home. You will work with a bunch of like-minded men and answer to me. But you will have to give up everything here: your current life will stop and you will work and do solely what I ask you to. I will call you soon, Charlie."

I stand and place my mug in the sink as I walk past it to the front door. "Oh, if you don't take the job, you will never speak of this conversation again. I am a woman you don't wish to cross, Charlie Worden, son of Debbie Tate and George Worden who live at 66 Rothermel Drive Ohio. And yes, I know exactly where they work, who their friends are and how to get to them. So, choose wisely, Mr Worden." And with that, I leave. His face was a picture when I left. I don't think he knew how much I actually knew about him.

I did call him two days later. He accepted the job, and I flew him to New York for training. He flew through it and became a close member of my team. He fit in and did exactly what was required of him. He did well with all that was asked. But some of the men didn't like the way he spoke about me, saying what he would do to me if he got the chance. I didn't hear anything of what he said, but K would always come tell me after I found him and X fighting. It got annoying after a while. I never had such fighting in my company; usually whoever I bring in fits well with the OG team.

One day, X came into my room without being asked, and I didn't have people in there. He came in and threw me up a wall, then forced his hand into my trousers while he had his horrible lips on my neck, his breath falling down my back, making me feel super cold.

For a few moments, my brain went numb. I couldn't understand what the hell was happening. No man has ever had the balls to even come close to me, let alone force themselves on me threw me through a loop. I kneed him in the balls. He doubled over before I brought my knee back up into his face, breaking his nose. He staggers back a couple of steps and his hand leaves my trousers. I then move my leg and sweep one of his legs from under him, causing him to fall onto the floor. Moving past him, I storm from the room. K, H, and A, all stare at me as I grab my brief case and keys.

"Give this to X. He goes alone." I give them a file; I need X to be away from the guys. And with that, I leave.

An hour later, I'm sat on a rooftop five miles away from where X is. I made sure he was here. His file was to watch Steadwell from a certain rooftop. I made it easy for myself. I have set up my sniper and I'm currently watching him; he is sat doing as he is told. He would have been a useful asset to me, but he crossed a line. I line up my shot and take it, the bullet passes through his skull. I watch as he slumps down and blood runs from his head. I sit there for a second longer, just watching as his blood pools and starts to run down the side of the building; his body lies there motionless. I call K and get him to collect X's body and clean the scene.

Coming back to the present, I look at M and realise that I killed X for less than selling me out, so I really don't feel bad about this at all. X did turn on me due to some sort of weird sexual need. But this is much worse. He didn't sell me out, he just tried to fuck me against my will. And if I hadn't killed him, what's to say he wouldn't have tried to do it again. I sigh and walk back upstairs; getting up there, I see everyone sat around the table eating.

"Grab some breakfast. I'm going to the gym. They should be out for a few hours, so I am not worried." I lean forward and grab some toast. Once I'm stand up, I squeeze Luther's shoulder and give him a wink. It's usually my signal that they are part of the crew, and Luther has been showing great promise. He has done all that was asked of him and has been loyal. Even if he did know it was me at the law firm, he didn't let on. Apparently, he also did quite well at the training, so Marcus said on the plane. I can teach skills. I can't however teach loyalty; you either are or you aren't.

I go into the gym which is in the basement and swap into my leggings and sports bra. The room isn't large, mainly because it's split between this and the cells just on the other side of the wall on my left. It holds a treadmill, rowing machine, weights and a workout area with hand weights and a punching bag. It also has a rock-climbing wall on the back, which I do enjoy using it's a fun way to build arm, leg and core strength. I stand on the mat and start taking out my anger on the punching bag.

"FUCK!" I yell repeatedly while I batter the hell out of the bag. I'm hitting it so hard the skin starts to leave my knuckles. My blood starts to coat the bag and over my hands. After a few minutes, I realise that this isn't going to quell my anger. But maybe something else will, well someone.

Chapter 26

I grab my phone and text H to send Luther to my room to collect my first aid kit; I know the one in the kitchen is empty. No one is clever enough to top it up, so mine is the only one that has anything in. Looking out of the window, I see what a lovely day out it is. The sun is shining brightly in the sky. The blue of the sky is radiant, giving a lovely pre-summer feeling. Birds tweeting all around, just makes you want to go out and enjoy the last of spring.

I hate the fact that my life is in such turmoil right now; the way that everyone is under suspicion of betraying me. M and Jasmine trying to get me killed, and the fact that I am complicating life with Luther isn't helping the situation. The last one however, I don't really care about. I have needs and for once in my life, I am going to give into them. I am going to get what I need to, to get through this time. Once it is all sorted with M and that skank, the pandemonium should calm down.

I don't have to wait long before he comes in. "Erm…E, I didn't realise you was in here. H sent me in for the first aid kit." I turn and look at him, his eyes hold a small amount of fear. I must have terrified him with my knuckles bleeding; they aren't anything too major. I've damaged them far worse in the past, but I suppose, when you haven't seen me like this before, I can be terrifying. The look in his eyes makes me sigh; the concern and fear mixed together irritates me. The slight shake in his hands as he shifts from one foot to the other perplexes me. I don't understand his nerves. We have fucked so why would you be like this?

"I know, I asked him to send you." I start to move towards him, my eyes never leaving his. I know I have a lust filled expression, my heart beating fast with anticipation of what is to come. I want, no I need him to dominate me. I want him to make me cum more than any time before. I think that when Xander dominated me, it changed something, allowing me to feel things I never have before. I found sex last time was a good stress relief, like the whole world outside didn't exist.

"Luther, I need you. I want to forget everything outside that door for a while." His eyes never left me. He is breathing just as heavy as I am as we stare at each other. His obsession and compulsion to have me evident in his demeanour. He stalks towards me, my legs making contact with the edge of my bed.

"How can I help you forget, E? But your hands are bleeding, they need treating." He looks at my knuckles as I slide them up his chest, blood trailing up him as I move my hands.

"Isn't it obvious? Also, don't worry about my hands, they will be fine." I grab his top, pulling his head down towards me; his voice turns me on more than anything right now.

"E, you need to tell me exactly what you want. That's the one thing that's the sexiest about you. Do you want me to lick your tight pussy? What about my fingers? Do you want them as well? Would you like my cock inside you? Or do you want me to just bandage your hands?"

"All of it, Luther, I want it all. But I also want to do something for you first." The moment I said this, his lips crash into mine. A low moan leaves my mouth but is muffled by his. His tongue delves into my mouth as I moan, making me hotter with need. My hands rip the thin top open, allowing me to move over his toned abs and chest, the feel of his hard muscles arousing me further. I start to kiss down his jaw and neck. I then start to trail kisses down his chest and kissing each of his abs. I roam my hands down his body until my lips reach his happy trail. Once there, I grab hold of his jogging bottoms. I pull them down. His cock springs free. I look up at him. I want to see how dominant he can be. I want him to tell me what he wants from me.

"Do you want me, Luther? Do you want my mouth on your cock?" I ask as I grip his ridged member in my right hand.

"Take my cock into that hot mouth of yours. I want to feel what it's like to have you around me," his voice has dropped and is filled with desire; my core is getting drenched with the way his eyes are looking at me.

I open my mouth and slowly edge my way down his shaft. His head falls back the further I go. His cock hits the back of my throat, but I keep going taking his whole length. A low moan leaves his lips as I finish taking him all the way in, his hands slide into my hair gripping it tightly. I moan around his cock as he holds me tight by my hair, he starts to move his hips slowly. I supress my gag reflex as he forces more of himself all the way into my mouth, my pussy is dripping wet feeling him forcing himself into me. I feel my mouth water as he pumps his delicious cock in and out, saliva begins running down my chin the further he goes. My eyes fill with more tears as I feel his entire length hit the back of my throat. The delectable feeling of Luther builds my height of pleasure.

"I'm going to fuck your mouth like the naughty girl you are. You're going to accept my cock in any way I choose and not complain once about it. Else there will be consequences for your defiance." He states while his whole cock is in my mouth, breathing becoming harder by the second. But the pleasure, however, is ten times better.

Fuck, this is such a turn on for me, even with Xander it wasn't like this. The way he spoke, the force he held my hair made me drip with need. Most people either stay the hell away or treat me like I'm going to break. But no Luther is taking charge, my pussy is quivering with anticipation. I nod slightly with his cock still in my mouth, his speed picked up and starts to savagely fuck my face. He keeps going harder and faster into my mouth, my hands clench his thighs as he picks up speed with each thrust of his cock. I love the way he feels as he moves faster and faster in my mouth, the enthusiasm in him shows how much he is enjoying this as well.

Each moan and grunt from him sends me a step closer to my impending release. His hand grips me tighter with every thrust, my head aches but in a delicious way. A way that is probably as sadistic and psychotic as I am. My need to be dominated and so sweetly punished is beginning to be sated, but I am a long way of being done. I want to be fucked until I cannot walk, until I am in need of a wheelchair. I have watched so much dom/sub things at the club, I want it, and I must have it. And right now, Luther is feeding that desire and desperation within me. He keeps going for a few more thrusts before he pulls out of my mouth with a pop.

His hand comes under my chin, pulling me to stand in front of him. He grabs my top and pulls it over my head, leaving me completely naked from the waist up. His lips clash with mine as his tongue fights me for dominance. His right hand goes into my hair, the feeling of his tight grip fills me. Luther pulls my head back by my hair, a gasp leaves my lips with the pain. His lips descend my neck; his eyes clocking the love bits littered across me. His face comes into my view. His left hand grips my chin, pulling my head so I can look at him properly.

"What the fuck are those on your neck?" Anger in his eyes, his grip tightening on my jaw.

"I…" I stutter as I watch his face contort with all his pent-up emotions.

"Don't fucking lie to me." His hand squeezing my jaw and my hair painfully tighter.

"I met someone…" Before I could finish, Luther moves his hand from my jaw to my throat, his grip tight on me. My core moistening as he shows me I am about to be punished. I pray he doesn't hold back.

"You are mine," he growls, his hand gripping me tighter. "I own your fucking pussy. You belong to me." I moan as he said that I am soaking with the way he is acting right now. The way he is brings out the deep need in me tenfold. My pussy clenches. Luther pushes me backwards with my throat until I am sitting on the bed, a deep hunger in my eyes as I look at him. His body ridged as he stares down at me, clearly upset with what I said. But the way he is running his eyes over me makes me think he won't be stopping; he still wants to fuck me. Maybe even punish me, teach me a lesson. The thought makes my lips twitch into a smile.

I lean back on my hands and watch as he kicks off his joggers completely, his body is fully naked, and his dick is standing to attention. His eyes roam my body, taking in the curves and edges of me. I'm not like many of the women Luther has been with, I'm dark haired and covered in tattoos. But he seems to be appreciating my body, his lust filled eyes are giving away how he is truly feeling. His hands grab the top of my leggings and panties yanking them down with a force, the cold air sweeps across my wet lips sending shivers up my spine.

"Centre of the bed, now!" Luther demands, and without thinking I immediately do as he has instructed. My mind clouded with lust and proclivity to do as I am told.

His body crawls up the bed resting his body next to me, his lips claiming mine again as his hand slides down and starts to play with my core. He slides a finger inside my wet core, my lip's part from his as my head flies back and a moan rips through me. My pleasure builds with every methodical thrust of his finger inside of me, his lips latch onto my neck moving slowly down my body.

"I am going to punish you. No other man will have you again. My cock will be the only cock you will ever have." Each kiss of his lips against my body has a small suck afterwards, clearly Luther is marking his territory. Showing me with his mouth what belongs to him, and right now I do. I will let him do whatever he wants to do to my body, I just need to have my desires fulfilled.

Luther's lips lock around my right nipple sucking it hard into his mouth, his thumb starts to massage my clit as he fingers me and plays with my nipple. My moans are loud as he pleasures me with his mouth and fingers. He's still sucking on my nipple when he glances at the door. "Don't worry, they can't hear us. Keep going," his eyes lock with me, his eyebrow raises, and his fingers leave me. I feel cold and empty without his pleasure inside me.

"It's, sir, to you, and how dare you tell me what to do. On all fours now." I look at him and see the deadly serious look on his face and move onto my hands and knees hastily. My ass in the air, a small amount of anticipation causing through me as I wait for him. "You are not in charge here I am, you will fucking learn how to respect me when we are alone." I sharp pain stings my right ass cheek; I gasp on impact and my back arches on instinct. My core gets wetter with this sweet punishment. His hand slowly strokes over the place he spanked me, soothing the pain slightly. My core clenching painfully with the overjoying feeling moving through me, the feel of being spanked sending me towards my release. I think right now I am loving being punished, I am enjoying being told off and being told what to do. A small part of me wishing I was in one of my sex rooms at Secret, grabbing toys and being fucked into oblivion. I would have loved to be tied up with rope or chains, Luther stood over me completely naked with a paddle in his hand. The thought turning me on, my pussy dripping onto the bed with wanton need.

"Now tell me, E, who's in charge?" Fuck, he is going to make me explode. He spanks me again, harder than before. My head flying back while I take a sharp breath in, pain flaring in my ass. I want more, so much more. And I think if I have to wait much longer for his cock I might explode, my core hurting with my yearning.

"You are, Sir. Oh God yes, you are," his hand spanks me one last time before flipping me over, my eyes on him as he looks at me with a cocky smile. His eyes flick over my naked body taking me in, I've never felt so desired in my life. His body crawling up to mine, his eyes boring into me. His maddening lust filled face mere inches from mine, his tongue darts out to lick his luscious lips.

"Yes, I am, when we are in a moment like this, I am always in charge. I will fuck you as I please, spank you as I want, and treat you how I desire. Some days we will be rough like today and others will be soft but know, E, that I will do all the choosing."

"Yes, sir, however you please, I'm all yours."

"Hands above your head and don't move them until I tell you to." I grab the pillow above my head, bracing myself for what Luther plans to do to me. He moves slowly down my body, his eyes never leaving mine. I bite my lip as I watch him reach his destination, the place I need him. The place he belongs right now. His lips land on my sensitive clit, I moan loud. I'm so glad it's soundproofed in here else everyone would know the sweet torture that Luther is giving me. I had it put in while I was away and now, I'm so glad I did. And I'm glad my decorator works so quickly, never would have known I had it done, the room looks exactly the same as when I left. He sucks my clit into his mouth making me moan again, my back arches as he licks and sucks me hard.

"Fuck yes…oh God," was all I could say as his tongue and mouth move over my sensitive area. If I died from this pleasure right now, I would die a very happy woman.

Chapter 27

Oh, fucking hell this feels great. This is exactly what I needed, Luther sucking my clit. Nothing better to take this stress away. I've never been so wet before; even when he took my virginity that was nothing compared to this. You don't have to say it I know it looks bad. I was with someone else last night and now I'm back in bed with Luther, but fuck, he knows what I want far better than Xander did. I've got years of a sexless life to catch up on. I move my hands into Luther's thick hair, pulling slightly at it. He moans against my clit, causing it to vibrate, making me even wetter, if that was possible. Suddenly he stops and looks at me, his brown eyes fixed on mine. "Did I say you could move your fucking hands?"

Oh shit, I forgot; I immediately move my hands back to above my head. Once he's satisfied, I'm doing as I'm told; he continues his devouring of my pussy. I've never been so hot for someone. It's more of a turn on that he's in control of me than what he's doing, although what he's doing is sensational.

I am so close to the edge, so close to coming when Luther slides in two of his fingers. My head moves back on its own and my back arches; my God, what is happening to me? "Oh, fuck I'm so close," I practically yell it; I don't know how much more control I have as his tongue's onslaught continues. Then all at once, when his fingers hit the right spot inside me, I start to shake, my orgasm slithering through my body. My mind goes blank, my head rolls even further back, and I'm panting like mad. Who knew something so simple as this could cause such a major reaction. I expect to feel him stop, but I don't. In fact, I feel his fingers start to move inside me again; a third comes inside to join the others.

"Did you think I was done? You will cum for me again. You will cum for me until I am satisfied you have learnt your lesson. Until you have learned who you belong to, whose cock is allowed inside this sweet pussy," Luther states as his three fingers begin to pump into me harder; my mind clouded by the sensational feelings passing through me. My breathing is ragged as I don't have a second to calm down from my last climax, before moving onto the next one. My head tossing from side to side as the intense sensations rage through me. Luther starts to move his fingers faster; my moans becoming screams with the vigorousness of him. My breath hitches when Luther stretches me further than before. Looking down, I see Luther has near enough his whole hand inside me. I know pussies stretch, but fuck me, I didn't know they went that big. His tongue starts to work my clit again, his eyes come up to meet mine. A wicked glint in them sets nervousness inside my stomach; that mixed with my need to cum again.

"Be a good girl, E, and cum on my hand," Luther states as his fingers curl inside me, my climax hurtling towards me at lightning speed. I grip the duvet hard, my knuckles turning as white as my sheets.

"FUCK," I yell as my cum gushes out of me, the force making me see stars. Luther drinks me up like a hungry vampire, sucking and licking my pussy while his fingers continue to move inside me, making sure he gets all my release. His groan against my pussy as he enjoys my taste vibrates through me, prolonging my climax.

"That's a good girl, give daddy everything," Luther grunts as I finally calm down from my mind-altering orgasm. I feel like I am unable to catch my breath; my eyes becoming tired. But when I look into Luther's eyes when I am calming down, I can see we are far from done.

His cock is still out from when I pleasured him earlier. A heavy desire written across his entire body; even looking at his cock, it looks painfully hard. A juicy drip just on the tip, and all the veins are bulging with the pressure of his impending release. His body moves back on top of mine, his lips claiming me with desire and mine replicates all on their own. My body seeming to move so effortlessly with him and his movements. Another more animalistic groan releases from my body as I feel his hard cock line up with my hole, and in one swift movement, his is completely embedded inside me. I've never felt so full before; I swear he's got bigger from last time. If our lips weren't completely locked together, I would have screamed with the force of his penetration.

"Fuck yes, you take my dick so well. E, I'm going to fuck you so hard, you would be able to walk; all the guys know what's happening between us, so I may as well make it worth knowing. I want you to scream my name when you cum for me. I want you to milk my cock." Now this is the Luther I need, a man who knows how to take charge of a woman like me. Someone who isn't afraid to fuck me stupid and then listen to me outside the bedroom. This is the guy I want to fuck right now.

He must see how much his words affect me because Luther looks down at me, a fire lights in his eyes. Much to my surprise, he pulls out of me and flips me onto my front. Grabbing my hips, he makes me get onto all fours again. His cock is thrust into me so hard that I am almost launched across the bed, but his hands on my hips keeps me still. Luther pounds me hard from behind, filling me even more than he did a second ago. Each pump of his cock is harder than the last, and each of his groans are louder than before. All my senses are gone as his hand comes down hard on my ass cheek, making me wet again and bringing me to the brink. I have never been so turned on; another hand comes down on my cheek hard before he massages the spot.

"Ah, fuck," I cry. This is amazing. I don't want it to end, yet I'm so close.

My panting gets louder with each of his punishing thrusts; his right hand reaches around me and starts to play with my clit, moving in a circular motion. My climax building again, the pleasure of Luther's hard cock and the stinging of my ass cheeks mix together, building me higher.

"Cum for daddy. Cum for me now," He grunts as his hand spanks my ass harder than before. My mind becoming blank, as I start to clench around Luther; my happy ending ripping through me harder than I have ever had before.

This sends me plummeting into my orgasm. It's so hard, I think I'm going to break him with how hard I'm clenching around him. Apparently, this is as intense for him as it is for me as he lets out a growl before I feel his hot seeds enter me. "Oh Shit! That's it, E, be a good girl and milk my dick with that tight pussy."

Luther grunts as he moves a couple more times before collapsing on top of me. I moan again as he makes contact with my back. That has to be the best sex I've had so far, not that I have much to compare. With Luther on my back, I feel like I won't float away with the intensity of all that happened.

Luther rolls off me after a few seconds of catching his breath, "Fucking hell, E, that was, erm…"

"Intense," I finish, that's because it was.

"Yeah, intense but amazing all the same. Maybe we could do that again sometime," Luther smiles, moving his head to look at me.

"Definitely Luther, anyway, didn't you come in here for another reason?" I chuckle to him; I know I wanted to use him to kill his father. And I am still intending to do that, but why can't we have some fun along the way? He might be a welcomed distraction from so many things, but that's all he is. I just need to keep reminding myself of that.

"Oh, Christ your hands, we best get those sorted." I chuckle again. My hands aren't a problem, they will heal quickly.

I get up and go to my bedside table and grab the first aid kit. I love my room. It's blue and white. Just like it was at Maggie's. I designed it to feel like it did back then. Made this place feel more like a home even though it's more like a base camp with all the men stopping upstairs and coming and going as they please.

"I'll get you some clothes to use, seeing as I ruined yours; glad it wasn't one of your expensive suits," I say, laughing again at the situation.

To the right of the bed are two doors: one to my bathroom and the other leads to the wardrobe. I do sometimes store some of the guys' clothes in here just in case they run out upstairs. I walk in and toss him something to wear while grabbing myself something new. I do have a meeting this afternoon. I hate meetings, but I need to speak to Freddy after what we discussed on Thursday. Throwing my clothes on and my hair up, I glance at Luther. He's dressed and got a smile on his face. I move into the bathroom, leaving the door open. I grab new contacts out of the cupboard. I lean forward and remove the old ones. My eyes catch Luther watching me.

"Hey, just because this happened again doesn't mean that we are an item, Luther, we are just having some fun. My life is turbulent at the best of times, so something serious isn't on the cards," I say with a raised eyebrow.

Luther just laughs and picks up the kit. He moves to the door and walks away. *God, he's annoying…*the voice in my head retorts followed by an eye roll and a small chuckle. I finish putting in my new contacts before following him into the dining room.

As I enter the room, I see all the lads looking between us. Everyone is smiling other than K, who seems to be narrowing his eyes at Luther for a second. I would like to think that is a hint of jealousy, but that would be a wishful thought. I know he doesn't like me like that. Maybe it's because I am fucking someone who is the son of a murderer. I don't know. I guess I will never understand.

Turning away from him, I roll my eyes at the lads. "Shut the hell up, you lot. I'm old enough to do what I want and not get funny looks from you. H just sort me out. I need to get a move on and not baby sit you assholes. That's why Marcus is here." Why the hell I deal with these men, I will never know. I guess it's because they are family, and I do care about them.

"E, what's the plan for today? Training, strategy meeting, something interesting. Also, what happened to your face? You have a split lip and some bruising on your neck?" K asks with a strange look on his face while H deals with my hands, which aren't such a big issue. I did however need a reason to get Luther alone and in my room. Wait, I completely forgot the split lip. Suppose because it doesn't hurt and I haven't really looked at it, but it's no big deal.

"Got into a fight while I was away, nothing important." I say with a shrug. "Sadly, nothing that interesting K, you, H and Luther are going to be sat here and baby sit those two downstairs. Make sure they get my famous traitor dinner. A and Q, you two will be staking out Steadwell. I want to know exactly what he's doing. If he speaks to someone, moves or even breathes differently, you inform me. And Marcus will be in my office making phone calls for me that we discussed on the way over. Aid will be joining you two on your steak out. He has brought your favourite car, A."

"Don't say he's got the dodge, with the awesome sound system and the heated seats?" A says with a childish grin. His light green eyes shine with anticipation, his dirty blond hair is still a mess from last night.

"Yes, he's brought that one. If you ask nicely, Aid may let you drive. Now go get ready. He will want to leave shortly." A basically runs upstairs to get his stuff. Q just chuckles, the feelings he has for A shows. His light brown eyes follow A. I wish they would just be open about their relationship.

"E, you know what to do to make him happy. God, it's like working with a child." Q chuckles again and follows him upstairs.

"Right, Marcus, you know what to do. Lads, enjoy your boring ass afternoon, and I will see you all in an hour. Keep your eyes on those two downstairs and send them some lunch. If they get out you, know what to do." And with that, I turn towards the door and grab my keys. I know Marcus will keep an eye on H and K, and Aid will keep an eye on A and Q. I know I don't have to worry about them; however, I have a sinking feeling right now.

Chapter 28

Getting to the cafe I use for meetings and the place I first met Luther, I take a seat; this place is practically dead. Usually, I shut the place for meetings but today, I decided against it as I won't be here long. Helen, a worker that keeps me informed in all matters of interest, walks over to me, a smile plastered on her face. "Hey, E, what can I get you?" I smile back.

"Coffee please, Helen. Anything I should know?" Helen contemplates for a moment.

"Nothing major. Hannah has sent you the CCTV this morning from the past month as always."

"Great, thank you." Helen turns and walks away to get my coffee. Hannah is the manager here, but seems she is off today. She always sends me footage of the café just in case there is anything interesting to see.

I'm always early to meetings and Freddy is always late; never known this bloke to be on time. After Helen brings my coffee, Freddy walks in, briefcase in hand. He spots me and takes a seat in front of me. "Hey, Freddy, want a drink?" He sets his briefcase down on the floor and takes the seat opposite to me. It's been three days since we spoke at Kugars, and he said that he had something to tell me. I received his text while I was waiting for Luther to come to my room. It's a bit of an impromptu meeting, but I need to know what he found.

"Coffee would be great, thanks. Now I have done what you asked of me, E, and I didn't find much on your men or Luther; however, I have heard that his dad is trying to follow him. Must have given him the slip, well, seeing as he's asking around about where Luther is because he didn't go home last night. So, wherever he is, he better get back to him so he's not suspicious of where he is. I did however find something interesting about Jasmine and you for that matter." He clears his throat before continuing, Helen puts his coffee down next to him.

"I know that you are aware that you and Jasmine are siblings, and that you were separated not long after your birth. But I found out that Steadwell knew where one of you was since then and lost the other. I would assume that he knew about Jasmine and lost you, seeing as he's none the wiser about you. Anyway, about six months ago, he contacted Jasmine and asked her to locate you, but you located her first. He asked her to feed him information about you, which she did, but it's strange; she fed him wrong information. She's sending him on a wild goose chase away from you. M is also in on this. According to their phone records, he has been telling her about someone else who is like you, and Jasmine has been telling Steadwell that. I don't know if she's aware she's giving him false information or not, but someone is trying to help you."

Wait what? Someone is on my side? I need to sort this out and sort it fast. Not that I care about them being on my side or not, they still told him information. They still went behind my back about this and that won't stand. All they had to do was speak to me, explain the situation and I could have used it to my advantage. Now they have just pissed off the wrong person.

"Anything else, Freddy?" I take a sip of my coffee and Freddy follows suit.

"There is one more thing. Jasmine is being followed so I would sort that out before the day is out."

"Thanks, Freddy, always on top of this for me. Pleasure as always, send my regards to your family." I get up to leave.

"E, it's your birthday coming up soon. I was wondering if you were doing anything for it. The grandkids were wondering if you would pop over. Apparently, they have something for you." I chuckle.

"After all these years, you know I don't do birthdays, but yes, I will pop by and see everyone soon, okay?" With a nod, we both say our goodbyes and leave.

I'm using Graham today as my driver, since Luther is at my place, I might as well. He knows when to keep his mouth shut, and he knows what to do if we are followed. He is a valuable asset to me. "All good, Ma'am?" I look up to notice him looking at me from the rear-view.

"It will be, Graham; I need Luther to get home to his fathers. Apparently Steadwell has been looking for him. I can do without him being followed. Make sure to drop him at his fathers, not his actual home," I say, receiving a nod from him. And with that, we make our way back to my house; the whole trip, no one says a thing. I like Graham. He knows not to say anything that could annoy me. It's one of the reasons I employ him. Also, he is a friend of Marcus' so that helps. In this game, everyone knows everyone. Doesn't matter where you are in the world, we all are connected by someone else.

Walking back into the house, I see that K, H and Luther are all sat in the living room watching the football game. It's strange. I didn't know they liked the sport, or that they were becoming that close. "I'm sorry to cut the game short, lads, but, Luther, you need to go to your father's house. He's looking for you and I can do without him coming here. I already know someone is following that bitch. He's been by your place this morning, go have a coffee there and then maybe I can see if we can sneak you back later," I say, taking a seat next to him. He turns to face me.

"Fine, I should see my mum. She's not been so happy lately anyway." I chuckle.

"Oh, she seems plenty happy to me. Oscar has been keeping her company for a few days now. She may just be pissed you haven't been to see her in nearly a month." His jaw drops for a second. I must have ruined the thought of his saintly mother.

"Oscar? Who's Oscar?" This really makes me laugh, like belly laugh. The type that is contagious.

"Oscar is the very nice gentleman that works in the bar your mum has been going to with her friends on a Wednesday night. You mum has about three, maybe four boy toys that keep her bed warm. And they all pass me information, and I keep them protected from your father. I don't know if he knows about her affairs or not, so it's better to be safe than sorry. And sorry I ruined the picture of your mother for you, best you know now." Patting his leg, I stand and point towards the front door. "Sorry, Luther, but Graham is outside waiting for you. I will be in touch soon." And with that, he stands and goes to leave, but not before he leaves one passing remark.

"I do hope to hear from you soon. It's not over what we spoke about earlier. And it's certainly not finished." And with a sly smile, he leaves. Rolling my eyes, I go back to sitting on the sofa, both K and H are looking at me.

"What?" I ask, slightly irritated by the whole situation.

"Oh nothing, E, just wondering what he was on about. Also, wondering what we are doing with M and Jasmine when they come round." I roll my eyes; of course they want to know what is going on in both situations. The latter one, they are welcome to watch, the first, however, is fuck all to do with them. I get up and walk towards the door that leads to the basement. Turning back to them, I nod my head in the direction I'm walking.

"You coming or what? Also, grab Marcus while you're there. I may need to tap out during this." My hands may be in bandages but for this, I will suffer the pain.

I make it down to M's cell, he's still out cold, which is a bonus; it means I can get him in the chair easier. I hate fighting to restrain people. I glance through the window opposite his cell, to see Jasmine still passed out on the mattress I left her on. Maybe I gave her more serum than I should have but hey, shit happens. I turn back to M's cell and put my thumb on the keypad. The thud of the bolt on the door echoes through the concrete basement. I push the door open and walk in, the cells aren't that accommodating; they smell and are just empty. Turns out, you can't get the smell of blood out of concrete, no matter how much you try. You get cold in here, but tough shit, it's not a holiday retreat. I grab a chair from the side of the room and move it into the middle.

"Put him in the chair," I command, to no one in particular. K and H move around me and haul his body on to the chair. I walk back outside and into a room next to his cell where we keep the tools. Rope hangs on the walls next to a plethora of other items of torture.

Today, I don't wish to use anything other than my fists. I want to feel it as I break his bones one by one. I want him to know how pissed I am that he crossed me, for him to feel all the hurt he has caused. We were supposed to be a team. I guess that went out the window. Walking back into the cell, I go to M and tie him to the chair, binding his arms round his back and to the chair followed by his legs. Marcus, K, and H do nothing but watch.

"How do you want to wake him up, E?" Marcus asks, although he already knows how I plan on doing it. I stand in front of him and punch him square in the side of the face. His cheek starting to bruise with the sheer force of my fist. M sharply takes a breath and looks up at me; his face is swelling already.

"What the fuck, E! What's going on? Why am I here?" M asks. He looks shocked and confused. Maybe I didn't hit him hard enough.

"Shut the door. No one leaves until I get my answers." And with that, Marcus shuts the door. Let's hope he doesn't take too long to spill his guts. I'm a very busy woman.

Chapter 29

"Fuck, E, why?" M retorts as his head snaps back from the force of my fist. I've hit him four times already, my knuckles hurting from the force. But I need to teach him a lesson; apparently the last one didn't register.

"Spilling information to Harry, are you? Got someone to try and kill Georgia in my own club, did you? Did you really think I wouldn't find out, you piece of shit?" I'm so pissed off, it's unreal. He thinks I am so stupid. My body filled with an all-consuming anger, and from the feel of it, I won't be quelling it any time soon. Maybe he thinks I'm slipping. I'm not, but maybe in his eyes because I fucked Luther and Xander, and I ran off to Washington at the drop of a hat. I don't care what he thinks. I'm not in the mood for games. I don't give a shit about his agenda anymore. He crossed me, and no one lives after that.

"E, I have no idea what you're talking about. Just talk to me. I'm your brother. I love you, just stop." My head falls back laughing at his comment. Love me? You're trying to get me killed. Marcus, K and H say nothing, just stand by the door. My fist connects with his face again, causing him to grunt from the blow. I grab a fist full of his hair and yank his head back. My eyes full of anger, I can't believe he would try to play dumb. His face is starting to swell, bruises are forming on his cheek and his right eye.

"Love me? You say you love me, but I can connect you to Georgia. I can connect you to the leak, and I can also connect you to Steadwell. You are a piece of shit, Matthew. You want my job, don't you? You think I would ever let that happen? And if you think teaming up with Steadwell would make that more achievable, you are dead wrong. And if you don't start talking, that's what you will be, dead."

"Connect me to Steadwell, E, I would never…" My fist makes contact with his gut, causing him to hunch forward.

"Tell me the truth, else you and that bitch you are fucking will both die." He looks me in the eye. I'm not buying this whole 'not involved' bullshit.

"I can't tell you a truth I know nothing about," M practically shouts at me. I laugh again.

"Fine, fine. Have it your way. Your darling girlfriend is just across the hall. Maybe I should kill her right now in front of you. Would that jog your memory? You and she may be feeding Harry wrong information but you are still going behind my back." A tear slips down M's cheek.

"Please, Emie, I'm begging. Leave her out of it. This is not what you think." Finally, he's getting it. I will kill her anyway; I can never trust her again and neither can I trust him.

"Explain and make it quick. I don't have all day." M sighs. I'm also impatient, have I mentioned that bit of me yet? I punch him in the face again, getting another grunt from him.

"You are weak, M, always have been. You were useless back in my company, and you are useless now. He has carried you all these years. If it was up to me, you wouldn't need carrying anymore," Marcus says, walking over and punching M himself. I've never seen him this angry with anyone. He's also never said this to M before. Yes, he's told me that I should have fucked him off years ago, but he was family. That means nothing right now.

"E, just talk to me. Get the others to leave. I deserve that, don't I?" Rolling my eyes, I walk to the door and let myself out. I walk over to Jasmine's cell and look through the window. She's still fast asleep which is great. I walk in and grab her top and use it to drag her into M's cell. His eyes go wide as I pull her in.

"Please E, don't," M pleads. I look at K who shuts the door and locks it. I slap Jasmine across the face, waking her up. She's shocked, eyes darting from me to the others. Then she clocks M, his face is swollen and bruised. He's still tied to the chair.

"E, please, what's happening?" Jasmine asks, a tear leaves her eye as the realisation that I'm not playing around dawns on her.

"Come on, lovebirds, tell me what's going on…No, neither of you wants to talk. Maybe this will persuade you," I say before stamping on Jasmine's lower leg, breaking it. Her scream reverberates around the concrete cell. "Each time you don't tell me what's going on, I will break another bone. The last bone will be the one in her neck, M. I suggest you start talking."

"Okay, okay. Just don't hurt her anymore, I beg you," M cries. I mean physically cries. Maybe it was love, a love that will be kept together forever. "Harry approached Jasmine months ago after I found her; we met a few months before I told you about her. It wasn't anything you think. I felt something for her. We spoke for a few months and even went on a few dates; I fell in love with her, E." I start to dry heave; my stomach turns at him falling in love with her. Not because he is in love, but because it is with a girl who looks just like me. I can't seem to understand why or wrap my head around him finding someone who looks similar to me. Maybe it's being very selfish of me, but it's weird, right? After I have composed myself, I look at him; my emotions for him are long dead.

"You really are disgusting and such a disappointment. You went out looking to fuck someone who looks like me; oh my God, you are fucking low. You found her before I knew she even existed and thought, 'hey she looks like the woman I have called sister since I was twelve. I'm going to stick my dick right in that.' You fucking repulse me, Matthew." I state while trying to hold back my churning stomach. Nausea sweeping through me.

"It's not like that. And you were okay with it the other day," M yells.

"When I thought this was just some fun, but you sought her out. You made it your mission to find her, this cheap wish knock-off of me. Fuck, I'm going to be sick. Have you always had some sick fetish about sleeping with family, or has it just been lately?" I put my hand on my stomach. I don't think I have ever known someone be like this.

Okay yeah, it weirded me out when I first heard about them. But to find out it's been months, longer than I knew this tramp existed. That sent me over the edge. Has he wanted to fuck me since we were younger? Has he always had some sick fantasy about me?

"What, no. We bumped into each other and just hit it off. We were sleeping together before I knew for sure she was your sister. I fell in love with her personality, her looks were just an added bonus. But I would never think about you in that way, you're my sister." I vomit straight onto the floor, the small breakfast I ate earlier leaving me. I have never felt so revolted and shocked in my life. 'Her looks were a bonus', those few words spun me. How? How can he be like that? We grew up together, and he has some weird tasteless fetish about what? Me? The fact she looks like me? I don't know, but it fucking disgusts me. Maybe this is an over-reaction, but to me it's the lowest thing he could have done.

"And she looks the spitting image of me now, does it turn you on more or less now she has the same colour hair as me? What about her eyes? Do you want her more with my eye colour? You are one sick fucker, not even as mafia have we stepped that low. You are unworthy of being my brother, or being alive." I grab her head and lift it by her hair, forcing her to look at the sick fucker I called a brother for so long.

"It never changed anything for me. I love her regardless. Anyway, when I knew Harry was speaking to her, I told her that he killed her parents, and he was the reason she was an orphan. I decided that she might be useful being so close to Harry, so we decided to feed him false information. We also spoke to the coppers he uses and some other contacts. They are all with us and giving him wrong intel on you."

He pauses and looks at Jasmine as she cries, clutching her leg. I drop her hair. She tries to curl up into a ball to make herself smaller. *Like that's going to help*...I think to myself.

Once I have calmed myself down, and the waves of nausea have passed, I turn to look at M again. "Why didn't you bring this up to me? Why am I finding this out now?" I ask, glaring at them both. I clock Marcus has a gun in his belt behind his back. I didn't put one on today, never usually wear one in my home. I am glad he is carrying though.

"It was nothing against you, E, just you have enough on your plate without this." No way, this isn't why he didn't tell me. I bend down and grab Jasmine's hand, gripping one of the fingers on her right hand. I move it back with such a force, I hear a snap. Holding the next finger, I turn and look at M.

"Oh, M, did you really think I would buy that crap. 'You didn't tell me because it would be too much stress', bitch please. My whole life has been stressful since I was nine. You have breezed through life. No war zones." Snap. "No death." Snap. "You have never even taken a life to protect anyone." Snap. With each statement, I break another of Jasmine's fingers. "But I guess I never really did know the real you, the vulgar, lowbrow and repulsive things you do. Not only do you fuck a dirty little version of me, but then you use her to get what? My company? My life? Or is it money you were after?" I grab her whole hand and force it back, breaking her wrist. Her scream is music to my ears, especially compared to all the nauseating and unutterable things to which I have just listened.

"E, I have always been loyal, why can you not believe me now?"

Right, that's it. I have lost my patience completely. I get up and walk towards Marcus and grab his gun. I know maybe a tad dramatic, but I have always promised to keep my men alive, and I sure as shit will keep it. I point it to M's leg and pull the trigger. An ear-piercing scream echoes around us. I've only ever shot one of my men before and let's just say I found shooting M was a waste of a bullet, but a point had to be proven.

"Now, M, please stop this shit. I've just shot you, and I've been good to you for over twenty years, haven't I? I've known your little lady love for all of five minutes. Quick question. Do you think I won't kill her? She is disposable, she always was. I will get to my revenge and no one, not even you and her, will get in my way. Do you understand?" I am getting angrier by the second. I turn the gun and point it at Jasmine's head; her whole body cowers and her arms come to cover her face. I pull the trigger and just miss her head; the bullet imbeds itself into the concrete floor.

"Take this as a warning. Next time, I won't miss," I state before flicking the safety back on and passing the gun back to Marcus. I never miss, so everyone in this room knows I did it more to prove a point.

Turning to K and H, I ask, "Either of you two want a go, as long as I get the info I need, I don't care how we get there."

K doesn't even bother to hide his anger and punches M five or six times. He even spits on him. I've known this bloke over a decade and never seen him ever get angry. Right now, I have a newfound admiration for him. He's managed to keep cool all this time, but the minute M crosses me, he loses it. Even H has anger written all over his face. "Please, E, I'll tell you everything. Just stop hurting him, I love him, and he's had enough." Jasmine grabs my leg with her left hand which I haven't touched yet. I laugh hard. Does she really think it stops here? K and H are going to town on M; he's bleeding quite badly from his face.

I crouch down to her, our similar faces mere millimetres from each other. "Oh, you stupid bitch. I will beat that shit stain to death if I have to." I grab her jaw and turn her face towards M and the lads. I watch as K and H cease their beating; everyone just watching our interaction. "You are both disposable to me, especially him. I have beat him worse than this before, sweetheart, so don't think I won't again. Once you become useless to me, you stop being an oxygen thief. And you two are losing your usefulness, therefore, I am losing my patience." I let her face go and stand, my attention solely on M.

"M, you are a complete waste of my time, money and energy. Your little love here will die if you don't talk. You didn't do this for me. You think you can take my place; you can't kill or protect anyone. If you became a mob boss, your whore over here is very much dead. Who am I kidding? She is dead anyway." I laugh, grabbing her hair I drag her in front of him. M's face becomes pale as he hears her scream, watching her tears fall down her face. I pull her head back roughly; I watch as her eyes meet his. The pleading in their eyes would make anyone else feel bad for them, but not me. My stone heart doesn't usually feel anything for anyone.

"Emie, please leave her alone. I will do anything, but please. If I meant anything to you, you would leave her out of it," M pleads to me, tears streaming down his face. The love he has for her is evident, but I can't see past the repulsion I feel for them both. The sickening feeling of them being together, it's disgusting.

"Oh, Matthew, you are so funny. You mean nothing to me now, do you want to know the moment you became nothing? It was the time you messed up and Marcus made me punish you. Each fist I laid into your body solidified this deep resentment. It also showed me what a complete liability you are. So no, she will be your punishment." With that said, I punch her in the side of the head. She slumps to the side. Blood starts to trickle out of her ear. I know she probably has concussion.

"I didn't do this to get your company. I did it to keep you safe. I did it to get Steadwell off your back, and Georgia worked for someone who knows him. She was going to cross you."

I have already looked into Georgia and her only connection was her boss from a previous job who knows Steadwell's secretary. "Do you think I didn't do my homework?" I grab my knife from my sock and run it across her face. Her blood-curdling scream rebounds off the walls around us. "Oh no, I cut that pretty little face. I hope you realise what lengths I will go to over this."

"You bitch," Jasmine yells at me, blood runs down her face. I cut from her left eyebrow down to her chin. She is lucky I decided not to take her eye. Bitch got lucky this time.

"You know what, you can both sit in your cells for a while and think about what you want to say to me. If I don't like it, you will both pay. I'm not above hitting a woman, Jasmine, clearly. And if you don't give me any answers worth my time, you will both die, sound fair?" And with that, I drag Jasmine back to her cell and dump her on the floor and lock her inside. Moving back to M's cell, I nod the boys to leave and again I lock the door on M and leave.

"You should have let me kill him, E. How dare that bastard go against you. How dare he cross you; he should have died for that just like X did. He's not worthy of being part of us," K says, visibly shaking with anger. I do really appreciate how loyal he is. He and H are my closest. I don't even know why I doubted them in the first place; they have always had my back, but I still have to check just in case. I found out that H and Willow are getting pretty close lately, which is nice; they both deserve to be happy. What's happening to me? I'm getting soft, and producing emotions. Eww! Next, I will be telling people I love them. And we certainly can't have that.

Chapter 30

Turning to the TV, I tap into the CCTV of the cells. This allows me to monitor everything from wherever I am. Jasmine is just crying laying by her door, whereas M is still sat in his chair calling out to her. I guess M would be, I didn't untie him. Listening to them, I hear faintly what's being said. I turn up the volume a bit so it's clearer. There is a small microphone and speaker inside the cells, I had them put in so people would incriminate themselves. Smart, I know. Most criminals are morons, and M is no different. Seemed to have forgotten I can also see and hear them. "Babe, listen, I know it hurts but we can sort this. It's my fault, it all is. I knew E would lose her shit if she ever found out, but I didn't think she would hurt you," M calls.

"But she did, Matt. God, it hurts so bad. I told you to tell her months ago when you told me about her. She's a psycho. I never in a million years thought she might do that to me or let her hounds beat you. We should have run away like I said. Got the hell away from Harry and E's bullshit. He killed people I didn't know, and I told you that. I can't be angry at him for it." Jasmine wanted them to run away? She wanted nothing to do with any of this.

Such a shame they know me, else I could have made that happen. He killed who she didn't know, I get that, but he still killed. Surely, she would feel something about that.

"I know, and I wish we had. I really do. Maybe if we just tell her what we told Harry, she may let us do that. I can't be without you, baby. You know you're my world now. You know I would do anything for you."

"She wouldn't believe us even if we do tell her the truth. She's fucking crazy."

I can't listen to this lovey-dovey shit any longer, or her bad mouthing me. I walk up to Marcus and whisper in his ear. "Keep an eye on them from your phone. I'm not listening to this shit anymore. Hopefully they may talk while I'm in the office. I need to call Scott. You know what for." With a curt nod, I say to the lads, "I can't listen to this shit anymore. If I do, I may vomit on the floor again. I'm going to the office." I grab K and H's arms and pull them with me into my office. I need to speak to them and come up with a game plan. Plus, I need Scott to come and clear up my mess; a mess I will be making shortly, if you know what I mean.

Once in, I open a bottle of scotch and grab three glasses. I can't believe this is happening. He's no longer family, he's not safe from Steadwell or me. Now he's just collateral damage, they both are. He chose his path in life, and being on my side was not his option. I could have laughed when he said I would have let them go, it was the most delusional thing I had ever heard. When has he ever known me to just let it be?

K grabs a glass from the table and fills it. "What do we do now, boss?" I'm not thinking straight at the moment.

"First, we need to know what M has been telling Steadwell. Then we need to know what coppers he's on about and see what's happened there. I also need to call Scott and get him over here, and Aid. I don't think he's too far away with A and Q."

"Sounds like a plan. Want me to call Scott?" H asks while reaching for his glass.

"Na, phone Willow first and tell her to see Steadwell when he gets there. I want her to ask him some questions. She's going to be the easier one to use as he won't suspect her. He goes at the same time each week. Then call Scott. K, call Captain Kenny. He will know which policemen are in Steadwell's pocket. Tell him I need those names now," I reply, grabbing my glass. I touch my earpiece; Luther is the only one who is active at the moment.

"Luther, can you hear me?" I set Luther's piece to be on ready for when I call. I asked Graham to give it to Luther when we took him to his parents. They do cause you to jump when you first wear them. Never expect someone to talk to you the first time and if someone doesn't tell you they are calling, it's worse. Although it's also amusing to watch, the jump is still funny no matter how many times you watch.

"Fuck, yes I can hear you." I laugh slightly and motion the boys to join the call so they can hear what Luther says. I hear something clink in my ears, like a phone has been placed over the earpiece. Someone must be watching, probably his father.

"Just a heads-up, Luther, K and H are also listening. Didn't mean to scare you."

"Scare me? No, of course not. What can I do for you?" He's being weird. His voice is slightly higher than usual. Maybe he is trying to be funny, but I don't think he is. I glance at the lads who just shrug. Their faces show their puzzlement. I don't understand why he's being like this.

"I assume you're going home or just leaving your father's. I do need to talk to you about a few things." He coughs and my phone dings.

I think my dad can hear me or someone is telling him what's happening, he's being really weird and said some strange stuff to me today. I don't know who I can trust.

Oh shit. I toss my phone to H who shows K. They look up at me and put my phone down on the desk. I take another swig of my drink. "Listen to me, Luther, and say nothing. Your dad goes to Secret tonight, so you can come here and talk to me in private. I will also run checks to see who's in your dad's pocket, but everyone who's working tonight works for me. I'll come get you myself later so it doesn't look suspicious, we will sort this." I touch my earpiece and disconnect the call. K and H do the same.

"E, what are you going to do about this? If Steadwell is onto us, then we need to act carefully," K states, worry evident in his eyes, and a deep furrow in his brow.

"I know. That's why Willow will find out the info that I need, and then I can act accordingly. Let's hope we can persuade him that Jasmine is actually the one after him; he may kill her for me." I was joking slightly, but if I think about it, it's not a bad plan.

"That's actually not a bad idea, E, saves us a job and Scott of disposing of her." K laughs, but that's the whole point. I already have to think of what to do with M let alone what to do with that snake as well.

"I'll call her now," H says and goes to walk away.

"Get B to keep her safe. Tell him that if it goes south to enact code seven." He nods and goes to the other side of the room, opening the door to leave. "Oh, and while you're at it, want to ask if she's coming over for Christmas this year?" I laugh. H rolls his eyes and leaves.

"You know?" K asks all confused.

"Of course, I know, mate. I'm not stupid. I see the way they look at each other, also I did background checks on everyone. It came up and confirmed what I was thinking."

K chuckles. He knows me, and he understands why I am the way I am. He still finds it amusing the way I react to other people's happiness.

"Find anything good on me?" K laughs, causing me to join in; his low gruff laugh is highly contagious. However, when I watch him closer, I see a small amount of hope on his face. I don't know why. Was he hoping I would find something?

"Na, mate, nothing I didn't already know. You're so strait-laced, I'm surprised you can breathe." We both laugh hard; a sly smile forms on K's face. I love the way he looks at me sometimes. I enjoy imagining it when we are alone in bed. The things he would do to me, but right now it's like he is hiding something. And he's happy to have something I don't know. Maybe one day he will finally tell me what it is.

A tap on the door grabs our attention. Marcus' head pops round. I beckon him in. He moves into the room and closes the door lightly behind him. "They didn't change their story, but M is getting queasy; maybe he's lost a bit too much blood." I laugh.

"Yeah, I don't care. What do you think about all this?" Marcus looked at me and raised his left eyebrow.

"You going soft, E? Asking my opinion?" he asks in a questioning tone. My anger flares again. I am right on the edge of killing everyone I know. Last thing I need right now is for someone to accuse me of losing my edge, because I know I am not. I just wanted advice; he has been doing this for far longer than I have.

"Fucking what? I'm asking because we both know you have been here before. We both know what happened, and I want to know if you would have done anything differently. I'm not going soft, Marcus. I need advice." Marcus just keeps staring at me like I've lost my mind.

After a few minutes of this face off, Marcus speaks again. "Look, E, I know you're not soft, but you know I wouldn't change anything. They both deserved it. You know what to do, E. You always have, you're my daughter. I taught you everything to get through this."

He was right. I knew exactly what to do. I always know what to do, but this time I was unsure. For the first time in my life, I was questioning myself, worrying whether I was doing the right thing. A feeling of unease fills me and has since I left Washington. But now I know what I need to do. I needed to get information, and I needed to get Luther here safe. Right now, I had a sinking feeling that something bad will happen to him, and I can't have that. Yes, I care about him but he's also fundamental to my plan, to my revenge. H makes his way back into the office.

"E, he's just turned up at Secret. Willow is going to sort him. And Scott is on his way, said he would be here around 11 pm." Right, that's two things sorted. I log onto the CCTV at Luther's and look at all the staff. Each of them work for me apart from one. Who is that? I don't recognise his face, and I am great at remembering people's faces. I don't think he is safe.

"Right, well I have a sinking feeling that the person walking around Luther's are either working for Steadwell or someone else, because they don't work for me. He needs to get out of there in case he isn't friendly. Then when I get back, I will deal with those downstairs. We all know that they don't walk out of here, whether they tell me the truth or not. They can be together in death."

"Very well, E. What shall we do?" Marcus asks as he gets himself a drink.

"B will keep his eye on Willow, and put her in room 5. It has the best cameras and audio. K, keep your eye on those downstairs and tell me if they say anything important. Marcus, get Aid up to date on what happened and what's going on. I'm going to get changed and grab Luther, before anyone says anything. He's imperative to my plan, that is all. I'm not fucking soft and I'm sure as shit not losing my touch. Understood?" Each of them all looked shocked at me.

"E, we weren't questioning you at all." K holds his hands up to me.

"It appears some people are, and I'm fucking done with being soft. Everyone has had too many free passes." And with that, I leave the room. I know I stormed out like a toddler throwing a tantrum, but I am done with being looked at like I am slipping. Like I am off my game. I am not, by the way; I have just awoken a need I didn't know I had. A need that I can't seem to satisfy. And I know the saddest part is it can't be quenched by the person I want it to the most; the only person I have ever desired. So naturally I sought someone else, someone who would be willing to help. I found two who were only too happy to help me. And maybe that makes me a whore, but if I was a man, people would call me a player.

Chapter 31

Walking into my bedroom, I grab the door to my walk-in wardrobe; I need to pretend that we have a date tonight. But I don't want to look like myself. I will dress like Jasmine. If I was Steadwell Sr, to think that Jasmine is after him, it would be better if I collect Luther looking like her.

My mind still reeling from what Matthew said; my stomach turning again, thinking about it. It might make me slightly egotistical, but who wants to sleep with someone who looks like their family. It's disgusting, well in my eyes, anyway. To others that might be fine – it might even be a turn on. To me, however, it was a vile thing. And for me to say that, it must be bad. No, I wasn't happy about it when I first found out. But I knew M, he never keeps a pussy for too long. So I assumed it would just be over before it got serious, so who was I to question. Moreover, he has slept with every girl at Secret, including Willow. So I just thought I would let it play out, let the cards land as they may. But contrary to my knowledge, he went for her, he made sure he found her. I just can't seem to understand how he knew about her, especially before me.

That's what I don't understand. How he knew about someone when I didn't. Who did he learn this from? Who did he know to find this out? And has he been selling me out for a while? A tsunami of questions consume my mind, and the lack of answers frustrates me. In spite of everything, I cannot focus on this right now. Luther might be in danger. And I need him alive; he is critical to my plan. So I push those questions aside and decide I need to get a wriggle on. I have to get Luther before anything disastrous happens to him.

Walking over to my wigs, I grab the side piece that I wear to go to the office, and grab the skin suit I use to cover the tattoos. If I'm going to do this properly, I need to know exactly what eye colour she wore when they met. How she dressed. I want Steadwell to think he's been talking to the one he is after all this time. I put on the skin suit and glue the hair on. I look in the mirror and bile rises in my throat; repulsion monopolises my mind momentarily before I manage to compose myself. Once M and that skank are dead, hopefully this feeling will fuck off.

Once I've done that, I leave the bedroom and walk into the main room; everyone is there just chilling with their drink. Suddenly, all eyes are on me.

"E, what are you doing? You don't wear that unless you're going to the office." I turn to H; he's got a confused look on his face; his grey eyes full of questions I don't think he wants to ask me.

"Well, if I'm going to sell the whole 'Jasmine being me' thing, I best look the part. I just need to know what colour eyes she wore when they used to meet. I want to know what style of clothes she wore, so I'm going to compare all her looks and find something similar."

Great plan, I know. I pull up all photos of Jasmine out and about when she's not here. T-Shirt and jeans mostly. That could work, and black heels. I can do that; her eyes are blue in all but one. Why the one time did she wear green? Actually, she's dressed just like me in that one photo. I need to know why. I don't understand she wasn't going to the office that day, actually she wasn't even working for me that day. I turn and look at the guys. The picture huge on the 68-inch TV. "Why does she look just like me in that photo; it was before I met her. Before all of this, did she know Matthew at this point?"

All the guy's shrug at me, looking at the photo. The time on it is about a month before I met her. I need to know what is going on. I know she knew Matthew, judging by the date and what he said earlier. Pure rage envelops me, knowing he was definitely stepping against me. He used her to show Steadwell what I look like. Was he hoping to get me killed without getting blood on his own hands? *Oh, I'm going to have fun killing him...*I think to myself, knowing I am going to break everything in him. Make him beg me to stop, and I won't. Not until I am bored of him, bored of his begging and pleading. I click print. I need answers and only two people can give me those.

Grabbing the picture, I walk to the basement. Once I reach her cell, I stand outside. I can hear them talking. I left the coms open so they could talk. I may be a bitch, but I'm not completely soulless. "Babe, E will understand. She loves me, let me talk to her and we can fix this," M shouts.

"I just want to go home. Away from this place, far, far, away. Where we can live happily ever after. And she doesn't love you. She called you nothing." I can hear the pain in her voice.

I open up her cell. "Now that's enough of that, don't you think?" I switch off the coms and walk over to her. She cries even louder than before. I can faintly hear M yelling through the corridor and open door, but with the coms off, it's not that loud. I am not worried about her escaping; I broke her leg so she wouldn't get anywhere fast. Although, I kind of hope she tries, I would very much enjoy the chase.

Crouching down, I show her the photo of her with Steadwell. "Why the fuck are you dressed like me in this picture? You had never met me. You knew nothing about me. Yet you have my green eyes, my clothes, and my ID, why?" Jasmine cries harder. I grab her broken leg and squeeze. Her yell echoes around the cell.

"I can't remember, I swear."

I sigh. "Oh, Jasmine, you think I'm stupid, don't you? You trying to be me here, tell Steadwell where to find me?" She's physically sweating. "Okay, Jasmine, I'll rephrase the question. Was this so you could lead him to me? Did you and Matthew plot to have me killed? And did he tell you to wear this?"

Her face pales. Bingo, my answer. I get up and walk out without saying another word. Locking her in, I hear her shout back to me. "Please, E, stop this. We want to live. We want a family and to be together forever. I love him."

"Do I seem like a woman who cares what you want? Answers are all I care about; you are just a thorn in my side. But I will grant you one favour, I will let you be together forever. Maybe just not in the way the two of you were hoping for." I hear her swearing and yelling in-between sobs as I move over to M's cell.

Chapter 32

I stand there for a second watching M still strapped to his chair, sobbing; he must really love her. Shame that their love will get them killed. Maybe Marcus was right. Love will be your downfall. It will get you killed. My heart clenches for a moment, not wanting to fully believe it. But as I look at Matthew, the realisation of this starts to set in. My mind closing itself to all my feelings of love for anyone. I can't allow myself to feel such things, for Luther, for K, or anyone. It's a weakness, and I can see that first hand now.

As I watch Matthew crying and trembling at the loss of that whore, it solidifies what I was taught all along. If I want my revenge, I cannot become this weak. I cannot allow love to enter me. I must stand strong and keep my heart secure. Mainly because if anything happens to me or someone I love. I don't want to look like this. I can't be consumed with the feeling of hopelessness; it doesn't help anyone. So love must stay away from me – revenge over love.

Opening the door and walking over to a sobbing, whimpering little excuse of a man. "Hey, Matthew, I have a question. Why does your little girlfriend look just like me, right down to her green eyes? She said it's you who put her up to this. Is it?" I flash the picture in his face and look at him. His eyes move down to the picture. When his eyes look at it, his Adam's apple bobs. I know he is hiding something from me.

"Look, E, it's not what you think. I did it to protect you."

I certainly am not buying this bullshit. "Protect me? Have I ever needed your protection? Have I ever needed you to do anything for me ever? I've protected you, more times than I would care to admit. You don't know the stunts I have pulled to get you out of all the shit you landed in. Marcus believes I should have left you in London, left you with Maggie. Maybe I should have, because all you have done is make one giant shit show for me to clean up again. Why did you do it?"

"Emilia, please, I'm your brother. We grew up together. Would Maggie like us fighting?" How dare he use my name and bring Maggie into this. I slapped his face hard, throwing his head to the side.

I grab his hair and force him to look at me, to see the unbridled rage in my eyes. "Emilia died years ago. That's not who I am. And Maggie would understand. She will understand." I emphasise the word 'will', while M just stares at me shocked.

"Understand? Understand what?" I let his head go and turn to the door walking away from him. Before I leave, I look back for a second.

"She will understand why you won't be visiting again. She will understand why you and Jasmine will be, how shall I put it, permanently indisposed. And I, as the devoted daughter, will be there to support her in this tumultuous time." And with that, I leave.

Everyone is still where I left them, but they have put the footage of the cells on the TV screen. "Do you want us to feed them? They have been down there a while," H asks. I know he cares. Matthew has been with us for years, but he's still pissed off with what's happening. I guess he isn't like me. I can switch off my humanity and just think business. That's what being a mafia boss is; it's just a business. We just aren't afraid to do what needs to be done.

"Sure, it will be their last meal anyway, such a shame really. She would have been useful. Oh well, I'm off to finish getting ready and grab Luther." I turn to look at Marcus, who's sat watching the screen while listening to me. I know how he's always felt about me having M around. Many times, he's called him a liability, a waste of my time. But he always understood why I kept him around.

"Marcus, you and Aid make sure that Steadwell gets information about Jasmine being the one after him. Drop a few hints to people he's using to find me. We need him to believe that she is the ones he's after and she's been lying to him all this time. Then hopefully, he will kill her for me. If he doesn't buy it, we will send her as a gift to him. Maybe do the normal mafia thing and send her head." That's a lie. We never usually send the head of someone to our enemies. That is definitely a movie cliché. Today, though, why not? It would certainly be a statement, and perhaps rattle his cage.

He doesn't stop looking at the screen. He just nods and grabs his phone. He types without looking away from the cells on the TV. I watch as Matthew keeps spitting blood on the floor and Jasmine just lying there like the pathetic bitch she is.

"Aid will be here in 15 minutes. Grab Luther then we will have a briefing on what's happening from here. If you're right about Luther, and he is in trouble, we will have to find a way of keeping him safe and keeping Harry off his tail."

"Oh, I didn't know you were in charge here, pops." I raise my eyebrow at him. His eyes snap to mine; my mouth twitches as he sees I am joking slightly.

"Well someone has to be." Marcus retorts back, making me laugh.

"I don't know how I ever ran my company without you, Marcus. Thank you so much for being here and taking charge." I bow sarcastically at him. Marcus' low chuckle echoes around us.

"Why, you are so very welcome, dear child." I laugh again as Marcus bows back to me. Sometimes we do like to wind each other up. We are kind of childish sometimes. "Anyway, hurry up. We both know shit can go south extremely quickly in our world," Marcus states, shooing me with a wave of his hand.

I nodded and moved to the room that Jasmine used. It's a good job we are roughly the same size. I can actually use her clothes to put my plan into action.

I grab a purple T-shirt and blue jeans and put them on. I also use a pair of her black heels. Glancing in the floor length mirror on the wardrobe door, I noticed how easy it is for me to look like her. It was a good job I got her to dye her hair; makes it easier for me to pretend to be her. I turn away from the mirror quickly, my skin beginning to crawl. I brush that feeling away, not wanting to think about it. About them. I take a deep breath, chastising myself for overreacting yet again.

Looking away from the window, I take in the rest for the room, my jaw hitting the floor; my OCD going into overdrive. Her room is a mess, her clothes are thrown everywhere and even some of Matthew's clothes are mixed in with them. She doesn't even make her bed; how can you go through life not making your bed? I guess that's Marcus in my head. He always said you can't start your day correctly until you make your bed. This shows exactly how different she is to me. I'm horrifically neat; everything in its place and all of my chores are done by 5 am in the morning. Whereas she doesn't wake up until 10 am and never cleans her plates or cups, tidies up or even makes her bed. I couldn't live like this, and I sure as hell wouldn't want to.

I shut the door before I start to clean her dump of a room. I have more important things to do than clean her shit up. Finally ready to get Luther, I move into the living room and grab my drink that someone must have brought in from the office. Taking a swig, I look up at the TV still showing the two cells. I know I'm cold-hearted because I'm looking at the man I called my brother for years and I feel nothing but anger towards him. I tear my eyes away, knowing they are on borrowed time. Matthew and Jasmine won't be darkening my home for much longer; they will be permanently indisposed soon enough. I however must sort out Luther first; I need him safe. Not just for my plan, but for a promise I made a few years ago; a promise I shall be trying to keep. Well, for now anyway. I may have promised to keep Luther safe from his father, but he isn't any safer with me. Anyhow, I best get going. Luther won't get here on his own.

Chapter 33

Pulling up at Luther's apartment block, I stroll past the front desk; a man is sat in the foyer with a newspaper. He is watching me over the top of it, but I don't recognise him. His dark eye moving with me. Is he is trying to be discrete? If he is, then he is epically failing. A blind man would have seen him looking, and I'm not even joking. His legs are crossed as he sits in a single seat chair in the lobby, his grey trousers aren't even ironed. They are wrinkles galore. Also, the paper is clearly yesterday's, not today's. The title reads 'Jackson's wife in sordid affair', and that was yesterday's headline. The New York Sun paper have a new affair allegation every other day, so yes, yesterday's paper. He's also an older man, judging by the flecks of grey in his dark hair. This is supporting what Luther is saying, making me think he really is in danger.

Stepping in the lift, I get a better look at the bloke; his grey hair is slicked back. He doesn't work for any of the mob bosses I know, and I know all six families. Well, the six major ones. I don't bother to know the smaller groups; they don't cause waves. Maybe just some inconvenient ripples, and they don't go anywhere to be honest. Mainly because the council and I handle them, and make their little companies disappear. I send a couple of text messages to each of the other bosses and see if he works for them. If he does, I can find out why he's here. But I have a sinking feeling he works for Steadwell senior, and if so, that means that Luther is definitely in danger.

The elevator doors open at Luther's floor. There are only two doors up here: one for him and one for Tyler, who lives in the other apartment. Tyler Flacks is a 29-year-old fuck boy. Mummy and Daddy give him everything. It's a good job they have plenty of money because he spends so much; I've never known someone spend money like it's water. He tried to gain access to secret, but he blabbed his mouth about it. So that was an automatic fuck-no to him joining; never heard from him again. Thank God, although B and K paid him a visit which might have helped. Rolling my eyes, I move to Luther's door and ring the door cam; his face pops up after a few seconds of waiting.

"Hey, Luther, I was in the area and thought we could grab a drink. Fancy it?" I give myself a sweet American accent, finding it easy to mimic Jasmine. His face is full of confusion; it's humorous that he hasn't worked it out that I am pretending to be her.

"S…Sure, Jasmine. I'll be out in a second." I decide to drop him a quick text, saying that it's me, and he should just roll with it. I watch as he reads my text, understanding moves over his face before his eyes meet mine. Luther seems more at ease, with an air of trepidation around him. Seconds later, the door clicks open, and Luther stands before me; a small glint in his eye. He says nothing, and neither do I.

He steps out and we get back into the lift; the silence is deafening. Clearly he is still on edge, and I can understand why. Stepping into the lobby, I grab Luther's arm and give him my sweetest smile; I could hurl with the thought of being like this all the time.

"Shall we? I fancy picking up where we left off the other night." I giggle, as the doors to the lift open in the lobby. I hate being girly but that's how she is, and I need people to think she was here.

"Sure, babe, then we can do that thing we were on about." I feel my cheeks getting hot, thinking about what he said earlier. I nod my head and grab his hand; his fingers slide in between mine. Our fingers interlocked is super strange. I've never held someone hand before. I usually drag people with me via their clothes, maybe even hair as I proved with Jasmine. I am not that into it, in all honesty, and don't even get me started on public displays of affection. I hate it, watching people kiss makes me want to hurl. I guess because I never have done PDA. I just don't like to see it.

We move out of the lobby; out of the corner of my eye I notice his eyes looking at the guy I spotted on the way in. I squeeze his hand, subtly letting him know that I'm aware, and that we can discuss it later. I can sense his tension as we pass the gentleman staring at us. The automatic doors open, and we are out; my mind still on the guy in the lobby. I haven't had a text message off any boss yet, but I only sent it a few moments ago. I walk over to the passenger door and open it for Luther. He gets in, and I take my seat behind the steering wheel.

"I'm assuming you saw the man with the paper?" I ask, my blue eyes holding his. She usually met Steadwell with her natural eyes, so I decided to put in my blue contacts so I looked as close to her as I could. His face scanning mine for any information I may have on him, but I don't have any.

"Yeah, I saw him. What do you think?"

"Look, Luther, he's not one of mine. I don't know who he belongs to. I don't think he belongs to any of the other mob bosses. But I am looking into it. There is also another man who was working in your house, and he isn't mine. I can only promise to try and keep you safe, and right now I can't, if you're not with the lads." I do want to keep him alive at least. I made a promise and I intend on keeping it. But right now, shit seems to be rising, and I can't stop what happens next. But I can make sure that my men are protected from the blast.

"I trust you, E, and I stand by your choices. I am scared if I don't, K and H will beat my ass." His chuckle fills the car, easing the tension slightly. I laugh with him as I pull away from his apartment block.

"Yeah, I think they would as well. I mean, of course they won't. God, we aren't animals." I laugh again. I know they would. Those two are as equally protective of me as I am of them; it's always been a quality of them that I have liked. I know I threatened H earlier, but that's been the only time he has ever questioned me. And from the look on his face, I think it will be his last. I've never seen him so pale or scared of me.

As I drive, Luther's eyes roam my face. I start to feel slightly uncomfortable. His penetrating gaze not leaving me. "You look beautiful when you laugh. You should do it more." This stops me dead in my tracks; my brain does not know how to respond.

"Thanks, I think." My cheeks heat up as I continue to drive. I take many side streets. I tap the screen on the centre console, loading the GPS. If I'm being honest, I'm just being petty.

"It's hilarious. Why are you writing a message with your car?" Luther chuckles, making my insides clench.

"I'm just being petty, honestly; I'm really hoping that your father is watching." We both laugh as I finish writing my message. Looking at the GPS, it reads, 'come get me.'

Pulling down an alley, I turn the car off and look at Luther. His eyes hold question and a trace of fear. It is sketchy around here, so I get why he is worried. "This is the most trust I will ever ask you to place in me, Luther. We are in your father's territory. I am going to be sending him a message, but this could get dangerous. I need you to call me Jasmine and follow my lead, then we may get out of this alive." Saying this, I grab two guns from my glove box. I hand him one and slide the other into my belt; Luther does the same.

"You do know how to use one, right?" I ask, the thought only just crossing my mind.

"Yeah, just about." His hands shake slightly as he grabs his door handle. I grab his left hand and squeeze it reassuringly. I know he went training with the lads the other day, but there is a dramatic difference between doing it in a controlled way and out in the world. I hope he doesn't have to kill anyone; it haunts you. It takes a strong person to take someone's life, and to be able to live with what happened. I can't see Luther being that person, and I hope I don't have to find out.

Nodding, I open my door and step out. Luther follows me shortly after. The minute we step into the alley, I throw Luther up the wall just behind him. I kiss him hard, and he replies with equal passion. "Fuck, Luther, I can't wait to finally kill your dad. He knows nothing about this or us. His face when we finally have it all, will be a picture." I smile, my American accent is on point, and it frightens me how much I actually sound like her.

"Yes, Jasmine, I know. He is so stupid; he will never know what we are doing."

"I know, baby, then we can have it all." I laugh hard at my comment before my lips claim his; his hands roaming my body. I keep waiting for somebody to disturb us, and lucky for me, I don't have to wait long as footsteps echo around the ally.

"Well, well, well. What do we have here, lads?" A bald man with full body tattoos states. His eyes are basically dead, not an ounce of light or life within them. I turn to look at him fully and notice he wasn't alone; two other men were just behind him. One couldn't be much older than eighteen, my heart would break but this is the world we live in. And a lot of the time it's not fair.

Giving them my sweetest smile, I pull away from Luther. "Hey, lads. So, what did I do to deserve to be graced by the presence of Steadwell seniors' men?"

"You are on our patch, and you have this deluded fantasy that you can take on our boss." The bloke stood in the middle of the other's states, amusement etched on his features. The young lad just stares at us; his face is full of fear and shock. Love how Steadwell's guys think they can act like they belong to a mob boss. Steadwell is just a wealthy jackass, nothing more. But if he wants to think like that, then who am I to stop him?

"Nothing delusional here, sweetie, but while I have you, could you do me a favour? Send a message to your boss for me."

A laugh erupted from the bald man. "You can send it yourself when we—" Before he could finish, I shoot him between the eyes; his body hits the floor with a loud thud.

"You were saying?" I smile at the other guys, their faces pale at my actions. Before the others could say anything, I shoot the middle guy in the chest, leaving the young lad the only one alive. With two bodies on the floor, I worry the young one will be with them soon, before I can get to him. He looks like he's going to pass out. He is deathly pale and physically shaking.

"What's your name, boy?" I ask, walking over to him.

"Tyler," his voice shaking as I move towards him.

"Well, you can send my message, Tyler. But I am sorry. You seem like a good kid." I slide a note into his pocket before putting my gun to his chest and pull the trigger. I watch as the life leaves his eyes. I catch his body as he falls.

Leaning down, I place his body on the floor. My hand goes to his face, and I close his eyes. It really is a shame, the world we live in. He seemed like a good kid, but sadly you always run the risk of dying for your choices.

"Did he have to die?" Luther asks as I walk deeper into the alley.

"Sadly, this is the world we live in. You always run the risk of dying for the side you choose. I wish he would have just stayed in school or done literally anything else. Oh well, we need to get moving." I continue to walk away from the car. I notice the confusion written all over his face, but he just follows. We walk for a minute or two, before my earpiece clicks on.

"E, two men are a couple of feet in front of you. There are two alleys coming up: one on the left, one on the right. They are in there." Marcus' voice flows into my ear. I signal for Luther to put his back against the right wall, while I take the left. Keeping close to the wall while moving forward, I can hear more footsteps than just ours; I lift my gun and aim at the alley in front of Luther. He follows my lead and raises his gun and copies my action.

"They are about six feet from the opening; be in your line of sight any second," Marcus states as we inch closer. I don't like to shoot in spaces like this. A bullet can ricochet and strike anyone, or you could miss all together. The space is tight, so the shot is even tighter.

A shot rings out catching me off guard. The man I'm aiming at comes into view. I raise my gun and shoot the bloke in his head. His body slams off the floor, I hear his head crack off the concrete. I watch as his blood begins to pool around him. Glancing at Luther, I don't see he's hurt; relief floods me.

However, that relief doesn't last long as the bloke in front me comes into view. Lifting my gun, I aim for his head. He also simultaneously lifts his towards Luther. We both must have pulled the trigger at the same time as two shots ring around us. The sound of both shots in this small space is deafening; my ears ring slightly with the power of the sound. He drops to the floor just like the other guy did, but a curse word or two grab my attention.

"Shit, Luther, you alright?" I rush over to him and look over him. I see blood trickling down his arm. "Fuck." I rip the bottom of my top off using the knife I keep in my sock. I move his left arm over his chest. I use my top as a sling. It should help somewhat with the bleeding. "Marcus, call Dan. Luther got shot."

"Christ, E, how did that happen?"

"Don't act like you can't see what happened. Just fucking get Graham here," I state while finishing patching up Luther as best I can; but with him flinching ever two seconds, it's difficult. "Luther, I know it hurts. But I can't do anything with you flinching every two seconds. Stay the hell still." I glare at him; he takes a breath to try and control himself.

Once he's all patched up, after much flinching and moaning on his part, I move us forward. It doesn't take long before we get to the end of the alley and see Graham waiting for us.

Opening the door, I let Luther into the car first. Then I move round the car and get in the opposite side. I keep glancing at Luther; he does look slightly pale. "Stop looking at me like that, E, or I swear you will get punished," Luther's voice turns me on with just that single sentence. I bite my bottom lip to stop a moan from escaping me. I've never been spoken to like that. "Are you trying to get punished, E? Are you trying to drive me crazy?" I put the divider up between us and Graham. I can do without him overhearing any of this.

While I lean forward, I feel something brush against my pussy through my jeans. It sends a shiver down my spine to my core, causing me to moan lightly. I go to sit down but Luther's hand doesn't move; his fingers keep grazing softly against my pussy. I can't sit down properly with his hand still between my legs. "Get on your fucking knees and suck my cock. Be a good girl, and I will reward you." I don't waste a second before getting on my knees in front of him.

I grab the top of his jeans and pop the button; Luther lifts his hips allowing me to pull them down easily. I watch him flinch slightly with his movements,

199

but he doesn't tell me to stop. His hard member springs free, allowing me to do as Luther commanded. I know it's the adrenaline making Luther horny, but I can't and won't deny him. I want him just as much as he wants me.

Gripping the base of his cock, I lower my head. Opening my mouth, I slide him all the way to the back of my throat. A deep moan spreads around the car. My core gets soaked just hearing him. I move my head up and down his shaft, taking him deeper each time. My right hand is gripping Luther's length while my left moves into my trousers. I moan as I suck Luther and stroke my clit.

"Get on the seat and take your trousers off." Taking my mouth off his cock, I undo my trousers and slide them down my legs. Climbing onto the seat, I go back to sucking Luther's cock; his right hand moved between my legs. I start to grind my hips against his hand, my orgasm racing towards me at an alarming speed. His fingers brush over my clit fast. I know he wants me to cum soon so he can do more things to me before he finishes himself.

"Cum on my hand, baby." The words mixed with the intense pleasure makes me finally fall into my climax. My head falls back as my orgasm rolls through me. Luther's cock leaves my mouth with an audible pop. My hand starts to move up and down Luther's cock while I ride out my climax. "Ride my cock, E, I want to fuck that tight pussy again." I don't waste another second. Crawling over, I straddle his lap. Luther lines his cock up with my entrance. I move myself down onto him. Our moans mingle together as Luther becomes fully embedded inside me.

I start to move my hips, riding Luther's cock. My head falls back as I keep moving my hips. I feel the car come to a stop, but I don't plan on doing the same. I start to move faster, chasing my orgasm. I ride Luther harder than before; both of my hands grab the back of the seat behind Luther's head. I feel as Luther begins to move beneath me; his hips fucking me faster, chasing his release. "Fuck, E, I'm going to come," Luther moans into my ear. I moan hard as my orgasm makes me clamp hard on his cock. "Oh God," Luther grunts as he spills his seed into me. I keep moving and riding the last of our orgasms out.

I lean my head on Luther's shoulder that isn't hurt as I catch my breath. "You guys done? Would hate for Luther to bleed to death," K's voice calls into my earpiece. The calm I felt a second ago is suddenly gone.

Luther chuckles as I pull away. "Come on, we should go," I state, putting my trousers back on.

"Wait, when did we get back?" Now it's my turn to chuckle. He should learn to feel and be aware of his surroundings.

"About five, maybe ten minutes ago. Come on, let's get you patched up." I open the door as Luther finishes putting himself away.

Moving into the house, I see everyone staring at us. Marcus is shaking his head at me. K has that same narrowing of his eyes at Luther again. H, A, Q and Aid all look like they are about to laugh at me. I don't pay them any mind and push past them. We walk into the living room. Spinning around, I let my eyes pass over each of the guys, trying to figure out what we are going to do next. Looking at Luther, I notice how pale he got; it's as if all the blood drained from his face very suddenly. His hand is gripping a dining room chair, but the way he is standing, I know it won't hold his weight. He seems to become extremely unsteady on his feet. Panic starts to seep into me as I continue to watch him.

Oh shit...my brain thinks as I watch Luther's eyes roll back into his head. Fuck, I definitely messed up. I watch Luther pass out. Now the car ride doesn't seem worth it.

Chapter 34

Oh, shit, I could see Luther going really pale and he was leaning on the back of the chair, darting over. I managed to catch his head before it fell back, and he hit the floor. "Christ, E, why didn't you bring him back quicker? Now he's out and we still have the problem of those two downstairs, and the fact that Steadwell is going to find his goons dead in that alley and you there. What are we going to do now?" Marcus says. He can be a tad of a drama queen. Rolling my eyes, I pick Luther up and lie him on the dining room table. H comes over to help me. I thank him before turning to Marcus.

"Right, first off, Dan is going to fix Luther up. A and Q, you will assist him with that. I know you love a little bit of gore. Marcus, you and Aid will keep your eye on Steadwell. Let me know of any developments and when he finds the bodies. Finally, K, H and I are going to pay Matthew a little visit and explain exactly what is going to happen to his precious little girlfriend. Now does that answer your question or are you going to continue acting like the world is about to end? Sometimes you are a complete drama queen."

With a huff, Marcus nods his head and walks back towards the chair he was sitting on when I left to get Luther. "But just so you know, none of this would have happened if you had brought him straight in, instead of doing unholy things in the car." Aid sits on the arm of the chair and nudge him with a chuckles.

"You're a fine one to talk. You're gay and you've killed people; you're also a mob boss. Can't get more unholy than that, pops," I state, causing Marcus to roll his eyes.

"Yes, yes, I know. Fine, I'm sorry for going off at you, E. It's just because I care." It's now my turn to roll my eyes.

"Yes, I know, and I'm sorry to go off at you and calling you a drama queen. Now shall we all get back to what's at hand? We all know what we are doing, right?" Everyone nods at me. Brilliant! Now that's sorted, I can have some more fun downstairs.

Turning to Dan, A and Q, I say, "Keep me updated on him, okay, and put him in my room when you're done."

"Yes, boss," A replies before I turn to leave with K and H in tow.

Once we are at the bottom of the stairs, K pats my shoulder. "Luther will be fine, you know. He's a fighter and has it bad for you. You seem happier, which is nice, especially after what you have been through." I turn to K; a look passes across his face, but I don't dwell on it for long.

"Yeah, I know he will be fine, and I am happy. He is a useful stress reliever at the moment. We have fun, and I don't have time for anything more. Also, you know I can't give him what he would want." That bit breaks my stone heart a little. This is another reason that I have never connected with a man because they will inevitably want children and sadly that is something I cannot provide. All the money I have and still I cannot conceive or carry my own. I know I could get a surrogate, but it wouldn't be the same. I wouldn't get to feel the kicks, and I wouldn't get to watch my stomach grow with my little one inside. It also still wouldn't be biologically mine. My eggs couldn't be saved. I guess that's another reason why I don't want a man. I would feel like I was disappointing them. Plus, if I had someone else do it, then that's another person to keep safe. Another life to watch over. And truth be told, I don't know if motherhood is really for me.

"I know, but that's a conversation with Luther for another day. Right now, we need to deal with these two," K states with a small smile. I can see the sadness he has always felt for me in his eyes, I know he feels guilt about what I went through. However, he has nothing to feel guilty about. He saved me and that's all that matters. That's all I care about. Yes, I feel sad, but I am alive and that's the main point. Children aren't the be-all-and-end-all for me. I have other things to keep me going and to give me a fulfilled life.

He's right though. We do have to deal with Matthew and Jasmine first. The rest can wait. It is imperative. We deal with this before anything else. Pushing my sadness away, I walk over and unlocks Matthew's door.

Walking inside, I watch as M slowly raises his head, defeat clear in his eyes. "Is it time for another beating now, E. Don't you think I've had enough?" Walking over, I crouch down in front of him, looking straight into his eyes.

"Yes, M, I think you're right. So this is what's going to happen. I've planted your girlfriend at the scene of killing Steadwell's men with Luther's help. She's on camera kissing Luther and telling him all about how she wants to kill him and tricked him into thinking that she was the person after him, blah, blah, blah. Then she guns down five men and escapes with Luther into the night. How sweet of her to take the heat off me for a while. I must go across the hall and thank her personally. Now the next part of my plan will kick into place because Steadwell will definitely fall for it, because I sound exactly like her, and when he realises the silly little girl he's been meeting, is the one trying to kill him, he will do my job for me."

Matthew starts crying hysterically. "God no, please, E, don't let him kill her. I can't live without her. She's my world. I love her." Smiling at him, I grab his face and make him look at me.

"Who said anything about you living, brother? You know what happens to those who cross me. You should have come to me with this. If you had, we would be having a vastly different conversation. But alas, you thought you knew better and look how that ended up. What we will do is let you watch the love of your life die right here in this cell. Then if you're, lucky we will allow you to join her. Sound good?" Matthew's eyes change from sorrow to hatred.

"You really are a cold-hearted bitch. No one will ever love you, E. No one. You were born alone, and you will die alone. Your parents had a lucky escape from you, you are pure evil, and I hope Steadwell gets to you first. Die, you evil bitch. Die alone. You will never be with him, and he will never feel the same as you." My heart breaks momentarily, knowing he is probably right. The look in Matthew's eye shows he meant everything he said; every word that left his tongue was his truth. But who said it was mine? Who said I would always be alone?

"It's cute how you think your measly little words will upset me, Matthew. I was resigned to the fact that I would die alone, from quite a young age. Your words have no effect on me, never have. You are a disgusting oxygen thief who should have died so many years ago. From your sick and twisted fetishes to your incompetence, you are worthless to me. Fuck, what am I saying? You were always worthless to me. But at least your death won't be. It will plug a hole which information is leaking," I state punching him in the face several times, taking my rage out on him.

Looking at K and H, I think they have heard enough from him and walk over to him. K grabs hold of his face and H cuts out his tongue. Matthew's screams bounce off every wall in the cell. Blood starts flowing from his mouth, pooling in his lap. If I were anyone else, I probably would have fainted, but I have seen worse, and done far graver things.

"Now you can't speak ill of E or anyone ever again. You always were a pathetic man, Mathew. You never were or would have ever been one of us." With that, H storms up to the door opens it and walks out.

"Maybe I will go drop this to your girl and see what she has to say. You are a waste of life, Mathew Cutten. Marcus was right. You should have stayed the hell away from E and all of us. You are no brother or friend of mine." After K had his say, he storms out of the room, leaving just Matthew and myself alone. Tears are falling from his eyes; blood is oozing out the side of his mouth.

I walk over and crouch down, bringing my face close to his. Venom in my voice as I speak to him, my eyes holding the hatred for him I've held all these years. "Matthew, I really never wanted it to come to this, but you left me no choice. Maybe one day you will understand. I have more than you to look after. More on the line than you ever realised, more than you ever will know. And you not falling in line like everyone else has put me here, brother or not, the team's safety comes first. It's nothing personal, it's just business. Sadly, Matthew, this is goodbye. Safe journey and all that." I can hear him try to yell something to me and I stand and walk away, but without his tongue, he just sounds all muffled. I pass one look back and shut the door on him, probably for good. I deadbolt it, locking away a part of my life that doesn't fit anymore.

Outside the cells, I see K and H looking at me. "Sorry, boss, but we couldn't have him talking like that about you. Family or not, he betrayed us and now he can't do that again," H says. I pat them both on the shoulders.

"I get it. If he spoke like that about any of you, I probably would have slit his throat, so I understand. Now why don't we play with his girlfriend for a little bit? I think we need the cheer up. Still have his tongue?" H holds it in the air like a trophy he won.

"Hell yes. Let's get this party started." They both skip over to her door and wait for me to open it. I know it sounds awful, but she has it coming.

Chapter 35

Opening her cell door, I noticed she has managed to shuffle her way to the back of her cell. After hearing us enter she looks up. Her eyes are puffy from all the crying, her face contorted in pain from the broken fingers and leg. Blood smeared down her face from the cut I gave her earlier. The blue in her eyes appears dull and lifeless, like all her hope and love has gone. She looks so pale, but I won't say it's because she hasn't eaten, because she's only been down here a few hours.

Maybe Matthew was right, and I was a heartless bitch. But this is nothing personal, it's just business. "What do you want now, E, to inflict more pain on me? To hurt me further, to scare me? Just do what you like to me. I don't care anymore. I just want to leave here with Matt. I want us to live our lives away from you, away from this shit show." K laughs at her and strolls over with H. They both stand before her, menacingly looking down at her.

"Well, isn't this sweet, H, Barbie wants to run away with her boyfriend and live happily ever after. How much would you love him knowing he could never talk to you again," K remarks, looking down at her.

"What have you monsters done?" she demands, suddenly getting a backbone; hats off to her. She has some guts.

"Nothing much, sweetheart, just this," H says with a laugh as he throws Matthew's tongue at her, eliciting a squeal from her. This makes them laugh even more. It was kind of malicious, but highly hysterical. My lip twitches as I watch on in silence, knowing this isn't the worst thing that could ever have happened to her.

"Yeah, H, I don't think he will be saying much to anyone these days, and I don't think he will be pleasuring you either. You two crossed us and no one crosses us. Didn't Matthew warn you about that? It's sad, really. But hey, chin up, sweetheart, at least he's still alive. Well, for now anyway," K follows.

"You psychos, how could you? He was a good man," she yells at us all.

"He was a coward, and a waste of oxygen. He deserves what he got for betraying the family. You're lucky he's not already dead. That's without the sick way he got with you. It disgusts me that he fucks you. It repulses me that he touches you, when you look like someone who is family. Worst part is, you're not even smart enough to know he used you. Matthew used not just your connection to Steadwell, but that disgusting pussy of yours. You were a toy in his game, and you will die for it. Well done, princess," H yells back. Meanwhile, I'm just stood there, leaning against the door behind me watching all this plan out. But what H states so matter-of-factly makes me think. He is right. She was a means to an end, clearly. He knew I would kill her for spilling information. He knew that he should have brought this to my attention. And alas, he didn't. She was disposable to him, at least in the beginning. Maybe on some deeper level, he does love her. But in the beginning, he used her. He found her and fucked his way into her life, corrupted her and now has left her for dead. And to think I thought he had already hit the scum level, but then he finds a whole new level of low. He ruined her life for nothing, and that's extremely sad. He knew what would happen to her if I found out, and if I knew she was speaking to Steadwell. Sadly, he didn't care enough; otherwise, she wouldn't be in this situation. Her life is now in my hands and ultimately, her blood also.

I suppose I will give him one piece of credit; this is the most diabolical thing he has ever done. The lengths he was prepared to go to, to achieve his naive little dreams; it is commendable. Such a shame he will never see them come to fruition, or get his lady love he is so desperately 'trying to save'. It's laughable, truly.

Then realisation hits me—she's already beaten up and broken—how would I play this to my advantage? Steadwell would know something is up when she has a broken leg and fingers.

K and H are still tormenting her when it hits me – car accident. What if we make it look like she was hit by a car being chased by his goons. Then he finds her unconscious on the floor with her broken bones and finishes her off for me. Perfect! Now I need to know what's happening with Steadwell, so we can get that plan sorted. "Lads, leave her alone; we are needed elsewhere. We can play again later." And with that, I open the door.

"You are the only coward here, E. You take what isn't yours and you kill for no reason. You are a murderer and an evil woman, and I can't wait to be rid of you," Jasmine yells at me as I begin to leave the room. Turning back to her, I look straight at her with no emotions.

"For your information, sweet pea, all death serves a purpose. As will yours. I may take what's not mine, but I never kill senselessly. And also, I can't wait to be rid of you either. Maybe that's why my parents didn't take you. They realised that you were the lesser of us. I had it all. The looks, the potential, the drive and what did that leave you with? A heart. Now if that's all I had, I wouldn't bother to live for long either. Goodbye Jasmine, enjoy your days. They are becoming fewer." And with that, we all leave and make our way upstairs.

A small part of me feels sorry for her. Within the space of a week, she went from her basic, mundane life to a living nightmare. Matthew destroyed her future. He killed anything she could have potentially had. I don't think I would have done what MaCall, one of the other mafia bosses, would have done. He found his brother a few years ago, from his father's multitude of affairs. And upon finding him he killed him, as he was terrified that he would come for his seat. Rumour has it that he never knew about MaCall, so he killed him senselessly. It created uproar within the families, no one knowing what to do. How to react to what happened. I, as lead council, had to call a meeting and sort them all out. It took weeks of meetings and hearings, weeks of listening to his bullshit justifications. Being at the top means I don't usually vote; I am more of the peace keeper. I make sure the bosses don't fight. And eventually, we all came to an agreement, but it wasn't without its issues.

Standing outside Jasmine's cell, I know I couldn't do that; I would have left her where she was. Maybe got her to move far away or done something to get her out of New York. But when Matthew came to me and presented her as a possible body double, I thought it wasn't a terrible idea. Little did I know, he had his own agenda. He had his own ideas, of which I had no idea. And now she must meet her end, and it's slightly saddening. But sadly, she made her choice, and she must die for that.

Chapter 36

Getting back to the living room, I notice that Luther and Dan are no longer in the room. A and Q are on the sofa watching some TV, and Marcus and Aid are watching the cameras from the alley in my office with the door open. Walking past them all, I make my way to my room.

Opening the door, I see Luther hooked up to an IV drip and a blood bag. He's also got a monitor on him, checking his heart rate.

"All is good, E; I got the bullet out with no complications, so he's all stitched and glued up. He's responding well to the blood I've given him and the IV fluid, so now we're just waiting for him to wake up. I'll leave him some pain killers on the side on my way out for when he wakes up.

"Any issues, call me straight away, okay?" I nod, turning to him.

"Thanks, Dan, don't know what I would do without you." And I do mean that. He's fixed me and the lads up far too many times.

"E, anytime. You have saved my ass more times than I can count. Stitching you and the guys up is the least I can do." And with a squeeze of my shoulder, he leaves, shutting the door behind him.

Walking over to Luther who is lying in the middle of my bed, I sit down and take his hand. I lift his bedding just to make sure there are no listening devices and grab my phone to scan the room. Once that is done and I'm satisfied that no one can hear me, not even Luther, I move some of his brown hair off his face.

His face has its colour back, sending a wave of relief through me. I don't love him, or think I am anywhere near that. I know on some strange level I care for him. I know I don't have normal feelings. How can you, when you have been raised as I have. With that being said, I know I have some sort of, not feelings but, compulsion to look after him. A deep seeded need to make sure he is okay, and when he was shot, I felt like I had let him down. I felt I had broken my promise.

I grab his hand and stroke small circles on the back; my eyes looking down at him. Taking in his peaceful state and watch as his steady rhythmic breathing makes his chest rise and fall. My eyes focusing on his breathing, keeping my own calm as I start to think about the past, and what's happening now. All of it eats away at me in this moment. The tidal wave of emotions and feelings envelop me.

My mouth starts moving before my brain can keep up; word vomiting all that I have held close to my heart for years. "You know I never wanted to be like this. I always thought when I was little, I would own a little cottage in a small Welsh village. I know, silly right, it would have a small amount of farm animals for me to tend to and a nice big back garden for my children to play in. I was always hoping for about five, maybe six children. I always wanted a big family. Going to see Mum and Dad on the holidays. Aunty Maggie and Uncle Rick would come by to see everyone if Mag's ever stopped drinking, that is." I chuckle to myself absentmindedly.

"I guess life had a different path for me. I always dreamed I would meet a man before I was 30. We would tend to the farm and the kids, plus take part in the local farmer's market. I would bake and he would sell plants, fruits and vegetable. You know all the normal things you find at one. We would be so in love and neither of us would ever be sad because we knew no matter what, we had the best life. We probably would have had a dog called Toby who we would take to the beach every summer with the kids and just enjoy our time together. But I guess that won't ever happen now, no man wants this. Why would they? I am a murderer. I am evil."

Looking down at Luther's hand, I run my fingers over the back of his. "Maybe when all this is over, I will move away; go find somewhere nice to live where people don't know me as the raging bitch E, and I can have a name. Maybe I can have a full name with a middle and surname, which would be nice. I could go straight and buy a nice house and get the dog that I wanted when I was a child, I could, you know, run away. But I would miss everyone: H, K, A, Q and the others. I would miss Marcus and Aid. And yes, I would miss you as well. For some strange reason, you make me feel normal. Like I can be a normal woman, not this trained hit-woman with a love for violence." Again I chuckle to myself.

"Thinking about it, I probably wouldn't do that. As nice as it would be, I can't see myself like that anymore. I'm not cut out to run a farm or live a mundane life. I love the hustle and bustle. Although I would love to go on

210

holiday, you know, somewhere hot and sunny. Somewhere where no one knows me and I can walk the streets like a normal person and do normal things, where no one knows me or cares who I am. Where I don't have to look over my shoulder all the time, wondering who is out there or have to carry a gun. Now that would be the life, Luther, maybe a month away to some hot remote island with the guys just chilling and being normal. I know Marcus is right. I can't do normal, but hey, why can't I try it? Why can't I try to be a girl for once?

"I could, you know. I even went shopping the other day and bought some clothes and shoes; that's no mean feat for me. I never go shopping. If I'm honest, I don't think I have ever been in a shop that isn't food in years. It always seemed like a waste of time, but if I'm honest, I enjoyed it. Well, apart from the woman at Christian Louboutin's who claimed I wasn't wealthy enough to shop there, but you know me, Luther, I showed her."

I laugh to myself; it was nice to get this off my chest. I've been holding these feelings in for years. Yes, the person I'm venting to may be unconscious but hey, I'm okay with that. The only other person I have said this to is sat out there, not thinking of me as anything other than his boss. I sigh. We have always been close, but only as friends and that's unlikely to change, no matter how much I wish it would.

"Anyways, I'll erm…leave you be, you know, to recover and all that. I'm just going to grab a shower real quick. Just hurry up and recover quickly, please." Leaning in, I whisper in his ear, "Please be okay, Luther, I erm…nevermind." Raising up, I brush his forehead again and drop a kiss on his head before getting up and walking around the bed and into the bathroom.

Closing the door, I take a breath; I feel lighter in a way to have said all that out loud. To actually let myself feel something for a short amount of time. I could have said so much more but I chose not to. Nearly twenty-five years of hidden feelings would take up a fucking long time to organise, and as always, I have shit to do.

Stripping out of my clothes, I move to the shower; my panties still smelling of what happened in the car. If I would have known he would pass out afterwards, I probably wouldn't have done anything. But, my God, he was hot, and Luther shooting that guy just made me all hot under the collar. I get it's the worst thing to be turned on over, but I have weird kinks, okay. Getting under the hot waterfall, I just think of what a roller coaster of a week this has been. I met three people: one I grew remarkably close to, to the point I would have taken that bullet for him if I was closer. A second one which was just a day of fun. And a third who betrayed me – I'm framing them so I can get some extra time and get Steadwell off my case for thirty seconds.

It's been crazy but I wouldn't change much of it – maybe bringing that bitch into my house, but other than that, probably not. As the hot water hits my skin, I feel some of my stresses washing away from me. The only thing I can't seem to stop stressing about is Luther and if he's okay. I care about him, a lot apparently. Even though I have only known him a week, he's wormed his way under my skin. It feels like everything I have done up until this point has been a way to get to him. Maybe this is the universe or fate or whatever you want to call it, telling me that there is someone out there for me. I mean, he's seen me kill. Maybe he's my consolation prize. He's killed for me and he's still here, and he's still trying with me. Either that, or I'm going soft. I'm not going soft. I know I'm not, but am I, for him?

Shaking that thought from my mind, I finish washing, being a little gentler around some of my sensitive areas. As much as he is amazing at pleasuring me, I am always a little uncomfortable after he has visited. It's a good kind of sore but still a little painful. After finishing up, I exit the shower and grab my white fluffy towel and hair towel to dry off. My bathroom isn't massive, but when I designed the house, I tried to maximise the space for what I needed. I have a small walk-in shower, sink and toilet, with all my cupboards built in. It works for just me and it's all white. My OCD is so bad that I put all my products in white bottles with black labels. Something about emptying them into tubs and bottles really chills me out. It's therapeutic. I know what you're thinking, super strange, and you're right, but I guess there are weirder things to enjoy doing.

Glancing at myself in the mirror, I noticed the bruises on my neck. Xander really did a good job with those. I know Luther isn't happy about them, and I guess in some small way, I understand why. I doubt I would be happy if he had been gone for two days and he came back with marks like this. When we were in here last, he did punish me for them. A strange feeling creeps up inside me, something I haven't felt in years. Guilt.

AGHH…why do we feel guilty? We weren't even serious with Luther. Wait, we still aren't serious with him, so why do we feel so bad…Maybe because we like him…oh shit! E, we are deep here, mate, so deep. Abort, abort mission. We need to leave Luther alone; we need to stop. My mind says, panic begins to mingle with my guilt. A war of feelings grips and dominates me. I can't be weak, and I have just watched how feelings make you vulnerable. But what if I don't want to? What if I like what's happening with him? I really need to think about all this, but first I need to think about what is going on with his dad.

Making my way into my bedroom with my fluffy towel wrapped around me, I notice he's still not awake. He's exactly the same as when I left him. Sighing, I drop my towel and walk to the door next to the bathroom. My small walk-in wardrobe is equipped with just a couple of draws for my underwear and a rail for my clothes to hang. It's nothing spectacular, but it does the job. Bending down slightly, I retrieve a set of pants, socks and a bra, all in black. I do have some in other colours, but usually all in dark and all quite simple. I also get a new top and jeans. As I'm doing up my bra, a low moan comes from behind me.

Glancing over my shoulder, I see Luther start to move while groaning. "Stay still. When I'm dressed, I will get you a drink and some painkillers," I say over my shoulder, grabbing my pants to put them on.

"Where am I?" Luther groans, still groggy and in pain.

"In my room. You passed out in the dining room. Dan sorted you out and brought you in here to recover."

Turning around, I noticed that Luther has moved his head to look at me. "E, did you catch me?" I smile; can't believe he noticed it was me.

"Yeah, I did. Couldn't have you hurting yourself. It's already my fault you passed out in the first place. I put my wants above your needs. I'm sorry, Luther." I look at the floor, that pesky feeling of guilt popping up inside me again.

"Hey, it's not all your fault. I was also part of that problem as well. I wouldn't change it. Anyway, I had the weirdest dream. I thought you was talking to me about owning a farm with kids and stuff. You didn't say anything like that, did you?" Oh, shit! He heard that. Blushing, I turn my head away and throw my top on.

"What? No. Why would I say anything like that? And you may have been part of what happened, but I should have known better. Now I'm off to get your pills." And with that, I hurry towards the door, only for Luther to stop me as the door opens.

"E, you're forgetting your jeans," he says with a smirk on his lips and a chuckle in his voice. Looking down, I notice I haven't put my socks or trousers on. Running back, I grab them, then basically jog out of the room. Why am I so embarrassed? So, I had dreams, so I told him about it. Maybe I'm embarrassed because I didn't want him to actually hear them or know about them.

213

Emerging into the living room still holding my trousers and socks, everyone stares at me. My hair is still in its hair towel, and I'm probably still looking red. "Everything alright, darling? You look a little frazzled," Aid asked with a kind smile. Everyone else has their jaws on the floor looking at me. I cough nervously. Glancing at K, I notice a look pass over his eyes. For a split second, I thought it was lust. I shake that thought away. Everyone was right, it would never happen.

"Yes, yes, I'm fine. I just erm…Luther is awake. Someone take him a drink and his meds. Also, he may be hungry so probably a sandwich. I'm going to sort something in the office and finish getting ready." And with that, I make my hasty escape.

Getting into the office, I slam the door behind me and lean back on it; trying to calm my rapid heartbeat. I've never felt like that, like I was a teenage girl running from her crush. It was beyond humiliating. God, I'm a mess right now. I feel guilty and conflicted. I'm confused about my feelings, and I am nervous about what's going to happen with the whole Jasmine situation. How did I get here? A week ago, I was a cold killer with no feelings. Now I'm confused and slightly scared of my feelings. I need to sort myself out. I need to work out what the hell I'm going to do. And most importantly, I need to get myself in check.

Chapter 37

Walking behind my desk, I open my computer. Logging in, I see an email. It's from Willow. I read it while continuing to get dressed.

Boss,

Here is what Steadwell told me. Firstly, he believes that girl you brought to your place that M is sleeping with, is actually the person he's been looking for. Secondly, he's coming for Luther. He knows that he's with her/you and he doesn't want him to get his hands on anything, so you need to keep him safe. And lastly, he bragged about someone telling him where you live. You aren't safe there. You need to move.

I've CC'd everyone in. They should be receiving this email as well.

Keep safe, boss.

Willow.

Fuck, okay. Hurrying out of the office, I look at everyone. I take a moment to look at all of them, each holding a spot in my heart. Not that I would ever say anything, I'm far too stubborn to. Each of my men have saved my life in more ways than one, each giving me a reason to continue. Every single one of them have been with me through hell and we are there again, and I know I need to keep them safe. I don't care what happens to me, they will all have letters from me upon my death. However, I care about what happens to them. They all see the panic in my eyes and know something is wrong, something has gone amiss. I waste no time giving out instructions for them all, knowing they will do everything without question, especially with the look I have right now.

"We are compromised. Get Luther and we are doing evac protocol 2. Let's move, people. This is not a drill," I say and move back into my office.

"E, what about those two down there?" K asks, pointing at the basement.

"Kill them and leave M there and move her to my room. Lie her on the bed and leave some of the files about Steadwell with her." With that, everyone nods and moves, collecting important items and files. I grab a memory stick, knowing it needs to be far away from this house. If this is found, I would be more than fucked. "Don't worry about anything else, let's just get the fuck out of here."

Walking to my bedroom, I open the door. Luther looks at me. "Sorry, Luther, no time to explain. We are evacuating the house. We are compromised. You need to get up. I'll help you." And with that, I remove the drip, blood bag and monitor cuff.

"Right, steady as you get up, okay? Really can't be hauling your ass with us," I say as I sit him up.

"E, what's going on?" Turning to Luther, I look at him.

"Listen, your dad has found me, which does work in our favour but also not. We need to get the fuck out. And as much as I would love a good old-fashioned gun fight, I have everyone's safety to think of. I'm going to get K in here to help move you. Oh, and FYI, if we don't make it out alive, just between me and you, yes, I used to dream of owning a farm. Happy now? We have to move." With a smile, he gets up.

"Maybe one day you will." I laugh at his comment.

"Probably not. I've changed a lot since then and I would miss the hustle and bustle of my life." Chuckling, he moves to swing his legs over the bed so he can start to walk. It would be a nice thought, to live a quiet life. But I know the truth, that once you are in this game, there is no way out. You can never hang up your gun and go straight. I have a territory, a company and all the things that come with that. So, leaving it all behind is a no go, unfortunately. But would I want to anyway? It's all I know, and I doubt I would be happy for long without this. Without the power and money.

"K, you done? So you can help Luther get moving?" I ask, tapping my earpiece to connect to everyone.

"Yeah, I'm on my way. Apparently Marcus has got into Steadwell's phone. He will be here within the hour." Shit, we really need to get moving.

K comes rushing in with a massive backpack on. "Yours is by the door, E. Which way are we going?" I look at K, with Luther still using my shoulder for support.

"Down and out. Has Willow made contact with H yet?" He just nods. Okay, this isn't good then.

"What?" I ask with a scowl. He looks away.

"She's hurt and H wants to go to her. He knows it's a trap. But he still wants to try and help her. He's waiting in the living room for you." Jesus! This is all I need.

"Grab Luther and move to the living room. We need to put everything in place before we leave." Just as I move to the door with K and Luther in tow, Marcus comes through the door with a dead Jasmine thrown over his shoulder. "Put her under the covers. Make it look like she's sleeping. He may not notice she's already damaged. Put the equipment in the wardrobe and throw clothes over it. Hopefully they won't notice. Then meet us in the living room." With a nod, Marcus follows my instructions.

Once in the living room, I see an impatient H pacing the room. "E, I need to help her. She is in trouble. Her email was hacked so they know we will be moving. Please let me go to her." I look at him. I know he loves her, but I need to keep them both alive. Grabbing my phone, I type to an old friend of mine, who coincidentally also hates Steadwell. He will collect Willow and wipe out all witnesses. No one but her lives. Looking back at H, I try to reassure him.

"B will know what to do, mate. He will get her to safety. I need you to trust me now more than ever." I glance around the room. "I mean that to all of you. Trust me completely, okay?" With a nod, they all agree.

"Right, you guys are going down and out. Go into my office and under my carpet is a door. Go down and follow it right to the end. A man will meet you there. He works for Del Stavo. He knows you are coming. Del Stavo owes me a huge favour, and I've called it in. I'll meet you there." They all look at me. Before any of them respond, I speak again. "And, boys, if anything happens to me, do me one favour, don't come for me. Leave and don't look back. You will all receive an envelope with instructions on what to do next. No matter what happens, just forget you ever met me. Live your lives and be happy, okay? Now go."

"No way, E, not without you. We have been together since you were eighteen. I didn't leave you then and I'm not leaving you now," K yells at me, hurt evident in his eyes. I knew he would defy me on this. I knew he would pitch a fit. But I also know he will do as he is told. This isn't the first time I have put them first. This isn't the first time I have thrown myself into the belly of the beast, all to keep him safe. And I sure as shit know it won't be my last either. I have always come back, and I pray to whatever is out there that I do this time as well.

"That's an order, K. Leave now. I will try my hardest to get to you. I promise you. I can't risk any of your lives over this. I started this so I will damn well finish it. Quickly, before it's too late."

Marcus walks up to me and wraps his arms around me. "You die, little bird, and I will bring you back and kill you myself, you understand? I taught you what to do. Use what you have. I love you, Emilia."

I whisper back, "I love you too, dad. Look after everyone for me. Make sure they are safe; someone is still leaking information, and I can't find who it is. Find them and finish them." Pulling away, he nods at me. Both sadness and determination flooding his eyes as he stares at me. Knowing he will do everything in his power to sort this, to keep everyone safe.

"Move, gents, we don't have all day."

"E, please come with us," Luther pleads to me, his eyes holding so much pain and sorrow. I walk up to him and grab his hand.

"I wish I could, but you guys always come first. My revenge has put you in danger, so I need to keep you safe. I will be back. This isn't the last time any of you will see me," I say with a smile. He smiles at me and then leans down and kisses my lips.

Once he releases me, I nudge him. "All of you now, else we are all dead." With that, everyone rushes into my office to escape. I follow them so I can seal the door once they are out. When all of them are in the tunnel, I turn to K, grabbing his arm.

"When you reach the man Del Stavo sends, tell him, 'The water is foggy tonight.' His reply should be 'Not as foggy as the sky this morning'. If that's not his reply, kill him." And with that, I shut and seal the door. I hope they meet the right man. Now I'm on my own and need to get the hell out of here, but how?

Chapter 38

The moment the door shuts, the perimeter detector starts to beep inside the house; they are closer than I thought. I walk into the living room and tap on the hidden button on the fireplace. The wall starts to descend into the floor, revealing a room none of my men knew about. It's full of weapons. Del Stavo told me to have something like this for just this occasion. It holds about fifteen guns and some grenades, even a few knives, swards and daggers.

Once I'm completely loaded up with weapons, I exit the room and put the wall back up. I glance at the CCTV camera, knowing that I don't want the lads to see this. I grab my phone and open the app to the cameras; I switch them off. A split second later, the front door blows open; causing me to stagger back slightly. Four men and a woman enter the room, guns aimed at me.

"Hey, Jasmine, you did well to get one over on our boss. But not well enough." The short chubby man says, holding his gun directly at me.

"Oh shoot, you got me." I chuckle before shooting him directly between the eyes. The others stare blankly at me. But its undeniable they are worried as I see the blood drain from their faces. The girl doesn't waste a second before she dives at me, the force sends me catapulting into the fire. My back burns and the pain takes my breath away for a second.

"That's it, bitch, you're so dead," I state before getting up and shooting the men next to her. They both hit the floor with a thud. I don't know if the shots are deadly, but right now, I don't care and if I'm honest, it doesn't matter too much.

I feel my side sting and hear a loud bang. A noise I am all too familiar with. Looking up, I see that bitch with her gun raised. Clearly, it was her that just shot me. I grunt at the pain as I feel blood run down my left side. I grab my knife and I jump on her; we fall to the floor my knife deeply embedded in her shoulder. She screams and thrashes beneath me.

"Is anyone else coming?" I demand, making her laugh at me.

"Like I would…" Before she can finish, I pull my knife from her shoulder and cut her pinkie finger off.

"I won't ask again. Are you the only four he sent?" She has tears in her eyes as she continues to yell and thrash around. I lose my patience and stab her in the stomach. I leave the knife impaling her because if I pull it out, she will most likely bleed to death before I get my answer.

"Fine, yes, he only sent us. We are the best he has." I grab her phone from her jacket pocket and open it. Her text messages confirm they are the only ones he sent.

"See, that wasn't so hard, darling."

"Wait, your voice is wrong. You're not Jasmine." The shock is evident on her face; it's an amusing sight.

"No, I'm not, but you won't be alive long enough to tell anyone. Jasmine was such a stupid girl, don't you think? Anyway, good luck wherever you end up." I chuckle as I remove the knife from her abdomen. Her eyes start to go vacant and blood pools on the floor beneath her. I move over to the other men and slit their throats, making sure they are dead. I could do without them getting up.

My burn and bullet wound are killing me, but sadly, I don't have two minutes to think about it. I walk into the basement to check that M is dead. Getting to his cell, I see him slumped over in his chair, but I don't see as much blood as I thought there would be.

Opening the door, I see his chest rise and fall, not too much though, but enough to know he's still alive. He looks weak and just clinging onto life. He lifts his head just enough to look at me. Clearly, there is no life left in his eyes. He looks at me like the world he once loved is gone, as if everything he held so dear is dead. The way his dark eyes have a haunted feel makes me sad momentarily. The paleness of his face allows the dark circles under his eyes to stand out. He looks so helpless, so pitiful. I sigh, grieving the loss of my brother for all of one second. Maybe he heard that bitch die, maybe he knows what's about to happen. I purse my lips together as I take one last look at his face, knowing full well that it will be the last time I will ever look at him. I know what has to happen. Doesn't mean I have to be happy about it. This is business, but doesn't mean it hurts any less.

"You have always known the rules in this world, Matthew. Why you felt the urge to go against me is beyond me, but now you must pay the price for your deception."

Tears roll down his cheeks. I walk over to him and grab his hair, forcing his head to come back and his eyes to meet mine. I stare at him my eyes and my face holds no emotion. "Sorry you couldn't put your ego aside and talk to me. Now you can join your precious girlfriend. Goodbye, brother." I raise my knife and plunge it into his heart; staring at him as I watch him take his last breath. That annoying guilty feeling edges its way back in, hating what I just did. I used to love Matthew, in my own unique way. That's probably why I couldn't leave him behind. Why even when I knew he was useless, I kept him around. And watching his life dissipate from him was hard. I never wanted this. I always thought he would die by someone else's hands, or a car accident with the way he drives. Sorrow and guilt fills me for a split second before I brush them away, unable to dwell on them.

As his head tries to fall forward in my grasp, I hold it while I remove the knife. Once the knife is out, I turn and walk away. I need Steadwell to believe that I am dead. I will miss this house, but I did buy a new one. I guess we could all move, but right now I need to get him off my case.

Making my way into my room, I see Jasmine lying in my bed. She is covered in my duvet and looks to just be sleeping. I move over to her and check her pulse. Thankfully, there isn't one, but I do notice there is a pool of blood starting to form. I bleed into the bed a little before grabbing a clean top and closing the bedroom door.

Getting back in my office, I make one last text message to a mob ally before setting my phone and house to self-destruct. This makes my phone and house explode and become engulfed in flames. I am sad to be losing this house, but it's needed. I can't have anyone finding anything here. Not that anyone could decipher my codes and encryptions on my files.

Opening the floor hatch that the men went down earlier, I start the timer for the self-destruct. I am going to have to make a hasty escape, and with my side and back, it's going to be a killer. I give myself six minutes, praying it's long enough.

Getting in the tunnel, I seal the door and run; pain coursing through me with each agonising step I take. My side all but screaming at me, but I can do without being anywhere near this place when it goes up.

After running down the tunnel for a few minutes, the whole place shakes. Small rocks and debris falls around me. For a moment, I miss a step, slamming into the wall, my burn hitting the sharp wall, causing me to curse and yell.

Regaining my footing, I run harder, knowing that that was just the first round of explosions. The next one will cause the house to completely collapse, then the fire will start destroying everything. I hope and pray that I will make it out, and that my contact is waiting for me.

Getting to the end of the tunnel, I see a silhouette standing there waiting for me. I keep running just in case the tunnel comes in, which isn't a bad idea but maybe when I'm not inside it. Rocks continue to fall around me; the sound of them hitting the stone floor echoes around me. With each second that passes, the stones begin to fall harder, making me all too aware that I don't have long. Dust and debris clouds my view slightly, making breathing slightly harder. But I cannot stop, else this tunnel will stop me for good.

As I make it to the exit, the last explosion erupts behind me. The shaking causes me to stumble, but I just about manage to stay standing. I watch as the entire tunnel collapses. A huge dust cloud consumes the space around me. I cough and wave my hand in the air, hoping to clear it a little. I watch as the realisation that my old life is gone hits me. My house, the tunnel, everything is gone. I can see a huge bellowing of smoke rising from where my house once stood. My entire life just went up in flames, and I feel a small sense of dread at my next moves. A cough pulls me from my thoughts.

"Hello, E, do we always have to meet under such dramatic circumstances?" Zayne Stark states as I finally make it out to him.

Once I have caught my breath, I chuckle. "I know, shit hit the fan, mate. Tell no one you have me, but I do need some help. So, I am calling in that favour. I need medical attention and somewhere to stay for a few days." I glance up at him, his face holding a big smile.

"Of course, I will get medics to the house and you some food ready. Let's go before someone sees you." I nod and start walking with him. I start to feel dizzy; I grab hold of Zayne's arm to steady myself. "E, are you okay?" My vision starts to come in and out of focus. It's so bad, I can't keep standing.

"If I die, Zayne, I will come back and haunt you." I chuckle as darkness starts to consume me. I feel my legs buckle beneath me. A strong set of arms wrap around me as my vison starts to dissipate.

"I would never let that happen; you are the only other boss I trust." I laugh before I finally succumb to the black abyss. I hope that the lads are okay.

Chapter 39

My eyes feel super heavy. My limbs also feel extremely sore. My back and side hurt like a bitch, and I'm not sure that's going to change any time soon. Groaning, I open my eyes. I'm lying on a queen size bed. The walls are dark blue, and the floor and furniture are a lovely oak, making the room brighter. The curtains are drawn, so it must be either late in the evening or early in the morning. I don't know how long I have laid here, but I could really do with a pee. I try to sit up, but the pain in my side makes that difficult. So I lie back down again, wishfully hoping the pain goes away soon.

"Hey, E, welcome back. You are still hooked up to the blood and IV drip, so try to stay still. Doctors want you to stay until you finish the bags," Zayne's voice calls from the dark blue sofa not too far from the foot of the bed. The fire is on, but it's making me too hot; I go to pull the duvet down, but realise I have no top on. Looking further down, I see I do have a big bandage wrapped around my middle, coming from my hip to just under my breasts.

"Can I have a top? I need to take my covers off. I'm really warm." I look at Zayne, who nods with a smile. Standing up, he grabs me a top and places it next to me. I then try to sit up again, gritting my teeth through the pain. I pull out the two needles in each of my arms and slide the top on.

"I told you to leave them in." I just shrug. Do I look like I care right now?

"When have I ever listened to the doctors, Zayne?" I chuckle. Everyone who knows me is aware of my inability to do as I am told. Zayne rolls his eyes as a knock comes from the door. A moment later, Tina, Zayne's wife, pops her head round the door. Her grey eyes complete her smile as she looks at me, her long platinum hair hangs around her.

"E, glad you're okay, sweet pea. Was worried there for a hot minute." I chuckle while trying to stand up. My legs feel a little weak, but I gain my balance quickly.

"You know, Tina, you don't have to worry about me, tough as old boots. Plus, I'm too stubborn to die." We all laugh; the pitter patter of tiny feet grabs my attention.

"Auntie, E." Aurora, their six-year-old daughter screams before running and jumping into my arms. She does this before any of us have time to react. For such a tiny dot, she nearly rugby tackles me to the ground. I hold my breath for a second to let the pain pass, but I don't care the moment I see her beautiful little blue-grey eyes and that adorable smile of hers.

"Hello, baby girl. I missed you," I say, cuddling her to my chest. Her giggles fill the room. My heart clenches slightly but I love this little peanut so much. She may be the daughter of a mafia boss, but she is the sweetest little girl I've ever met.

"I'm not a baby. I'm six, Auntie."

"But you will always be a baby girl to me, peanut. Anyway, I love you. Have you been a good girl for your mummy and daddy while I've been away?" Her smile is contagious, causing me to smile with her. Her blue-grey eyes sparkle, and her freckles and blond hair make her the prettiest peanut ever.

"Yes, she has, but you know, Auntie E is hurt. So, you can't be jumping and getting excited," Zayne states while coming over and taking Aurora off me. Her face falls, and a pout forms on her lips.

She is the only person in the world who has me wrapped around their little finger. "Peanut, I'm hungry. Why don't you come with me, you can tell me all about school and your friends?" Rory squeals and tries to wiggle out of Zayne's grasp. I laugh slightly as I watch her kick Zayne hard in the side. A small grunt leaves his lips as he sets peanut down on the floor. Once he has put her down, she runs from the room and down to the kitchen. Tina, Zayne and I all chuckle and follow her.

"Big bad E is wrapped around my daughters' little finger." I look at him and shrug.

"What can I say? I can't say no to that adorable face. But I do need you to do something for me. I want to call a meeting of the treaty. My men are currently with Del Stavo and don't know if I'm alive. Also, I'm hoping most will help keep Steadwell occupied."

"Sure, I will call them." Zayne nods.

"Call Marcus as well. Him and the lads should come." We make it down to the kitchen and Zayne goes off to call the other bosses. Tina and I sit with Rory and eat.

"Tina, how long was I asleep?"

"Twenty-eight hours roughly, so you have been out a while. Also, it's Wednesday. What are you going to do today?" I haven't thought too much about what I'm going to do, but I need to be with the lads.

"I'm probably going to chill here today, then tomorrow I will go home with the lads. Rory is too important, and I am in hot water. I don't want to be here too long. If anyone finds out I'm alive, they could come here. I wouldn't forgive myself if anything happened to peanut."

Tina looks at me with understanding and appreciation. "You are always welcome here. You're family and have done so much for us. But I do appreciate you putting Rory first. You're her godmother and we would help in any way we can. Thank you." I put my hand on Tina's and smile at her. She smiles and nods back.

We start to eat breakfast; I didn't realise how much I needed food or how hungry I was until I started eating. I devoured all my food and Sonia the chef made me two pots of tea. After about thirty minutes, Zayne walks in and joins us at the table. He bends down and kisses Tina and then Rory. "Hey, where is mine?" I tap my cheek with a mischievous glint in my eye. I always love winding him up.

Zayne's blue eyes flicker as he laughs at me, Tina shakes her head at me with a smile on her face. "K would only get jealous." I look down and cough with awkwardness. I wish he would, but he hasn't ever gotten jealous. Even with me fucking Luther, so why would he now?

"Wait, you two still aren't together yet?" I just shake my head; my heart sinks slightly. I still wish I could have the man who stole my heart and held it for fifteen years. But I shouldn't hold onto a love so hard, especially when I doubt it will ever happen; but I can't seem to let it go either. K will never give me my heart back, but do I really want it back? It's so broken, pain filled and undesirable, wouldn't having it back just hurt more? They say it's better to have loved and lost, then to never have loved at all. But I never lost my love. I just gave it to someone who doesn't reciprocate it. Shoving the feelings down to the depths of my soul where they have always lay, I decide to move the conversation on.

"So?" I raise my eyebrow, hoping Zayne will speak about something else. God, anything else would be better than K and my feelings.

"Anyway, I've told everyone to meet at the warehouse at two tomorrow. You sure you want to do this?" A look of concern passes across his face.

"Yes, I need to get back to the lads. But most importantly, I need to keep peanut safe. And right now, I can't promise safety. I can't and won't risk anything happening to her. Del Stavo's kids are all grown up, so being there isn't as bad." Zayne nods, but he still has a sullen look. "When this has passed, I will spend time with Rory, and be more present like before." This brings a small smile to his face. Rory has been colouring for the past twenty minutes; her little face so full of concentration.

We sat for a while and chatted; Rory telling me about her time at school and what she did with her friends. I laugh and enjoy my time with her. One day, I plan on having kids. I need someone to take over my empire and maybe I would be a good mum. I mean I love Rory and looking after her. Maybe that is something I can look into when my life is less complicated and more stable. Who knows what the future holds?

Chapter 40

"E, it's one-thirty. We should get going." Zayne pokes his head around the door. I had spent the past day and a half with Rory and trying to figure out my next move. I was awake most of the night, my mind consumed with thoughts of what to do. Plus, the pain was terrible, but Rory helped in the day to keep my mind off it. Rory looks up at me, sadness evident in her little eyes.

"You're coming back aren't you, Auntie E?"

"Not this time peanut. I'm in some trouble and I need to keep my special baby girl safe. But when this is all over, you, daddy, mummy and I will go out. Anywhere you want." She smiles and comes to hug me; her arms go around my neck. For a six-year-old, she is damn strong.

Tina walks in and tries to pull Rory off me. I chuckle as she fights to stay in my arms. "Okay, peanut, you can stay with me until Daddy and I leave, then you have to go with Mummy. Alright?" She nods. I stand up and put her on my left hip trying to not have her on my burn. She clings to me like a baby monkey to its mother, I do hate leaving her. Since the moment she was born, I knew I would die for her. I would burn the world to the ground just to keep her safe. And the trust and love she gives me; it melts my long dead heart.

When peanut was born and I met her for the first time, she gripped my thumb in her tiny hands. And in that moment, I knew I would never say no to her. I was definitely under her thumb. Her little blue-grey eyes looked at me and I had a new person to protect, someone else whose life meant more than my own. But if anything happened, I am one hundred percent using her father as a human meat shield; I wouldn't think twice about it. But don't tell Zayne that, he doesn't like knowing he is less important. His ego is far too fragile.

Once we are downstairs, I pass Rory back to Tina and give her a kiss on the forehead, before moving to the car. I wave at Tina and Rory as we pull away. Rory's tiny little hand flailing about as she watches us go. A lone tear leaves my eye, a sinking feeling envelops me thinking this could be the last time I see her.

Zayne and I are in one car with two of his men in the front. Four of Zayne's men are in the second car behind us.

"I don't know how this is going to go, E, not all the men are happy I called this meeting."

"I don't fucking care; I am the lead council member. And it is my right to call meetings whenever there is conflict. If they wish to go against me, then they are in violation of our laws. Laws in which their ancestors wrote, and they are all so insistent we uphold. You and I both know the price of breaking our laws. Not to mention each and every fucker there is petrified of me. I was called Reaper before I was a boss for a reason. A reason they all know far too well." I know it's true. I worked for all the mob bosses before I created my company. And I still do the odd jobs for them now, so they would hate to lose my help. Being the lead councillor has so many responsibilities. My main one is that I keep the peace between all the bosses. I was elected a few years ago and none of them would want to cross me. I have too much standing for them to; also, I doubt any of them are stupid enough.

"You're right, but just so you know, I am with you all the way, not because I am scared. I mean I am low-key terrified of you, but that's not the point." We both laugh before he continues. "But because you have saved my ass too many times, so naturally, I will stand with you even if no one else does." I appreciate what he is saying. I have helped him out a lot. I have done jobs his men couldn't, and I spent time training them and teaching them to be better in combat and shooting.

After about an hour, we pull up to a huge container yard. This is on neutral land, so we can't, by mafia law, fight here. So, we have to remain civil with each other, and the containers means that no one who isn't in the alliance can find us. We all have our own unit to get to the meeting point; it's underground. Sometimes, I feel like we use too many movie clichés. I chuckle. This causing Zayne and the driver to look at me with raised eyebrows.

"What? Sometimes I think we have taken on too many books and movie clichés. We meet in underground bunkers; we use riddles, so we know who's calling, and the best one is code names. It just makes me laugh. Maybe we should stop watching so many movies and get some original thoughts for once." Zayne sniggers as we pull up to the container we use to get to the meeting.

Walking into the pitch-black container, one of Zayne's men bends down and opens the floor panel; a dim light starts to illuminate the darkness around us. If you have never been before, this can seem very ominous and a little unnerving. We descend the steps into the meeting room. I am a little slower with all the pain. Luckily, it's not as bad as yesterday, but I am still not back to full health either.

As we get down, I can hear arguing about Luther being here. Zayne raises his eyebrow at me. I just shrug.

"Why is that son of a bitch's offspring here? He could go against us; he can't be trusted." I hear one of the bosses yells over all the murmurs.

"He is here because of me, so you better respect my choice. You would hate to go against me, Lucius," I state, walking into the meeting room. All voices stop dead, and all eyes move to me. I know my home going up in flames was all over the news. I watched them dig out M and Jessica bodies. I've been MIA for nearly three days, so people would naturally think it's me. Looking around, I see everyone but Zayne is shocked to see me standing here. The room is in pin-drop silence; no one saying anything, just staring at me, mouths agape.

"E, you're alive." Relief flashes across K's face. I know he was scared I was dead, but we have both been in worse situations.

"Did you doubt me, K?" I smirk. I can't believe he underestimated me.

"Of course not. But we never saw you leave on the CCTV." I just roll my eyes and move into the middle of the room to address each of the bosses. They all watch me move slowly across the room. My right hand clutching my side, slightly hoping the pressure will ease some of the pain. And FYI, it doesn't.

Once I'm in the centre of the room, I sit on the table and look at each man in here. I flinch as I hoist myself onto it. I should have tortured her ass a bit before I killed her for this. I fucking hate being hurt; it's highly inconvenient.

"So Steadwell sent people to kill me. This is a violation of laws we have had written for years. Seventeen generations have stood here, and never once has an outsider tried to threaten our integral peace, which we hold so dear. Steadwell is a loose cannon, a snake in our grass. We need to eliminate him; we need to set an example. As the lead council, I ask you all to consider standing with me, standing against someone who is a threat to all we stand for. I ask you to really think about his motives, because it might be me today he is after. But what is to stop him coming after all of us? What is to stop him from trying to kill your heirs? Your wives, your family. And what is to stop others from thinking the same. We have spent years keeping the peace, let's not allow someone to try and take that from us." The room explodes with questions and people shouting over each other. I can't hear anything over the noise. It's impossible. I knew they would all be outraged over this; they hate anything disturbing the status quo. "Now who stands with me?"

"Stark house will stand with you." Zayne winks at me, a look passes over K and Luther for a moment. It did not go amiss when he said house not family. He has always said I am part of his house. Zayne is a forward-thinking man, who doesn't give two shits about our old traditions. He has always believed we need to move into the twenty-first century and doesn't believe in 'inbreeding' – his words, not mine. Basically, family makes it sound weird to him. Also, he doesn't believe in marriage alliances, like most of the others do.

"Trudo family will stand with you. We cannot let this pass; he is poison in our well. My forefathers would not have let this continue, and neither will I." Lucius nods, his jet-black hair with wisps of grey scattered through it, is slicked back. He is wearing a crisp black suit with white pin stripes, and he has fine wrinkles around his bright blue eyes; looking like a classic mob boss – told you, too many movie clichés.

One by one, all the companies fall in line and agree to work together, and I get why they call me the mafia queen now. They will always follow me and stand by me; it's satisfying to know I am the ultimate boss.

"Brilliant. I will be in touch soon." I get off the table, flinching again slightly. Zayne comes over to help me. Turning to look at him, I smile. "Look after peanut, I will come by as soon as it's safe."

"Of course, E, Rory will be excited when you get back." We do a half hug, and he pecks my cheek. We say our goodbyes before turning to my men and Del Stavo. They all look at me as I walk over, concern written plainly across their faces.

"Hey, Del, great to see you again. You mind if we crash at your place for a while longer?"

"That's fine, princess, glad to see you're not dead. You had us all worried." I roll my eyes.

"I've been having that effect on people lately," I state and move towards the stairs to Del's car. Halfway up the stairs, I clutch my side tightly. Since I woke up this morning, I have been in pain, but now I know I've split my stitches. A hand rests on my other side, taking me by surprise. Looking back, I see K. I watch his face contort with worry and concern.

"E, what's wrong?"

"Just that stupid bitch was a shit shot, but I think my stitches have popped as I feel the blood running down my side. Don't worry, let's go." I suck in a deep breath before continuing up the steps. A hand touches my burn and I yelp. A tear slips down my cheek. I had tried to keep Rory off my burn and stitches all morning, but two minutes with these guys and they have me in pain.

"E, you sure you are okay?" H asks, his eyes roaming over me, clearly, he is trying to assess the damage.

"Yes, now everyone get the fuck in the car," I grunt. "And don't fucking touch me." No one says anything. They just follow. I slowly make my way up the stairs, my pain intensifying with each minute movement I make. My breathing becoming heavier as I climb the stairs, but I try to not show weakness.

I get to the car and get straight in. If I'm honest, it's more like a van than a car. K sits next to me on the right and Luther sits on my left. I lean forward slightly so my back doesn't touch anything as my burn is starting to hurt badly again. "Marcus, call Dan. I need stitching and a burn wound sorting."

While we are driving along, we hit a bump in the road. It makes me jolt and pain shoots through me. I yelp in pain, clutching my side. "Little bird, what happened to you?" Aid asks, grabbing my hand.

"Just a burn from the fireplace and a small bullet wound. If that bitch wasn't dead, I would kill her again." My head starts to spin, maybe the bleeding is worse than I thought. Once I lift my top, I see quite a bit of blood running down my side. My head starts to feel heavy, and I slump to my right. I fall onto K and his arms wrap around me; I feel the darkness consume me before I completely pass out.

Chapter 41

Waking up, I feel very warm and my side is killing me. I also notice that I could hear a strong heartbeat under my ear. Moving my head, I look up and notice I was lying on Luther. I strangely felt content. I also felt safe for a second like everything outside of the bedroom door doesn't exist or matter. I didn't have a phone or communication with any of my team. I just wanted to make sure that all of them were okay. I think I am starting to care for him, like I care for the other men; nothing more, as I'm not capable of that.

"Hey, you okay?" his low husky voice called from above my head; looking into his eyes, I smile.

"Yeah, I'm okay, just in pain. How are you?" I ask, rubbing his shoulder.

"Yeah, a little sore as well, maybe we should go downstairs; it's probably close to dinner time," he says while glancing at the clock.

"It's a bit late to be honest, but I think chef will still cook for us," I say after also looking at the clock.

"You're right. But first," Luther's lips descend onto mine, the kiss slow and passionate, like all the feelings he wants to say are being portrayed through his lips. My heart rate increases with each movement of his soft lips, my hands resting on his chest. A warm feeling penetrates me as I realise I kind of missed him. Breaking the kiss, he looks down at me. "I've been wanting to do that since I knew you were alive." He's not the only one. I've been thinking about him since I sent him away.

"You aren't the only one." I shyly smile at him.

"Good, because there is so much I want to do with you and to you. Also, I do have one thing I want to say. Now I don't expect a reply or you to feel the same way, but I need to say it. I love you, E, I would kill again for you. I would tear this world apart for you." I place a finger on his lips.

"I care for you as well, but I don't want you to kill for me, but I really appreciate the sentiment." And saying my feelings aloud is weird, but definitely true.

"Bit late for that, baby. Anyway, let's go get some food," he says with a chuckle. What does he mean a bit late? Has he killed again?

"What do you mean by that? What's happened in literally three days?" He chuckles again.

"Don't worry, I'm sure Marcus will tell you." And with that, he grabs some clean clothes that Stavo has provided and gets dressed. What the fuck has happened? What's changed? Looks like someone has been in while we were asleep because there is clothes here for me as well. I hate that people just walk into your room in this place, and I remember that part from last time I stopped here.

"Oh, quick question. Did you really kill someone with your favourite toothbrush?" What! How does he know?

"Yes, why you ask?" I really don't understand what's happening. Did I actually die, and now I'm in hell?

"Oh K, H and Marcus where having a 'E killed better in front of me' war. Was fun and interesting; was nice to hear more about my girlfriend." My jaw hung open; I care for him but am I ready to be his girlfriend? Panic starts to set in. *NO...oh no no no no no*...my mind just repeating the same word, over and over. This is what I didn't want to happen. He can't love me or want something other than sex. It could ruin everything, fucking hell.

"Did you just call me your girlfriend?" He laughs, his face full of humour. Mine however, hold nothing but complete anxiousness and terror. This cannot be happening.

"Hell yes, I did, do you have a problem with that?" He strolled towards me with a challenging look in his eye, not perturbed by my state of pure panic.

"I don't know if I am quite ready for that yet." I state with a sad look in my eye. He stood inches from me, his face holding nothing but love.

"That's fine. I can wait as long as you need." His hands come up to cup my face. This does fuck all to quell the rush of emotions that rush through me. "Just so you know, I'm not going to fuck you later; I'm going to make love to you. I'm going to take it nice and slow; I'm going to have you screaming my name for me to the whole house." His words sent shivers directly to my core; my legs threatened to buckle at his words.

"Hmmm, how do you affect me so much? Do I still have to call you Sir when you make love to me?" I ask, closing the gap between us.

"Yes, in private, I am Sir to you. I will follow you in everyday life, but in bed, you will follow me and do everything I say." I grab his collar and pull his lips back to mine, sealing them in a hot passionate kiss. The thought of us having a title scares the shit out of me, but I cannot deny I have some form of infatuation with this man. I just want fun for now, no strings. At least now, while my life is in complete shambles.

Pulling away, I look into his eyes, "Well, we best go downstairs, sir, I'm starving. And yes, for both food and you." He just chuckles and grabs my hand.

"Let's go then, babe. I best feed the queen." And with that, we head downstairs, I won't lie, it's weird holding someone's hand. I haven't held one since I was a child holding my dad's hand to cross the road. The feeling of our interlocked fingers seems to enhance how I was feeling earlier. A cold sweat consumes me the closer we get to the dining room. I take a couple of controlled breaths to try and ease my beating heart. I don't know why I suddenly can't control my feelings. I always knew it might come to this; I've seen it many times. I guess I was just too stupid to see, or maybe hopeful it wouldn't. It was all meant to be fun, stress relieving, but now. Now it's all so much more, to him anyway, and I don't know if I have it in me to say no. To break his heart.

Getting downstairs, we were still holding hands. When we reached the dining room, I tried to drop his hand but Luther just looked at me.

"They all know I love you, and they all know that you feel somewhat similar. So, I don't think we need to bother hiding it from them." I'm shocked again.

"How?" He just chuckled.

"I sort of got angry and yelled it at them and that I would do anything I could to protect you. It's a long story. I'm sure everyone will be happy to share with you." God, I'm just full of questions today. How can so much change in a week?

Chapter 42

Walking in, all eyes descend on us, smiles broke out on everyone's faces except K's. Something flickers across his face, but I don't register what it is. "Fucking hell, someone catch me up, please. This one is speaking in riddles," I say, nudging Luther. "Q isn't here, so I am assuming that he is my mole. So where is he? And why are you warring over who I killed better?" Everyone including Stavo laughs hard at me. What is happening?

"Little bird, you better sit down. It's going to be a long story," Aid says with a smile. Luther and I grab a seat at the dining room table. I look at everyone. Everyone apart from K is smiling. He just sits there, glaring daggers at Luther. I managed to unlock our hands, much to my relief. I know I am over thinking, the same as when I found out about M and Jasmine. But I can't do this, and I know that for a fact. I can never love him; I can only care. I knew going into this I was using him, playing him like a puppet to get what I want. And yes, okay, he got under my skin a little bit. Just, nowhere near as much as I got under his apparently. The thought of us being officially together, it makes me want to run. I know, I'm dramatic, no need to tell me.

But watching K narrow his eyes at Luther, it gives me a weird feeling. Like he doesn't trust him or something. He is the only one who seems to have taken a dislike to him. It's like X all over again. I just pray he doesn't fight him over whatever is going through his mind. I'm not ready to be in the middle of another one of K's smack downs. I turn my attention away from him; it's not worth prying into it yet.

"Well, if it's going to be a long story, can I have something to eat while I'm here? I won't lie, I'm starving and haven't eaten since breakfast at Zayne's." Stavo just clicked his fingers and chef came running in.

"E, pleased to see you again. Yes, sir, what can I do for you?" her pleasant voice spoke.

"E and Luther need food, please." Nodding, she ran back to the kitchen.

236

"Well, someone better start talking. I'm getting impatient." Looking at Luther, he just smiles. K looks at me and starts to explain everything.

"Well, when we all thought you were dead, Luther came barging in here after going for a think and said that he was going to kill his dad and stuff. Then Marcus said 'well kill Q then.' Marcus started telling us what happened, but Luther didn't give two shits what he did and just shot him straight between the eyes. Then went into a big speech about how you started something, and he was going to finish it. Won't lie, it was cool to watch, but also, we were all pissed that Q betrayed us." Luther did that? Well, that was unexpected.

"That's why you said it was too late." Looking at Luther, he just smiles. His brown eyes holding a glint of mischief; my core pulsating with need at the thought. Told you all, I have weird kinks.

"What can I say? I was angry, and he deserved it." He leans close to my ear. "And you love it, don't deny it, baby. It turns you on that I did it." And he's right, I know I'm so strange and probably wrong for feeling this, but each to their own.

Looking at him, I just nod. "Right, now, I'm sort of caught up on all the shit that's happened here. And we will be coming back to the whole 'who I killed better', and just so you know, no one has seen my best kill. I will be going for a shower after I have eaten and get Dan here to fix my stitches." As I say that, chef brings in my food. I would remember her name but Stavo fires all his workers so often, I can't keep up. "Erm…Thanks," I reply as she places food in front of me and Luther. I have chicken and salad. I guess it will do, but I would have loved a KFC or something deep fried and smothered in chocolate.

As I start to eat, I realised how hungry I am. Usually I'm conscious about how I eat when people are around, but right now, I don't care. Everyone is staring at me. "What?" I ask with my mouth full of food, I know lady like or what. Everyone just smiles like I'm some sort of show for their entertainment.

"You are eating like an animal, my dear," Stavo says with a slight chuckle to his voice.

"You would too, if you had been shot, thrown into a fire, killed two of your family members and dealt with a very hyper six-year-old for twenty-four hours. You would be hungry too," I reply. Luther just laughs at me; I love hearing his laugh. It puts a strange feeling in my chest. The same one I had when I watched him leave my house, but it's a good feeling. I always want to protect all my men, but I want to protect him more, mainly because his mother asked me to. That's what I keep telling myself, anyway.

We chatted for a while. The guys fill me in on many things and how they are finding it living with Del Stavo. But then a smell hits me and I remember that's me. I haven't washed since the attack, so I know I must smell like a sewer. "Now if you will excuse me, I stink like a sewage pipe. My room is still as I like it, right?" I ask Del Stavo.

"Of course, E, I knew you would need it at some point." I just nod.

"Call Dan. I will be down in a bit." I don't even talk to Luther as I get up. I just pull his shirt and practically pull him out of his chair. Once in the hall, I let go of his shirt and make my way upstairs, turning left instead of right.

"Where are we going?" Luther asks, grabbing my hand.

"My room, Stavo keeps all my favourite things here in case I need them when I pop by. Sometimes when I do him a favour, it gets a little messy." Walking down the corridor, we take another left at the end of the corridor. I do love how everything is painted white with gold decorations. It's simple yet elegant.

Coming to my door at the end of the hall, I grab my keys and open it. Looking around, it's exactly how I left it. Although I know Del Stavo will have had it cleaned. "Wow! This is beautiful," Luther remarks from behind me. But when I look at him, his eyes are on me.

"Do you mean me or my room?" I ask, walking over to him.

"Mainly you, baby, but this room is also lovely," he remarks, placing his hands on my sides gently. "We best get you washed, I won't lie, E, you do smell a little."

"A little, that's putting it nicely, don't you think?" I wasn't wrong. I smelt like the worst thing known to man. I have smelt corpses better than me, and they are disgusting. All I can smell is burnt flesh, old blood, sweat and something I don't even want to identify. I've never felt more gross in my life, and before you ask, no one gave me a bed bath. Mainly because all of Zayne's house keepers are terrified of me. I have a reputation of being violent when I'm hurt. It's a long story. With a chuckle, I tug him towards the bathroom just to the right of the door we came in.

Chapter 43

The bathroom here is huge with a free-standing white bath in the centre of the room; a wall-to-wall shower to the right of it and a sink and toilet on the left wall. All my cabinets are built in with more than enough storage, maybe when I get the new house done, I will give myself something like this. "Do you want a bath, E, or do you prefer a shower?" Luther holds my gaze as I look at him. A shower would be nice but right now, the bath is calling me. The time to soak and relax is now.

"A bath please. I could use the relaxation. I will jump in the shower quickly first to wash all the blood and grime off me." Shutting us both in the bathroom, Luther goes over to the bath and starts to run it. I strip my clothes and look at myself in the full floor to ceiling mirror.

Looking at myself, I can see all the scars and injuries I've had over the years. But the one on my stomach suddenly has so much more meaning and feelings. I run my hand over it. I jump when I feel a pair of hands grab hold of mine from behind.

"A penny for your thoughts?" His voice is so quiet and soothing like all my troubles have melted away.

"It's nothing, just this scar has more meaning to me now. It's never bothered me before. But now that you're in my life, it's changed. Because there is one thing I need to tell you." I turn in his arms and look into his eyes; they're full of so much question and anticipation. "Luther, I can never give you children. I understand if you want to walk away." I avert my eyes as I say the last bit, I can't see the disappointment in them I was expecting.

His fingers lift my chin to look at him. "E, I love you; do you know what that means? It means that no matter what, I will always be with you; children aren't a massive thing for me. And we can always look at other ways in the future, but right now, I want you all to myself. Also, it doesn't stop us trying," he says with a wink and a grin on his lips.

239

"Really? You will stay?" I'm shocked. I always thought that whoever would be with me wouldn't stay after knowing I can't give them children.

Luther rolls his eyes and gives me a quick peck. I know I don't want serious, but knowing that he won't leave me, it's removed some of the weight on my shoulder. "Now if you are done being silly, I need to get you clean before you have a bath," Luther leads me towards the shower. I walk in and turn it on. It feels so nice to have all the grime and stress from the past forty-eight hours run away.

Running my hands over my face, I sigh. I never thought I would feel like this, I'm so used to being strong and in control. But right now I feel like I am crumbling, like I am barely keeping my head above water. With all the Luther stuff, my brother crossing me, and my house going boom, my head is in shambles. I can't seem to think about where to go from here, and what my next moves are? I groan and rest my head against the cold tiled wall, allowing the warm water to run down my back. I try to organise everything; I try to quieten the raging storm inside me. Unfortunately, nothing seems to.

While washing my face, I feel Luther behind me. His smell and presence has a calming effect on me. "Where is your wash stuff?" he asks into my ear, leaning over a little, I push a tile and a draw emerges from the wall.

"I hate people stealing my stuff, so Stavo built me this. I'm thinking of putting one in my new house," I say while I grab the special washcloth and body wash. Luther lathers it up and starts washing me off, starting from my shoulders and neck. Moving down my arms, then moving to my chest. Who knew that being washed by someone would be so intimate and erotic. He moves lower with the cloth until he reaches my ass, making sure to not hurt my wounds. Running the cloth over my plump ass, I lean forward so he can clean me better.

"That's a good girl, lean a little further forward," Luther says while pushing my back further forward and slightly down. My breasts touch the wall; it's super cold against my hot body.

He puts the cloth between my cheeks and slowly rubs it between my backside; it does feel good. But I also want him to go further. This is the worst form of teasing, it's like torture. Moving the cloth slightly lower, he just grazes my hole, my core dripping with need. His movements are horrifically slow, and my ability to hold on diminishing by the millisecond. "Luther, listen, I've had my fair share of torture but right now, this is beyond that. I don't think I can take much more of this." And I know I can't. It's awful, like I'm waiting for rain in a drought.

"I'll take as long as I like, and there is nothing you can do about it. I am going to show you the difference between fucking and making love. I'm going to go slow and you're going to accept that." The way he said that while slowly cleaning my ass made me wetter than Niagara Falls. I bite my bottom lip as I think on his words. This man could literally talk my panties off. He would just say some smooth words and my pants would grow legs and just leave.

Finally, the washcloth made it to the desired destination, a relief passed through me as he slowly washed my pussy with such precision. Small moans leave my lips, each time he passes over my nerves. While Luther cleans me in the most erotic way, he lowers down and peppers kisses all over my back; they are so light, they mix in with the water from the shower.

"You are so beautiful, E, you don't understand how much you turn me on. You're mine now, today, tomorrow and always. I'm not letting this beautiful body, mind and soul go. You belong to me, E. Tell me you belong to me," he says, rubbing me a little harder and faster – maybe I could settle for Luther. It wasn't a bad runner up prize, I guess.

"Yours, Luther, I'm all yours," I moan as the pleasure starts to build inside me. I know I don't fully mean it, but if it gets me what I so desperately need, I will say it. Hell, I will say whatever he wants me to, just so I can cum already.

Once I said that, he spun me around and his lips smashed into mine. The kiss was softer than he's ever given me. It emanated all his feelings that he couldn't express with words. His tongue pushed through my lips, and I opened slightly to allow him access. I couldn't stand the small gap between our bodies, so I wrapped my arms around his neck and pull him closer, his arms wrap carefully around my middle, hugging me even closer to his body while simultaneously trying to not touch my bullet wound or burn.

"I think we are clean enough for the bath baby," Luther states. We could definitely go in the bath now. If he keeps teasing me like this, my legs may just give out. We turn off the shower and move over to the bath. Putting my toes in, I realise it's at just the right temperature. This bath is extremely large but so is the whole house. With it being so big, it means that Luther with his over six-foot height means he isn't going to be cramped. A content sigh leaves my lips as I settle into the bath and rest my head on the side, my eyes open just enough to watch Luther in all his glory get in. He slides down next to me.

"Hey, come here baby." I slide over to him, and he just picks me up and puts me between his legs with my head resting against his chest.

"You know I've never shared my bathroom even when I'm not in it, let alone have someone in here with me. It's nice, I can relax for five minutes. Don't think I have ever chilled since I was a child," I say mindlessly to Luther just allowing the water and his hands rubbing over my stomach to sooth me.

"That's good, baby. I want you to be relaxed around me," Luther says while circling his hands lower with each movement.

"Maybe I should choose a name for you to call me when we are alone apart from, baby, something that fits the person I am with you." His chuckle makes me shake slightly. I am not a fan on him calling me baby. I know it's meant to be a sign of his feelings. But it's really grating my tits in all honesty.

"Call yourself whatever you want. I love you as E, so what does a name matter?"

This stumped me. I guess he's right. I will never understand how or why this man loves me, but people fall in love in stranger ways. "My birth name is Emie." I look up at him, his eyes just shone love and felicity at me.

"Emie. It's beautiful. But I guess after what my father did and what you have been through, Emie stopped being who you are. So, I understand why you go by E these days." My jaw drops. He was totally right. That's why I faked my own death and became this monster. I never thought he would have such a deep thought. Throughout my time of looking into him, I never heard or saw such thought-provoking moments from him. The way he just understood the way I was, the fact that I am so damaged yet so together. Luther didn't strike me as the person to think much deeper than sex. Yet here he is changing my opinion completely. Each moment with him showed what he is truly like, and the playboy is clearly a front for a much more meaningful man. His lips meet my forehead and his fingers stroke over my clit as he says.

"I love, E, not Emie. I will be making love to you, E, as you are. With all your flaws and all your bad sides. I will be showing who you are now, and what it's like to be loved by a man. I will make you forget any other man that turned your head." Hold on, the way he said 'turned my head' and the knowing look on his face made me instantaneously know.

"Aid and Marcus told you about Kieran when I was a kid, didn't they?" He laughs.

"Yeah, they mentioned about you putting them in hospital; even back in the day you were my type of woman." I blush at him. I put him in hospital more than once, and his friends to boot. He was a cocky prick who always thought he was better than me, always wanted me and everyone else to think he was the best thing since sliced bread. But sadly for him, I was better. And I proved that countless times. Now he's a bitter nearly forty-year-old man, sad really.

"That's how I got the scar under my eye. That's where Marcus cut me. Aid had to stitch me up, stopped me looking at any other man until you." *Not every man*...I thought. His fingers went back to stroking me. My eyes closed, and my head went back onto his chest.

"Good, and I want you to do a lot more than look." His deep raspy voice rings in my ears, my core moistening with each syllable he speaks and movement he makes. I bite my lip as my orgasm creeps towards me slowly, my core begging for Luther to give me sweet relief faster. His movements are horrifically slow, my head on his shoulder as I feel each and every pass of his fingers on my sensitive clit.

After a few seconds, his fingers entered my hole, a long moan leave my lips, and my hips start to move with his fingers, as he slides them in and out of me. With his right fingers inside me, Luther moves his left hand to my breast and starts rolling my nipple between his fingers; the sensation feels amazing, driving me crazy. I'm getting annoyed that I can't get to him because I'm lying against his chest, but I might just lie here and enjoy him playing with my body. His fingers start to move faster and faster inside me, while he tugs my nipple harder.

"Ah, yes, Luther," I moan at Luther. The low utter of my voice causes Luther to twitch behind me. The way he is making me feel right now, between his words and his actions, portrays all the love and desire he has for me. Having never experienced something like this before has my mind reeling, but that thought is soon obliterated by my need as I become closer to my impending climax.

His fingers just weren't enough for me, I need more. No, I demand more. The delectable feeling of his fingers just isn't giving me the satisfaction I so desperately crave. I pull him out, and before he can say anything, I spin round and climb on top of him. He always makes me cum, always takes charge and maybe today, I want to make him cum. Maybe I want to be the one that gets him over the edge first. Lining up with the tip of his cock, I slide down on top of him. As I take him fully inside me, he lets out a gruff moan, shooting pleasure straight to my core.

"You naughty girl, you know when we are alone like this, I'm in charge," he says as I start to rock my hips on top of him. The way he said it with a deep sense of need made me moan. That mixed with the look in his eye was soon going to be my undoing.

I don't say anything as my hand grips his throat. I will have what I want from him, what I need more than oxygen itself. I grip his throat tightly, shock and lust flood his features. "Fuck, this is new," he moans as I start to ride him faster while I choke him harder. His moans are mixed with gasps for air, but he doesn't move my hand. The water from the tub starts to splash up the side of the bath. Riding him faster, his moans get louder. I can feel myself getting closer to the brink.

"Luther, cum with me; I want you to fill me," I whisper into his ear; his hands grab my ass. With his firm grip on my ass, he moves me up and down faster than ever. Water is going everywhere. After a few seconds, Luther stops moving me and just holds me still while he pounds me from underneath. My head flies back at the onslaught from him; he feels amazing and I'm so close. I grip his throat even tighter, causing Luther to moan harder as he pounds my pussy. "Oh God, yes…I love you inside me, Luther…I'm so close." He just grunts in response; his pace never wavers as he pounds me.

My orgasm hits me like a train, my breath comes heavy from me and my heart rate spikes. I let go of Luther before I lean forward, making sure that my head doesn't land on his damaged shoulder. Luther doesn't stop moving inside of me, he only slows down as my orgasm washes over me, waiting for me to finish coming down from my high.

"I will make this round quick, baby, but only because you need looking at. When we come to bed, I'm sure as shit going to make you come at least three times before I even put my dick in you," he whispers in my ear before moving harder inside of me. I get on my knees in the tub while Luther pounds me mercilessly. I can feel my next wave of pleasure come barrelling towards me. I throw my head back enjoying every second of him inside me; his grunts and my moans echo around the bathroom as we both reach our orgasm. After a few more seconds, I feel Luther twitch inside me as he finds his release, sending me hurtling into mine. We both sit there for a few seconds, catching our breath.

"Okay, I think that definitely made a mess." I chuckle, looking him in the eyes. Luther laughs and looks over the side of the bath.

"Erm yeah. I think someone is going to need to clean that up." I laugh again and Luther joins me. "Right, baby, let's get you dressed and downstairs. I'm surprised your stitches held up after that." I step out of the bath and Luther follows; neither of us caring that we are dripping water everywhere.

Walking into the bedroom, I see two sets of clothes lying on the bed. I roll my eyes; I wouldn't get used to this. I like my privacy and in Stavo's house, people always walk in. I know they are here to help me, but I like to do things myself. I always have and don't plan on stopping now.

"Well, whoever walked in knows what happened then." Luther chuckles while he dries himself. Yeah, that's the worst part, nothing is a secret in this place. Most of the staff will know I'm fucking Luther by the time I get downstairs. I produce an audible groan and I grab my towel; this is the last thing I need.

Drying myself off, I flinch when I rub my side. I forgot for a second, I have a scratch there. I should have cut her into tiny pieces for shooting me, but I was running out of time.

"Here, let me do that." Luther grabs my towel and starts drying me off. It's weird having someone take care of me. But I'm also not going to knock it either.

Once we are dried and dressed, we make our way downstairs. Fiona walks past me with a bucket and a mop. "I assumed the bathroom will need cleaning," she retorts before making her way past us. I've never been so embarrassed in my life. Especially when I catch the smirk on her face, causing my cheeks to begin to blush.

"Yep, everyone knows." Luther laughs as we get into the dining room where everyone is still sitting with a drink in their hands; they are laughing and chatting casually.

"E, Dan is here for you. He's just in the next room," Stavo says with a smile on his face.

"Thanks, I'll grab a drink while I'm there. I will probably need it."

"I should say. I can see why you sound proofed your room at home. It appears you do most things very loudly." H chuckles and I just turn my back and walk into the living room to get my stitches done. God, I hate men sometimes.

Chapter 44

Walking into the living room, I nod at Dan and remove my top; my side is still bleeding but not as much as before. Relief passes through me when I see that. I was worried it was worse. But I guess because I didn't pass out, that should have shown me it wasn't that bad. My burn also doesn't look as large as it feels. I listen to the lads while Dan starts assessing my wounds. I don't know who tried to stitch me up while I was unconscious, but they did a terrible job.

"Nothing man, just next time, try to keep it down. We were trying to have a conversation and all we could hear was you two. E's room is directly above us." My face burns with my blush. I forgot they were beneath us. I can hear them all laugh. My hands come to cover my face; a small groan passes my lips.

"Don't encourage them, Luther. Ouch, mother fucker," I yell as Dan starts to remove my split stitches. I keep flinching as he pulls on them. It really fucking hurts.

"Well don't move then. We both know this is going to hurt," Dan yells as I keep flinching and taking in sharp breaths.

"I'm paying you all back for everything you guys put me through; my room wasn't soundproof. You would be surprised what I hear when you think I'm sleeping." I hiss as Dan pulls out another stitch.

"Sorry, E." Both K and H shout to me, even though K has never brought a woman back. And judging by how H reacted to Willow being in danger, I know it was just her that he was bringing back with him.

I watch as they all move into the living room; I don't have my top on. If they were anyone else, I probably would be self-conscious. However, most of these guys have seen me like this or with even less on. I have been treated in front of these guys more times than I can remember.

"You doing okay? Want a drink?" Luther asks, grabbing my hand.

"Yes, please, scotch would be great," I say with a smile.

"Fucking hell, Dan, what the hell did I ever do to you?"

"You keep flinching. I'm nearly done. Just stop wiggling and it won't hurt as much. Just stay still for two pissing minutes," Dan states while stitching me painstakingly slowly.

"Pour us all a glass, mate. I think we are going to need it," H states as he plonks down heavily onto the three-piece couch. K sits next to him while Marcus and Aid sit on the two-seater. The rest of the lads just dot around the room.

"Will you stop that, it hurts!" I yell while he stabs me again. I glare at him. If looks could kill, he'd be riddled with bullets.

"Sometimes I prefer it when you're unconscious. You're so much easier to cope with. You and that attitude do my head in. Maybe Luther can fuck that out of you." We glare at each other for a few seconds. I could smack him for that comment. But Luther bursting out laughing breaks the tension, everyone else joins in and I just sigh before hissing in pain again.

"I'm not living this down, am I?" H chuckles at my comment before taking a swig from his drink, I love the fact that we can chill and forget the shit storm that is kicking off around us.

"We are just all happy you are okay, and back with us, little bird." Aid smiles.

"Thanks, Aid, but I do wish you would stop calling me that. I'm not fourteen anymore," I state with a pointed look. Aid chuckles like this isn't meant to bother me. I'm meant to instil fear in my men, and little bird does the complete opposite.

"Sorry, E, but you're our little bird and you know Aid has always called you that; doubt it will ever change. He calls me babe and you know how I feel about that," Marcus says as he squeezes Aids leg. I roll my eyes, frustrated at the fact he calls me that, but I know he won't stop. I flop back on the table and run my hands over my face. My back hurts but right now my head hurts more.

"Wait, you two are a thing?" Luther asks, causing Marcus and Aid to chuckle.

"Yes, we are married. Have been for twenty years now."

"E was our flower girl," Aid, adds causing me to groan. Why would he mention that? I was thirteen, my dress was light pink, and I looked really pretty.

"I bet she looked gorgeous," K says with a light, carefree sound to his voice. I bet he's smiling that smile that could light up the whole of New York and sends butterflies around my stomach. I chastise myself for thinking like that, knowing it will only hurt me.

"Oh, K, she looked adorable. Pink sundress and a flower head piece. Her smile lit up the room as she walked down the aisle – best day of my life." I covered my face with embarrassment as Aid said this.

"Ah, E, I can't imagine you in a pretty pink dress. Or smiling for that matter," H says with a chuckle.

"Okay, yes. I wore a pink dress and flowers, I also danced on Marcus' feet as I was thirteen and couldn't dance. Now if everyone is done embarrassing me, I will go and enjoy my drink after all this torture." I sit up and take my drink from Luther. Everyone erupts into frenzied laughter, including Del Stavo, Dino and Don. I down my scotch in one go and get up to get another one. I cringe as my side hurts while I move.

As I'm pouring my drink, Willow struts into the room. Anger passes over me as I clock the black eye and sling she is sporting. "I'm so glad you're okay, Willow. I'm so proud of you holding your own. You are one badass bitch."

"Thanks, E, they could have done whatever the hell they wanted to me, but I sure as shit wasn't telling them a fucking thing. You have had my back all these years, so I will always have yours." I nod and sit on the coffee table next to Luther. I give him a small smile. I don't do feelings but the fact that Willow did that made my heart swell with pride. I care about her more than I would ever say as she has become like family.

Everything feels like it has changed. I don't cope well with change. I stand and walk out of the room; I feel very suffocated. I move through the house aimlessly as I try to clear my head. I don't know what I want right now. I don't know what to do. A little over a week ago, I had all my ducks in a row, now the ducks have been blown to smithereens, just like my house. My men are taking the piss out of me, and Luther is in love with me. Like what the actual fuck has happened to me? What could have happened to cause my life to be in such turmoil? I can't understand. And come to think of it, I don't know if I want to. After a few minutes, I hear a conversation which catches my attention. Slowly, I move to the wall and keep out of sight. My curiosity peeked.

"No thank you, I'm looking for the gym," Luther states. I assume that's where he thinks I am. It is usually where I go when I need to calm down. Either that or he just plans on working out, but I don't think he has workout clothes.

"Sir, you don't need the gym. You're right just the way you are, so muscular and strong. Just how a man should be," Courtney's sickly sweet voice states, clearly thinking she is flirting with him. She is such a man eater. But what got my heckles up is Luther is mine, and she needs to keep away. I stop dead in my thought train. When did I become so possessive?

"Don't touch me, and I'm definitely not interested in you or your opinion. Now tell me where the gym is before I tell Del Stavo you are being inappropriate while on the job."

"Do you think that he will believe you over me? You're Steadwell's son. I'm his trusted employee. You should be lucky I want you. Any man would be grateful I show them any attention. You will give me what I want." My blood boils at this. I don't care who you are. You don't do this.

Creeping up to the corner, I watch as Courtney pushes Luther up the wall behind him. She brings one hand up and starts massaging his peck and the other descends to his crotch. My mind flashes red and I grab her collar and throw her about six feet back from Luther. I take a defensive stance in front of Luther. If this bitch wants what's mine, she will have to go through me. I don't stand for sexual assault in any form, no matter who it is. No means no in my eyes; it should always be consensual.

"Stay the fuck away from what's mine, or I swear to God Stavo will be the least of your worries. Who the fuck do you think you are, forcing yourself onto someone? You are nothing, you will always be nothing. Touch him again, and I will paint the walls with your insides." I fucking mean it; my anger is radiating off me. My breathing is rapid as I stare at her. I am going to kill this bitch.

"Why would he want you, bitch? You're psychotic, you kill and have no emotions other than anger. I can give him a woman; I can give him everything his heart desires. We both know I'm the better choice." She is causing my anger to rocket with every second of this conversation.

"Why would I want you? E is so much more than you, in each and every way she is better. Stay the hell away from us. And disrespect my woman again, and I will teach you a fucking lesson. E may be bad when she is angry, but when someone upsets my woman, I'm fucking lethal. Now go back to your job before I do something you will regret." The anger in his voice sends a shiver down my spine. I can feel his body shaking with rage behind me. I grab his hand to try and calm him now without taking my eyes off her.

She scoffs and stands up; she has been yelling at me and Luther while sitting on the floor. She really is coming across as desperate right now, but I will give it to her though. That look of determination hadn't faltered for even a second. "He will be mine; I will be making sure of it. I will have my way, and there is nothing you can do to stop me." I snap. Her attitude is pissing me the fuck off. I punch her directly in the face. The force of the blow sends her back to the floor. "You bitch, I will make you pay for that," she yells at me; I laugh but stop abruptly when she pulls my hair. Does she really think this is how I fight? I just grab her throat, squeezing just hard enough to get her to let go of my hair. Her eyes bulge as I tighten my grip; her eyes lock with mine. I watch as fear creeps into her, a look of pure shock overtakes the look of determination.

"I won't warn you again. Stay the fuck away from what I own. I will end you if you even think about him again. Hell, I'll end you if you even so much as breathe near him." Her face is turning red, and her eyes are wild as she claws at my hand around her throat. Panic starting to set in as she realises she can't escape my grasp.

"You can't stop me. He was promised to me. And I intend to collect what is mine." Courtney gasps at me, each breath seems harder for her to take. I can't take the riddles. I throw her at the wall using her throat. As she makes contact with the wall. I hear the air leave her lungs, making me know I threw her with a force. I watch as her body hits the floor, and she begins gasping for air.

"What do you mean he was promised to you? Who said you could have him?" she states, trying to stand; it takes a few moments. When she is up, she uses the wall as support while staring at me, a wicked twinkle in her eye. My stomach sinks as I realise who she is referring to.

"Who do you think? I told him where you lived, and he promised me Luther. I've wanted him for years, he belongs..." Before she can finish her sentence, I pin her back against the wall with a knife to her throat. Now I have her full attention. Right this second, I want to kill her more than anything. She threatened everybody's life. I will protect my team with my life, and she nearly killed them all.

"E, she has information. She is useful; don't kill her yet," Luther states. I hadn't even noticed that everyone had turned up. All eyes are on me, anticipating my next move, even the staff are watching.

"She sold us out. She tried to kill us all. And for what? A man? How pathetic. She should die, and I will make sure it happens. And don't even get me started on what she did to you. I should cut off her fucking hands."

"E, please. Don't you dare get blood on my walls; they haven't long been painted. Take her downstairs. You can do whatever your heart desires. But for heaven's sake, don't paint my walls red. It's not the aesthetic I am going for,"

Del Stavo states, clearly bored of me playing with my new toy. I remove my knife and grab her hair before pulling her over to Del Stavo. I then throw her at his feet.

"Get her out of my sight before I redecorate your house." Don steps forward and drags Courtney away, her skull splitting scream reverberates down the hallway. "Right, I think we all need to chat. There are a few things we need to discuss. But right now, I need a stiff drink before I do something that will either get me killed or will fuck up my entire plan." Turning, I look at everyone; their eyes are glued to the floor. Well, everyone but K. He's never been afraid of me when I was angry, he just takes it in his stride. Never complained, or got upset at my outbursts; he always just understood and moved on. I guess that's why I've always been so close to him, because he knew that whatever I did was to keep everyone safe. But all the others are terrified of me when I am this angry.

"What can I say, my men know not to mess with her. They have all either seen or heard what she is capable of, but it's a good job you were here. Else she would have painted my walls red already, so don't hurt her, Luther, else I may paint my walls with your blood." I heard Stavo state to Luther behind me. I roll my eyes, but we all know it's true, and I love that they are so scared of me.

Chapter 45

Walking into the living room, I head to the bar and grab a bottle of scotch. I twist and flick the lid off before swigging straight from the bottle. I don't usually do this, but right now I'm on the edge of blowing my lid at someone. Luther's hand grabs mine that is holding the bottle before taking it off me. He pours me a glass instead. "You okay, babe?" his voice whispers into my ear. I always thought that someone calling me babe would send a shiver down my spine, wanted to think it would awaken something inside of me. But right now, it doesn't do a fat lot; if anything, it turns me off. Maybe that's because it's not the guy I've always wished would call me that. Another reason might be because I only like having sex with Luther, but I don't have feelings for him. Well, not the feelings he has for me anyway. How can I when my heart belongs to another?

"Yes, I'm just not great with change. This is the largest change I have had without having a choice in it. She also tried to get us all killed, so that doesn't bode well with me either. Who the hell does she think she is to do that, and to think that she could force herself on you? Even I have higher standards than that. Plus, change stresses me out, especially when it's out of my control," I whisper back, and it's true, I don't always cope well when things change.

"Do you regret us? Have I forced something on you that your either not ready for or feel uncomfortable about?" His eyes hold pain and fear at how I will respond. I don't understand, but maybe he has greater feelings for me than I realised. And maybe he realises I am not as into this as he is.

"No, I don't regret sleeping with you. But I have to be honest, it is a big change for me; one I may have to spend some time adjusting to." I watch as a small amount of relief passes across his face. I look at everyone who is staring at us. I guess I should speak to them. "Okay, so right now I have no idea where we go from here. All my files, tech and information went up in flames with the house. My…"

Oh, E, you're so thick, I chastise myself. My old brain is so slow and stupid. I dart to my room and into the bathroom where our clothes are still lying on the countertop. Grabbing Luther's trousers, I dive into the pocket. I find the USB where I stashed it before the attack. As he was kissing me goodbye, I took that moment to slide this into his pocket. I thought if anything happened to me, K or H would use it. Now I need it, and I am so proud of past self; I am brilliant.

Sprinting back into the living room, I go straight to the laptop; I know Del has never changed the password just in case I pop by and use it. "Sometimes I surprise even myself." I chuckle to no one in particular. I load it up and scroll to the file I am after, praying it's still here. Clicking on it, I enter the password and unlock it. Everything here is exactly what I need. "Now we are cooking with gas."

"Why are you so awesome?" Luther asks, coming to a standstill behind me. He clearly is trying to read my files over my shoulder. However, I am fluent in five languages and right now, it's in Italian, one of my favourites. I find it so romantic and a very sexy language, plus it reminds me of the time I met K's family, but that is a cute story for another time.

"Well, while you were leaving, I slipped this into your pocket. I just needed it away from the house just in case I died there. H and K would have known what it was. Anyway, it holds enough of my information on your father as well as some files on other people who do things for me or are my contacts. But most importantly, it holds my plans, and also everything your father has done since the day you were born, and the most important time just after I was born." The whole room is silent. I completely realise that not everyone knows my birthday; only Marcus, Aid and K.

"When were you born?" Luther asks, looking at everyone.

"Don't look at me. I couldn't tell you," H states with a shrug.

"Twenty-seventh of November nineteen-eighty-six," K states without missing a beat. I glare at him. I don't tell anyone that.

"Hold on, that's the same date as mine but a year later. And how does K know but H doesn't?" Luther says, shock written all over his face.

"Well, that would be because K was with me in the force and with Marcus and they use to celebrate it with me, but when I moved over here, I stopped. It was never important. Plus, I have more money than sense so why would I want people buying me shit. I obviously won't like. It's not a big deal; it's just another day." I lock the computer and go sit in the chairs opposite A, K and H.

I really lost my enthusiasm for my birthday when Rick died; it became unimportant. He used to make it special: cards, presents and a cake. We would go hunting at the crack of dawn trying to catch dinner for us. One year, we tried fishing, but it didn't go so well. After that, we never tried again. We changed from fishing to hunting. It was so much better. I loved it; truth be told, I loved the time I spent with Rick more than the hunting. Then we would spend the afternoon sorting out whatever we caught and then cooking it. Maggie would get sober for the day, and it was always a welcomed relief. She would talk about mum and dad, telling me funny stories about them. It was nice to sit in my special place with them, just having family time. But when Rick died, it wasn't the same. Maggie tried, but it just wasn't. Not that I didn't love her trying, but how could I replace the times we had together? Now, it's not a day I care to think about, but I still phone or visit Maggie, and that's all that counts. I just wish we could drop this; my heart hurts the more I think about it.

Chapter 46

"Nobody bother to even wish me a happy birthday. I haven't celebrated in years, and I don't plan on starting now. I stopped for a reason, and I won't dredge up the past. Now please drop it; feel free to celebrate your birthday, Luther, but forget you know mine." I'm looking sternly at them all. Del Stavo has a look that passes over his eyes before looking away; something is up and for the life of me I can't understand why. Yes, he's always treated me better than most of the other mob bosses other than Zayne. Gave me my own room, let's me crash here when I'm injured and don't want to go home. But by his face, I think there is something more.

"E, will you come with me please?" Del Stavo says while standing. He had been sat on a single couch watching us. I nod, standing and making my way over to him. As he leaves the room, we pass Don, who gives me a nod and a smile. Don has always been so nice to me, like he cares about me, which is nice. If I'm honest, I used to like coming here because Stavo always treated me well and looked after me. I had all my own stuff and my own room. It always had new sheets when I came to stay, and all my things were left exactly how I like them. I've never questioned it until now.

We move through the house until we reach his office. Opening the door, we move in. "Take a seat, E, you're going to need it," he says while getting a Pepsi Max out of the fridge for me. I dubiously take a seat, watching Stavo intensely.

"Del, talk to me, you're starting to worry me." And he was. He has a worried look like what he's going to say will upset me.

"E, please don't hate me for what I'm going to tell you." He takes a deep breath before continuing. "I know you have found out that Kathy and John aren't your biological parents, but neither is Harry Steadwell. Sarah is your mother, and…" He pauses before grabbing something out of his desk and placing it on the table. I didn't interrupt him; clearly what he said was hard enough but deep down I think I know what he's going to say. "And I'm…"

He can't say it, so I finish, "You're my dad." He just nods and looks away from me. To say I'm shocked isn't quite right. I'll be honest. I'm not shocked he is my dad; I'm shocked it's taken him all these years to tell me. "Why did you tell me?" I don't understand why he's telling me now; he's waited seven years. Now that he's told me, I can see the resemblance between us. I have his jet-black hair and skin very similar to him. And I have the same green eyes as him and Dino. Also, it's funny how we are both mob bosses – what are the odds.

"I told you because I don't want to hide it from you anymore. Every year I write you a card. These ones are from when you were a child. I used to write them, but I never knew where to send them after Kathy and John did a runner from Steadwell. I was going to take Jasmine in, but he threatened to kill Sarah if I did. I couldn't let that happen." He took a deep breath, telling me all this clearly distressing him. His eyes shine with unshed tears, moisture collecting in the corners. Clearly he is heartbroken.

"You loved her, didn't you?" I could tell he did or maybe still does. His face moves back to look at me.

"I do. She was my childhood sweetheart and I loved you girls. I still love you; you are my baby girl. Once I heard you were back in the US, I was thrilled and super proud of where you were in life, but I didn't want to disturb you or your life. So, I asked you to be my prized hit-woman. I gave you job after job so I could see you. I wanted you to be in my life any way that I could. I knew Jasmine was in the city and been watching her, but she never did much in her life. But then I saw she was selling Steadwell information, I got in touch with Freddy, who you sent to find out what's happening. I've been trying to keep an eye on what's happening in your camp, trying to keep you safe." I didn't know he did all this, but now I'm holding him in a better light. I mean I already held him in a good light, but with this insight, I feel differently towards him.

"So, you didn't tell me because you didn't want to fuck with my life? Did you not think that I would have wanted to know? Luther doesn't even know that Kathy and John are his biological parents and not only that, but that Harry killed them when I was nine and he was ten. He also doesn't know that the woman that raised him is my mother and now I know that you are my father. Oh, fuck's sake, could this get any more confusing. Next you will be telling me that Steadwell forced Sarah to marry him and that's what he took from you." I chuckle, but Stavo doesn't seem as amused as I do.

"Yes, that's what he took from me. He took Sarah and my babies from me; she married him to keep me alive. That's why I built my empire in hopes to take him down, and now I can take him down with my little princess. I will make him pay for what he did, for all the pain he put you through and all he put Sarah through. She was my world, and the way Luther looks at you, reminds me of the love that Sarah and I shared. And if he hurts you, I will kill him without even thinking about it."

I understand now his hatred for Steadwell. I never knew before why he had these feelings for him. He used to just say he took something from him. Looking at him, I know it pains him to tell me this. I can see the hurt coursing through him. Walking around the table, I sit on the table and grab his hand. "Now, I'm not going to suddenly start calling you dad, but if we both get out of this alive, maybe we can work out our relationship."

He looks at me with a genuine smile, like the weight of the world has been lifted off his shoulders. "I would like that. I best give you these," he says as he passes me a stack of envelopes. Glancing at them, they have Emilia, but the rest isn't my name.

"Is this my birth name?" I ask, glancing at him.

"Yes, your birth certificate states your birth name is Emilia Alexia Del Stavo. I remember holding you in my arms when you were born. You gripped my finger in your hand, and I knew I would burn this world to the ground to keep you safe. But when I lost you, my world imploded, and I turned vengeful. But seeing you now, I couldn't be happier. I'm so grateful for Marcus and Aid for what they have done for you. And Maggie, Rick, Kathy and John for raising the wonderful woman you are."

I never knew I had a different name. There is a lot over the last few days I never knew about myself. "Come on, we best get back. I also need to get a phone so I can start making some phone calls and get things moving." As I get up and walk out, a picture on his wall grabs my attention. It's a photo of Del Stavo holding a baby with the same eyes as me and a little boy stood next to him. Looking closer, the boy looks super familiar. I recognise him.

"That's you in my arms, and Dino stood next to me. These were the best days of my life; I had all my babies and my love with me. I wanted to give you the world, but look at you, you already have that. And yes, before you ask, Dino is your brother." I turn to him shocked. I have a brother, like some biological family. Jasmine might have been biologically related to me, but Dino has been there a lot for me over the years. He's even picked me up when I've been in trouble or injured.

Chapter 47

Walking out the office, I make my way back to everyone, but I'm looking for someone in particular; he's sat with the lads chatting. Marcus and Aid on the love seat, H and K on the two-seat couch, Luther and A on the three-seat couch and Dino and Don leaning on the bar. They are all chuckling about something as we walk in. I still have all the envelopes in my hand when I move into the room and all eyes fall on us. "Everything okay, boss?" Dino asks, his eyes moving between me and Stavo.

I look at Stavo and smile. "Yes, Dino, all is good. Can we have a chat outside?" I want to ask him if he knew about me. He nods and we move outside. Once outside, I look into the well-trimmed garden. I always loved this place. It is so beautiful out here. "So did you know about me?"

I don't know what to think about it, and I am worried about what he's going to say. I don't want to take Stavo's company. I have my own, but if he is fine with me being around, I would love to have the backing of him in the future. "Yeah, I knew, so did Don. He's our half-brother. Dad made us keep it from you over these past few years, thinking you would run away from us. It was hard for him to keep it because he was devastated you weren't with us; as was Don and I. We know you won't come here and steal our company, seeing as you have your own. We would love to work with you though. And I know Dad wants you around more. I'm sorry I hid this from you. I did what Dad wanted."

I'm not mad in the slightest. I understand their trepidation with telling me. I just smile at him. "Dino, I just want us to work together and maybe we could build a relationship. But only if you want." Dino smiles and hugs me. It's nice knowing I actually have family that cares.

"I would love that, E." He pulls away and calls Don over. He moves out to us with a smile on his face.

"She finally knows then?" Don says with a chuckle and pulls me into an embrace. Looking behind them, I see Luther with a twisted look on his face.

"Think we need to explain to Luther what's going on. I think he's jealous." I chuckle loudly, then Dino and Don look at him before joining me. Is this what I'm going to have to deal with, the thought makes me laugh harder. "We should go back in before he starts a fight for getting the wrong end of the stick." I laugh with a tear in my eye.

Moving over, I sit on Luther's lap; he wraps his arms around me in a possessive move. "Chill, Luther, you are definitely getting the wrong end of the stick. It's far from what you're thinking." I chuckle to him.

His arms squeeze me before saying, "Probably not, but I'm still possessive over you."

Dino chuckles. "Mate, never in a million years would I see my sister in that light."

"Same here. We are just happy she knows now. It's been horrid hiding it for the past, nearly eight years. We are proud of her. She definitely took after Dad, even not being raised by him," Don says with a smile, leaning against the bar like he was when I entered.

Everyone's jaws basically drop; their eyes pass between Stavo, Dino, Don and me. I don't bother to explain. I'm still digesting it myself. Grabbing an envelope off the pile I have been holding, I open it, and look at the contents. It's a birthday card. It looks like it would be for when I was very little. Opening it up, I notice inside it was signed.

To my princess,

Happy 1st Birthday.
All my love, Dad and Dino.

I haven't had a card for years and to have thirty-two of them in my hands dating right back to my first, my eyes start to fill with tears as I look down at the card. Grabbing another one and opening it, it reads the same but with Don's name next to theirs. The more I opened, the more furious I got. But one card caught my attention, it was for my twenty-fourth birthday. The inside read:

To my princess,
I hope that one day you will finally get to read this. I am beyond proud of you and glad that you are finally back on home soil. One day, we may be reunited and be able to get to know each other. You have been back for a few months and

already you are making waves. I know it's you because how could I forget those beautiful green eyes. I hope that one day I will be able to explain to you why I am not in your life, and maybe you will be able to tell me all about your life. I want you to remember how much I love you, and how much I will always love you. I do hope that when you find out about all this that you will forgive me and your brothers. We wanted to find you sooner, but you are like smoke and extremely hard to find.

I love you, my baby girl, today, tomorrow and always.

Dad x.

This made my heart stop. Steadwell crossed a line by swapping me with Luther. I hated him for killing Kathy and John, but now I want to kill him for a whole different reason. I'm going to make sure it's slow and painful.

"E, what's wrong?" K asks. I hadn't realised that everyone had stopped talking and were watched me read these cards. Quickly, I wiped the tear away before putting the card into the envelope.

"Mhm." I nod before getting up and moving to the bar and getting a drink. My mind is going a million miles an hour; to say I'm furious is an understatement. I'm seething. I want to go into his house right now and kill him so slowly, he begs me to end it for him, which I will be all too happy to do. I'm struggling to hold my anger in. I want to break things and smash shit up. Before I can even think, I throw my glass straight into a wall, watching it smash all over the place. Gripping the table, I try to calm my breathing. *Breathe, E...breathe in...breathe out...in...out...*

My mind tells me before I do something I'm going to regret; he's fucked up my life one too many times. He's also fucked with Luther's life one too many times. I haven't even told him what I know. How do I tell him? "Stavo, do you have my glasses. I need to take these contacts out?" My eyes are slightly irritated, but I'm going to use it as an excuse to explain the crying.

"Yes, princess, they are in the cupboard by the front door. So is your guns and knives, just in case you need them," he says with a smile. I nod and move my way through the house till I get there.

Opening the door, I see that all my stuff I left last time I was here, is all neat and tidy. Grabbing my glasses and closing the door, I walk into the living room and throw my contacts in the bin. I need to get some more. I hate glasses, not because they don't suit me just, they get in my line of sight when fighting.

Putting them on, I sit back on Luther's lap. He pulls me closer, whispering in my ear, "God, when I thought you couldn't get sexier." I chuckle at him. How does he calm me down so easily? How is it when I sit with him, or he even touches me slightly, I'm a hell of a lot more chilled. I look at all the lads sat around me.

"Go chill for the night and get some sleep. Tomorrow will be a long day." They nod before all moving out of the room, I get off Luther, turning to him. "Go with them. I have a few things to sort out. Go to bed in my room. I'll meet you there in a while." He looks reluctant but nods. He bends down and kisses my lips before leaving.

I know he knows I'm hiding something, but right now isn't the place to tell him. Turning to Dino, I look into his eyes. "Where did you put her?" I'm going to take this anger out on someone who deserves it.

"Cell 3. Need some help?" I would love some help, but I also worry I will disturb them with what I plan to do.

"You sure you want to see this? I'm pissed and she's going to get the full force of my anger. I'm not pleasant when I'm pissed."

"Hell, yes. I've always been curious how you get your information. Also, she deserves it." Don chuckles, while Dino nods.

"Fine, let's go then."

Chapter 48

Looking at Courtney in front of me, she looks like she's petrified. And damn right she should. I stand before her, fists clenched. Del Stavo, Dino and Don stood by the door watching me. They look too excited to see what I will do. Grabbing the chair next to the door, I move it to the middle of the room, while Courtney cowards on the cot in the corner. "Sit, or I will make you sit," I say, pointing to the chair I just moved. She scurries into the chair. Does she think this is going to be easy? She's stupid if she thinks I'm going to let her off this lightly.

"Well done, now I'm going to ask you some questions and if I don't like what you say, I will make you regret it. Does that sound okay?" I ask while walking to the door. I know Stavo has a cabinet full of stuff I can use to extract information. "She bolts, break her legs. She goes nowhere," I say to my brothers who nod. Opening the cupboard, I gaze on the plethora of equipment displayed in meticulous order before me. I opt for a pair of scissors, pliers and a hammer. I know I'm barbaric, but I'm angry, so I'm going to make this shit hurt. I'm going to go back to my military days, the days where I would use whatever I could to get what I need.

Walking back in, I hand the hammer to Dino, and Don the pliers. I'm going to start with the scissors. She thinks she is so pretty, so why don't we change that. Walking behind her, I grab a chunk of her hair and cut it off. She screams. I've not even started yet, and I already think I could get her to spill in seconds. "Right, now I have your attention. So, I want to know why you told Steadwell where I live."

I grab another chunk of hair. She starts crying. After a few seconds of no response, I cut another chunk of hair off and drop it in her lap. "Please, if you think this is the worse it will get, you are sadly mistaken," I say, walking past her, grabbing the hammer from Dino and slamming it down on her knee. A loud crunch echoes through the room. Her scream is even louder than before.

"So do I have your attention now? Are you going to answer me? If not, I can always start removing limbs. I do hate doing that though, means I'm on limited time before you bleed to death." Courtney looks at me. She tries to muffle her sobs. "Good girl, now answer my question. Why did you sell me out?"

"I've wanted Luther for years. He's…gorgeous…Steadwell said he would make it happen if I gave…if I told him the address of the person after him…I never told him who you were…I swear…just your address," she says between sobs. I want to believe her, I do. But I still need to know things.

"How did Steadwell get in touch with you?" I stand in front of her with the hammer still in my hand.

"He knew I worked for boss; he met me in a supermarket. He paid me ten thousand to give up your address. My mum's sick, I needed the money," she says with pleading eyes. I knew this was bullshit. I knew this was a lie and her mum is completely okay, because she was at the fundraiser last week. I bring the hammer down on her other knee, shattering it. Her scream was blood-curdling, and it was like music to my ears.

"Your mum was working the fundraiser on Wednesday last week; I spoke to her and she's actually in very good health. Even has a new man on the scene. Do you think I'm stupid? I would hate to think you are going to underestimate me."

Her eyes move to Stavo, pleading with him. "Please, boss, make her stop. I'll tell you anything but get her to stop this." Stavo says nothing. His face doesn't even waver as he looks at her. She cries hysterically.

"Don't look at them for help. By the time I'm finished, you will be begging for death. I promise you will regret every life choice you made to get here. I'm your worst fucking nightmare and the last person you will ever see," I say, getting in her face. She grabs my hair and tries to pull me. This bitch is really getting on my last nerve. I smash her in the chest with the hammer, breaking a few of her ribs and maybe her sternum. This gets her to let go. Standing back up, I clock her in the face with my fist. Right, breaking things isn't getting the job done so why don't we start removing things.

Walking over to Don, I swap the hammer for the pliers. Pulling my knife out of my belt, I put it through the back of her hand and into the chair arm. This isn't to torture her, but it does add to my aesthetic. "I must say, Courtney, you're definitely going to make my night interesting; I may have been a hit-woman for years, but before that I was very used to torturing people for the government. Maybe I should electrocute you next. I know it's a bit medieval, but it is fun. Or should I start pulling out your fingernails? Maybe I should try water boarding. That one could always get someone to talk; acid is also equally effective. I'm not into shooting people, too messy and loud. We are also in a small room so could cause some issues. Which sounds best to you?" Her face pales again. If she went any whiter, I think she would pass out. "Not so big now are we, Courtney! But you were right about one thing. I am emotionless." A maniacal laugh erupts from my chest. Maybe I am sadistic and psychotic, because I am enjoying it all too much.

That was the best part of being in the government, going to places of war and torturing people. I know it's sick, but it was great having that power over someone. Men always underestimated me until I extracted information that they couldn't. I'm not any normal woman, I'm a power-hungry bitch who enjoys doing things like this. Putting the pliers on her right-hand index finger, I grab her finger. "Tell me the truth. You went to Steadwell, didn't you? Did Del Stavo not treat you right? Did you think that you could make a few quick bucks? Do you hate me?"

"No, boss, is great, and I love my job...I just needed money...this was nothing...against you...I'm sorry, E...please believe me...I'm so sorry..." She sobs as pains ravages her body. I pull and dislocate her finger; I'm really getting board of her now. I'll be honest, I just want to take my anger out on her.

I grip her fingernail and rip it out; her screams are enough to make my ears bleed. "I know how much you get paid; you and I both know you don't need the money. Why did you sell me out?"

Her sobs get louder, but still no answers, so I grab another nail and repeat what I did to the last one. "Luther should be mine; he is hot and rich. If he fell for me, I would be rich and can do whatever I want. Steadwell senior promised me this, said that I can do what I want once I have him and you are gone."

Oh, that's it! She is greedy. I detest power hungry and money hungry people. They are stupid yet ruthless people doing whatever they please for a buck. I know, so hypocritical, but I am power-hungry in a completely different way to this bitch.

"Did you tell him anything else?" I ask looking at her, her eyes are red, and skin is pale. She shakes her head quickly, but unfortunately for her, my patience is wearing thin. I need to let off some steam and her being like this and not listening or answering me isn't helping. I just start beating her up, throwing my fists into her, anywhere I can. Her face starts to swell almost instantly with each impact. Blood is dripping from her hand as she moves against the blade cutting her further with each movement; her screams and grunts don't even resonate with me while I'm in my rage.

After about ten minutes of me beating the shit out of her, I turn to the lads. "Anything you gents when to ask, because I'm bored of her now. We aren't getting anywhere. I'm wasting time here." Gripping her next finger with the pliers again. Her sobs get louder. "She's clearly no use to me anymore, just a selfish bitch who is greedy as fuck. That's all you are, isn't that right, Courtney?" I pull on her next finger.

"YES, I'M SELFISH. PLEASE STOP, I'M SORRY. I'LL DO ANYTHING YOU ASK, BUT PLEASE MAKE IT STOP," she yells as I pull. She really is a stupid girl. Does she really think I'm going to let her live? No one lives after they cross me.

"No, princess, she has nothing of interest for me," Stavo says over my shoulder.

"Oh, of course I will make it stop, Courtney. But I don't think it will be the way you want." I laugh as I look into her swollen eyes. Pulling the knife out of her hand, I plunge it into her chest and twist. I watch as the life leaves her eyes. Blood is running down my hand that's still holding the knife in her chest. I wish I hadn't had got so bored so quickly, but I couldn't be bothered to go round in circles. Putting my fingers on her neck, I don't feel a pulse; she's definitely dead.

Pulling my knife from her chest, I turn to the door. "You okay?" asked Stavo. I just nod before opening the door. Some of my all-consuming anger quelled, but I am still in raging bitch mode. I guess it would take more than beating that skank up, to squash this feeling, to sate the need to kill. Something I have been feeling for years, like a demon that travels with me. I could see myself becoming a serial killer in another life, if I didn't learn to channel my anger.

Stepping out of the cell, Luther, K, H, A, Marcus and Aid are all looking at me. I have blood dripping from my hand and from my knife that I am still holding. I also think some of the blood has gotten on my top. They all just stare at me. What have I done now? Are they jealous they weren't there? Did they want to know something from her? I don't say anything just move past them and make my way upstairs. I don't even care I'm dripping blood all over the place; it's not the first time, and I doubt it's the last time either.

Chapter 49

Apparently, everyone had followed me. I walk into the kitchen and turn on the taps to wash the majority of the blood off. All I can hear is whispering behind me. "What, what the fuck do you all want from me?" Turning to my men, I look at them all. "You know that crossing me ends in death. I don't care if you're sorry. I've held that philosophy for many years." Turning to Stavo and my brothers, I say, "And what did you expect? I'm not the most notorious killer in the USA for nothing." Looking between all of them, still fuming from what Steadwell did to me and Courtney selling me out. "I am not changing how I run things for any of you. She's lucky I went easy on her. The next person to cross me will feel my true wrath. I'm just getting started. So does anyone have anything to say before I find it out myself?" I'm literally on the edge of killing all of them. I'm so angry. I need to rain my temper in. I feel like I am a bomb waiting to explode; the pressure of my anger building higher and higher. Then I will just go boom, and that is scaring me a little.

"E, we are just worried about you, that's all," K says, approaching me. I get they are, none of them have ever seen me so angry. But they never saw me when X was around; he got me this angry and paid the price.

"I'm fine. Stop worrying about me. Now go to bed. In the morning, we have some T's to cross and I's to dot before we make our next move. That's a fucking order. Bed, NOW," I yell the last word, all of them including Stavo, Marcus and Aid move upstairs. I hear them talking quietly to each other, but I pay no attention. If they are down here, they will only annoy me, and right now that will be the worst thing they could do.

Moving back to the cells, I look in the guards' room and see that Courtney's phone and other items are there from being stripped. Grabbing her phone, I walk back into her cell and look at her lifeless body. She's slumped over in the chair, blood still dripping from her chest. I move to her and put her thumb on the screen to unlock it. I do love that people use thumb print or facial recognition to unlock things these days. They say it's safer, but when you're dead, it's the easy way in; I don't have to crack your password. Opening the phone up, I go straight to the text messages. One stands out. I recognise the number, but there is no name attached.

She lives at 56 Fair oak Blvd.
Brilliant. Anything I should know?
She will probably come here or another mob boss's house if she makes it out. You will want to kill her on sight. I don't know how good at fighting she is, but be prepared.
Thanks for the heads-up; the money is in your account. Now delete these text messages.

She definitely deserved to die; she even told them where I would be heading. Her phone pings again; it's from the same person.

Get out. We are almost there.

Fuck, shit, balls! We are under attack; they know I got out and they know I'm here. Who the fuck tipped them off? If it was her, I will have to get her phone to H. If not, I will have to find out who it is.

I have no time to waste. Getting upstairs, I find the button that arms the house and alerts everyone we are under attack. Hitting it, a loud siren bellows through the house and the grounds; all the window and door shutters start to come down. "What the fuck is going on. Why are the shutters coming down?" Stavo yells as he runs towards the front door. Everyone hot on his heels.

"Whoever is texting Courtney's phone just text her they are almost here. I'm sorry, guys, I've put you all in too much danger. I am so sorry." I move and open the front door and look at K. "K, you know what to do." And with that, I roll under the shutter just before it shuts; leaving my men inside.

I see four guys running to me. "E, what's going on? Why is the alarm sounding? Also why are you out here instead of being with the others?" Will asks, one of Stavo's trusted. He's been with them since I can remember and has taken a bullet for me once or twice. I've been shot at a lot, so my memory is blurry at who took what bullet for me.

"Courtney leaked my location to someone and now they are on the way. I'm going to assume it's Steadwell coming. We need to protect the house," I say before running to a small door on the side of the house. This one doesn't need a shutter; it's near enough impossible to get into unless you have fingerprint access. I know I made fun of it before, but I can't be arsed to get him to change it right now. It's also convenient when you need quick access.

Opening the door, I grab out some guns and extra ammunition; also a couple of knives and a large sword. I'm extremely skilled with all these weapons. I'm just thinking about how many may actually be coming. But no one is getting through those fucking gates, I'm going to make sure of that. Walking back, I see all thirty of the outside guard huddled together. "E, what's the plan?" Will asks, making the whole group look at me.

"Right, Sam, Louis, and Frank, you guys protect the house. If we let anyone through, kill them on sight; only step in if we need you. Tyler, Rich, Owen and Logan get in the towers and shoot down any fucker coming towards the building. The rest of you, work with me. No one makes it through that gate. Will, stick with me and keep my back safe, rest split into pairs and work with your other. This is how we will stay alive. If any of you die, I'll bring you back and kill you myself. Got it?"

"YES, BOSS!" They all yell in unison. Nodding, we all move into position.

"FIVE CARS ARRIVING, E," yells Tyler from his perch near the gate. Five cars with probably about five per vehicle, that means about 25 people coming. Could be a few more, but no more than 30. This seems too easy.

"KEEP YOUR EYES PEELED, THIS SEEMS TOO EASY!" I yell back to all the men. Will stands just next to me, his gun in his hand but I haven't reached for mine yet. I want to get some blood on my hands. "Don't die on me, Will, and don't let me get shot. That shit hurts, and I am not in the mood for it." I chuckle and so does Will.

"It's more than my job's worth to let you get hurt. You're family to us, so we are all here to protect you." Just as he said that, the snipers start shooting, causing me to look at the gate as a car smashes through. As soon as the car skids to a stop, four men jump out. I spring into action, running at one of the men. Grabbing my knife, I swipe and slash his throat before turning to another one. His gun is on me and even from a few feet, he misses me. I slash his wrist quite hard; he drops his gun, and I plunge my knife into his throat. I watch for a second as he hits the floor, before turning around.

"E, 4 o'clock," Will yells. Turning, I see a guy raise his gun and shoot, hitting the car just next to me. I grab the blade of my knife and throw it at him with all my strength, getting him straight between the eyes.

I'm now starting to get pissed. More men are making it through the gate. Right, this is going to stop, and I'm the one that's going to make it happen. I walk to where they are. I shoot three down without even thinking about it. I'm the best for a reason and whoever came here looking for me, was dead the minute they got in the car. I need to get some blood on my hands; taking my sword out, I take off one guy's hand as he brings his gun up. I'm so used to combat that even the sounds of guns ringing and men shouting doesn't bother me. I notice about 15 guys lying on the floor. There aren't that many left standing. This was a suicide mission for those men. Stavo clearly made sure they were all well-trained and were masters at what they do.

Turning around, I feel only what I can describe as my insides being ripped out. My chest hurts like a bitch, and I feel liquid running down my chest, soaking my top. I halt my movements, seeing a man with black hair and dark eyes look at me with his gun raised and a smile on his face. I shoot him before falling to the floor. It all happens in slow motion; the pain is excruciating, and I can't hold on much longer. My vision is failing. My whole body is starting to go numb. I can just hear Will shouting my name before darkness consumes me; if this is death, then I will greet him like an old friend.

To be continued…